Ursula's

Maiden Army

Ursula's Maiden Army

by

Philip Griffin

Reno, Nevada

Ursula's Maiden Army

 Beagle Bay Books,
a division of Beagle Bay, Inc.
Reno, Nevada
info@beaglebay.com
Visit our website at: http://www.beaglebay.com

Cover Design: Doug Andersen

Library of Congress Cataloging-in-Publication Data

Griffin, Philip, 1957-
  Ursula's maiden army / by Philip Griffin.-- 1st ed.
    p. cm.
  ISBN 0-9749610-1-9 (trade pbk. : alk. paper)
  1. Ursula, Saint--Juvenile fiction. 2. Huns--Juvenile fiction. I. Title.

PZ7.G881364Urs 2005
[Fic]--dc22

2005004097

Book design by Robin P. Simonds
ISBN-13: 978-0-9749610-1-9
FIRST EDITION
Printed in the United States of America

12 11 10 9 8 7 6—1 2 3 4 5

Dedicated to the real women whose incredible exploits sowed the seeds of the legend of St. Ursula.

Also, to the memory of my grandfather, Edward "Ted" Griffin, and all his comrades, who, while in service to their country in the Second World War, were taken by the cruel sea.

ET VIRTVTIS MAGN MAI IESTATIS MARTYRII CAELESTIVM VIRGIN
IMMINENTIVM

". . . in honor of virgins who had suffered martyrdom. . . ."
(Extract from the "Clamatius Stone." See Historical Note)

Contents

Ursula's Maiden Army

Cordula's Tale

"*AAAHHH!*" the young girl screamed. There, framed by the gap in the curtains through which she was peeping, were the grotesque remains of a woman's head with vivid red hair. Startled by her cry, the visitor let go of the sacking that had carried the gruesome object all the way from Colonia. The cloth fell away, revealing the face in full. It was staring straight at the girl with sightless dark caverns that had once been living eyes.

"*AAAHHH!*" she screamed again, grabbing her older brother for protection.

"Come here *at once,* young lady!" The girl's mother commanded angrily. She looked unnaturally small standing beside the tall, robed stranger, "How long have you been hiding? And *you* can come here too, young man! I know you're there!" She glared into the shadows behind the curtain. "How long have you two been there? Have you been eavesdropping on us? What have you heard?"

The sobbing young girl burst from behind the curtains and ran into her mother's arms for comfort. Sheepishly, her older brother followed; his eyes transfixed upon the monstrosity on the table.

"And who might these young folk be, Cordula?" the visitor asked quietly after the young girl's sobs died down. His cultivated voice was heavily accented, but had a warm and friendly tone.

"Oh, I beg your pardon, Your Grace." Cordula ushered the two children around in front of her to present them, slapping their heads gently as she did so to stop them staring at the head. "Children, this is Bishop Clematius of Colonia. Your Grace, this is—"

"A very special young man," Clematius interrupted. "One of only two living Britannic witnesses of the martyrdom of the province's best—though he was still a small babe in arms at the time."

The boy bowed politely.

The Bishop returned the gesture with deferential respect. Then he took hold of the boy's shoulders. "Tell me, young man, I'm curious." He looked deeply into the child's eyes. "Do you have any memories of that day? Any recollections at all?"

The boy looked questioningly at his mother.

Cordula was staring at the Bishop and her son intently, her expression tense and guarded. Her face, though aged and lined from the responsibilities of motherhood, still had some of the glow of youth. Her eyes had lost none of their inquisitive stare. Her brown hair, now streaked with gray and tightly constrained in polite, domestic braids, threatened to cascade loose and fly free in the wind, as it had once done long ago.

Reluctantly resigning herself to the inevitable, she nodded her permission for her son to answer.

"Yes . . . I do, Your Grace," the boy said tentatively. "I remember seeing something white and beautiful slowly being smothered by something black and ugly. As if . . . as if the black thing was eating the white thing. But the main thing I remember is . . . ."

He paused and looked again at his mother, unsure whether to say more. The Bishop did the same. They both caught a fleeting glimpse of the suffering in her eyes.

"Go on," Clematius said gently.

The Bishop's reassuring manner gave the boy confidence. When he spoke again his voice was stronger. "The main memory I have, Your Grace, is sounds. I remember a wailing noise coming from the people all around me. And I remember Mother shouting. But most of all I remember the sound of a bird—a hawk I think—screeching above my head."

"Incredible!" The Bishop stood to his full height and addressed the Heavens. "God be praised for granting such a gift!" He looked back down at the boy with a smile that was so full of warmth the boy smiled back in reply. "God gave your infant's mind such powers, my son, so that you would truly remember that which should never be forgotten."

Then, with an even broader smile, Clematius turned to the boy's sister. "And you must be the lovely Brittola, named after one of the most revered of the martyrs."

Brittola needed no further bidding. Boldly, she stepped away from her mother's side and thrust out her hand to the Bishop.

Clematius, barely managing to suppress a grin, bent forward to kiss it with formal solemnity. "I apologize if the . . . if our little item of business scared you. I know it looks fearsome, little one. And, once—long ago—it did, indeed, have life. But all life is long gone. It has no power now—believe me. It really is nothing for you to fear."

"There are many worse sights in life than that, Your Grace," Cordula said firmly. "They will need to get used to them sooner or later."

She placed her hands on her children's shoulders and turned them around to face her. "I thought you two were going to be out playing all afternoon. Now that you're here, you might as well stay. I want you to be good and keep quiet. The Bishop has little time and we have much to discuss. Is that clear?"

"Yes, Mother," the children said in unison. The boy took his sister's hand and obediently moved her to the other side of the table.

Cordula looked up questioningly at the Bishop.

He nodded, encouraging her to proceed.

She glanced across at her children and forced a smile. *Oh, what a crooked piece of work you are, cruel Fate! What a conundrum you place before me! Here is both Life. . . and Death. My wonderful children, and this . . . this thing. Both stare me in the face. Both together, when they should be far, far apart.*

Cordula sighed and returned her gaze to the grisly object before her. As she reached her hands out to grab hold of it, Brittola began to groan with revulsion. A quick, sideways glare from Cordula soon hushed her.

Cordula paused and closed her eyes. *What if it really is her? Or worse still—what if the hair has been dyed? What if the roots of this very red hair are white?* She felt her own scalp tingle as nightmares she thought long vanquished came rushing to the fore: armies on the march and whole peoples on the move; skirmishes and tactics; frantic rides; long, long journeys; monstrous storms; the beating drums; and then—the greatest fear of all—*the Huns!*

The nervous rustle of her daughter's frock snapped her back to the task in hand. Cordula coughed, regained her composure and stared once more at the head. Then, very deliberately, she placed first one hand, then the other just below the ears on either side. With a firm grip, she slowly lifted it up to eye level.

Having been crudely embalmed, the skin was shriveled and crinkled like a dried fruit. It was gray all over except for yellowish patches where the flesh was loose from the bone. The neck had been set in tar and placed on a dark wooden base like a trophy. This had been done quite recently; the tar was still soft to the touch—unlike the head itself, which felt hard. Cordula could tell that, in places, it was brittle, and as she moved it in her hands she could feel the odd loose flake about to return to the dust.

So much death . . . such, foul, foul death! There was so much death that day. Did this woman die there—on that evil field? But, how could she have done? There was so much death that day . . . yet—somehow—she seems so far from death . . . .

The most striking part of the head, and in some ways the only facet of it that suggested it had once been alive, was the hair. Arranged in Britannic braids about the forehead and ears, its roots had, indeed, been a vivid red when its owner was living and breathing. Now, though, it was dull and lifeless.

"It could be her," Cordula said quietly. She turned it around to survey the back. "The cheeks are in the right proportion to the forehead and jaw. The hair *is* how she was wearing it that day." She touched the braids around the right ear. "But then, many of the women wore it that way, and hair can easily be re-arranged after death."

"I must admit," Clematius said, leaning forward to peer closely at the hollow eye sockets, "there is some merit to the owner's claim that it has an officer's bearing."

"Well—there is only one way to be sure." Cordula cupped the back of the head firmly in her left hand and thrust the forefinger of her right hand through the slightly parted lips.

The children gasped. Even Clematius was shocked by her action. Like the children, he continued to watch open-mouthed with astonishment.

Cordula closed her eyes as she felt systematically around the inside of the dead mouth. While she worked, the head made hollow, eerie crackling noises—like a damp fire in the cold. After a while, she opened her eyes, pulled her finger out and wiped it on her tunic. Then, very carefully, she placed the head back on its crumpled cloth.

"That's not Pinnosa," she said decisively.

"B-but how do you know?" Clematius spluttered. "How can you be so certain?"

Cordula smiled and moved over to the window to look out at the kitchen courtyard. "This woman has all her teeth. Pinnosa had one missing."

"Which one?" Clematius blurted.

Cordula turned to face him. "I think I'd rather keep that to myself, Your Grace. Just in case any more of these . . ." she nodded at the head on the table, "poor women come in search of being put to much-needed rest. Would you please see to it, Your Grace, that she is buried—with honor—amongst her own?"

Bishop Clematius coughed and regained his usual authoritative tone, "Of course. You may be assured that she will be laid to rest with the dignity she deserves. May I ask how you came to know which of Pinnosa's teeth was missing? It's not that I wish to imply . . . you understand, but I *am* accountable to others in this matter, and . . . ."

"There is no need for you to feel uncomfortable about asking, Your Grace. I shall be more than happy to tell you."

She paused and looked at her children. Their faces were brimming with eagerness to hear what she had to say. *They should go to their room. They're too young. The time has not yet come for them to be told these things. Anyway, their father isn't here.*

"This was once her home, you know . . ." Cordula said distractedly, "Pinnosa used to live here." She turned to look once more out of the window, oblivious to her children's exclamations of surprise. "This was built by her father to be the family home, and its name was the Villa Flavius . . . but that was a long, long time ago." She stared for a while at the secret shapes formed by the lost objects that lay hidden beneath the carpet of glistening snow. Then, slowly, she began to speak in hushed tones, more to herself than the others. "Can it really be that long ago? I remember the day Pinnosa lost her tooth so vividly . . . it seems like only yesterday. Ursula, Pinnosa, and I—Martha and Saula weren't there. They were probably off with some of the young officers as usual—had just returned to Glevum after our first ever hunt. Brittola, who was still too young to hunt at that time, joined us as we came through the gate. I was only in my seventeenth year, which means Ursula and Pinnosa must have been in their eighteenth and Brittola in her fifteenth. We were so full of ourselves as we paraded around the Forum arm in arm! Pinnosa had two deer tails and a hare's paw strung in her hair, Ursula had another deer tail and a foxtail in hers and I had two hare paws in mine. Brittola was twanging Pinnosa's bow, and we were all singing *Off We Go* at the tops of our voices—"

She paused and looked across the kitchen courtyard toward the opposite door of the West Room. As she did so, Clematius thought he saw her give an almost imperceptible nod, as if someone were standing in the doorway, watching and listening, and whoever it was had just given Cordula their approval to continue.

"We were laughing at being shooed away from a glassware stand by a funny old woman with a missing ear. She's still there to this day I believe. When, suddenly, Pinnosa cried, 'Damn!' She had her hand to her mouth and was wincing with pain. 'What is it?' I asked. She said, 'Wait here. I shan't be long.' Then she ran over to where one of the surgeons was washing his kit in the water trough and spoke to him briefly. He reached down into the water and produced his tooth-puller. Pinnosa helped to work it into position. Then she knelt before him. They both gripped the handle and started pulling—hard! It was a tough struggle, and she seemed to be doing most of the pulling. The next thing I knew, he was polishing a new piece of silver and she was splashing her face with water." Cordula laughed. "Typical Pinnosa! When she came back to us she tried to carry on with the singing as if nothing had happened! It was only at Ursula's insistence that she opened her mouth wide and showed us all the bloody hole."

"Incredible!" Clematius said. "She pulled the tooth herself. Most *men* couldn't do such a thing."

"Come now, Your Grace. Our job is to dispel myth-making fabrications, not add to them! I only said it seemed that way. We were about six stalls from the trough and I couldn't see clearly enough through the crowd. On the other hand, as you well know, Pinnosa—God rest her soul—was capable of many things well beyond the reach of many others, including most men."

"She truly had a man's heart and spirit. And yet . . . ." Clematius joined Cordula by the window. "Although she was a big woman, she was not a masculine one. Indeed, I found her surprisingly feminine at times. How vividly I remember when she took her Vow of Chastity. She bowed her head forward to take my blessing. Her hair, which for once was loose and not braided, fell across her face. For the briefest of moments I saw before me a vision of pure womanhood in its most genteel form. She was looking at the chalice and her eyes—eyes that had seen so much—had an expression of such innocence, such purity . . . ."

He looked troubled by a thought that had occurred to him and turned to face Cordula before asking very deliberately, "You mentioned Martha and Saula being 'with the officers as usual.' They were . . . um—weren't they? Oh, how in God's name can I broach such a sensitive point? They were—"

"'Worthy of their Vows'?" Cordula laughed mirthlessly. "Oh, you need have no fear of that, Your Grace! It was because Martha and Saula enjoyed the company of men so much that they valued their virginity more highly than any of us!" Still smiling an empty smile, she returned to the table. As she drew the cloth over the head and tied the sash, her smile waned. "Believe me, Your Grace, I can attest to the purity of all my fellow officers, as well as most of the women in the ranks." Her eyes filled with tears. "For as you know, that is why I am not with them in Heaven."

"Forgive me! I did not mean to suggest . . . ."

"There is nothing to forgive, Your Grace," she said quietly, failing to hide the tremor in her voice. Cordula drew a deep breath, regaining control. Looking Bishop Clematius in the eye, she added, "There is nothing *left* to forgive."

She glanced across at her spellbound children. "Now, much as it is an honor and a pleasure to see you, Your Grace, the snow lies thick and the sun *is* getting low."

II

"Why didn't he stay, Mother?" Brittola complained, as they bolted the doors and windows against the night. "He was a nice man. I liked him."

"Your father isn't here, and it wouldn't be proper." Cordula avoided her daughter's gaze as she busied herself with the fire. "Anyway, the Bishop was in haste to return to Londinium and then to Colonia, where he is much needed."

"Are all Batavian horses as big as the Bishop's, Mother?" her son asked.

"They are not all as big as that, but they are generally of a good size." She placed the fish in a pan on the hob, a flat shelf at the side of the fireplace, poured in some water, plucked some herb leaves from the bundles that were hanging nearby and started laying them along its body. "Your father tells me that your grandfather used to have some Batavian mares in his stock, but no stallions. He found the stallions too thick-set in the shoulder and he was breeding for speed." She paused, looked up at the rising smoke and smiled. "'Moving fast is better than holding fast when danger comes a-calling,' was his motto."

"I love it when you tell us about the past, Mother. Oh, do tell us more!" Brittola pleaded. "Please tell us about—"

"Tell us about Aunt Ursula!" her brother interrupted. "You *never* talk about her!"

Brittola gasped at her brother's request. He had mentioned the forbidden subject.

Cordula visibly froze. From behind, the children could see their mother tightly grip the handle of the pan, and her knuckles tensed and whitened. Then, slowly, she lowered her head, let out a long, tortured hiss of breath, and turned to face them. They braced themselves for a tirade. They knew it was wrong to broach anything to do with Aunt Ursula. Brittola wheeled on her brother and was about to berate him, her face fierce with a scowl; but before she could utter a word, Cordula spoke; and much to the children's surprise, her voice was quiet and calm.

"Aunt Ursula? You want me to tell you about Aunt Ursula?"

"W—well . . ." Brittola bravely started, "We know we shouldn't ask, but we . . . ."

"Yes, we *very much* want you to tell us about her." her brother said boldly. "Very much!"

"I see." Cordula frowned and stared hard at her children. *They're not ready. Now is* not *the time.* She scrutinized their faces and could see such curiosity burning hot in their hearts; could see how they desperately wanted—needed—to know. *Maybe now is the time. Maybe that head was one of the women coming back to tell me now is the time.* She turned back to the fish and resumed wrapping leaves about its flesh. *All they know is life. They are full of it . . . They* are *it. Is it really for me to tell them of death?*

Yes, it is. The sound of a familiar voice—a pale, quiet voice—filled her mind. *It is for you—the giver of their lives—to tell them. After all, both life and death are part of the same thing. Each is meaningless without the other.*

Cordula sighed resignedly, *You are right . . . as ever.* She drew a deep breath and started to speak.

"Aunt Ursula was—Ow!" Cordula snatched her hand from the fish as if it had bitten her. One of the bones had nicked the tip of her middle finger. She squeezed it to make the blood flow and held it over the fish pan to let the broth catch the drips. While she was waiting for the bleeding to stop, she stared at her children, taking measure of their readiness. *Their father should be here for such questions.* The thought of her husband helped to calm her racing mind. *Oh, why isn't he here for this? Such burning curiosity can't easily be quenched!*

"Your Aunt Ursula was my cousin," she began, attempting to adopt a matter-of-fact tone. "Like Docilina's children are your cousins."

"Yes, Mother, but what was she really *like*?" her son persisted.

"Yes, Mother, please tell us!" Brittola implored.

"What was she like? Well, to me . . ." Cordula's voice took on a quality her children had never heard before. Gone were the brusque tones of a busy mother and villa keeper with much on her mind. Gone was the reassuring resonance of a woman who had seen and done much in her youth, and who spoke on every topic with measured authority. It was, instead, a light, dancing voice, not dissimilar to that of her daughter's. A voice full of passion and wonder. As she spoke, she stared above their heads into the fathomless distance. "To me she was life itself. In a way, she gave me my life just as assuredly as I gave you yours. But she did far more than just give me life—she molded it, shaped it, defined it. And not only mine, for there were many others, thousands, for whom it was the same. And then—"

"You mean she was like a big sister?" Brittola interrupted, clearly struggling to understand.

For a brief moment, Cordula looked dazed, as if she had been startled from a dream. Then she looked down at her children and saw them both staring up at her with expressions that were so quizzical she started to laugh. With the laughter came an overwhelming sense of relief. And as she laughed, the children laughed. She bent down to give Brittola a hug. "Yes, my little lovely, just like a big sister. Did I ever tell you she had the same eyebrows as us?"

"No."

"Well she did! And, like you and me, whenever she was concentrating hard on something, she used to crease them up—just like we do."

"Then she was *funny* sometimes; not all serious like they say she was?" Brittola became so carried away with her racing thoughts, she didn't give her mother a chance to reply. "What about Aunt Martha and Aunt Saula? They were funny too, weren't they?"

"Oh, they were the *funniest!* I can tell you a thousand stories about those two!"

"Oh, *yes*, Mother, please tell us more!" Her son jumped up and down with anticipation.

"All right you two, I'll tell you the story—"

"Hooray!" They joined hands and started dancing with joy.

"But not right at this moment!" She waved them quiet. "After we've eaten. We have to cook and eat first and then clear away. Then, if you're not too tired, we'll go to bed, and I'll begin the story of Ursula and Pinnosa and—"

"And Aunt Martha and Aunt Saula?" Brittola cried.

"And the First Athena?" Her brother pleaded.

"And Aunt Brittola?" Brittola blurted excitedly.

"And the Great Expedition?" Added her brother, tugging at Cordula's sleeve.

"And—that's enough!" She clapped her hands for silence. "Now while I finish the fish, you, young lady, can prepare the vegetables. While she's doing that, you, young man, can lay the table and fetch the wine."

"Yes, Mother," they said in unison. They hurriedly set about their errands with an enthusiasm she had never seen in them before. She watched them for a while as they busied themselves with their tasks. Then she continued preparing the meal.

Just as she was salting and squeezing citron onto the fish, she heard the children behind her starting to hum a simple tune. It was an old hymn that people often sang while they worked. But under Cordula's orders it was banned at the villa, and nobody—not even her husband—was allowed to sing it. As soon as she recognized the refrain her smile dropped, her face became tense with anger. She spun around. "What is *that* you're humming?"

Brittola looked stunned at the sharp rebuke. "It's *Praise the Lord,* Mother."

"I know that!" Cordula snapped. "Where did you learn it?"

"At school." Brittola's voice quavered and her lips started to quiver.

Cordula scowled and was about to berate her when there was the familiar voice again. *If it's all coming out, it's all coming out. Don't try to stand in its way.*

Cordula hesitated. *I suppose she means no harm.*

Of course she means no harm the voice said, *It is a happy song . . .and she is happy. That's why we used to sing it. Remember?*

Yes, I remember. Slowly, she smiled. "It is a beautiful song. Do you know the words?"

"Yes, Mother."

"Then please sing it properly. Don't just hum it."

Brittola tentatively started the opening lines. Her brother soon joined in and by the end of the first chorus they were both in full voice.

Cordula was about to return to what she had been doing when a flicker of movement outside the window caught her eye. She went over to see what it was. The tiny opening offered a clear view of the kitchen courtyard and as she neared it she realized that it had started to snow. The sky was thick with cloud, robbing the courtyard of most of its remaining daylight. As she looked out through the flickering flakes, a trick of the fading light made the courtyard seem alive with fast moving shadows of cold blue and gray. The shapes were ever changing: jumping here, racing there, disappearing and reappearing. Although they took no specific form, she knew exactly what they were.

At that moment the old hymn reached her favorite verse and to her ears the sound of her children's voices seemed to fill the entire villa. *The music is chasing out all the old demons, and replacing them with a spirit that has long been denied.*

She looked upward. The distant mountains were lost in the whirling flurries. All that was visible above the villa's roof was a vast canopy of shimmering gray. It did not appear to her, though, as something oppressive and overbearing, as it might have done to most. Instead, in her mind's eye, it was an endless sea of a wondrous silver light whose power, once so awesome and strong, was now beginning to wane. She heard the children start another chorus.

The familiar voice sounded again. *In less than ten winters from now, they'll be as old as we were when we first came to this place. And in a further four winters they'll outlive us.*

"I shouldn't be telling them the story," she replied out loud. "They are not yet of an age when they can fully comprehend the meaning of it all."

Oh, I wouldn't let that bother you, said the voice with a gentle laugh that was full of the innocence of lost years. *Neither were we when it all began.*

Suddenly, there it was, in the swirling blues and grays, the stark image of Pinnosa's face rendered hideous with anguish and fear. And there was her piercing cry, echoing and reverberating throughout all eternity, shrill with urgency—"URSULA!"

The face rose up through the falling snow toward the sky, which had begun to brighten. The cry became fainter and fainter until it was engulfed by her children's singing. At that moment they commenced yet another round of their happy song, and as they did so, Cordula began to cry.

Praise Him
Praise Him
Praise Him
Praise the Lord

Christ our Lord
Teach us
Teach us to be right

Christ our Lord
Lead us
Lead us to the light

Cordula's tears fell upon her sleeves as she reached for their platters. *Not these old words again! Not now!* She clasped the platters to her breast as if to protect herself. The lilting, rhythmic round and the haunting verses of the song welled up from somewhere deep, lost and forgotten in her heart.

Jesus
Take us
Feed us
Make us good
Oh Lord

She tried to resist, but the tune overwhelmed her. She succumbed, and allowed herself to join in.

You came
You saw
You knew
You understood

Oh Lord

Your love
gives power
like
no other could

Oh Lord
Our Lord

Praise Him
Praise Him
Praise Him
Praise Him
Praise the Lord

As she sang, its melody filled her mind—and freed it. It all came flooding back. Dreams, thoughts, hopes, fears, plans, tears, horrors and anguish. It was all there in flesh, mind, body and spirit. All of it. And, with the memories came the words she needed to tell her children.

III

"Long before you were born, when I was not much older than you are now, there was a time when it seemed as if the whole of the Roman Empire was in turmoil. Massive hordes of the fearsome Goths were on the rampage and were even threatening Rome itself. They forced the Emperor, Honorius, to take refuge in his fortress city of Ravenna where, together with his army commander, Stilicho, he plotted and schemed against his many foes.

"At the same time, much further to the north, on the other side of the Alps and far beyond the Empire's borders, tribal warfare was raging amongst Rome's barbarian neighbors. Whole peoples were driven from their native lands and forced to migrate in search of new homes and fortunes. Many of them headed for the safety and rich pickings of Roman territory where the already over-stretched armies were unable to contain them or keep them at bay.

"At about this time—when I was enjoying my seventeenth and eighteenth summers—a host of Germanic tribes, in particular the Suevi and the Burgundians, succeeded in crossing the deserted frontier along the Rhine and Danube. They ravaged the northern and western provinces, especially the cities and estates of glorious Galliae. Stripped of its soldiers and left virtually undefended, Galliae offered the invaders an enticing and irresistible bounty.

"Britannia wasn't safe either. It was not to be long before the first of the Saxon landings, adding to the constant threat of Hibernian and Pict raiding parties, and stretching our defenses to their limit. Yet, just at this time of urgent need, our men were needed elsewhere; along the frontier, keeping war-hungry tribes at bay, or deep in the southern provinces dealing with others that were running amok. And, with the men away—the people felt defenseless.

"And finally—although we were blissfully unaware of them at the time and it was to be a while before we were to hear their chilling name—a new enemy was on its way. From distant lands far, far to the east there came a fierce, war-like tribe, which posed a truly formidable threat—a foe more terrible and terrifying than any other . . . *the Huns.*"

Brittola shrieked at the sound of the dreaded name. Both children were sitting bolt upright on the bed and staring at Cordula with faces full of alarm. She smiled and held out her arms. They needed no further bidding and dived for her protective embrace.

"There, there," she said soothingly. "There are no Huns here. There are no Huns in the whole of Britannia. Have no fear. You're safe here."

"What about Ursula?" came the muffled voice of her son from somewhere beneath her sleeve.

"Yes, Mummy, what about Aunt Ursula?" Brittola's face peeped out from the bundle of blanket she had gathered around her. "When did *her* story begin?"

Cordula couldn't help laughing at the look on her daughter's face. With her laughter all three of them relaxed—the chill of fear that had momentarily gripped them already forgotten.

"When did Ursula's story begin? That *is* a good question. Hmmm, let me see. I think I'll tell it to you as she told me, in the long, long late-summer evenings, while we were waiting for news of that monster, Mundzuk." *She must have known that it would need to be told one day, and that I would be the one to tell it.* The children could sense that the real story was about to begin, and shuffled into comfortable positions. Brittola snuggled herself under her mother's arm, and her brother lay on his side next to them both, head propped upon his hand.

"It all really began one hot May day, in Corinium . . . ."

Part One

Britannia

BRITTANIA

Pict Country

Hibernian
Country

Segedunum
(Wallsend)
Hadrian's Wall
Cilurnum
(Chesters)
Uxelodunum (Stanwix)
Vercovicium
(Housesteads)
Luguvallium
(Carlisle)

Eboracum
(York)

Lindum
(Lincoln)
Metaris Aestuarium
(The Wash)

Deva (Chester)

Causennae
(Ancaster)

Ratae Corieltauvorum
(Leicester)

Viroconium
Comoviorum
(Wroxeter)

Luentinum
(Pumsaint)
Magnis
(Kenchester)

Maridunum
(Camarthen)
Glevum
(Gloucester)
Tamesis
(Thames)
Londinium
(London)
Rutupiae
(Richborough)

Corinium
(Citencester)
Durobrivae
(Rochester)

Sabrina Fluvius
(The Severn)
Calleva Atrebatum
(Silchester)
Dubris (Dover)

Lindinis
(Ilchester)

Durotrigum
(Dotchester)
Venta Belgarum
(Winchester)

The Channel

Chapter One

The Men Depart

The relentless *crunch, crunch, crunch* of the soldiers' feet as they marched though the city and past the Palace was so strong it shook the small, traditional figurines of the house gods—the *lares*—in the corner of the ladies' chamber on the upper floor. One of the old, domestic deities toppled over and leaned awkwardly against the side of the shrine. The thunderous marching, shrill horns, blaring trumpets, rata-tat-tat of drums and roar of the crowd forced the young women in the room to shout at the tops of their voices in order to be heard.

Martha and Saula, who were right beside the balcony, had to cup their hands to each other's ears and bellow to be heard. They were trying to see out without being spotted by the people below. Being lean and willowy with long, loose straight hair, they looked like a pair of long-necked herons peering out of reeds.

Cordula, her brown locks pulled back and braided into a waist-length ponytail, stood alone on the other side of the window. She knew she wouldn't be the first to see the highlight of the parade—the approach of the Commanders. But it gave her a clear view of the Londinium Road as it traversed the small rise outside the city gate. That way, she would be the first to see her darling Morgan on his black horse, Hermes, should they appear.

The attendants, busy with preparations for the Great Feast welcoming the returning Commanders, were constantly coming and going. Some were collecting the various table spreads and ornamentations that were to adorn the feasting tables. Others relayed important orders for the kitchen from their mistress. In between directives, Ursula, on the other side of the room, was carefully selecting her robe for the evening. She was seated with her back to the window, picking through her large oak chest of robes and togas. All the while, Oleander, her old attendant, combed her mistress' white-blond hair, readying it for arrangement by fluffing it up into wispy ruffles like a soothsayer's beard.

Brittola was hovering at Ursula's side, eager to be involved in things but equally desperate to avoid getting in the way. Her wild and wavy black hair had already been tamed into plats about her ears, exposing her youthful face. The style allowed her bright, hazel—almost green—eyes to be seen clearly for once, rather than being lost behind her usual tangle of curls. "How will you wear your hair tonight, Ursula? To the back or to the sides?"

"I haven't decided yet, but I think . . . ." She paused and looked up at the younger woman out of the corner of her eye.

"Yes?" Brittola said, eagerly leaning forward.

"I think I'll wear it to the sides."

Brittola beamed.

Ursula, turning to face her, was unable to prevent her own broad smile. Her deep blue eyes flickered with merriment. "Which means I won't be needing my gold and onyx hairpin. Would you like to borrow it, Brittola?"

"Oh, *could* I?" She started clapping excitedly, but then managed to restrain herself. "That is, if none of the others would like to wear it."

Ursula reached out and clasped Brittola's hands. Beginning her sixteenth summer, Brittola was the youngest of their group and a full three winters younger than Ursula or Pinnosa. For a moment Ursula allowed herself to share her young friend's excitement at the return of the army, and they exchanged a private grin. "Oh, I shouldn't think they'll want it. Besides it'll look far more effective in your dark curls than in their horse tails!" She produced the hairpin from her accessory casket and handed it to her young friend. Brittola took it with the wide-eyed wonder of a child receiving a prize.

"Oh, where *is* the Vanguard and the senior officers?" Saula groaned aloud during a momentary lull in the cacophony from the crowd outside. "Where's Constantine? Why does he have the army pass first? Why doesn't he lead the parade like other Roman Commanders?"

"The men are his glory, so they share his glory," Ursula called across the room without looking up from the fine cloth she was examining. "He always says, 'those who work hardest should rest soonest.' It's his way. His men always come first. The only time he goes ahead of them is when they march into battle. And besides . . ." she turned and held Saula's diverted gaze before continuing, "he's a *Britannic* Roman Commander."

"It's not Constantine she's so eager to see, Ursula!" Martha shouted in reply. "It's the Vanguard she's anxious about. And a certain young officer called—"

Martha!" Saula cried, tugging Martha's sleeve to shut her up.

Martha retaliated by tousling Saula's hair. Saula grabbed a nearby wall hanging and pretended to smother her best friend. Their unusually boisterous play soon became so unruly that Ursula gave them a censorial look. They reluctantly calmed down and returned their attention to the scene outside, sulking like scolded children.

After a long pause, Martha leaned over and said to Saula, "I *love* watching the men on the march. See how handsome and smart they all are! Is there a sight to be more proud of in the entire Empire?"

"Especially as most of them are single and extremely eligible!" Saula added, nudging Martha in the ribs. "And I'm not the *only* one with someone specific in mind!"

They both giggled. Martha peered over her shoulder to see if Ursula was watching, and, seeing that she was fully engrossed with Oleander, she cupped her hand to Saula's ear. "I wish I was a bathhouse slave tonight!" They erupted into raucous laughter.

"Please!" Cordula protested.

Martha and Saula both poked their tongues out at her in reply before looking out once more at the street below.

"Look!" Saula cried. "The Commanders' standards!"

Ursula leapt to her feet, her work momentarily forgotten. "Is Constans . . . ."

Cordula glanced at her cousin and caught a fleeting glimpse of naked fear. She knew the word on Ursula's lips was 'there?' But then—somehow—Ursula managed to control herself and say, "the first?"

Brittola ran past Ursula to stand in the full frame of the window, becoming partly visible to the crowd below. "Yes, is it Constans or Constantine or someone else who has the position of honor?"

Martha and Saula had the best angle to see along the Palace wall, and both were straining their necks as far as they could. It was Martha who spotted them first. "I can see the leading horse's head! It's . . . It's . . . ."

"Gerontius," they groaned in unison as the huge, thickset man came into view.

"The ugly, fat bull!" Saula hissed.

"But wait! There're two of them abreast!" Brittola cried. "No, *three!* All three are leading together. And the one in the center is . . . *Constans!* Constans has the greatest honor!"

Ursula closed her eyes and shuddered with relief. As she did so the crowd below saw the Commanders and cheered with an almighty roar.

"Well, well, well," Cordula moved behind Brittola and spoke into her ear. "Constans *is* becoming popular."

"That's because he's so handsome!" Brittola shouted over her shoulder.

"True. Ursula will have to be careful there!" They both laughed. "And Constantine's getting on a bit. It's good to see his son shaping up well. He'll need to be strong to finish his father's work."

"What do you mean?"

"Re-building the army. You're too young to remember when we were defenseless, and we—"

"Oh, Ursula, *do* come and look!" Brittola interrupted excitedly. "Constans and Constantine are riding side by side, father and son—great heroes both—like Phillip and Alexander! And your Constans is at the heart of the glory. Oh, *do* look, Ursula, please! You'll be so proud!"

"*Ursula!*" A rich, clear voice rang out from the street below: the familiar and welcome sound of their great protector, Constantine. "Come out on the balcony, Princess, and let your people see you! Come! And all you other beautiful young ladies—I know you are up there keeping discreetly out of sight. Cast aside undue decorum! Come forward and greet us with your majesty. Let Constans see his beloved bride-to-be and let the men know that we are truly *home!*"

Martha and Saula needed no further bidding. They threw aside the wall drapes they were hiding behind and led Cordula and Brittola out on to the balcony. They were met by rapturous cries from the crowd. The legionaries let out a great cheer at the sight of the four young noblewomen.

Brittola squirmed with embarrassment.

The cheers died down. Everyone's lips became stilled with expectancy.

Slowly, Ursula emerged from the shadows. Being taller than the others and with her mane of white hair falling loosely over her shoulders, she filled the window with her presence. Having reached the full bloom of womanhood since the army left on its expedition almost a year before, she looked a picture of serenity. With her commanding dark blue eyes she carried all the dignity and authority of her fondly remembered mother, the late queen Rabacie. Upon her appearance, the people in the crowd re-doubled their cheers.

She smiled in acknowledgement and briefly took in the scene before fixing her gaze upon her Constans. He, too, had matured since they had last met. The final residue of boyhood had left him. His hands held the horse's reins with a firm grip and his wispy beard had filled out into the same thick, black gorse as his father's. His skin had the weatherworn look of a seasoned campaigner and had lost its supple shine. His broad smile was now a knowing one; not so full of questions.

The whole assembly witnessed the look of love that passed between their handsome young hero and their beautiful princess.

Then, Constantine slowly reached up, removed his helmet and bowed.

Constans followed suit. So, too, did Gerontius, but only after a pause and with ill-disguised impatience at what he clearly regarded as a frivolous waste of his time.

"Behold, good people of Corinium! Behold *all* the folk of Britannia!" Constantine grabbed his son's arm and raised it high in triumph. "Behold your *future!* Behold Constans and Ursula!"

"*Constans and Ursula! Constans and Ursula! Constans and Ursula!*" The cry was picked up by the crowd and seemed to fill the city. At the height of the chanting, the Commanders gave another graceful bow, replaced their helmets, and urged their horses on, resuming the parade.

Just as the officers' standards were disappearing from sight, Cordula grabbed Ursula by the arm. "Look," She pointed over the roofs to the hilltop beyond the city walls. "Pinnosa!"

Even at such a distance there was no mistaking Pinnosa. She was riding her huge, black mare, Artemis, and dressed in her usual attire—hunting clothes. Her bright red hair was tied back and up so that it wouldn't get in her way. A string of game was slung over her right shoulder. A deer was draped across Artemis' rump. Her bow was strapped behind her back. She carried her long hunting spear in her left hand. As her friends watched, she turned the great horse away from them and rode out of sight.

"She must have heard the noise and known the army was on parade," Brittola's voice was heavy with disappointment. "Why didn't she come to join us?"

"She was probably too busy with that deer," Martha said. "You know how nothing can keep her from the hunt, especially once the chase is on."

"I think you are right, Martha, but I wish she would change her ways," Ursula said with a sigh. "All the more so now that she has official responsibilities and needs to be here performing her duties—just like us. She is sometimes far too comfortable in what she calls 'the civilization of the wild,' and regards 'the wilderness of the city,' with far too much disdain. Oh, Pinnosa . . ." she said more to herself than to the others, as she continued to stare at the now vacant hilltop. "Why do you prefer the world of nature so? And why do you take such delight in shunning the world of men?"

"The truth is she envies men and their world," Saula said jokingly to Martha as they turned to leave the balcony. "She's like a wolf obsessed with the hawk's wings!"

They all chuckled at the observation. Even Ursula smiled as she returned to making preparations for the Great Feast.

II

Ursula turned to Brittola, who was seated beside her at the ladies' head table. "Where are all the men?"

The Great Feast had already started, due to the presence of some important Roman officials from Londinium, even though most of the men had yet to arrive. The officials were at the head table, along with King Deonotus, Morgan the messenger, Bishop Patroclus and three local noblemen. There were still six empty seats reserved for Constantine, Constans, Gerontius, Brittola's father, Conanus, and two more senior Commanders. Most of the women, at both the head and lower tables, were present. The wives of the officials were with Ursula, Brittola, Cordula, Martha and Saula at the other head table. The lower tables, which were supposed to be a pleasant mix of men and women, were still half-empty and occupied by the wives, mothers, and sisters of the junior army officers. The only important woman missing was Pinnosa.

The food was lavishly presented and smelled tantalizingly delicious. There were whole calves and pigs on spits, huge mounds of cooked game, shellfish and fruit on great silver platters. The aromatic wine was beginning to whet everyone's appetites. Indeed, the ample-framed Bishop Patroclus—after breaking the bread and blessing the feast—had already given full rein to his hunger and accumulated quite a pile of debris from his ravening.

Meanwhile, the entertainment had begun. A fire-eater, clad in a striped animal skin of some kind—which Cordula thought might be called 'zebra'—kept the women so well amused by his acrobatics they did not seem perturbed by the absence of the Commanders.

Ursula took advantage of the diversion to slip over to her father. "Where can they be, Father?" she whispered into his ear. "They should have been here long ago!"

"Don't fret, my dear. For men to whom we owe so much, a little patience should be easy to give."

"But, Father! Their baths would have been complete well before sunset. What can they be doing? Surely they are hungry and thirsty." An awful thought occurred to her.

Her father's anxious glance confirmed her fears. "Don't trouble yourself so, my dear. Your work is done. The feast is magnificent. Be patient. They'll be here soon, I'm sure you—"

"They're at the *altar*, aren't they?" she hissed. The glare she fixed upon her father, made his congenial smile freeze.

"Hush!" King Deonotus quickly turned her away from Bishop Patroclus. He need not have worried, since his old friend was wholly engrossed in getting at the juicier parts of a succulent young partridge. "It is not easy for good leaders to leave their men. Their sense of duty is too strong. Allow them to complete their work."

"I'm going to put a stop to their—work—and fetch them here!"

"No! You mustn't do that. These are men's matters. You shouldn't concern yourself with them."

"Anything that concerns men is of great concern to women—as well you know, Father."

He smiled. "You have the same fierce resolve as your mother," he said. "I know I can't do—or say—anything to stop you once your blood's up." They exchanged a glance of understanding and she left.

At that moment, with a sudden flash and a crackling sound, the fire-eater made a white dove appear from a flaming hoop and fly across the gathering. Several women gasped in amazement, Cordula shrieked excitedly with surprise, and even Bishop Patroclus put down his partridge to join in the round of applause.

Almost no one noticed the Princess' departure, except Brittola. She had watched the hushed conversation between her friend and the King. As soon as Ursula slipped behind the screens, she picked up her cloak and quietly followed her out. At the same time, Oleander sidled out into the antechamber, determined, as ever, to keep her mistress in her sight, just as she had done since Ursula had been old enough to walk.

Back at the head table, Cordula—who had observed the three sneaking out—took advantage of Brittola's absence to make herself more comfortable. She stretched her legs, reached for a clutch of deep purple grapes, and proceeded to consume them with succulent delight.

III

Ursula walked quickly down the empty main street toward the Officers' Hall. The lane, shadow-filled during the day, was flooded with a warm pink glow of an early summer sunset. An unseasonably cool breeze blew her white-gold hair around her shoulders. She could hear how the wind agitated the animals in some of the enclosed kitchen gardens and building yards nearby: geese grumbled and half-honked; pigs shuffled and snorted; some dogs barked whilst others whined. Apart from these noises, the only other sound was the *flap-clap-flap* of her sandals on the deeply rutted, stone road.

"Wait for me!" Brittola cried breathlessly, running to catch up.

"Brittola?" Ursula stopped and turned. "You shouldn't be out here. Go back to the feast. I shan't be long. I'm just going to fetch Constans and his father. They've probably been caught up with something and forgotten the time."

"And I'm going to fetch Father. He's probably been caught up, too."

"I'll make sure he comes with them. Now please—go back."

"I'm coming with you. They're up to something, aren't they?"

"If they're up to what I think they're up to, then you must stay behind. Your father would most certainly not wish you to see it. It's not for young eyes like yours."

"Ursula! How can you say that to me? We are both only children. When our mothers died, you were the same age as I am now. Did you shirk your responsibility to your father? Wouldn't you have been just as determined as I am to check on him and, if needs be, put him straight?"

The last rays from the sunset enabled the two women to look deeply into each other's eyes. "You're right. I would," Ursula said. "When my mother died, my father was my life, even though Constans was my love."

"And I don't even have a love. Father is all I have."

Ursula smiled. "Very well. You may come," she said. "But be prepared. *This . . . .*"

Brittola knew what she was going to say next. It was a phrase they always used when bracing themselves to face any difficult or unpleasant task, and they completed it in unison, *"May not be easy!"*

They laughed, put their arms round each other and set off together.

IV

The front of the Officers' Hall faced outward from the city center, which meant that Ursula and Brittola approached it from behind. They were just passing the rear of the huge building when the sound of men chanting caught their ears. They paused. As they listened, the refrain, which seemed to be coming from the alley that led behind the hall, grew—culminating in a loud, guttural roar.

"Come on!" Brittola cried, running off to investigate. "Let's catch them at it!"

"Brittola! Come back! Come *back*, I tell you!" Ursula shouted to no avail. Her friend had already disappeared into the alley. With an exasperated, "Oh, Brittola!" she ran after her.

The alley opened into an old courtyard. The long, solid wall of the Officers Hall formed one complete side of the yard. It had no openings of any kind, except for a small window that was high up in the center and well beyond reach. Beside the wall and immediately outside the window was a large, old chestnut tree with strong branches reaching well above the hall's roof. Ursula and Brittola knew it well, having climbed it often in their childhood. The people of Corinium had a superstition that the little window looked into a room where dead soldiers' shadows lived. It had always been a big dare among the city's children to climb the tree's creaky boughs to peer inside and see if the shadows were moving.

Ursula caught up with Brittola at the entrance to the courtyard. The chanting had started again. The sound was coming from the small window, though the thickness of the wall rendered the words indiscernible.

"Come on! Let's see what they're up to," Brittola whispered. Before Ursula could respond, she ran over to the tree, leapt for the lowest bough, and started to climb.

"We're not children now you know," Ursula muttered to herself. Reluctantly, she followed, and set about seeking the toe holds and hand grips she had used as a young girl.

While she was making her way up to the long branch that gave a clear view of the window, the chanting climaxed with another roar like the one they had heard from the street. "Brittola!" she whispered loudly. "Come down! It's not safe!"

But Brittola could already see what Ursula feared.

By the time Ursula reached her, Brittola was transfixed, with one hand gripping a branch overhead to steady herself and the other clasping the large, silver cross she always wore, brandishing it high to ward off the evil before her eyes. Ursula sidled up beside her and looked down into the room.

She saw a hooded figure with its back to her, swathed in black cloth, wearing a red and gold headband. The figure was bent forward as if preparing something, and it was surrounded by a congregation in similar attire. Standing in front of the hooded figure and facing the window squarely was Gerontius, clean-shaven and naked to the waist. As the two young women watched, the figure straightened and thrust a large, jewel-encrusted, gold goblet into the air. The red liquid it contained splashed out and down his bare arms. Gerontius reached up, took the vessel, and held it in the air for the duration of the guttural roar the gesture had elicited from the congregation. As the noise subsided, the bull-necked Commander lowered it to his lips and drank. Some of the red liquid ran down his cheeks and trickled from his chin. His draught complete, Gerontius placed the goblet on the altar and moved out of view. As he did so, the men resumed their murmurous chant. The hooded figure lifted the freshly severed head of a calf into the air by its ears and refilled the goblet with its dripping blood.

Brittola gasped. Ursula feared her friend was about to faint and reached out to grab her. At that moment Brittola's father, Conanus, who was also freshly shaven and naked to the waist, came into view and stood before the altar.

"Come on. We've seen enough. Let's get down," Ursula urged. She tried to shield Brittola from the awful sight.

"Oh, dear sweet God!" Brittola cried. "What is he *doing*? He isn't even wearing his cross! Oh, God! *Oh, God!*"

"Shhh! Brittola!" Ursula tried desperately to calm her. "Come on! Let's climb down and put a stop to all this."

Brittola shook her head violently in disbelief and squealed. "God! Make it stop! Make it stop! *Please!*"

Ursula managed to grab Brittola around the waist and began coaxing her back down the tree. As she did so, she caught a final glimpse of the scene inside the hall. All the men, including the hooded figure, were looking up toward the window. The hood on the robed figure slid back, revealing the stern face of Constantine. Next in line for the ceremonial rite, also cleanly shaven and naked to the waist, was Constans.

V

Ursula was still helping Brittola descend the tree when the men, now dressed in their togas and carrying torches, emerged from the alley. Filling the courtyard, they surrounded the gnarled old chestnut, sneering and cursing.

"Come down here to me, you hysterical young wench! I'll give you something to scream about!" Gerontius shouted.

"Hold your tongue, Gerontius!" Constantine made his way through the men. "Can't you see it's Princess Ursula?"

As he spoke, Ursula eased Brittola onto the bottom-most bough. Constans, who had pushed his way to the front, reached up to lift her down. The moment he let her go, she fell to the ground, weeping.

"We are truly sorry to have disturbed you gentlemen!" Ursula snapped, as she leapt from the tree. Although she addressed the entire gathering, she kept her eyes firmly on Constantine and Constans. "We simply came to remind you that the Great Feast, being held in your honor at the Palace, awaits your presence." She bent down beside a sobbing Brittola. Taking her friend in her arms, she began rocking her gently to and fro, saying quietly, "There, there. Don't cry. It's all over."

A murmur ran through the assembly, "It's young Brittola."

Her father, Conanus, made his way to the front and stood next to Constantine. He was the army's most senior statesman when they were on campaigns, and was older than the other Commanders. His aged gait showed all the more when he was out of uniform. "Come, my dear. Pull yourself together. You've made enough of a spectacle of yourself this evening, and we've got a wonderful feast to attend yet." He stepped forward and, smiling kindly at Ursula, picked his daughter up by her arm.

"Let me go!" She waved his hands away and scrambled to her feet. "Let me go!" Once standing, she flicked back her hair and stared at him defiantly. "How could you, Father? I noticed you took off your cross. Why was that? Because you thought you could hide your shame from God?"

Visibly upset, he tried to reach out and take hold of her, but she shied away again.

"It's bad enough *they* should do such a thing!" She made a wild sweep with her arms to signify the surrounding men. "But why *you* should do it is beyond my comprehension! You don't need to prove anything to anybody—other than to God. You of all people! You who were blessed as a baby by Constantine the Great himself. How could you do such a terrible thing, Father? *Where is your faith?*"

"Come. There are better times and places to have such discussions, my dear." He tried to lead her away, but again she resisted.

"*No!* I want to know why you and these other 'Christian' men can't keep faith with the *true* God!"

"We keep faith with whichever god or gods we please, young lady!" Constantine stepped forward and forcibly took hold of her arm to prevent her from embarrassing her father any further. "Why, even you have the old gods by your hearth at home, don't you?"

"Yes, but, that's just tradition—it's not—"

"And, you give thanks to Zeus and Athena when its appropriate, don't you?"

"Yes, but that's not—"

"Do you know *why* you do that?" Constantine paused, but then continued before Brittola could answer. "I'll tell you why . . . because you are *free* to do so . . . . "

"I know, but—"

Constantine raised his voice to address his men. "And your freedom to worship whatever you please in the manner of your choosing is part of the true glory of Rome. Only Rome is powerful enough to embrace more than one religion and any number of gods. For all gods yield to Rome's superior power."

He paused to glance around the gathering, but his gaze was captured by Ursula's intense stare. "Brittola, your father is absolutely right. There are better times and places for such talk, and I'll tell you why. The freedom you enjoy, which gives you the luxury of having such discussions—about whether we are ruled by God or the gods, or about whether Faith or Fate weighs heaviest in the balance . . . ." He allowed a note of mockery to enter his voice. The men responded with sniggers and smirks. "This freedom is hard won and needs to be constantly defended against a whole multitude of hostile forces. So before all else: before God, before Faith or Fate, before even Freedom itself, must come *Duty!* It is every able-bodied Roman's duty to defend the Empire and *all* that she stands for." He looked pointedly at Ursula and Constans. "And, it is only after he has performed his duty—successfully—that he can retire to the company of his family and friends, sit down at peace and enjoy his hard won freedoms such as wonderful feasts and discussions about—"

Sensing his grip relax, Brittola wrestled herself from Constantine's grasp, grabbed her silver cross with both hands and thrust it high into the air. "No!" she cried. "That's not right! You must be clear in your mind—and your heart—that your only *real* duty is to God! The *one* God. The *true* God! Why be content just to live in a free world? What kind of 'hard won' freedom is it that makes you free to drink the blood of the beasts? Seek to live in a good world, too! You can only do that by subjecting yourself to God's Will. And you can only begin to do *that* by rejecting these false gods, and by ceasing to act like . . . like *animals!*"

Constantine bristled. His men wouldn't dare to interrupt him once, and now this young girl had done it twice.

"As your father rightly says," Ursula stepped in front of Brittola with her back to Constantine. "This is neither the time nor the place for such discussions." She turned to face Conanus. "I think you should take her to the feast where such topics are more appropriate."

"Come. Let's take a slow walk together." The old man gingerly placed his arm around Brittola's shoulders.

She lowered her head and allowed him to lead her away. For a moment it looked as though her outburst was over. But then, just as they were entering the alley, she pulled free and spun around to face the gathering. "Your first duty is to God not Rome!" she shouted. "You are a *Christian* army first— and a Roman army second!"

The men simply stared at her. None of them spoke; none stirred. She glared back defiantly, begging confrontation, until she encountered Ursula's stern expression of disapproval. She bit her tongue, turned and finally departed, followed by her father. The sound of her sobs could be heard, echoing around the dark alley, well after she disappeared from view.

As the sound began to fade, Constantine gave a decisive nod and his silent order was immediately obeyed. The men dispersed, leaving him alone in the old courtyard with Constans and Ursula.

Ursula broke the silence. "I can see how it must be difficult for you to reconcile leading an army which is both Roman and Christian. What puzzles me, though, is how you can fight any battle or wage any campaign unless you are clear in your own mind exactly what you are fighting for."

"It's often knowing what you are fighting *against* that is the most vexing question," Constantine replied in the warm tones she had known and loved since childhood. He paused and held his torch closer to her. "Ursula, you have gained many responsibilities since you took over from your dear mother. You should know by now that there are often many different reasons for the duties that befall us; usually more reasons than we're aware of. If we tried to think of them all, we would go mad. In the end we fulfill many of our duties simply because we know they are things that must be done, not because we know why we are doing them."

"But what about our personal reasons? Surely we have a duty to ourselves, too." She looked at him defiantly. "You, for example. I'm curious; what exactly do you—you *personally*—fight for when you go into battle?"

They stared at each other silently for a while. The prolonged gaze continued, making Constans look uncomfortable.

"I thank goodness that you're a woman," Constantine said, finally breaking the long silence. "That means you'll never have to go into battle. Even though I'm a man of war, and I have seen both God and the gods in action, I can't answer your question. All I can say is this: Whenever we go into battle, if God is with us he gives us Faith. If the gods are with us they give us Fate. Both make excellent weapons. Both make excellent shields."

He turned to Constans and slapped him on the shoulder. "I believe we have better things to be doing than play games with words! Will you please take our Princess back to her Palace and to the Great Feast where she belongs? I'll be along shortly."

Constans took Ursula by the hand and led her from the courtyard. As they left, Constantine laid his torch on one of the old chestnut tree's boughs, clasped his hands behind his back and stared up at the now dark window in the rear wall of the Officers' Hall.

"Ursula!" he called, just as the young couple were about to enter the alley. They paused. "If ever I make a decision about whether it is God or the gods, Faith or Fate I truly believe in, I'll make a point of letting you know."

VI

Constans and Ursula walked the length of the alley in silence. As they entered the street, they slowed and stopped. Then—at long last—she was looking into his beloved eyes. The rest of the world with its burning issues and its constant demands was completely forgotten. All that mattered—all that existed—was their love for each other.

As she offered herself for his embrace he hesitated. "How could you allow such a scene like that in front of Gerontius and the others? Couldn't you control Brittola? Please remember you are soon going to be my wife. One day they will be our subjects, and we will need their respect."

For a second, Ursula had difficulty taking in what he had said. "Brittola has good reason to be upset at what you were doing, and for that matter—so do I!" He tried to speak, but she cut him off. "I don't want to be the wife of a blood-thirsty pagan! You were about to drink from the chalice, too. Don't deny it! I saw you—with my own eyes! Where is *my* Constans? The Christian Constans I was baptized with? What kind of man are you becoming?"

"A man shaped by his *work!*"

She was surprised at the new-found depth and assertiveness in his voice.

"See these hands? These hands that you love to feel so gentle upon your tender skin? You should see them at their work. Oh, how much you would admire their skill! Thrusting a spear into a man's gut. Slashing at an enemy's throat with a sword. Carrying a comrade from the gore and yanking arrows from his flesh. That's my place of work—the battlefield! And in battle, believe me, it is the gods of war—the gods without—who are beating the drum. Not the personal God within. When the arrows fly or the enemy charges, each man prays to the only gods that count—those who control fortune and destiny. Fortune does not distinguish between Good and Evil as it works wild in the fray."

"What you speak of has nothing to do with God, and everything to do with luck! How can you say that the battlefield is your place of work? Your true place of work is in the hearts of men, as their leader, as their Commander and, one day, as their King. Your hands weren't meant for killing, but for signing decrees and greeting visiting dignitaries, and—"

He had begun to smile as she was speaking, and now he started to laugh. It was the deliberate laugh of someone using laughter for its effect on the listener. She had never heard him laugh like that. "And holding my wife, and caressing my children. Oh, how I love you when you are bursting with ideas. Your forehead becomes furrowed and your face always says far more than your voice." He tried to pull her close.

She resisted and pushed him away. "Don't distract me so Constans. This is important. I mean it! I will *not* marry a pagan! Not even a half pagan who is pragmatic about his worship like his father. Brittola is right. You must be as true to God as you are to me or to our children."

He stopped laughing and grabbed her by the shoulders. She had never known him like this. He was her Constans—her familiar Constans, her beloved Constans—yes; but, now, for the first time ever, she was with Constans the man. And this man—her man—had his first thing to say to her, man to woman. "Ursula, listen to me. You know yourself how strong this new army is. You know how disciplined we are. How, with my father at its head, we are the most powerful fighting unit in all Rome! The Emperor couldn't *wish* for a mightier hand to do his work, and . . . ." He saw the concern in her face and paused. "And I think our time has come. I think we will soon have to serve on the Continent."

Even though her mind was racing, and her heart was welling with fear—the same dark fear, a fear full of menace that she had felt earlier—she managed a reassuring nod and smile to indicate that he should continue. "We're on full alert. Our numbers are higher than ever. We've mobilized all the reserves from the standing units and drawn them into the field army. Things are looking bad in Germania and Galliae, and I think . . . ." He took a deep breath and stared deeply into her eyes. "The situation on the Continent is dire. The Governors of the provinces are desperate. The number of German invasions is on the increase. Barbarians are breaking through the frontier defenses, laying waste to land, towns, and even a number of cities. But, just when the Governors need to increase their defenses, units of cavalry and infantry are being re-deployed from the frontier garrisons to the south to defend Italia against the Goths. Because of the threat, even the Imperial Court has moved south to Arelate. All of this means that the only way the frontier defenses can hold is if the Britannic legions embark on a campaign to rebuild them and restore order." He swallowed awkwardly, "I think we will be setting forth any day now."

She lowered her head to hide her look of horror as she struggled to come to terms with his news. "I . . . I remember the last time our army went to the Continent, don't you? When your father was just a centurion? Remember how splendid and proud the legions looked when they departed? We all watched them leave, their weapons gleaming in the sunshine as galley upon galley slid quietly away from the safety of the long, white cliffs, heading for Gesoriacum." Her eyes filled with tears. "They were so full of shame when they returned years later, only a handful of men, their horses lost, virtually without any weapons and their uniforms in tatters. There were barely enough of them to recruit, train and rebuild the army in order to regain so much lost strength. But rebuild they did. And now look at you . . . ." She raised her head and looked him foursquare in the eye. "The best army this province has ever had."

They both managed a weak smile, but Ursula's faltered. She was close to tears. "Oh, why are we cursed on this island? Why is it that every time we manage to build a strong army—an army that is the envy of all—an army that can truly defend Britannia—that it is then taken away from us? Why is it that the fruit of all our hard work is to be wasted on preserving the privileges of those in Galliae—and elsewhere—who are too indolent to organize and protect themselves properly? Why is it that Rome with all its twisted politics and trickery . . . . Why is it that Rome always reaps our harvest?

He held her in his arms. "We won't fall prey to the politics of Rome, my love. We are more than a match for this task. We can accomplish even *more* than the Emperor expects. I believe we will be so decisive in our campaign that the frontier will be stronger than ever before. They say that some of these northern peoples can be made into useful federal allies. We will settle the most civilized of them along the outer edge of the Empire to act as guardians against further invading tribes. The others we shall send back where they came from or escort them to areas where they can do no harm. In the process, through our leadership and example, we will teach those wastrels in Galliae how to organize their own defenses more effectively. Galliae, Germania and Hispania need to stand with Britannia as equal pillars of the West, instead of whimpering every time there's a threat of invasion and relying on us to do the dirty work. When we've accomplished all this—and we will—we'll return home, to a safer home, where a man can retire to his estate and be with those he loves."

She nestled her head against his shoulder. He lowered his voice to the soothing tones she heard so often in her dreams, and while he spoke she could feel his heart beating. "When this time comes and I believe it will be sooner than we think—when no more campaigns need to be waged, no more battles fought. When a lasting peace reigns, my duty will at last be done. I shall devote myself to my true life. Our life together. Our family. Our kingdom. And in that life I shall put all gods aside but the true God we share in our hearts. Forever and ever. I promise."

They kissed a long, gentle kiss, breathing as one. Then, suddenly, she pushed him away.

"That still doesn't forgive you for your blood-drinking idolatry!" She punched him hard on the arm. "But, that will have to wait for now! Come on . . . ." She grabbed his hand. "Let's join the feast!"

They walked off briskly towards the Palace, filling the familiar old streets of Corinium with the sound of their jokes and cheerful banter. As they rounded the corner, Ursula caught sight of Oleander emerge from the shadows and sneak along behind them with a hand clapped over her mouth to conceal a wry smile.

VII

Once everyone was finally assembled, the Great Feast went well. The quails were so appetizing and the wine flowed so freely that Bishop Patroclus burst into song. The Roman officials—now quite enjoying their cups—joined in the choruses. Everyone was settled and relaxed. Constantine, Constans, King Deonotus and Conanus were listening intently to Morgan as he relayed more details of events on the Continent. Only occasionally did one of them interrupt the messenger with the odd comment, which usually made the whole group laugh.

Looking distinctly awkward and uncomfortable, Gerontius had been seated on the other side of the table with Bishop Patroclus and the officials. Ursula, who was with the officials' wives on the adjacent table, smiled to herself as she watched him straining to hear what Constantine and the other Commanders were saying.

"He's like a pig wondering what the spit's for!" Brittola whispered in her ear. They stifled outbursts of laughter. Since her walk with her father, Brittola had calmed down. She seemed to be enjoying the evening as if nothing had happened.

Just then, the sounds of a scuffle broke out behind the dining screens. Some of the attendants could be heard making protests. "Out of my way! Get back into the kitchen and stoke up the fire!" Pinnosa swept in and stopped in front of the head tables. She was still in her hunting clothes and had a young deer—complete with its first growth of antlers—slung across her back.

The singing and laughter stopped. Everyone stared. Some of the Roman officials and their wives were open-mouthed with astonishment.

"I'm sorry I'm late," she said deferentially to King Deonotus. "Only it crossed my mind you might need some more meat for your larder after such a feast. At first I thought I'd get a big, fat boar . . . but then I remembered you already had Gerontius!"

Everyone laughed, except, of course, Gerontius, who scowled into his drink.

Pinnosa unloaded the deer into the hands of two nearby attendants. Then, pulling out her hunting knife, she grabbed hold of one of the deer's antlers and hacked it off.

"Here, Gerontius!" she cried, strolling over to the heavily-built man. "This is for you. From what the bath house slaves tell me, you need all the help you can get!"

The reference to sexual prowess and aphrodisiacs made the officials' wives hide their faces with embarrassment. The men roared with laughter at the Commander's expense. The hatred between Pinnosa and Gerontius was well known by most present, but even the Roman visitors could feel it now.

She threw the antler down into his food, glaring at him with cold-eyed aggression.

The laughter stopped.

Gerontius stabbed his eating knife so hard into the tabletop, a dish of oysters toppled and cascaded into Bishop Patroclus' lap. Slowly, he stood up, turned around, and snarled in his guttural northern accent, "I'll not let good company and the need for manners stop me from thrashing an impudent young brat, whatever the sex!"

"You?" Pinnosa was now less than an arm's reach from Gerontius. "Thrash me?" She laughed defiantly. "You're a big man in the army, where you can get others to fight for you. But on your own—you're just mouth and flab." She puffed out her cheeks and mimed a caricature, taunting him to the limit.

"*Why you!*" He dived forward and tried to grab her. She ducked nimbly to one side, avoiding his clutches with ease.

Then Pinnosa turned on Gerontius. Leering at him with a mixture of defiance and disgust, she raised her hunting knife and brandished it with threatening menace. She started to circle him—poised ready to strike.

"That's *enough!*" Constantine shouted. "Remember our guests. Save your petty squabbles for the street. Don't bring them in here!"

"Come and join the ladies!" Ursula hurried across the room to grab Pinnosa. She called to the attendants. "Bring her a dining robe!"

"I'm not an impudent young brat now, Gerontius!" Pinnosa snapped before Ursula could reach her. "I'm full grown and more than capable of shifting your bulk—which is more than you did for my father! Furthermore, I intend to prove it." She turned to address the head table. "I hereby challenge Gerontius to a contest!"

"What?" Gerontius cried. "A contest with *you*?"

"Come and sit down Pinnosa," Ursula pleaded.

Pinnosa slowly and deliberately sheathed her knife, then moved forward to stand directly in front of Gerontius, sneering right into his face. "What's the matter? Not man enough to test your strength against a mere woman! Pah!" She spat at his feet. "Just as I said—all mouth and flab!"

Gerontius, clearly trying to contain his rage, and, at the same time, desperate to be spared further embarrassment, looked across the table at Constantine.

Constantine said nothing. He simply raised a questioning eyebrow and shrugged, barely able to conceal his amusement.

Slowly Gerontius turned back to face Pinnosa. "If it's a lesson you want, then a lesson I'm happy to give you." He forced a strained smile, bowed to the ladies' table and sat down, once more turning his back on his adversary.

"Tomorrow morning in the south meadows after morning bells!" Pinnosa snarled.

"Tomorrow it'll be," he replied begrudgingly without bothering to turn 'round.

Pinnosa seemed satisfied. She bowed gracefully to the two head tables, politely acknowledged the Roman officials, and allowed Ursula to escort her to join the ladies.

"Hello. How nice to see you," she said to several of the guests, as she made her way around to her allotted place, grabbing food and wine as she went.

VIII

News of the contest spread rapidly. Riding down the narrow path from the city to the south meadows, Ursula found herself surrounded by officers, off-duty soldiers and townsfolk. Her friends and Cordula were with the Roman delegation under a large elm by the river. Servants offered dainties taken from a small skiff moored nearby to them. She dismounted and made her way to join the party.

A few minutes later, Constantine and Constans arrived carrying flasks of the finest wine from the Palace's cellars. "It's a perfect morning for a contest," Constantine said, obviously refreshed and in good spirits. "Come! Let us drink to poor Gerontius and his bane—the girl who would avenge her poor father's maiming."

"May the best fighter win!" Constans added while their glasses were filled.

The revelers toasted.

Ursula loved the Palace wine. As she drank, she sucked the crisp May air in deeply through her nose and mixed it with the vintage against her palate. She could feel its tangy aroma awakening her taste buds and filling them with a sense of anticipation. She swallowed, and as she did so she noticed the morning sun beginning to glisten through the mist-laden treetops.

A hunting horn sounded from the upper branches of a huge oak tree by the entrance to the meadows. Ursula smiled to herself as Brittola cried excitedly, "It's Pinnosa! She's up in the tree!"

It sounded again—a long, shrill note repeated three times—the signal that game had been spotted. The branches rustled and Pinnosa emerged, sliding down a rope to land on one of the lower boughs. She blew her horn three more times and sprang to the ground, shouting, "I can see my prey! I'm coming to get you!" She made her way through the assembly with purposeful strides, clearly intent upon her quarry.

With the contest looking imminent, the people in the middle of the clearing moved aside to create an arena for the action. As the crowd parted, Gerontius became visible. He had just arrived with some other officers on a small boat and they were getting out at the opposite end of the meadow.

Pinnosa reached the center of the newly cleared space and came to a halt. She stood absolutely still, waiting for the approach of her adversary.

Gerontius stood staring at her for a while, like a fighting bear sizing up its opponent. Then he adjusted his helmet, straightened his sword and started to advance toward her at a slow march.

King Deonotus stepped forward and addressed the gathering. "Pinnosa of the House of Flavius. You have the honor today of having your challenge accepted by the great centurion and High Commander of the Britannic legions, Gerontius. Speak first young woman, so that we might know your cause."

"I am here, Your Majesty, to avenge the tragedy of my father, the great commander Marcus Flavius. He wasn't only abandoned by this man in his moment of need in the midst of battle, but was reduced to great shame by being crippled for the rest of his life by his wounds. His injuries weren't so deep to kill him and grace him with the honorable death of a hero. But they were crippling wounds that could have been avoided had it not been for Gerontius—who ran from the fray in blind terror like the scurrying, bloated rat that he is!"

Pinnosa caught sight of Ursula in the crowd and they exchanged a quick nod of acknowledgment. "My cause, Your Majesty, is to give my father— who now lives the life of a helpless invalid—the satisfaction of knowing that the cause of shame and suffering—this loathsome coward, Gerontius—was bested by a mere woman!" She took several steps toward Gerontius and glared ferociously into his eyes. "For it was Gerontius who should have mustered the men shoulder to shoulder around my father when the first arrow struck. It was Gerontius who chose instead to withdraw to the safety of the main line and wait for a full re-grouping. And, it was Gerontius, again, who preferred to declare Marcus Flavius dead rather than join the search party, who—long after the battle was over—eventually found my poor father almost drowned in his own blood!" She turned to address the crowd. "I hereby swear that I shall finally give my father satisfaction." She raised her voice and shouted her cause for the heavens to hear. "The honor of the House of Marcus Flavius!"

"Marcus Flavius! Marcus Flavius!" The cry was quickly picked up by the crowd— including several of the junior officers—becoming a jubilant, ear-splitting chant.

Gerontius glared threateningly at the chanting officers, but as Constans had joined in, he had no hope of controlling them.

"And you, Gerontius, Commander of Legions!" The King had to raise his voice in order to be heard over the chanting. "What is your reply to this slant upon your honor?"

The crowd fell silent. For a moment only the birds could be heard.

"I've got nothing to say that hasn't already been said! I just want to teach this young wench a lesson she's long had coming to her and put her back in her place! Oh aye, her father were a great man all right, and I feel sorry for him. Or what's left of him. But, on the day she's talking about, the fighting took me one way—and him another! That's all there is to it! If she can't face up to the truth, then that's her tragedy, not her father's plight." He fidgeted impatiently with his sword. "Now, let's get on with it! I've got more important things to do with my time than teaching young women about men's work!"

"Very well," the King said. "The contest shall commence. As the challenged, Gerontius, it falls to you to nominate the first round."

"Horses—shields and spears!"

Pinnosa's horse, Artemis, and Gerontius's brown stallion were brought onto the field without trappings. The protagonists were handed identical weapons and shields.

While the preparations were being made, Ursula led Constans a little away from Constantine and the others.

"Trust Gerontius to choose spears," she said. "Swords would have been fairer."

"Gerontius isn't concerned with playing fair. He's only concerned with winning—by whatever means. He's very good at it. Which is why he is where he is."

"Do you ever have to fight alongside him?"

"Not under normal circumstances, no. Our contingents have completely different places in the formation Father uses. Only if we had to come around in a wide sweep, or if he was pinned down and driven to the right, would we find ourselves fighting side by side."

Constans became engrossed in the preparations for the contest. Ursula stared at him, her heart full of concern.

At that moment, Pinnosa mounted Artemis and everyone, including Constans, gave a loud cheer.

There it was again: the fear that gripped her without warning. Her insides felt as if they were tying themselves in knots. "Don't trust him!" she cried suddenly. "Don't *ever* trust him!"

"Hmm?" Constans smiled at her distractedly. "Don't trust who?"

Another cheer came from the crowd as Gerontius mounted his steed.

"Gerontius, of course! You're his greatest rival now. As you say, he'll do anything to win—use whatever means. I'm warning you, my love, no matter how closely you have to work with him on campaigns, never, never trust him, especially if . . . ."

"If what, my love?" He lowered his head so that his ear was by her mouth.

"Especially if your father should die," she whispered.

He looked lovingly at her and was about to say something when yet another cheer from the crowd forced his attention back to events. "We'll talk more about this later," he said with a confused smile. "Watch this! They're ready to make the first pass."

Gerontius took off his Commander's helmet and plumage. Like Pinnosa, he wore only a simple tunic with a leather belt around his girth. They both had short spears and small, circular shields.

"This will be a test of their horsemanship," Constans explained, knowing that Ursula had never seen such a contest before.

"In what way?" she asked, putting her arm through his and holding him tight.

"They're riding bareback, and they aren't allowed to grasp—or even touch—their steeds with their hands. I didn't know Pinnosa could ride like that—did you?"

Ursula didn't reply. Instead, she simply nodded. *Oh, Pinnosa—do you never know fear? Must others fear for you, as I fear for Constans?*

Pinnosa and Gerontius maneuvred their horses into position at opposite ends of the clearing. Without a word or signal, they began their charges simultaneously.

The crowd roared in anticipation of the clash. The cry "Marcus Flavius!" reached new heights.

Nearer and nearer they rode. Then they were close enough to strike. Iron struck leather. Artemis reared. The crowd gasped.

"If she falls off—it's all over." Constans said, more to himself than Ursula.

"Stay on, Pinnosa!" Ursula shouted to her friend.

Pinnosa remained mounted—but only just. Ursula could see that it was all she could do not to grip Artemis' mane. Pinnosa had dropped her spear, which Ursula knew she had been using to keep herself steady.

Gerontius rode on, waving his spear in triumph as he urged his horse around for a second pass.

Artemis had barely settled down, when Gerontius was upon Pinnosa again, attacking her exposed, weaponless side. At the last moment, Artemis responded to Pinnosa's will and back-stepped, leaving Gerontius thrusting into mid-air. He was off balance and his horse, too, began to rear. Pinnosa came alongside and lunged at him with her shield, forcing him to pull away. As the horses separated, he lurched forward and gashed his cheek on his own shield.

The sight of blood enthused the crowd and their cries were tumultuous as the two combatants positioned themselves yet again—ready for another pass.

"A third pass!" Constans exclaimed. "I've never seen one of these go to three."

They rushed headlong at each other. Pinnosa swerved just in time to force him to pass on the spear side. As Gerontius made his jab, she veered away. It made him lose both balance and control. His horse started sidestepping frantically. Much to the delight of the crowd, Pinnosa managed to wheel Artemis around and make a play for his spear. Just as she leaned out to reach for it, however, his horse reared again and she gripped his arm instead. Both riders toppled and fell.

"A *draw!*" Constans shouted excitedly, giving Ursula a rib-crushing hug.

Badly winded and gasping for breath, Pinnosa was the slower of the two to pick herself up. Gerontius came up behind her and struck her hard across the back with his shield, pushing her face down into the trampled earth. The crowd booed.

Constantine shouted, "Gerontius! Play fair! Remember she's only a wench!"

"Short swords!" Pinnosa pulled herself to her feet and spat out dirt. "Short swords and shields! I'll get you now, Gerontius! Let's have a *real* fight!"

The crowd was intent on the prospect of a good sword fight. No one took any notice of a messenger who, at that moment, rode into the clearing at full gallop, dismounted, and headed straight for Constantine. No one, that is, except Ursula. She pulled herself free from Constans's embrace in order to watch as he delivered his message.

It was clear from his manner that the news he bore was of great import.

Constantine's smile dissolved. His shoulders drooped. As she watched, she felt the icy tentacles of her nameless fear return. Instinctively, she turned around to catch the eye of her beloved, but he was still engrossed in the contest. She left Constans's side, went over to her father and led him to Constantine. She remained with her father, the King and the Commander of the Brittanic army, while the messenger repeated his dispatch from the Continent. As she listened to him speak, she knew with a horrifying certainty that his words were the resonant missives of Doom.

"Three tribes of Burgundians and two huge tribes of the Suevi have broken through the *Limes* (which he pronounced *LEE-miss*). They crossed the Rhenus in several places between Mogontiacum and Castra Region. The frontier defenses have been broken asunder. What was left of the Colonia, Mogontiacum and Treveris garrisons after the Imperial Court had left for Arelate has been scattered to the four winds. The Germans are pouring in, and all the cities can do is shut their gates. The whole of Germania and northern Galliae are exposed to attack by the invaders."

Constantine and her father stared at each other silently for what seemed an eternity to Ursula.

Then, with a grim sigh of determination, King Deonotus finally spoke. "The time has come. We can't wait for the Emperor's orders a day longer. We must put our plan into operation at once."

"We'll leave tomorrow," Constantine declared with grave resignation. "Constans will depart at morning bells with the First Horse. They'll need to ride hard to the coast and cross the Channel as fast as possible. That way, they can make a good start in rallying whatever forces are left in Germania and Galliae before the rest of us arrive. I'll commence the march with the main body of the men around mid-morning. We'll head for Londinium where we'll be able to make the necessary arrangements before heading for the Channel ports and undertaking the main crossing."

"Marcus *Flavius!*" Pinnosa cried, signaling she was ready for the second bout of the contest. The crowd roared.

"We'll prepare to leave," Constantine said, looking about him and forcing a smile, "just as soon as we've enjoyed our sport." He put his arms around both King Deonotus and Ursula and turned them back to face the contest. "Come my friends! Let us take pleasure in what we shall soon be fighting to defend!"

Pinnosa hacked twice at Gerontius's shield, inflicting deep cuts before he responded. Their swords clashed. Gerontius was caught off-guard by her wrath and her surprising strength. She forced him back four or five steps with her furious attack before he regained his footing and managed to make a stand. His counter-thrust was almost overpowering in its brute force. He struck hard with five powerful hacks that dented and cracked Pinnosa's shield. Just as he was about to deal the decisive blow, however, Pinnosa managed an upward swipe. Even though it was partly deflected by his shield, it made a deep gash under his arm.

The sight of more of Gerontius's blood whipped the crowd into a frenzy.

The combatants broke apart to regain their breath. As they returned to the center of the meadow, Pinnosa screamed a fierce battle cry that was full of rage and the threat of mayhem. She lunged forward, her sword flashing in a swirling blur and seeming to come at Gerontius from every direction. She managed three downward hacks in quick succession, despite Gerontius's frantic left-to-right sweeps. He was forced to his knees. She threw aside her shield. Using both hands, Pinnosa hit him so hard with a side-swipe that she split his shield in two. The blow opened up another wound—this time on his forearm. His defensive upward thrust met thin air as she leapt to one side.

The crowd gasped at her nimbleness.

He dropped his sword and fell at her feet. The fight was over.

Pinnosa put her blade to his throat and forced him to lift up his sweaty head so that they were facing eye to eye. "I call upon all those present this day to witness this contest. To say, without equivocation, that the house of Marcus Flavius has been avenged upon this vile and evil man called Gerontius. And let it be known that though he might achieve some measure of fame and glory in the anonymous army, amongst strangers . . . ." She looked back down at Gerontius, who was still spluttering to catch his breath. "Amongst his own—where he is known—in our hearts—he shall know only the eternal shame of being bettered by a mere *wench.*"

The crowd began chanting, "Pinnosa! Pinnosa!" and "Marcus Flavius!"

Ursula made her way back toward Constans. He saw her coming and put down the flask of wine he was holding so that he could embrace her.

She was barely a few steps away when two of the Roman officials' wives came between them. They were bursting with excitement and questions.

"Can all you young Britannic women fight like that?"
"How old is Pinnosa?"
"Where does she come from?"
"Who is this Marcus Flavius?"

Ursula did her best to answer them politely. While she was speaking, she could only watch as Constantine broke away from the crowd and beckoned his son to follow him. He shouted orders for all officers present to assemble at the Officers' Hall without delay. All Ursula could do was look on as her beloved gave her a wave and then walked away to be caught up in events.

"Do all you young noble women ride bareback?"

"What do you wear when you go hunting?"

The questions kept coming. As if from far away, she could hear her voice, sounding calm and controlled as it answered. Inside, however, she was being consumed by the dark flames of fear. Her inner voice screamed, *Don't go, Constans! Please don't go!*

IX

The rest of that day saw Corinium a-buzz with activity. Every single man, woman and child was busy with some aspect of the army's preparations. Wheelwrights and carpenters repaired wagons. Blacksmiths, cobblers, tailors and tanners worked through the night repairing old uniforms or making new ones. Attendants cleaned everything that was about to depart with the army. Children ran about fetching water, relaying messages and carrying goods of every description. Ordnance crews wandered the city, procuring this, checking that and storing everything. Doctors saw to every infection, and made sure that any wound, major or minor, was properly dressed. Horse doctors did the same for their equine patients. Even the guard dogs were checked.

The barbers pulled over five hundred teeth that day. Later they were put in a special box made of bone. It was placed in the Basilica at the base of the statue of the Emperor Claudius, the man who had made Britannia part of Rome.

Messengers and other ordnance crews were sent ahead to secure provisions, clear camps and barracks. Others were sent to procure the huge transport galleys and their crews ready for the mass Channel crossing.

This last task was Morgan's responsibility as Head Messenger, which meant he was one of the first to leave. Ursula just happened to be looking out of the window from the Ladies' Chamber with its clear view of the Londinium Road when the moment came for Morgan to depart. The gate trumpet sounded with a long, shrill note followed by three short ones. A loud cheer went up from the Messengers' Yard just inside the gate. Morgan appeared outside the city walls, already at a full gallop as he headed up the gentle rise on his way to Londinium.

As Ursula watched she saw a figure leap out from behind a tree at the top of the rise and flag the messenger down. She knew at once it was Cordula.

X

"Whoa!" Morgan cried, as he reined Hermes to a halt.

"Ha!" Cordula said playfully. "Thought you could slip away, did you? Thought you could leave without a proper goodbye?"

Being still within sight of the city, Morgan couldn't dismount. To do so would have been a very bad omen for the many eyes that the messenger knew were still on him. Instead, he leaned forward as far as he could toward his beloved, who was straining to reach up to him for a farewell kiss.

"Cordula, you mustn't stop me on my errand like this. I must make haste. We have little time, and—"

"Oh, hush! I'm on *my* errand—to catch a wisp of the wind and pin him down." Cordula tried to make light of things, but couldn't disguise the anguish in her voice. Her heart was bursting with love for the handsome young man who had only joined the garrison two winters before. Morgan was the son of a horse breeder from the wild frontier country. His father had been killed when their farmstead had been attacked by Hibernian raiders and burned to the ground. Morgan had been away on his first trip to the army barracks at Deva at the time. He had returned to find his entire family murdered and his home completely destroyed. All he had left was the strong, young, black stallion he had been riding, Hermes. The two of them had been in the army's service ever since. The cautious, intelligent and well-spoken young man with his amazingly fast steed had not only rapidly won a reputation in Constantine's eyes as the best messenger in Britannia, they had also ridden into Cordula's life like the tumultuous winds of March. The dark haired youth and the freckle-skinned, brown haired maiden had filled each other's hearts with the most passionate of loves. "Why don't you ride off out of sight, then double back and meet me at Hog Bottom Well?" she suggested. "I can be there shortly—all alone—and I have a surprise for you . . . ."

It was Morgan's turn to interrupt. "I can't," he said sternly. But, his face betrayed the tone of his voice. She could see how much he wanted to say 'Yes.'

"Oh, please!" she pleaded. "Just for a short while."

"No!" Morgan wrestled his arm free from Cordula's grasp as he resisted her attempts to caress his face and kiss him. Hermes shied at his master's restless movements and Morgan struggled to control the horse. "Not now, my love. I must go."

"Then take me with you," she said recklessly. Even though she knew it was impossible, every sinew of Cordula's being was longing to ride away with him—to be with him constantly and never let him out of her sight.

He finally managed to break free from her grasp. Hermes quickly settled, and Morgan was able to look her firmly in the eye as he answered tenderly, "I wish I could."

With that, he gave Hermes a slap, and the great horse set off—over the crest and away from the city. Morgan waved at Cordula one last time before disappearing from sight. She was wearing a bright red shawl, which she took off and used to wave back, and continued to do so even after he had gone.

Eventually, long after the speck of the rider on his black steed was lost in the distant dust, she stopped waving. The shawl flopped against her raised arm and fell to the ground, crumpled in a heap. Then, she, too, fell—into a sobbing heap, her heart rent asunder.

XI

Ursula knew that as soon as Morgan disappeared over the horizon every living moment would be torture for Cordula. She wouldn't be able to think or dream about anything other than his return. Ursula knew all this because that was how she felt about Constans.

Will I have another chance to be alone with him before he goes? She remembered how many plans the officers had to go over to make sure the Channel crossing and the operation on the Continent went smoothly. *It will be impossible for me to see him till very late tonight, if at all. Then, at first light tomorrow morning he and his contingent will leave.* The panic-stricken thought that the only chance she would have to say good-bye would be at the formal and public farewell gripped her again.

"Oleander!" she cried. "Run over to the Officers' Hall and take a message to Constans. Tell him I'd like to see him when they pause to eat."

"I'm sorry Mistress. I've just heard that the officers and your father have asked for morsels and tidbits to be prepared. They won't be stopping for a meal."

"Then tell him I'll wait for him in the Palace garden around midnight."

"Very well, Mistress."

Ursula returned her attention to the scene outside. She could still see the figure of her cousin lying by the side of the road, weeping. Ursula slowly took a deep breath, dabbed her eyes with a piece of cloth, and resumed working on the small trinket she was holding in her lap.

XII

Midnight found Ursula dressed in her finest summer toga and seated on a stool in the Palace garden colonnade. She stared up at the stars. There was Ursa Minor, her namesake, doing its eternal dance with Ursa Major around the North Star.

"Will it only be in Heaven," she said aloud, "that we will find our true home—where we can be alone together in an endless embrace?"

All through the night she sat her vigil, until the pre-dawn glow stirred a cockerel and it's cry snapped her from her thoughts. Oleander was a little way off under a small, ornamental willow, snoring gently. The cockerel's crow marked the start of the day and within moments the slaves' quarters to the rear of the Palace's kitchens were bustling with activity. The night's peace had ended.

Ursula finally heaved a long sigh and stirred. "Come on, Oleander." She eased her stiff joints into a standing position. "It's time to get ready for the farewell parade."

Yawning, Oleander slowly rose to her feet, then set off as fast as she could to catch up with Ursula. As she was crossing the colonnade, she spotted a small object lying next to the abandoned stool and stooped to pick it up. "Mistress!" She cried. "You dropped your picture!"

XIII

Constans looked magnificent in his full regalia. His uniform and equipment had been well cleaned and burnished. Their bright colors gleamed vividly in the bright, early morning light. He was freshly shaved, which made him look less tired than he was. He, too, had been up all night, poring over maps and documents with his officers.

His men, a full contingent of two hundred on horseback, were mounted. They were arranged in ranks of twenty, five abreast and four deep, in Corinium's Forum—which was just big enough for such a force to assemble, complete a circuit and depart. Later that day, only Constantine's Vanguard would be turning out in dress uniform for the formal farewell speeches and a parade through the town. The main body of infantry and cavalry would be commencing their march in their regular uniforms, and wouldn't be assembling into a single force until they reached a large clearing by the road to Londinium—a full two miles from the city. For the sake of the formal farewell ceremonies, King Deonotus' throne was placed on a platform in the center of a large purple carpet at the end of the Forum. The Royal Party consisted of the King himself, Princess Ursula, the visiting Roman officials plus their wives, and several members of other local noble families, including Brittola, Martha, Saula, and Cordula. Pinnosa was also there, for once, dressed in finery—a pure white toga with gold trim. Her long red hair was braided in yellow and orange ribbons.

Constans stood at full attention at the base of the steps to the platform, his helmet and plumage held correctly against his right shoulder plate. Constantine and Gerontius were on horseback, positioned on either side of the Royal Party as Guards of Honor. Both mounts wore ceremonial parade masks, which were so heavy and cumbersome they had to be removed before the horses could be ridden anywhere. Gerontius had a dressing on his arm protecting the wounds he had received in the contest the day before.

Ursula's friends couldn't resist the prospect of having some fun at his expense. Martha led the others over to him. "Fancy a big, important army Commander being beaten by a simple frontier country wench!" They all began to giggle.

Gerontius went bright red and stared straight ahead, pretending they weren't there.

"You know what they say, don't you?" Pinnosa said teasingly. "Even young roses have thorns!"

By now, Gerontius was barely able to keep his composure. He began to splutter with rage as she continued.

"And there are plenty more thorns on *this* young rose, Gerontius!"

The young women were now laughing so loudly the rest of the Royal Party started to mutter with disapproval. Ursula was forced to leave her father's side and 'shush' them.

At that moment, a fanfare of horns sounded to silence the assembly and King Deonotus stepped forward to address the crowded Forum. "People of Corinium, most noble visitors, and men of the army of Britannia! I stand before you humbled by this magnificent display of disciplined soldiery. Men of the First Horse—I salute you!" He raised his hands high above his head. His palms had been coated with a special mixture of gold dust and ground glass. As they opened against the rays of the morning sun they sparkled and flashed. The crowd gasped with amazement and delight.

"Today you leave us. Soon you will bravely go forth to help our beleaguered friends across the Channel. There, no doubt, you will meet great challenges and grave dangers. But there will be nothing that heroic, fighting men like yourselves can't handle with the ease of a baby at play. Let our cousins in Germania and Galliae know that the disciplined units of the armies of Britannia are indeed the most powerful in *all* Rome!"

Tumultuous cheers from the crowd interrupted him.

"Go forth men of Britannia! Go to the rescue of Germania and Galliae and perform your great deeds! Become heroes—conquerors—even legends and myths!" He paused, waiting for the Forum to fall silent before continuing in a more somber tone. "But remember these words, men of Britannia. As you depart this beloved isle we call home, remember that no matter how honored and exalted you become on the Continent, you will always be strangers to them. Only to us—only here—will you ever be sons, cousins, family and true friends. So, return home heroes! Return home rich in triumph and glory! But above all . . . ." He paused again. "*Return home!* Return home safe . . . and return home soon!"

For a moment there was silence as many of the cavalrymen exchanged glances with their loved ones.

Ursula watched Constans while her father was speaking. Even though he was standing rigidly to attention facing the Forum, she knew he could see her out of the corner of his eye. As the King's speech came to a close, she saw a tear run down her beloved's cheek.

"See his tears?" she whispered, almost inaudibly, to Cordula who was standing alongside her. "I wish I could wipe them away."

"And kiss him? And caress him?"

The two cousins looked at each other. Tears rolled down their cheeks. Their lips quivered.

Ursula reached for Cordula's hand and squeezed it tightly. Her entire being was filled with an overpowering yearning to hold Constans, and the formality of the occasion was preventing her from doing so. Coupled with the prolonged silence that followed her father's speech, Ursula began to feel she was suffocating in the stillness and inaction. She was about to burst with frustration. Then, slowly, as if in a dream, she found herself dropping Cordula's grasp, raising her hands and clapping. Within less than the time of a breath, the whole assembly followed her lead and erupted into rapturous cheers and applause. Even the men on horseback banged their shields with their spears.

Constantine unsheathed his long sword and waved it through the air in a wide arc to command silence. "People of Corinium, honored guests, and men of the First Horse! I humble myself to the honor of serving our great King . . . *Deonotus!*" He bowed graciously while the crowd cheered. "I also humble myself to the greater honor of serving truly the bravest and most noble people in all Rome . . . the proud people of Britannia!" He bowed again in acknowledgement of even greater cheers before continuing. "Men of the First Horse. Always remember this. Britannia is more than your home. It is your life's work. It is your sworn duty to protect this province from all its enemies, whether they be here on our island or overseas. And, no one can fulfill that duty better than you. *I salute you* men of the First Horse! *Britannia's Bravest! Britannia's Finest! Britannia's Best!*"

The cheering forced him to pause again. While he was waiting for it to die down, he glanced at his son and the young woman who would one day be his daughter-in-law. Then he continued. "You have long honored me, my fellow citizens, by entrusting me with the duty to defend you from peril. In return, my fellow Britons, I have long given you my most cherished possession . . . my life's work. I now give you something even more precious to me. I give you my son . . . Constans!" Another great roar erupted from the crowd. Constans acknowledged it with a wave of his hand. "I say to you, my son: Do as your King tells you! Return home. Return home safe. Return home soon. But in addition—and most importantly of all—return home to your future. To your beautiful bride-to-be . . . *Princess Ursula!*"

To the ecstatic cheers were added shrill whistles, tooting pipes and the frantic banging of drums. Ursula lifted up her arms. A white dove flew out from each of her sleeves. As they did so, Ursula winked at Pinnosa. It was she who helped to devise the trick.

The crowd's applause intensified.

Constantine lifted his sword once more for silence. "I wish you both a future filled with much happiness together. A future blessed with many children and grandchildren. Then, I might be able to take a rest from my duties, and finally allow myself to be protected by somebody else for once!"

While the crowd were still laughing and enjoying Constantine's joke, Ursula strode boldly down the steps to Constans, clasped his face in her hands and kissed him full on the lips. The hoots and shouts for "More!" were almost deafening. She needed no further bidding and did as they demanded. This time he wrapped his arms around her and held her tightly in his embrace. Unmindful of the crowd's roar, she pulled back slightly and handed him the small trinket she had been working on.

"What is it?" he had to shout.

"It's a tiny portrait of me, which Brittola painted. I had it set in a silver frame and encased in wood. I decorated it myself. It's something for you to remember me by." While she was speaking, she placed it around his neck. For a moment it dangled awkwardly on its black cord against his breastplate, looking a little silly. She smiled and tucked it inside against his chest. Then she looked up at his face.

"I shall never take it off. Even when I'm bathing." He took her firmly by the shoulders and looked deeply into her eyes. "Always remember this. Only in your voice—I hear family. Only in your eyes—I see home."

There were so many things she wanted to say, so many things she had to say, but all she could manage was, "Come home soon." They kissed a third time, taking the crowd's raptures to new heights.

"*Attention!*" Constantine bellowed.

Constans let her go. With a forced stern expression, he spun around to face his men. As he did so, Ursula whispered, just loud enough for him to hear: "Please let our eyes meet—just one more time!"

She watched, powerless to stop him, as he put on his helmet and straightened his cloak. She stared helplessly, sadness and longing etched into her heart, as he mounted his horse, adjusted his sword and moved out to take up his position at the head of the procession. His attendant handed him the standard. He raised it on high, producing the biggest roar from the crowd yet.

"Commander! Lead your men out!"

"Yes, sir! Men of the First Horse! *Forward!*"

He wheeled his horse around and—as he made his parting salute to the Royal Party—their eyes did, indeed, meet. They only had a fleeting second to look at each other, and in that precious moment they both tried with all their might to say so many things with their hearts and their expressions: 'Take care of yourself and be ever mindful of your enemies' 'Remember me' 'I'll always be here waiting for you' and 'I'll always be true to you'; but their time was up. His salute was complete and his horse started to pull him away. He put his hand to his lips—his sweet, warm lips—and blew her a farewell kiss. She barely managed one in reply before his horse turned and he was off.

The men circled the Forum, saluting the Royal Party as they passed, and exited down the main street toward the Main Gate, Londinium and the Continent. To Ursula the cheers from the crowd now seemed to be coming from far away, from another time and place. The standard was all that was visible of him now as it floated in a haze on a sea of the First Horse's bobbing plumage.

Cordula and her friends, along with the rest of the crowd, ran across the Forum after the men, crying their farewells. Brittola's shrill voice rose above all the others. "God goes with you!"

Pinnosa, however, remained behind. She put her arm around Ursula's shoulders. "Come," she said gently. "You're tired. You should go back to your room and have a little sleep before Constantine's departure. By the time that's over it'll be around midday and we'll still have the whole afternoon in front of us. I'll make the arrangements and we'll go for a ride—you, me and the others. We'll get away from the city. We'll leave all this behind, and go up into the hills to the north. You'll be able to find a nice quiet spot to rest if you wish, and I . . . ." She smiled to herself. "I might just do a little hunting."

Ursula nodded and allowed Pinnosa to lead her back to the Palace.

As they exited the Forum, Brittola, Cordula, Martha and Saula ran after the pair and caught them. They formed a group—six young women, arm in arm—and set off together, each looking their finest, and heading in the same direction.

Chapter 2

Defenseless?

Led by Pinnosa, Ursula, Brittola, Cordula, Martha and Saula went on an overnight hunting expedition deep into the luscious, green hills of King Deonotus' hunting estate. Early the following afternoon, feeling refreshed and invigorated, but ready for the luxuries and comfort of the Palace, they emerged from the forest to rejoin the Corinium Road a few miles southeast of Glevum.

As they crested a hill, they spotted what appeared to be a family on a farm wagon. Even from a distance they could see that the person driving the team of donkeys was an old man. There was a young woman sitting next to him, comforting two small children who they could hear crying loudly. Two older children, both girls, sat in the rear with the belongings. Three figures, presumably their slaves, were walking ahead of the wagon, each with a heavy load on their back; bundles of clothing, water flagons, even small pieces of furniture.

Pinnosa signaled to the others to hold back while she and Ursula went ahead to investigate. As they neared the wagon, Pinnosa recognized the family. "Aelwines Galicus? Heulwen?" she called out. "What's happening? Where are you going?"

"Pinnosa? Is that really you?" The young woman, Heulwen, looked back anxiously over her shoulder. She hugged the youngsters close and said to them, "Hush, children. These are friends."

The old man did not seem to notice the two noblewomen approaching them on horseback. He stared straight ahead, remaining silent. His eyes were full of fear, telling of some unspeakable horror he had witnessed and was intent on leaving far behind.

As Pinnosa and Ursula drew up to the wagon, Heulwen said, "They came down the valley, from the direction of the coast, two days ago. Hibernian raiders, murdering, pillaging and setting fire to anything they couldn't carry. We were lucky to get away. Father here was fishing upstream when he heard the hideous cries of Gynreth the potter as they tormented the poor man to death. Father ran as fast as he could back to the farm. We just had time to throw our things in the cart and escape before they were upon us. When we got to the high ground and looked back we could see smoke . . . . It was coming from our burning home . . . ." She had to pause. The memory was still torture to her. The children started to whine again, and she coddled them to quieten them down.

She took a deep breath and continued. "By the time we got to Magnis it was already filled with people fleeing from the menace. We didn't feel safe there, so we continued on to Glevum. We got there just before dawn this morning. As soon as we arrived, we went straight to the Garrison Centurion and pleaded with him to send a force to go after the murderous fiends! He couldn't do anything though. He only has fifty men, and they're needed to guard the city. The only real help we got from him was when he told us that the field army was at Corinium. So we're on our way there now to find our Gildred and—"

"He's gone," Pinnosa interrupted. "They've all gone. The army has left for the Continent." She leaned forward, an intent expression on face. "Heulwen? What of my family? My parents? My brothers? Did you see them? Are they all right?"

Heulwen looked at her. The Galicus homestead was only a few miles upstream from the Flavius villa. After a long pause, she shook her head and mumbled, "I'm sorry . . . ."

Sensing her mistress' sudden tension, Artemis stopped. As Pinnosa dropped back, Ursula saw her stiffen like game before the chase—her eyes staring wide.

"Please listen carefully," Ursula said urgently to Heulwen. "I am Princess Ursula, daughter of King Deonotus, and a friend of Pinnosa's. I must ask you to take our attendants with you to Corinium. Will you do that?" Heulwen nodded. "Thank you. You will be well rewarded. Now, when you get there, I want you to go directly to the Palace with our attendants and make sure the King himself hears your story. Tell him you met Pinnosa and me on the road, and that we have gone to Glevum. Is that clear?" Heulwen nodded again.

Looking back and seeing that the others were almost upon Pinnosa, Ursula wheeled her gray mare, Swift, around and went to intercept them. As soon as she reached the group she said in a hushed voice, "It sounds like Pinnosa's family might have been attacked by Hibernian raiders."

"No!" Brittola exclaimed. "How do you—"

"*We ride!*" Pinnosa's powerful voice filled the air. She forced Artemis to turn so violently, the poor horse had to rear. As she flew past the others she glared at them with a face like one of the old gods of war. "*Come on!*"

"Follow her! Don't lose her!" Ursula shouted. They were already turning their horses around and urging them into a gallop as she spoke.

As the others rode away, Ursula paused to address Oleander. "We have to go to Glevum, and probably into frontier country to make sure Pinnosa's family is safe. I want you to go with these people, the Galicuses, to Corinium. Tell Father that I'll return in a few days' time, and that I'll bring the others back with me safe and sound." She pointed to the supplies her attendant was carrying on her back. "I'll need some of that food and those water flasks."

Oleander hastily unpacked the provisions and began tying them to Swift's straps, muttering to herself, "It's all very well you making sure *they're* safe and sound, but who's going to be making sure *you're* safe?" When she finished, she grabbed Ursula's leg and said, "There's no stopping you once your mind's set on something. That made you a formidable child, and it's going to make you an even more formidable woman."

Ursula, who had been anxiously watching her rapidly disappearing friends, looked down at Oleander. They shared a smile. Then, Oleander stepped back.

"Glevum and beyond!" Ursula cried as Swift leapt into a gallop. "Here I come!"

II

They rode hard and were in Glevum in a short time. As soon as they entered the city gate, Pinnosa and Ursula dismounted. They ran to the Guard Station to find out what was happening, leaving the others to take care of the horses in the Messengers' Yard.

"News of the raid first reached us last night." The Garrison Centurion was a gruff old man; an old campaigner who had been the army since well before Constantine was a young recruit. It was clear he had little time or patience for troublesome young women—no matter how high born. "A messenger rode in from Magnis just before evening bells. He said some travelers had seen the raiders coming over the mountains from the coast two days earlier. He said him and the other Magnis guards reckoned it was probably a three-boat group about twenty-five to thirty strong. It's obvious they're out to plunder the Wye valley. And they're probably heading for Magnis itself. Then, this morning, two families, the Galicuses and the Valenses, arrived, looking for—"

"Looking for their families. We know. We met the Galicuses on the road to Corinium," Pinnosa interrupted, then asked impatiently, "Where are the Valenses?"

"Oh, they are still in Glevum, Mistress. They've been taken in by—"

"And, what exactly have you done about the situation in the valley?" Pinnosa couldn't contain her exasperation any longer. "Have you sent out a patrol? Reinforcements to Magnis?"

"Not exactly, no, Mistress. We—"

"Why *not?*" Pinnosa began pacing.

"Give the good man a chance to answer you properly, Pinnosa," Ursula intervened.

"Thank you, Mistress." The old soldier lowered his voice as he fought hard to maintain a civil tongue. "There are only fifty of us. We are needed here to—"

"So, what have you done? You must have done *something!*" Pinnosa lunged at the Centurion in her frustration. Ursula had to grab hold of her arm to hold her back. The Centurion instinctively went for his sword and almost unsheathed it.

"Yes, we *have* done something, Mistress." He spoke through clenched teeth. "We sent six Wye valley men to the main garrison at Viroconium to muster a thirty strong cavalry unit. They're to ride to Magnis at once." Seeing Pinnosa turn away in exasperation, he turned to address Ursula. "They should be setting off from Viroconium first thing in the morning. They'll be at Magnis by mid-afternoon at the latest."

"That's far too late!" Pinnosa groaned. "You're giving those Hibernian scum virtually a whole day to do as they please. They could attack another dozen homesteads in that time, torturing, raping and murdering the families! Or, if they're not too drunk on Roman wine, they might even find their way back to their boats and escape with all their rich pickings before any legionaries *finally* show up!"

"Don't you think my men who have families and friends in that valley wanted to go to their rescue as fast as possible, Mistress?" the Centurion snapped. "Of course they did! But they obeyed orders and went to Viroconium instead because they knew it was the only wise thing to do. We are desperate for good fighting men here—especially now that the main field army has gone.

I can't go losing units of my men every time there's a raiding party! If I let that happen, by the return of winter, we'd have no men left!"

Pinnosa sighed. She looked first at Ursula, then back at the Centurion. "Then maybe it's time for the *women* to do some of the fighting!" She made for the door. "We're heading for Magnis right now. If my friends and I meet up with any of these raiders on the way—even though we are only carrying hunting weapons—I'm sure we wouldn't be afraid of taking them on." She looked at Ursula before adding derisively, "And there are only *six* of us."

The Centurion growled. "I can't order you not to go to Magnis, Mistress. But—with all due respect—there's a big difference between hunting game and tackling murderous Hibernian thugs." He turned to Ursula. "I implore you, Your Highness, not to do anything rash. The men from Viroconium will arrive in the valley tomorrow and they will deal with the problem properly. I understand how Mistress Pinnosa must feel, but I wouldn't be doing my duty if I didn't strongly advise you to stay here in Glevum tonight. If you do decide to proceed to Magnis tomorrow, I'll happily provide you with an armed escort—indeed, I'll escort you myself."

Ursula did not answer. Instead, she stared intently at Pinnosa.

After watching their silent clash of wills, the Centurion added tentatively, "In any case, Your Highness, you would never make it to Magnis before dusk. It's well over thirty miles."

"He has a point," Ursula said, without taking her eyes from Pinnosa. "If it were only you and I on Artemis and Swift we might be able make it. But think of Brittola and—"

"Hell's teeth! Think of *my family!*" Pinnosa shouted.

Ursula seemed to waver with indecision for a moment. Then she turned to face the Centurion. "Thank you for your information, and for your kind offer. I assure you we'll give the matter careful thought. If we do decide to continue on to Magnis, we'll most certainly proceed with utmost caution."

Both Pinnosa and the Centurion tried to say something, but Ursula cut them off, adding firmly, "Now would you be so kind as to tell us where can we find the Valenses?"

"In a fishmongers' of the same name, by Fisherman's Quay, Your Highness."

"Thank you." Ursula moved over to the door and was just about to lead Pinnosa away when she remembered something. "Oh, I meant to ask . . . . Where were the galleys that are supposed to be patrolling the coast and preventing these raiding parties from landing?"

The old officer was caught off guard. "Well, Your Highness, we *are* short of men. It's possible that there are as few as three out at sea on patrol. There could be as many as ten or twelve at Maridunum being re-fitted and cleaned."

"Hah!" Pinnosa barked. "What good are clean galleys, when it's *fighting* ones that we need?"

"That's enough," Ursula said sharply. She led Pinnosa away, thanking the Centurion again over her shoulder.

The Valenses had no news of Pinnosa's family, and could tell them nothing about the situation in the valley that they did not know already. Like the Galicuses, all they could do was recount with terror their narrow escape. They lived even further upstream from the Flavius villa than the Galicuses did. In their flight, they had cut across the hills well before the bend in the river where Pinnosa's family lived.

Thus armed with all the information Glevum had to offer, and with the sun already low in the sky, Ursula and Pinnosa returned to their companions.

Pinnosa's face was as dark as an approaching storm as she entered the Messengers' Yard and leapt up onto Artemis' back. She started heading for the gate without uttering a word.

"What's happening?" Brittola cried. Like the others, she obeyed Ursula's urgent signal and began to mount her young brown mare, Feather. "Are we leaving?"

"The authorities can't do anything to help my family," Pinnosa shouted over her shoulder. "So we'll have to!"

"We're heading for Magnis!" Ursula called out, turning Swift around to head after Artemis.

"Magnis!" Saula yelled. "Frontier country! We'll never reach Magnis before dark!"

"*This* . . . ." shouted Martha from the rear as they rode through the gate.

"*May not be easy!*" they all cried in chorus.

III

Magnis only had three stone buildings and one paved street. All the other buildings, like most frontier structures, were wooden. The town's defenses were of wood, too. It was encircled by two extremely deep dikes over which the only way to cross was by a long and lonely ramp leading up to the town's single gate. The horses' feet echoed on the wood.

"Halt!" the night sentry cried from the palisade in the dark. "Who goes there?"

"Pinnosa, daughter of Maximus Flavius. Princess Ursula, daughter of King Deonotus and four friends!"

"Come forward to the gate to be identified, Pinnosa, daughter of Maximus Flavius! All you others—stay on the ramp!"

Within minutes, the gate was opened and the six women with their tired horses were safely inside. The town's Centurion barked orders for suitable arrangements to be made for the young noble ladies. Then he led them to their makeshift quarters, a small dormitory adjacent to the Officers' Hall. While a flurry of attendants rushed to take care of the young women's needs, Ursula and Pinnosa took the Centurion aside and asked him for the latest information.

"We have over twenty-six families from the valley taking shelter here. We know the Galicuses and Valenses have moved on to Glevum. That leaves your family, Mistress, and four others unaccounted for. Flavia Lucilla isn't here because her villa was spared. She has a staff of over thirty. They put up a spirited resistance with just farm implements and hunting weapons when the murderous mob came their way. They managed to kill two of the raiders and turn the rest back. That was late this afternoon. We haven't received any more reports since."

"Why haven't you responded?" Pinnosa cried in exasperation. "Haven't you even sent out a patrol to check on the missing families?"

Like his fellow officer in Glevum earlier that day, the Centurion, a kind-hearted elderly man whom Pinnosa had known since childhood, looked embarrassed by her questions.

"As you well know, Mistress, there are only fifteen of us here. We have to be capable of defending the town, if necessary. We sent a rider to Glevum yesterday, asking for reinforcements, but none came today. In fact, when we first heard your horses, we thought you might be them."

"Six Wye Valley men have been dispatched to Viroconium." Ursula cut off Pinnosa, who was about to berate the man further. "You should expect about thirty on horseback sometime tomorrow. Hopefully, soon after midday."

"Good." The Centurion sighed. "A bit late—but good. Then we'll be able to go out there and deal with the murdering swine."

"A bit late?" Pinnosa was about to say more, but then saw Ursula's censorial look and managed to contain her comments.

"Thank you, Centurion," Ursula said. "You've been most informative and most kind. Now, if you'll excuse us, we've had a long day."

She was about to walk away when the Centurion coughed and said, "Your Highness?"

"Yes?"

He shifted uncomfortably from side to side, obviously troubled by what he had to say. "You and mistress Pinnosa and these other young ladies are not thinking of going up the valley to the Flavius villa by yourselves, I hope?"

"Pinnosa is understandably concerned about her family."

"Yes, of course. But, surely you wouldn't do anything foolish, Your Highness? These Hibernians can be extremely dangerous. The cavalry unit is on its way from Viroconium. I'd rest much easier if you and the other ladies would at least wait until they get here. Then preferably wait a little longer until we've secured the valley."

Ursula smiled. "I appreciate your concern, Centurion. I assure you, we do not intend to do anything that will add to your burden of responsibilities."

"Thank you, Your Highness." He saluted and made his way out, pausing briefly by the door to add, "I bid you a pleasant night's sleep."

The women were so exhausted, they took their baths and ate their meals in almost complete silence. Afterwards, Martha, Saula, Brittola, and Cordula went straight to bed. As soon as they had settled, Pinnosa leaned over to Ursula and whispered, "I'm not ready for sleep yet. I'm going to check on the horses."

"I'll come with you." Ursula followed Pinnosa outside, even though all she wanted was to curl up in her bedroll like the others.

The Magnis night was still, with just the gentlest of warm breezes caressing the world into sweet slumber. The horses were tied to the side of the women's quarters. They had been watered, fed and covered with blankets. Swift and Artemis were nearest the door, resting their graceful necks against each other. A night sentry patrolled past on the nearby palisade, silhouetted clearly against the bright yellow disc of the newly risen moon.

"We'll find them tomorrow," Ursula said reassuringly. She leaned against the rail and looked at Pinnosa. Her friend stood on the steps, staring at the moon. "Don't worry. I'm sure your brothers devised a clever scheme and hid your parents somewhere safe, away from the raiders."

Pinnosa heaved a sigh. Ursula could tell she had something to say but was finding it difficult. After a long silence, she said, "I . . . I had a terrible dream last night."

"Oh?" Unlike the others in their hunting camp, Ursula had been sleeping too deeply to hear her friend's restless groans.

"I dreamed we—Father and I—were out in the mountains on our horses, just like when I was young. He was . . . he was his old self." She smiled and turned away again to look back at the moon. "We were having great fun, hunting a deer and splashing our way along a fresh mountain stream, when suddenly—" Her smile disappeared. "The sky turned from blue to silver. The water in the stream dried up. We looked up and rushing toward us out of the sky were four black riders—riders in black hoods and capes, riding four powerful black horses and galloping hard, coming directly at us. Then, there were more black riders, dozens and dozens of them. More and then more until the sky was full. Hundreds of black riders—thousands!" She paused and shivered.

"Go on," Ursula said quietly. While Pinnosa had been speaking she had felt the icy tentacles of her dark fear rising up from within to chill her soul, making her shiver, too.

Pinnosa took a long, deep breath and continued. "Just as the black riders were about to overwhelm us, they disappeared. There in their place, standing absolutely still, facing away from us as if they were about to depart, were . . . four, lone, white riders. They were in white hoods and capes astride white horses." She paused and took another deep breath. Her voice choked with emotion. "I don't know why, but I became terrified of their leaving. I shouted, 'Don't go!' as loudly as I could. They turned around, and it was then that I saw their faces." She turned towards Ursula. There were tears running down her cheeks. "It was Father and Mother, Julius and Titus."

Ursula reached out and took her hand. They held each other tightly as if holding onto life itself.

After a while, Pinnosa pulled back and continued, "They each gave me loving smiles, waved good-bye, then turned away and began heading into the bright, white light which now filled the sky. Just as they were disappearing from view, Father turned around once more. I heard him cry, 'We shall be waiting for you, Pinnosa! We shall be waiting!'"

"Have you ever had such a dream before?" Ursula asked gently after Pinnosa had contained her welling tears.

"No, never." Pinnosa coughed to stop herself from sobbing. She pulled away from Ursula in order to look into her eyes. "But that wasn't the end of it."

Ursula felt the hair on the back of her neck rise. Somehow, she knew exactly what Pinnosa was about to say next.

"I turned around and the person next to me—the companion I had been hunting with—the person who had been my father . . . was now you." Ursula felt as if she was going to faint and had to grab hold of the rail as Pinnosa spoke.

"Next to you were Martha and Saula and Brittola . . . though curiously I don't recall seeing Cordula. All of us were dressed as white riders, and—"

"*Don't!*" Ursula gasped and unconsciously began to shy away from Pinnosa. "Don't say any more."

Pinnosa stepped toward her, looking concerned, yet at the same time smiling. "But Ursula, the nightmare was over. It had become a beautiful dream. The white light was now all around us. It felt so warm—so beckoning. We all held hands and started to laugh. We had become so free and happy together. In some strange way, we had been liberated from the nightmare, so that we could finally be happy. Stranger still, the happiness wasn't limited to our friends and ourselves. We were sharing it with a whole *host* of white riders. Hundreds of them. Thousands. And the strangest thing was, all the white riders were women. There wasn't one man amongst us."

Pinnosa paused and they each looked into the others' eyes. A tiny creak drew their gaze downwards. They both saw the whiteness of Ursula's knuckles as her hands unconsciously tightened their grip on the rail.

"I am sorry, but I'm too tired to think about what this means." Ursula forced a smile. "I . . . I desperately need to sleep."

Pinnosa turned away to look again at the moon, now well above the palisade.

Ursula, her head reeling, carefully made her way back toward the door. She was just about to go inside when Pinnosa spoke again. "It was a dream about death, wasn't it?"

"Yes," Ursula said in a flat, feeble voice.

"My parents and brothers are dead, aren't they?"

Ursula spun around. "No!" she cried desperately. "That's not true! They were in a dream! We were in the dream! We're not dead! Why should they be?"

Pinnosa continued to stare up at the moon. "They died at the hands of the Hibernian scum yesterday."

Ursula looked at Pinnosa standing tall and proud with her face so pale in the soft light of the night. "We'll find out tomorrow," she said wearily. She went inside and gently closed the door behind her.

IV

"Wake up!" Pinnosa called. "Come on! We've got work to do! We can't wait for sleepy heads!" She went from bunk to bunk, shaking her friends awake and dragging them to their feet. It was still dark, but through the open window they could see the eastern sky beginning to redden along the horizon.

Ursula shook the tiredness from her head and drank some water from a goblet, which had been placed on a stool by her side. She watched Pinnosa as she roused Brittola, who was curled up in a ball at the foot of her bunk. It was clear that Pinnosa had not slept all night.

"It's still dark. Why have you woken us so early?" Cordula sat up, rubbing her eyes "Are the men from Viroconium here already?"

Pinnosa dragged a heavy sack in through the door. "We're not waiting for them."

"What do you mean, we're not waiting for them?" Martha asked before she bit into an apple. "You're not suggesting we go up the valley *alone*, I hope?"

Pinnosa let the sack drop with a loud clatter and stood up straight. "I'm leaving before the cock crows. Those of you who wish, can stay here and wait for the men from Viroconium. If, on the other hand, you decide to come with me—" she pointed to the sack, "there are your weapons."

For a moment there was silence as Martha, Saula, Brittola, and Cordula exchanged dazed looks. Then they looked instinctively to Ursula, and Brittola asked pleadingly, "But last night I thought I heard you say to the Centurion that we wouldn't be a worry to him?"

Ursula looked each of them in the eye before replying. "I told him we wouldn't add to the burden of *his* responsibilities." She heaved a sigh, looked at Pinnosa and stood up next to her. "But we can't stop Pinnosa from going—and I, for one, am not letting her go alone." She turned to look back at the others. "*I* take full responsibility for that."

"Oh, silly me. I forgot," Martha said with a mock smile, nudging Saula playfully on the arm. "Didn't you say yesterday that there were no good shops here in Magnis—nowhere I can find fine clothes or jewelry?"

Saula nodded.

Martha stood up. "Well, in that case, I've changed my mind. If there's nothing better to do around here, I'd love to come with you for a brisk early morning ride deep into wild frontier country. How about you, Saula? Fancy an early morning jaunt?"

"Me? Miss all that fresh air and fun?" Saula said with a staged laugh as she, too, rose to her feet. "You can count me in."

"I'm with you Pinnosa!" Brittola leapt from her bunk. "All we're doing is riding up the valley to Pinnosa's home and visiting her family. It's not as if we're actively *seeking* the raiders. Is it?"

"Precisely," Ursula said emphatically.

They all turned and looked at Cordula. She smiled and said, "Well, don't expect me to be the only one left behind—full of worry. Besides, I'd rather fight the Hibernians than have to explain to the Centurion what you're up to."

While they were getting dressed and snatching morsels of food, Pinnosa started distributing the equipment she had gathered from the armory while they were sleeping. They were each given a small, round shield, a hunting bow with a full quiver of arrows, a hunting spear and a short, legionary's sword like the one she always wore. When they were all ready, Pinnosa leaned around outside the door. She produced a full-length officer's sword with an ornate hilt, then strapped it around her waist.

"Where did you get that from, Pinnosa?" Brittola exclaimed.

Pinnosa smiled and tapped her nose. "Don't forget I know this town well."

"What do think you'll need it for?" Ursula asked.

"Extra protection." Pinnosa replied. She strolled to the door and asked in a loud voice, "Shall we be off?"

They found their horses already saddled. A sentry, who had been waiting for them to appear, was positioned nearby with an oil lamp. At a nod from Pinnosa, he hurried off toward the town gate while they mounted their horses. The eastern sky shed just enough light to penetrate the blackness as the young women settled into their saddles and set off. Within moments, the gate was wide open and the six young women were flying across the ramp at a full gallop. The sound of their horses' hooves reverberated like thunder in the deep defense dikes below. It woke up the whole of Magnis. Dogs started barking, cattle mooed and cockerels crowed with all their early morning might.

Once they were off the ramp, they headed straight for the river. With Pinnosa in the lead and Ursula guarding the rear, the group took the rough valley road that led them upstream toward the Flavius villa—and whatever the hills had in store for them.

V

They reached the last river bend before the Flavius villa just as the fiery rim of the sun started to appear above the mountaintops. Pinnosa signaled a halt. She had them dismount and led them to a small glade by the river, where they could tether their horses and keep them well-hidden from the road's view.

"We go the final stretch on foot—and very, very quietly," she explained in a whisper. Then she led them back over the road and into the undergrowth. They soon picked up a deer path that enabled them to creep unseen toward the villa grounds. As soon as they could make out the estate's main buildings, Pinnosa whispered, "Wait here. I'll go ahead." To Ursula she said quietly, "I'll be back as soon as I've made sure the front grounds are safe." Then she disappeared into the undergrowth.

After Pinnosa had gone, the others remained motionless for an agonizingly long time, listening intently for some sign of her return. Eventually, Ursula decided they should wait no longer. She signaled for the others to follow her. Slowly, step by step, they crept toward the edge of the woods. As the trees started to thin, they saw a steep path leading from the river to their left up to the villa buildings on their right. Just a few more steps and they would be out in the open and fully exposed to view. They scoured the landscape for any sign of activity. All they could see was the peaceful beauty of a sleepy frontier estate languishing in the morning light of what promised to be a glorious early summer's day. The dense foliage of the surrounding woodland was alive with the small noises of busy birds and animals. But there was no sign of the kind of disturbance that would be caused by people, especially loud Hibernian raiders moving around.

After yet another long pause, Ursula turned to the others, signaled that they should raise their shields and led them from the trees. As soon as they joined the path, their view of the villa buildings became clear. It was then that the horror was revealed that none of them would ever forget.

There, just in front of the first building in the middle of the path, was Pinnosa, kneeling motionless before a badly mutilated and naked corpse. It was hanging upside down like carrion from the branch of a large oak tree. Entrails and strands of congealed blood dangled over its face from huge gashes that were slashed across its front. They could see it was the body of a boy about to become a man. It had to be one of Pinnosa's two younger brothers, and from his red hair they guessed it was the youngest, Titus.

Ursula discarded her weapons and shield, bent down beside Pinnosa, put her arm around her shoulder, and bowed her head to join her in silent prayer. Martha, Saula, and Cordula briefly knelt on one knee behind them and gave quick bows of respect. Then they sat upright, crouching purposefully, with their shields raised and bows primed—on the alert against attack.

Brittola was the last to join the group. Deep in a state of shock, she came around in front of the others and knelt beside Pinnosa. For a short while she just stared open-mouthed at the corpse above her head. Then she dropped her weapons with a clatter and grasped her silver cross, mumbling a prayer.

"Hush!" Pinnosa hissed, spinning angrily round. Her sudden and fierce outburst made Brittola burst into tears. Cordula dived forward and put her hand over her mouth to silence her.

Pinnosa stood up, nodded at the main buildings, and headed off toward them accompanied by Martha and Saula. Brittola, who had regained control of herself, followed with Cordula. Ursula brought up the rear.

They reached the rear wall of the large barn flanking the outer courtyard and found themselves looking upon the villa's entrance, where, in better times, visitors would arrive to a warm reception. Now it was eerily silent. Not even the cluck of a chicken or the shuffle of a cow could be heard. Pinnosa pointed toward the opposite rim of the courtyard and indicated she intended to approach from that side. Ursula nodded. Pinnosa stepped out into the sunlight and crossed the yard, completely visible to any eyes that might be watching from the villa.

Ursula led the others up the side of the barn, which was still shrouded in shadow. She knew Pinnosa was acting as a decoy to distract any lookouts and give them a chance to escape, if necessary. As they advanced on the main villa building, Ursula found herself praying for an entirely different scene—one, which she already knew in her heart was impossible. *Perhaps there are survivors in the house. And, when they see Pinnosa coming, they'll run out to greet her with loving words . . . instead of war cries.*

They all made it safely to the portico outside the main entrance without so much as a mouse stirring. The door was ominously ajar. Pinnosa slipped inside, taking care not to move it in case it creaked. She signaled to the others that they should do the same. Pinnosa's boldness gave the others courage, and they all entered the dark unknown of the villa's interior together.

They stood in the Entrance Hall for a few moments to allow their eyes to adjust, as well as their stomachs, for the room stank of gore. At a signal from Pinnosa, they moved toward the west antechamber. As they did so, Cordula slipped on something wet and sticky. She barely managed to stifle a scream.

There was a huge pool of blood at her feet that had spread out from beneath the staircase.

Pinnosa went over to the alcove and, leaning forward, looked inside. "Mother's attendant," she whispered as she withdrew. All the others could see of the victim was one sandal-clad foot poking out from the shadows.

Merciful God! Ursula fought hard to control her emotions. *What hell did she experience in her last few minutes?*

The antechamber led into the West Room. It was a large, private room that Pinnosa's parents had made theirs ever since her father had been crippled. It extended out from the main building to the rear and had a windowed terrace, which faced east and opened into the kitchen courtyard.

The last time Pinnosa had been in the West Room, she had come running in full of excitement to tell her parents about Titus' latest hunting triumph. He had successfully wounded and chased off a wolf, which had tried to attack him as he had gutted a smaller kill. *Perhaps he thought he could do that to Hibernian marauders.* Pinnosa rounded the pillar at the entrance. This time there was no warm greeting, no gentle hug from her mother, and no squeeze of her hand by her father. There, at the far end of the room, were two dead bodies who could no longer do such things. The morning sunshine was pouring in through the terrace windows and filling most of the room. The bodies were fully robed and lying together in the shadows. One was seated on the floor, leaning back against the wall. The other was slumped forward across the first's legs, face downward.

Pinnosa strode the length of the mosaic floor with loud steps, all caution forgotten. The others, however, still trod carefully, remaining fully on the alert against the threat of attack. The seated figure was Marcus Flavius. His eyes were open wide, staring sightlessly at his beloved mountains framed by the window. A spear had been thrust deep into his heart. He looked serene, as if all his pain and suffering had been lifted. The other body was that of Pinnosa's mother. She had impaled herself on a long sword. It was clear they had killed themselves, rather than face the terrible death that had come pounding on their door.

"*Look!*" Brittola hissed. She was at the rear of the group and had the clearest view of the kitchen courtyard. Simultaneously, they all turned, saw what Brittola had seen, and leaped for the safety of the shadows. Pinnosa and Ursula were together next to the window by the corpses. Martha was by herself between that window and the next. The other three were huddled together on the far side of the second window. Ursula frantically signaled that they should stay absolutely still. Then, she and Pinnosa carefully peered round the window frame. In the courtyard were the Hibernian raiders—and they were all fast asleep. Scattered about them were dozens of empty wine urns, which explained why the women's noise had not woken them up. Not one of the inebriated louts stirred. Ursula looked back at the others, put her finger to her mouth, and nodded, indicating they could look as long as they kept quiet.

The Chief, a grotesque beast of a man with a broad, bearded face, was flopped across a stone chair in the center of the yard. He was wearing a large, grimy leather cloak. Beneath it they could see several knives and two huge swords strapped across his bloated belly on even grimier leather belts. His guards—two huge, thick-necked dolts—were stretched out on the paving at his feet. Some of his men were lying in clusters against the walls of the courtyard as if they had been heaped together. Others were sleeping flat on the ornamental borders or flowerbeds, where they had collapsed the night before in their drunken stupor. The ground was littered with weapons. They were mostly of a crude nature: bludgeons, swords, knives and axes. Stacked against the walls were sacks of plunder, each full to the brim with looted goods.

Pinnosa gathered the others in a group and, using gestures and whispers, outlined her plan. Then she and Martha made their way around to the East Room on the opposite side of the courtyard.

As soon as they were in position, Pinnosa raised her hunting horn, which she always wore around her neck, to her lips—and gave a single, short, high-pitched call.

Six arrows flew. All six hit their targets and went in deep. Five of the men, including the Chief and both his guards, screamed themselves awake in terrible agony. A sixth couldn't scream because Saula's arrow had pierced his neck. His bloody gurgling and writhing added to the wild panic that ensued.

Pinnosa's horn sounded again. Another six arrows flew. This time the guards were pierced a second time. They fell back to the ground. A further three men were hit and they too started to scream with pain. There was pandemonium in the courtyard as the unharmed men scrambled about like crazed beasts. A third call rang out and more fell. By now, only a few of the men were unscathed.

"*Drop your weapons!*" Pinnosa shouted. Her voice thundered over the wails of the wounded. "*You are surrounded!*"

She repeated the order in their own tongue, which she had learned as a child from some of the Hibernian merchants and travelers who would occasionally visit Magnis.

All the men, including most of the wounded, turned to face the window where Pinnosa's voice had come from. Some of the able-bodied shouted abuse and waved swords or bludgeons.

The horn sounded again. Six more arrows. Four made their targets.

"Drop your weapons!" Pinnosa's voice was firm. She repeated herself in Hibernian. The sound of dropping weapons showed their obedience.

"Drop *all* your weapons!" Ursula let fly another arrow. It ran through the arm of an older man who was holding a huge iron axe behind his back. It fell with a heavy thud onto the paving stones. It was rapidly followed by the clatter of yet more weapons being dropped.

Pinnosa emerged from the shadows and strode boldly into the center of the yard. She had discarded her bow and shield. Instead, she wielded her short sword in her left hand and the long one in her right. Martha also entered the courtyard, but remained in the shadows; her bow drawn and poised ready to fire at the slightest movement. At the same time, Ursula and Cordula moved into the courtyard from the West Room, and Saula and Brittola appeared in the doorway. They all had their bows drawn.

"All of you that can still move—go over to the end wall and lie down flat on your stomachs! And *no talking!* If any one talks, he gets an arrow in the throat!" Pinnosa held out her long sword at arm's length, pointing it to where she wanted them to go and repeated her orders in Hibernian. The six remaining able-bodied men and several of the wounded obeyed as best they could. The Chief, who had just yanked an arrow from his thigh, made as if to follow them. "*Not you!*" she shouted. "You stay right there!"

She went over to one of the guards. He had turned white with pain and was shivering with agony. He was trying to pull an arrow from his side. She bent down and, without hesitation, slit his throat with her short sword. "That's for Titus." Then she stood up and turned to face the Chief.

"Pick it up!" She pointed to his long sword. It had fallen from his belt and was lying near his feet.

"We ain't got no trouble to be making with you, Mistress." His voice was shrill with fear, exaggerating his thick accent.

"I said *pick it up!*"

"You wouldn't be harming a wounded man now would you, Mistress?" He winced with pain as he bent down. "Now, that wouldn't be a fair thing to be doing."

"*Quiet!*" Pinnosa threw down her short sword. She circled him menacingly with her long sword held forward in both hands. He raised his sword and readied for her attack.

"I don't want to hear your foul voice!" she snarled. She dragged the tip of the blade across the paving stones raising a shower of sparks and sharpening its point. "In fact . . ." she tossed the sword from hand to hand. "I never . . ." she tossed it again. "*ever* want to see your vile face . . ." she gripped it with both hands, ". . . *again!*"

She leveled her sword and ran at him. He brought his blade up to counter her attack, and at the same time attempt a back swipe. She lunged downward and flicked the tip. His sword flew from his hand and slid across the paving with a sickening, rattling clatter. He went for one of his knives, but he was too slow. She thrust her blade deep into his huge belly. His eyes bulged, and he started to gag.

"*That's* for my mother!" She cried. "And *this* . . ." She took a deep breath, and pushed again–hard. Her blood-soaked blade came clear from out of his back, piercing his rank and tattered cloak, ". . . is for my *father!*"

She stepped back and yanked the sword free, tearing his bowel open as she did so. His quivering bulk flopped to its knees, then toppled forward. It landed flat on its face, lying motionless in a rapidly spreading pool of its own blood. One gaping eye was still visible, full of hate—even in death.

The able-bodied men were clearly petrified of the ferocious Roman woman. Ursula, with Cordula by her side, did a quick circuit of the court-yard, making an assessment of the situation. In one of the flowerbeds they found a man very near to death. He lay on his back with an arrow through his stomach. He was bleeding badly, and twitching violently. Ursula picked up the Chief's long sword that was lying nearby, put the tip to the man's throat and leaned on the hilt. There was a muffled crack, and his suffering was over.

"Martha," she said calmly. "Go back to Magnis and fetch help. You'd better bring leg irons for twenty—no make it twenty-five. And wagons for the wounded."

VI

At mid-afternoon on the third day of their long trek across the mountains toward the coast, Ursula found herself exhausted. She was riding side by side with Cordula, two lengths behind Brittola, who was in turn another two lengths behind Saula. Martha had dropped back to join the rear guard behind the wagons containing the seriously wounded. She wanted to take a rest from monitoring the prisoners as they shuffled along in their ever-rattling shackles.

The sound was also grating on Ursula's nerves. "Oh, that *awful noise!*" she groaned in exasperation. "I can hear it in my sleep."

"Sleep?" Cordula replied wearily. "I can't remember what sleep feels like—not proper sleep anyway. None of us have really slept for days."

"I know. It's the same for the men, too. They've been on the go as long as we have—especially the Wye valley men from Glevum. One of them was saying to me earlier that—"

"Look!" Cordula interrupted her cousin, pointing straight ahead.

Away in the distance, Pinnosa appeared from behind a rock at the side of the trail, on Artemis. She had been shadowing the deportation party ever since they began their long trek. Sometimes she disappeared for a long while. Then, they would spot her up high on a bluff, or riding away into an adjacent valley. This time she galloped hard across in front of them and down into a narrow cut in the land, which took her out of sight.

"She needs to be alone," Ursula said. "She has a lot of pain and grief in her heart. But she's not the type to express her feelings—even to us."

"I would be the same if such horror came into my life," Cordula said quietly. They lapsed into silence. "I wish Morgan was here," she added eventually, looking sorrowfully at Ursula. "The same questions keep going round and round in my mind: 'Where is he now? What is he doing? What dangers is he encountering? Is he all right?'"

"You should try to put such thoughts to rest. They will drive you to distraction."

"I can't."

"I know you can't," Ursula reached out to touch her cousin's arm. "I can't either." They looked each other in the eye and both managed to force a weary smile. Then, they lapsed once more into silence and resumed their seemingly endless ride, each lost deep in thought.

"Pinnosa's trapped in a madness from which only she can escape," Cordula said after a while.

"Yes, but, thank goodness we're here to help," Ursula replied. "Without us, she would have absolutely no one." Ursula shivered as her own fears stirred deep in her heart. She thought back to the events at the Flavius villa two and a half days before.

The hours while Martha had been away had been extremely tense and difficult. Ursula and the others commenced their cleaning up by searching the Hibernians for concealed weapons. Without their leaders they were so terrified of the armed women, especially the fearsome, Hibernian-speaking redhead, that they'd put up no resistance. None of them spoke as they were stripped to their tunics and had their hands bound. Then, as Ursula turned her attention to dressing the men's wounds, Pinnosa began searching the villa and its grounds for her brother, Julius.

Thorough and methodical at first, her search became more and more frantic. They heard her calling his name, sometimes in the buildings, sometimes far away by the river or in the forest. Her voice often echoed in the courtyard like the haunting wail of a banshee.

They had just removed the last arrow when she returned. Bursting into the courtyard with both swords drawn, she screeched in a hoarse voice, "Where *is* he? What have you murdering swine done with him?" Before Ursula was able to reach her, she pinned one of the unharmed men to the floor. She cut his bonds, forced him to outstretch the fingers of his right hand, and placed her blade across the knuckles. "Tell me right now," she growled, "or you won't even be able to count your blessings."

The man was too frightened to speak, and Ursula was too slow in pulling Pinnosa off to save three of his fingers.

A young lad, barely sixteen, who had been unharmed in the attack, bravely rose to his knees. He said in clear Britannic, "Excuse me, Mistress. Are you looking for the other young Roman boy who defended this house?"

Pinnosa freed herself from Ursula's grasp and wheeled round to face the red-haired youth. Ursula noticed something astonishing—he was brandishing a simple wooden cross that he had been wearing around his neck.

Brittola was riding next to him now, talking about God and occasionally breaking into a psalm or hymn with him, when they discovered they knew one in common.

They are mortal enemies, Ursula mused as she watched them. *He a Hibernian raider, and she the daughter of a rich Britannic Roman family. Under normal circumstances, he would be cutting her throat intent on stealing her riches. Instead, they are together, sharing the same God, singing the same songs. Even joining in worship.* "Don't you think it's strange, Cordula? We think of these Hibernians as uncivilized primitives, yet we have one here who knows the scriptures. I wonder how many more there are like him beyond Rome's borders. I wonder if he senses God the same way as we do."

"I imagine they're some of the questions she's asking." Cordula nodded toward Brittola and smiled. "After all, he is a very talkative young man."

Ursula laughed for the first time in three days. She looked at the Hibernian lad afresh. He was quite handsome in a farm boy kind of way, with a loose mop of red hair sticking up in tufts. Brittola's unruly, black bundle of curls provided a nice contrast. It was then she noticed Brittola was wearing the gold and onyx hairpin she had loaned her for the Great Feast. She pointed it out to Cordula and they shared a chuckle. "It'll be quite a time before the next feast. I don't think I'll be needing it for a while. Anyway, it looks good in her hair. I'll let her keep it. It goes well with her cross . . . ." Ursula grasped Cordula's arm.

"A cross!" she exclaimed. "I've just realized . . . he's the lad I saw fumbling in his tunic during the attack. I thought he was going for a hidden weapon. It's lucky I missed. He was simply reaching for his cross—just like Brittola does when she's frightened or upset."

"It's a mistake to conceal a cross under a tunic," Cordula said. "People are bound to think you're going for a weapon."

Ursula's tired mind started to wander. If you do conceal a weapon on your body, it's difficult to reach for it inconspicuously. Now if you wanted to be able to reach for a concealed weapon without creating suspicion, how could you do it? She was still looking at the back of Brittola's head and suddenly her eyes opened wide. "Why, of course . . . ."

A splashing sound brought her mind back from its meandering thoughts. They were fording a sizeable stream. The Hibernians were up to their knees. Swift seemed to be enjoying the cooling sensation. At that moment, Pinnosa reappeared off to their left. She was galloping hard away from them, water splashing in every direction. The clatter of stones momentarily added to the constant rattle-clink of the prisoners' chains.

The boy's words came rushing back. "He's dead, Mistress," he had said. Ursula admired his courage in risking Pinnosa's wrath. "He was killed like the other one. But, instead of hanging him from a tree, they"—he nodded toward the dead Chief and guards—"threw him in the river."

Pinnosa went deadly quiet at the news. Ursula braced herself to control another outburst. Instead of ranting and raving, however, Pinnosa slowly lowered her head and walked back into the West Room, where her parents lay. The next time they saw her was later that morning. Martha had returned with much more than shackles and wagons. While she had been at Magnis, the contingent of men on horseback from Viroconium had arrived. She had brought twenty of them back to the villa. With their help, the women had shackled the able-bodied Hibernians and loaded the seriously wounded onto the wagons. They had been just about to set off for Magnis, when Pinnosa had appeared at the villa entrance.

Her eyes were swollen and bloodshot from weeping. She was still wringing her hair with grief, and it was tangled in a mat. "Where are you taking them?" she cried, her voice shrill and hoarse.

"To the cells in Magnis, Mistress," the Commander, an elderly man who had seen many campaigns, replied.

"Oh, no, you're *not!*" She wrenched her hand free from her head, pulling a big clump of hair out, which she threw to the ground. Then she reached for her sword. "They're going back where they came from. Back where they belong. I'll not rest until this land is rid of the likes of them."

"But, Mistress—"

"But, Pinnosa—" Ursula moved toward her.

"Or . . ." she raised her sword, "I run them through with this *here and now!* By God's Will, I'll cleanse these hallowed stones—made foul by their evil deeds—with their blood!" Her eyes glared wild with such fury the Commander was completely at a loss for words. "What's it to be, Commander? A bloodbath of these steps—or a cleansing of the land?"

"I would need special orders, Mistress."

"You would obey orders from Princess Ursula, daughter of King Deonotus, would you not?"

He nodded.

Pinnosa turned her mad stare on her friend. "Well?"

Ursula knew that beneath Pinnosa's rage she was in deep torment. *If I don't follow her some way into her madness, I won't be able to pull her back from the awful abyss gaping before her.*

Finally, without taking her eyes from Pinnosa's, she said, "Commander, you are to use half of your men to escort these prisoners back to their boats. The rest are to assist with cleaning up and with helping the other families return to their homes." She looked across at the others, who were near the wagons for the wounded. "All six of us will accompany you."

The Commander frowned but then graciously bowed his consent. "Yes, Your Highness."

VII

The long journey to the coast had started badly, with some of the less seriously wounded prisoners incapable of keeping up with the pace, despite numerous whippings. Then, late in the afternoon, they found an additional four-wheeled cart. It seemed to have been abandoned, and, fortunately, its team of donkeys was nearby at a deserted homestead. They loaded the slowest of the men onto it, and from then on they began to make better progress.

From the outset, Pinnosa had adopted her eerie shadowing behavior. When the time came for them to make their first camp high in the mountains—she was nowhere to be seen. During the night, however, Ursula woke to find Pinnosa standing over her. Despite gentle coaxing, Ursula was unable to get her to talk or lie down to sleep. Eventually her own exhaustion had forced her to close her eyes, leaving her distraught friend to the darkness.

On the second day, the military road they were following took them over the highest ridges of the mountains, and they began the long descent to the coast. Their second night was spent in the comfort of a fully stocked and provisioned army camp. Just before dark, Pinnosa appeared and tethered Artemis up with the rest of the horses. She waved her friends away and insisted on sitting apart from the group, but she did eat some food and even drank a half flagon of wine. Ursula was relieved when she eventually saw her lay down to sleep for what must have been the first time in three nights.

The third day, they experienced their only serious trouble on the journey. While passing through the gold mining town of Luentinum, they attracted the unwanted attention of a large group of the burly miners. Despite the best efforts of the Commander and his men, they surrounded the deportation party, jeering and jostling the prisoners. More worryingly, the miners lunged menacingly at the young noblewomen. Ursula had just drawn her sword in defense when Pinnosa appeared. She came racing up the road from their rear, galloping on Artemis with her red cape flying out behind. She charged at the miners, shrieking war cries and brandishing her long sword menacingly. She singled out a big, fat brute, who was obviously their leader, and went straight for him, forcing him to scurry away backwards. He stumbled and fell. But still she was upon him. In fear, he turned and ran from the rearing horse and wild, sword-wielding woman. Seeing this, the rest of the miners backed off, content to limit their molestation to jeers and taunts while the prisoners and their escort went on their way.

Since then, although she had continued to keep her distance, Pinnosa checked on them more frequently.

"Slowly but surely she's coming back to her senses," Ursula said to Cordula. "Maybe soon the nightmare will be over and—"

Suddenly, there were loud shouts of excitement from the front of the line of prisoners. Ursula urged Swift forward. She reached the head of the line at the same time as the Commander. The Hibernians excitedly explained in broken Britannic that they had spotted the rock formation that marked the track to the cove where their boats were hidden.

VIII

"See over there, Your Highness?" the Commander indicated a nearby headland. "If you ride to that bluff yonder—the one that looks like a bear's head—you'll see an old temple complex directly below you. Some say it was built by the Druids. Not long ago, a group of Christian monks from Glevum and Viroconium cleaned it up and started using it as a kind of retreat. But they had to abandon it when the frontier legions were cut. We couldn't guarantee their safety. I think you'll find it's still in good repair though. It should provide you and the other young ladies with somewhere suitable for you to rest and clean yourselves up. It has basic bathing and cooking facilities. All the equipment should still be there."

"Thank you. I don't think we're needed here any more," Ursula replied. She glanced back at the others who were waiting patiently for her in the lengthening shadows on the beach. "We'd best be going before the darkness beats us."

"Very wise, Your Highness."

She looked anxiously about the rim of the cove, hoping to see some sign of movement—some sign of Pinnosa. *What if she didn't see us leave the road?* She turned back to the Commander. "If Pinnosa appears, would you please inform her of where we have made camp?"

"Of course, Your Highness." The Commander looked uncomfortable and hesitated for a second, as if deciding whether to say something. After checking that none of his men was near, he said in hushed tones, "I'd just like to say, Your Highness, that Britannia owes you and these other fine young ladies a great deal. You did the work of twenty men. And what's more, if men had done what you did, they would be heroes worthy of the greatest honors."

"Thank you, Commander." She smiled. "Coming from you, that is, indeed, a compliment."

"One more thing, Your Highness. The Lady Pinnosa's had a terrible shock. I've seen grown men twice her age go the same way after a battle, including officers of the highest rank. She's strong, though. She'll get through it. And when she does, she'll be tougher than ever. I've seen it work that way many a time."

"I think you are probably right." Ursula had come to respect the old officer a great deal over the past few days. She cast her eye over his men, and was struck, yet again, by their age—not one had seen less than forty winters, and many had seen over fifty. Some of them were supervising the able-bodied Hibernians as they dug their boats—shallow-drafted with six oars apiece—out from the sand. Others were helping the seriously wounded from the wagons and leading them down the path to the beach. The rest were preparing the camp at the back of the cove beneath a small bluff. The prisoners would be chained firmly to the rocks throughout the night, and would remain shackled when they were put out to sea at first light the following morning. It was the only way to ensure they would go back to Hibernia and not attempt a second landing, even with so many wounded.

She looked the Commander in the eye, took his hand and shook it firmly. "Thank you for all your help, Commander. I assure you that I will fully commend you and all your men to my father, when we return to Corinium."

As she turned to walk back to where her friends were waiting, he stood to attention and said loudly for all to hear, "On behalf of our Legion, and of the people of these mountains; Your Highness, I salute you—and your brave companions!"

IX

At the heart of the temple complex was an overgrown grotto, where hanging vines dangled over a well by a shallow pool. They were so struck by the beauty of the setting they decided to sleep in the open on the long terrace beyond the pool, instead of in an antechamber. The grotto looked out over the sea, and when they lay down they could hear the waves lapping gently on the rocks below.

The monks had built a simple altar with a plain wooden cross in the center of the terrace.

"You can imagine them in their sack-cloth, and with their shaved heads, at prayer," Cordula said to Brittola. Brittola nodded and smiled.

The group had bathed and were just finishing a quiet supper when they heard someone coming through the grotto. Pinnosa emerged from the shadows and went over to the altar. She stood facing them, silhouetted against the blood red sky, fully cloaked with her long sword hanging to one side. She appeared to be clutching a small sack.

"It's over and done with." Pinnosa's voice was more than tired. It was eerily flat and lifeless.

"Where have you been?" Ursula and the others stood up to greet her. "We've been worried about you."

Without saying anything, Pinnosa walked over to Ursula and hugged her. Then she started hugging each of the others, one by one. *Has she finally returned to her senses?* Ursula wondered as Pinnosa moved slowly round their group.

When she finally spoke, however, her voice sounded strange. "I waited until you'd all left the cove before I went down to . . . to say my farewells."

Ursula could sense that something was wrong. Pinnosa's face was racked with conflicting emotions.

"Here." She offered the sack to Ursula.

"What is it?" Ursula tentatively took hold of the dank object.

Pinnosa stood awkwardly for a moment like a child caught in the act of some mischief. She turned and spoke to Brittola instead. "Don't worry, I spared your young friend." She faced Ursula again. In an unconvincing attempt at sounding defiant, she declared, "They'll never blight this land again! And all their Hibernian friends will think twice before joining any more raiding parties."

"What have you *done*, Pinnosa?" Saula cried. "What, in God's name, have you done?"

"With the help of the Commander, I . . . I cut off their thumbs."

Brittola screamed. The others gasped.

Grim-faced and speechless with rage, Ursula strode to the edge of the terrace and slung the sack as far as she could into the night. She turned to Pinnosa and shouted, "You're right! It *is* over! Are you happy now that you've had your revenge?" She glared at Pinnosa.

Pinnosa attempted to scowl back, but she could not. She lowered her gaze and bowed her head.

Ursula continued to glower at her, prolonging Pinnosa's agony, until eventually she turned to the others and ended the awful silence. "I think we *all* ought to get some much needed sleep. Tomorrow we head back to Corinium and *civilization*."

Ursula cupped her hand in the pool and took a sip of water. Then she went over to where she had laid her bedroll and prepared herself, at long last, for some much-needed rest. The others, including Pinnosa, followed suit, and within a few moments they were all settled and ready for sleep.

Then, just as they were beginning to drift into slumber, Brittola stirred. She rose, walked over to the altar, and knelt to pray. "Dear Lord and merciful God," she said in a clear voice. "Terrible deeds have been committed in the past three days in the name of revenge. We have seen how sin begets sin, and how those who are sinned against, in wanting to redress the sin, become sinners themselves. For this, dear Lord, we ask . . . nay, we *beg* your forgiveness." She lifted her head to the heavens. "Amen."

They all said, "Amen." The loudest voice was Pinnosa's. As Ursula and the others watched, silhouetted against the stars, Brittola went over to Pinnosa, and, after a slight hesitation, patted her on the shoulder. Then she returned to her bed. Before long, the only sound that could be heard was the gentle lapping of the nearby waves.

X

Ursula was awakened by the sound of seagulls squawking as they dived down for the rich pickings left by the departing tide. Not wishing to disturb the others, she rose quietly and walked over to the edge of the terrace.

The morning light shimmered on the gentle waves and a refreshingly cool breeze was coming in off the sea. She left the terrace and picked her way across the rocks toward a large boulder that was well out into the water. She climbed onto it, sat down, tilted back her head and let the breeze take her hair, enjoying the occasional splash of spray on her legs and feet. For a long while, she sat motionless, enjoying the peaceful scene.

A curious feature caught her eye. About fifty cubits out, in the middle of calm water, a turbulent eddy was causing the waves to crest prematurely. *Probably a hidden rock*, she thought, *or some quirk of the undertow.* Her dark fear returned, making her insides churn. *Those hidden currents are just like events on the Continent. I hope Constans doesn't become engulfed in some lurking mire of treachery. We've seen for ourselves these past few days how easy it is to be charting apparently peaceful waters only to be—*

"Looking for a nice fish for breakfast?" Pinnosa's voice made Ursula jump. "The others are still sleeping. I saw you out here, and thought I'd join you. Or would you rather be left alone with Contans?"

"I was thinking about our Hibernian 'friends' actually." Ursula smiled as she moved over to let Pinnosa sit down, then put her arm round her to give her a friendly hug. "In fact, I think I owe you an apology." Pinnosa looked at her quizzically. "You were right to do what you did last night—cutting off their thumbs."

Pinnosa flinched and looked down at the water by their feet. "Well, I'm not so sure. I was acting in anger and not really thinking clearly."

"Whether you were thinking clearly or not, thank goodness your thirst for revenge got the better of you." She stared unseeingly at the nearby rocks. "These are truly dangerous times. I think Constantine exaggerated the readiness of the defenses in order to put people's minds at ease. We've seen for ourselves how over-stretched the garrisons are. Only fifteen men in Magnis—and old ones at that. Only three galleons patrolling this area. It must be the same all over the Province." She pointed out to sea. "Every potential raider—Hibernian or Pict—is going to try his luck sometime in the coming harvest season. We simply can't afford the luxury of deporting prisoners who are capable of returning to wreak more havoc." She frowned. "In fact, I think I should speak to Father and ask him to declare a 'no prisoners' policy, at least until the men return."

Pinnosa, who had been slowly nodding in agreement, sighed. "Actually, there are even greater dangers with deportation than just the risk of freed prisoners returning to make further raids. When they return home, they'll tell stories of a weak Britannia: of empty army encampments; of very few legionaries; and, of Roman estates only being able to defend themselves with slaves and women."

Pinnosa scrutinized the western horizon as if expecting a raiding party to appear at any moment, heading straight for them. "The word will spread all over Hibernia and probably back across the sea to the Picts. Within barely two cycles of the moon we could see them forming another Grand Alliance. Then, they'll attack on two fronts at the same time—and in large numbers. With no mobile Britannic field army here to tackle them and force them back, hundreds, if not thousands of people will end up like my family." She turned to Ursula. "What is it?"

While Pinnosa had been speaking, Ursula was looking at her with a curious expression on her face. "'Only able to defend themselves with slaves and women,' eh?" she said teasingly, punching Pinnosa on the arm. "I think we gave a pretty good account of ourselves back there. You with your little toots on your horn. Our arrows finding twenty-two out of twenty-four—mostly moving—targets."

They smiled, then sniggered, and soon they were giggling like Martha and Saula. Pinnosa put her hand to her mouth and made little toots. Ursula fired make believe arrows with comical 'twang' sounds. They were soon laughing so much they could hardly speak.

"I've just had an interesting thought," Pinnosa said, when she could catch her breath.

"What's that?" Ursula asked, becoming more serious.

"A hundred or so hunting women like ourselves patrolling along the coast and chasing off the Hibernians would make an extremely formidable force, don't you think? Or even going on a Grand Tour along the Wall, Pict hunting." Pinnosa laughed again. "We would certainly give the raiders—and the old guards—something to think about!"

"We certainly wouldn't be defenseless." Ursula sat up straight. "Do you know something, Pinnosa? It might just work! A force of hunting women—fully armed—patrolling the coast. Even making a tour along the Wall—as you say. Why not?" She took Pinnosa's hand. "The men are going to be away for the entire campaigning season. That means we have to find a way to bolster the defenses for at least the rest of this summer . . . ." She paused, then continued in a subdued voice as she resigned herself to something. "And probably well into the next, too."

"You're right!" Pinnosa cried. "Think of all the hunts we've been on. There are plenty of able-bodied hunting women. They would be more than capable of dealing with bands of raiders in the same way that we've just done. Remember that Baetica from Lindinis? She could handle a horse as well as any man in Constantine's cavalry. Better than most—including her husband in Constans's Vanguard. And we've seen many a woman who can fire an arrow or throw a spear with as much accuracy as any man." She pummeled her leg in her excitement. "We could raise a hundred *easily*."

"More," Ursula said. "Remember last summer's hunt? We could find a hundred hunting women in Corinium alone. If we included the Glevum women, it wouldn't be too difficult to raise two—even three—hundred." She looked back out to sea. "In fact, if we issued an invitation throughout the entire West Country, we could probably create a force of several hundred."

"The only difficulty would be finding enough horses," Pinnosa said thoughtfully. "But that wouldn't matter. We could organize ourselves into infantry and cavalry units—foot soldiers and horse riders—just like a regular, mobile field army."

A noise from behind caused them both to glance back at the temple. The others were beginning to stir. Cordula and Saula were already rolling up their beds.

Ursula looked at Pinnosa. "Do you really think it would work?"

"Forming a mobile field army of several hundred West Country women?" Pinnosa mused. "Something like two or three hundred on horseback? We could bring them to frontier country to train. That way, they would be here, on the spot, ready to deal with any more Hibernian raiders who came trying their luck." She raised a quizzical eyebrow.

"It sounds feasible . . . ." Ursula said tentatively.

"Let's see. It would take about a cycle of the moon to organize. Another to execute." Pinnosa started counting the cyles on her fingers. "By then we would be in high summer. Once we were fully trained, the few men there are could be spared to man the empty galleys and make a show of force along the Hibernian coast. That would be harvest time—the time we are most at risk. Perfect timing."

"Couldn't the women take some of the galleys out?"

Pinnosa shook her head dismissively. "No. The extra training for handling a galley would take too long. The galleys themselves would probably need to be re-fitted to accommodate three per oar instead of two.

"Come harvest time, we could take some of the women on a full campaign up the east of the Province and along the Wall. We could make several skirmishes into the Pict homelands to deter them from attempting an attack. Then down to Eboracum by the end of the harvest. We could even make a slow return circuit and be back in our homes before the Hunter's Moon. The borders would be secure and we would certainly have given the men food for thought while they're away. Indeed, it should encourage them to come home early, before they're out of a job."

"*We'll do it!*" Ursula proclaimed. "We'll form a mobile field army of women."

"A force of women like the Amazons of old," Pinnosa cried. "Fighting side by side with our men against the enemies of Rome—whoever they may be!" She stood up, obviously excited.

Ursula stood up, too. "No, *not* the enemies of Rome." she said, becoming serious. "The enemies of *Britannia*. It's because the men are fighting the enemies of Rome that we're having to do this." She took Pinnosa by the arm. "While the men are fighting for the greater cause of Rome, the women shall be fighting for a cause which is much closer to their hearts and just as important—for their homes." She looked back at the temple complex. "We are having to fight, Pinnosa, because we—the able-bodied, fighting women of this island—are the only hope this Province has left."

Pinnosa gripped Ursula's arm in return, her face solemn with intent. "They will only fight if they trust their leader."

Ursula smiled. "We already do."

They both found their laughter again, and gave each other a hearty pat on the shoulder.

"Come on." Ursula started heading back to the terrace. "Shall I tell the others—or shall you . . ." she said, adding teasingly, "Commander?"

XI

"An army of women, eh?" Martha said playfully. "I'm all for it. We'll show the men a thing or two!" She winked at Saula and the two of them started giggling.

Cordula, however, looked worried. "Have you really thought this through? It's not just the fighting women, is it? What about things like messengers, and provisions, and . . . and all sorts of things I can't even think of right now."

"You can't, but you will, Cordula." It was Ursula's turn to wink—at Pinnosa. "We'll put you in charge of the ordnance crews."

"And the messengers." Pinnosa added.

"Yes, *and* the messengers." Ursula confirmed with a nod.

"Me? In charge of the messengers?" Cordula couldn't prevent herself from smiling at the prospect of working with Morgan. Ursula and Pinnosa both laughed and put their arms round her.

The only one not laughing was Brittola. She had gone very quiet while the others discussed the plan, lowering her head and letting her hair fall over her face. Then, as Ursula and Pinnosa embraced Cordula, she broke away from the group and ran out onto the terrace.

Ursula signaled to the others to stay where they were, and rushed after her.

She caught up with Brittola by the altar, where she was kneeling in prayer.

"What's the matter?" she said gently. "Don't you like the idea of women forming an army?"

Brittola looked up. Her face was full of anguish. Her eyes were brimming with tears. "Isn't there enough blood spilled by the men?" she cried. "I don't think women should be adding to all the maiming and killing. It's not right."

Ursula paused for a long moment. "Do you know something, Brittola? I think you have an important point."

"You do? I mean—do I?"

"Yes . . . a very important point. An army of women doesn't have to be the same as an army of men, does it? At least, not in every respect. For instance . . . ." They began talking animatedly to each other.

After a while, Ursula led Brittola back into the antechamber, where the others were busily discussing their plans.

"Attention, everyone," she said, clapping her hands. "Brittola has an important announcement to make." She smiled encouragingly at Brittola and nudged her forward.

Brittola took a deep breath, looked back at Ursula, then blurted, "There'll be no killing!"

"No killing?" Pinnosa exclaimed incredulously.

"None," Brittola said slowly. "We'll only use our weapons to wound and disarm. We won't aim to kill unless it's absolutely necessary—in self defense." She glanced at Ursula who nodded for her to continue. "It won't be our mission to add to all the misery and pain in the world. Instead we'll concentrate on being a show of force—a *magnificent* show of force—acting as a deterrent to would-be attackers, and nothing more. In this way we'll show the world the true power and goodness of God. We'll be a force acting purely in His name!"

"Is that all right with everyone?" Ursula looked pointedly at Pinnosa.

"Is it all right? It's *perfect!*" Pinnosa walked over to Brittola, arms outstretched. "Without you acting as my conscience, Brittola, I'd be nothing more than just another blood thirsty, red-haired frontierswoman!"

Pinnosa gave Brittola a huge hug, and the others rushed to join in.

Chapter 3

A Clarion Call

Ursula, Pinnosa, and the others were completely unprepared for the reception that awaited them upon their return from the mountains. News of their exploits had spread far afield. Their first taste of renown came at Magnis. When they appeared on the road from the river, a loud cheer went up from the palisade. As they crossed the long ramp and entered the gate, they were engulfed by a large crowd.

"Well done, Pinnosa!"

"Well done, Princess Ursula!"

"You beat off over thirty of the swine!"

"More like sixty!"

"What are you talking about? There was over a hundred of the murdering swine!"

Amidst the clamor, everyone wanted to see, and to thank, the six young noble women—their fearless heroines—who had certainly beaten off one of the more dangerous Hibernian raiding parties seen in the wild frontier lands in recent years. They were festooned with flowers and had many gifts of food, cloth and wine thrust upon them. Later Brittola and Cordula arranged to distribute the gifts among the families who had fallen victim to the raid.

On their way back to Glevum the following day, they passed through a metal-working yard. The road filled with cheering craft-folk calling out blessings and praise at the tops of their voices.

"If ever you go fighting raiders again, and if you need good, women's body armor which is as strong as a man's, but lighter—remember the name *Balig!*" cried a big man with a booming voice.

"I'll give you a better price than he will!" shouted another. "Remember the name *Haleseth!*"

"I have three daughters. You only have sons, Haleseth. Mine's sure to be the better fit!" Balig retorted, and the whole crowd laughed.

In Glevum, they were met at the city gate by a mounted Guard of Honor. It was led by the gruff, old Centurion who only six days earlier had tried to dissuade them from embarking upon their desperate errand. He saluted the young noblewomen formally as they approached. When Ursula and the others came to a halt he said, "Your Highness. Your safe return to our city brings us great joy and cause, indeed, for celebration. I fear I must offer you my fullest and most humble apologies for wrongly under-estimating your zeal and courageousness—which are clearly matched only by your prowess."

Ursula smiled and bowed. The others did the same, apart from Pinnosa, who remained completely impassive and contented herself with patting Artemis. Her disdain was palpable. It was clear that she still regarded him as having failed in some way.

"In addition, Mistress Pinnosa," the Centurion continued more than a little uncomfortably. "I would like to express my deepest sympathy for the loss of your family, which must—"

"Save your flowery words," Pinnosa interrupted. "You know they're wasted on me."

The Centurion coughed, bowed awkwardly, then resumed his well-rehearsed welcome speech. "It now gives me great pleasure, on behalf of all Glevum, to welcome you back safe and sound, and to greet you . . . in triumph!" He gestured towards the open gate. "Your Highness . . . Ladies . . . Glevum salutes you!"

Escorted by their Guard of Honor, Ursula and the others paraded slowly down the main street, through cheering crowds, to the Forum. A delegation of city nobles dressed in their finest robes was waiting for them. Once again they were showered with gifts, including fine silks; even pieces of jewelry. This time, they decided to keep some of their bounty.

The biggest and warmest welcome, however, was waiting for them at Corinium. When Ursula and her friends reached the point where the forest ended and farmland began, they were amazed to find the road was already full of people. The first to spot them was Oleander.

"Mistress! Mistress!" she cried as she came running up to Ursula, her eyes streaming with tears of happiness. "Thank goodness you're back. You're father *will* be relieved. We've been so worried. The messengers said you were safe, but they didn't say whether those foul Hibernians did you any harm. Are you all right? Were you, or any of the other young mistresses, wounded?"

"Not a scratch, Oleander," Pinnosa interrupted before Ursula could reply. "Except for some scars that won't heal."

"What does she mean, Mistress?" cried the old attendant anxiously. "Are you hurt, or aren't you?"

"We're all fine, Oleander," Ursula said, reaching down to allow the old woman to kiss her hand. "But Pinnosa's family were all killed by the raiders, along with seventeen other poor souls from a valley that was completely unwarned and unprotected."

II

So many people wanted to praise, bless, or, simply to touch them, it took Ursula and her friends a long while to complete the final stretch of their journey. As they rounded the last bend in the road, they saw King Deonotus himself at the gate, waiting to escort them into the city. He was surrounded by a small contingent of the Royal Guard in full ceremonial dress. Ursula was later to learn that the twelve men present were the unit's entire strength—less than a tenth their usual number. The rest had been seconded to Constantine's personal guard to replace those who had ridden ahead with Constans's special advance unit.

The King's anger was tangible from afar. As Ursula and the others approached him, their smiles withered against his steely cold stare. He waited until they had pulled up in front of him before speaking. "You could have *all* been killed," he growled.

"But Father—"

"What demon—what *madness*—possessed you? Taking on a gang of cold-blooded killers who were hell-bent on murder . . . or worse, hmm? What would we—your families—be doing now if the raiders hadn't been in a drunken daze, hmm? What would we be doing now, if it had been *them* with the upper hand in a deserted villa instead of you? Did you pause to think about that before rushing headlong into your appointment with Fate?" He deliberately looked each one of them in the eye. Only Ursula and Pinnosa could return his gaze. The others were forced to look down in shame.

"It was I, who—" Pinnosa began.

"Father, we—" Ursula meant to cut her friend off.

The King raised his hand for silence. "Hush for now. Save it for later." His tone lightened. "As it is, God in His Wisdom has seen fit to reward us with cause for celebration—rather than punish us with cause for mourning and despair."

Ursula saw the slight twinkle in his eye. She knew they were forgiven.

"Simply to welcome you home would be blessing enough. To welcome you home safe and sound would be a double blessing. But that's not all. God has seen fit to bless us three times over . . ." He raised his voice and lifted his right hand. "We welcome you home safe and sound and—God be praised—*in triumph!*"

At the King's signal, a hundred trumpets blared forth an ear-splitting fanfare from the battlements, heralding the noblewomen's return and announcing the commencement of their parade through the city. As the King and his guards led them through the gate, from high above on the city wall dozens of children, squealing with joy, threw handfuls of colored feathers and petals into the air to shower down upon the procession like multicolored snow. Once they were inside the city, the refrains of the official trumpets were lost in a cacophony of horns, pipes, drums, bells, cheers and cries. There were so many people intent on touching them, it seemed to take forever before they could make their way through to the Forum where their formal reception awaited.

At the Forum's entrance they tried to dismount and proceed on foot. Instead they were hoisted on the shoulders of enthusiastic townsfolk and carried the length of the square. They were taken to a high, wooden dais that the King had specially constructed on the steps to the Basilica. Deonotus reached it long before his daughter and her companions. Donning his crown and royal cloak, and sitting astride a finely dressed steed covered with polished leather and bronze regalia, he positioned himself in front of the dais and waited to receive them. "People of Corinium!" He cried as soon as Ursula and the others were up on the platform above him. The crowd's cheers were so loud and persistent it took more than ten blasts on the royal horns before the King could continue. "Good people of Corinium! They have come home at last!"

A deafening outburst of cries, drums and whistles prevented him from saying more. While the horns were desperately trying to quell the noise he stood up on his mount and shouted to Ursula, "They're not going to let me say much! They want to hear from you!"

Ursula stepped forward to the edge of the platform and raised her hands for silence, but by now many of the townsfolk were far too excited to be quiet.

"You showed the ugly Hibernian swine, Princess Ursula!" a young girl nearby shouted. "Their brawn was no match for your brains!"

"When are you going to go raider-hunting again, Pinnosa?" an old man cried next to her. "How many are you going to kill next time? A couple of dozen? A hundred?"

"People of Corinium! We are truly humbled and overcome by your reception . . . ." Ursula began, but the exuberant cries of praise from the crowd persisted, forcing her to pause. She glanced back at the others, her eyebrows raised in a crooked crease of exasperation. Then she looked down at her father who, with a broad smile, mouthed, "Be patient."

Eventually, the cheers started to quieten down, but before Ursula could speak, the old man near the front stood on an up-turned wooden pail and addressed the crowd.

"God be praised!" he shouted. "That six young ladies should do the work of thirty men and escape unharmed!"

"Where were the men?" a large woman near the front bellowed. She was the miller's wife, and was renowned for her loud voice. "It's not right that our young noblewomen had to do the work of armed men! Where were the guards from Magnis? Or the ones from Glevum for that matter?"

"There aren't any fighting men left! Constantine lied!" one of the Forum potters boomed with the resonant voice of a market vendor. "All the army's gone! They're down to fifty at Glevum and a hundred a piece at Deva and Viroconium!"

Ursula shared an anxious glance with her father as the short, thick-set man continued. "We're defenseless I tell you! We don't stand a chance if the Hibernians and Picts form another alliance!"

Both Ursula and King Deonotus made to say something to calm the surge of fear and anger that had suddenly gripped the gathering, but they were cut short by the miller's wife.

"That's right! We *are* defenseless! Where are the fighting men—the cavalry units and the archers—we need to keep back the murdering Hibernian swine and their Pict cousins? We can't defend ourselves with young women!"

"That's where you are *wrong!*" Pinnosa stepped forward, her powerful voice forcing all others into submission. She cast her fierce gaze around the Forum, commanding silence, ending her sweep with a long, hard look at the miller's wife. "There are plenty of women who are capable of fighting and keeping the invaders at bay!"

"*Pah!*" The huge, red-faced woman, folded her arms with disbelief. "The best of our fighting men have gone and now some soft-handed women with horses think they can take their place."

"'Soft-handed women with horses?'" Pinnosa exclaimed, becoming red-faced with anger. "Just what do you—"

Martha rushed forward to grab Pinnosa by the arm. "Wouldn't it be a good idea if we reminded people of what 'soft-handed women with horses' can do with a little training?" She tapped her bow and quiver and, with a nod of her head, diverted Pinnosa's fierce gaze toward the far side of the Forum. Pinnosa looked puzzled for a moment, then realized what Martha had in mind. She nodded in reply.

Martha turned to face the miller's wife and grinned. "If you think all the best archers and all the best horsemen have gone, leaving us defenseless—then think again."

The miller's wife and the potter looked at each other and scoffed.

"Move back and make room!" There were exclaimations of surprise as, with a dramatic flourish, Pinnosa drew her long sword from its scabbard and thrust it high into the air. Then, keeping her arm outstretched, she slowly lowered it to eye level and pointed down the centerline of the Forum. "Move back and make room, I say!"

An open space began to appear down the entire length of the square as the townsfolk obeyed. Pinnosa put her fingers to her lips and gave a long, shrill whistle. From the far end of the Forum, Artemis neighed in reply. The crowd turned and saw the great horse rearing and punching the air with her powerful hooves. Pinnosa gave a second whistle. The huge, black mare thundered through the clearing toward her mistress, forcing any stragglers to leap out of her way.

"You are right when you say that there aren't enough fighting men in Britannia to keep the Hibernian and the Picts at bay," Pinnosa shouted, as Artemis came to a halt immediately beneath her. "There aren't enough men who can do *this!*" She sheathed her sword and leapt from the platform onto Artemis' back. The crowd gave a small cheer and began to applaud. "And there aren't enough men who can do *this!*" She grabbed an arrow from her quiver and strung it to her bow. Then she turned Artemis around and, side-kicking her flanks, urged her into a full gallop. Halfway down the Forum, she took aim and let the arrow fly. It hit home, piercing a leather flagon, which was hanging just above people's heads from a shop front awning. It started spinning and spraying water in every direction. The crowd cheered loudly and began chanting her name. Pinnosa wheeled Artemis around and commenced a second run. "And where are the men who can do this?" she cried, letting a second arrow fly just as she reached full gallop. It hammered so hard into the spinning flagon the strap broke and it fell to the floor with a loud *splat!*

Pinnosa halted her horse at the base of the podium. In an effortless move, she stood up on Artemis' back and leapt across on to the platform.

While she was waiting for the deafening cheers to cease, she noticed Ursula and her father exchanging glances.

As the cacophony began to subside, Pinnosa attempted to resume her address. "Though there mightn't be enough men left who can—"

"We all know what *you* can do, Pinnosa!" the miller's wife interrupted. "But you're special. You grew up on a horse." She turned to shout to the crowd. "There aren't many women like her, who can fight like a man! Without more men we're defenseless!"

"That's right!" the potter boomed. "We're defenseless against the invaders!"

"That is *wrong!*" Pinnosa roared, glaring at them both, "There are plenty of women who are capable of dealing with invaders."

"What women?" the miller's wife scoffed. "Who?"

"Hunting women, of course," Pinnosa snapped.

"Why, there are hundreds of hunting women in the Corinium and Glevum areas alone." Brittola blurted, rushing forward to stand at Pinnosa's side. "There are certainly enough to form a field army to patrol the frontiers."

"*What!*" King Deonotus exclaimed.

"Brittola and Pinnosa are right." Ursula stepped forward. "You've seen what a woman can do with training and practice. If there aren't enough able-bodied men left in the Province to defend us against invasion . . ." she paused and looked very deliberately at her father, "the women will have to do it."

She turned to face the gathering and cried out. "We are going to send out a call to all the West Country for hunting women to assemble here and form a temporary field army!"

"An army of *women?*" the potter cried incredulously.

"An *army* of women?" murmured the miller's wife and the old man simultaneously with wonder.

The same mix of astonishment and disbelief was echoed around the Forum as the exclamation was repeated and relayed through the crowd.

Pinnosa made to say something, but Ursula held her back. At her insistence, her friends stood still while the idea took root in people's minds. Then, as the murmur dissipated and the crowd became silent, she turned calmly to the others and said, "Ladies?"

Following Ursula's summons, her friends moved forward to join her at the edge of the dais and form a line. As soon as they were in position, Ursula, who was at the end nearest her father, very deliberately placed her hand on the hilt of her sword. This was one of many silent signals they had been working on since their adventure. In response, they drew their weapons and held them low, pointing to the ground. Following Pinnosa's lead, apart from Ursula, they all raised their blades upwards and thrust them high into the air.

Ursula kept her blade low and waited, staring down at her feet. As soon as the gasps of amazement had ceased, and the crowd had settled once again into an uneasy silence, she lifted her head and made her bold proclamation. "Out of our love for our land, our people, and our beloved home! For the defense of the Province, and to the glory of God . . ." She lifted her sword to join those of the others. Together they shone in the bright summer sun like a dazzling metallic ray of light.

"*The women of Britannia shall fight!*"

III

"I know they only departed a week ago, Father, but has there been any news?" Ursula asked eagerly as King Deonotus finally joined their welcome home feast. *Please have something to tell me about Constans—please,* she thought while her father settled into his seat.

"All we know for sure is that both Constans and Constantine's departures went well," the King replied, once he was comfortable. "A messenger arrived from Rutupiae this morning. He said Constantine's departure was a magnificent sight. Over one hundred galleys in full sail on a steady sea, heading straight for the northern beaches of Galliae." He looked at his daughter and added pointedly, "We haven't received any reports from the other side of the Channel yet." He raised his glass. "To the success of Constantine's campaign. May they all return home safe . . . and soon."

Everyone toasted his words. At the feast were three young children: Martha's brother, Uricalus, and Cordula's younger sister, Docilina, both in their tenth summer; and Saula's younger sister, Trifosa, who was in her sixth.

"Why did all the men have to go, Your Majesty?" Docilina asked after the adults had completed their salutation.

"To fight off the German tribes—stupid." Uricalus sneered, giving his cousin a punch. "Where will the first big battle be, Your Majesty? Treveris? Mogontiacum?"

"Ah, the battle lust of young boys! Where would we be without it?" The King smiled. "You are right, Uricalus. In a way they have gone to fight the

German tribes, but, unfortunately, it's not quite as straightforward as that. Let me try to explain it as simply as I can to you . . . ."

He cleared the table in front of him and arranged three knives in a line, end to end. On one side of the line he placed a platter of fruit. On the other he scattered some quail bones from an appetizer they had been enjoying.

"Think of your villa estate and the wilderness beyond. Your villa has beautiful gardens: flower gardens, kitchen gardens, even hanging gardens, all well kept and the envy of your neighbors. In addition to your gardens, you have your fields for growing crops, your grazing land for livestock, your yards for poultry and your stables for horses. In other words you are surrounded by the riches and pleasures of Mother Rome. Are you with me?" The spellbound children nodded. "Now, beyond your estate, in the wilderness, are the wild beasts of the forest. What are they?"

"Bears!" Uricalus cried. "Big bears and wolves!"

"And foxes," Docilina said.

"And the monsters of the night!" Trifosa squealed. "Like dragons and witches!"

"Well, let's not worry about monsters for now," the King said with a reassuring smile. "Let's think about the foxes and the wolves. What do they want from your estate? What do they try to grab?"

"*Lambs!*" Uricalus shouted excitedly, provoking a 'shush' from Cordula, who was seated with the children. She'd asked that they be included in the gathering, promising the children would be on their best behavior.

"And calves and foals," Docilina said.

"And baby birds," Trifosa added excitedly. "And . . . and, even big birds."

"That's right. The foxes and wolves are always trying to sneak into your estate and steal tasty morsels. And so it is with Rome herself. The Roman Provinces are like large estates in a way, and the great cities, including Corinium, are the villas. The creatures of the wilderness are the barbaric tribes beyond our borders." He looked up at Ursula. "They can be very fearsome and dangerous. They are constantly lurking in wait for a chance to take advantage of a breach in our defenses and rush in to grab their plunder." He returned his attention to the children. "Here in Britannia, the Hibernians and the Picts are the creatures of the wilderness. In Germania and Galliae it's the German tribes. In Italia, and elsewhere, it's the Goths—"

"The *Goths!*" Uricalus repeated in a silly voice. He pulled a funny face and leered at Docilina.

She frowned and turned her back on him dismissively, as if to say, 'don't be so childish!'

The King continued. "Now the problem is that, in recent years, the frontier armies have been busy elsewhere. That has meant that there haven't been enough guards on border patrol and the defenses have been weak. As a result, the number of raiders has risen tenfold. Worse still, they have all tried to cross into Roman territory at the same time and at many points along the frontier—from Galliae in the west to Thracia in the east—stretching our already weakened defensive forces well beyond their limit."

"So Constantine's gone to put them all to the sword!" An excited Uricalus jumped up and began smiting enemies with his imaginary sword. "Take *that*, slimy Goth! And *that*, verminous German! And *that*, and *that!*"

"Uricalus!" Cordula snapped. "Quiet! Your King is talking. Sorry, Your Majesty."

"I wish it were that simple, Uricalus. You see these raiders are not really raiders any more. They're not content to simply sneak in and make off with their rich pickings, back into the forest where they came from like a lone fox or a small pack of wolves. Now they are intent on coming in large numbers—men, women, children like yourselves, and grandparents—on wagons and carts. They are even bringing their livestock with them. Whole tribes are on the move. They're breaking into Roman territory in order to make it their home. They want to make our homeland their homeland."

"Why do they want to take our homes?" Docilina asked. "Because they're so beautiful?"

"I'm sure that's one reason. But the main reason is because they are safe. You see, they want to be inside Rome where they feel guarded and protected. That's because they themselves are afraid of other, more barbaric, tribes beyond the frontier. The new monsters in the wilderness."

"What kind of monsters?" Trifosa asked, her voice quivering.

"Well, no-one knows for sure, but I keep hearing the same name being mentioned more and more—especially in reports from the east—of a war-like and godless tribe with big heads and long, hideous faces, called . . . ." He leaned forward and opened his eyes wide for emphasis. "The *Huns!*"

Trifosa burst into tears and started to whine.

"That's enough, Father!" Ursula said. She too had felt a sudden surge of terror like an ice-cold flash of lightning when he uttered the name.

"The Huns!" Uricalus said in a silly voice, then pulled a funny face, and leered at Docilina once again.

She punched him hard on the arm to make him stop. He clasped his arm and punched back, harder still. "Ow!" she cried and started pulling his hair. Within seconds they were rolling on the floor. Cordula and Martha scrambled to pry them apart.

"The boy's got spirit!" The King laughed. "He'll be a good fighter when he grows up."

"So will she," Pinnosa retorted. "Anyway, Your Majesty, how do you imagine things are actually going over there?"

The King took a thoughtful sip of his wine and sat up straight. He was obviously wary of Pinnosa. "I imagine Constans'll be finding it hard to muster a significant number of men in Germania and Galliae. The Imperial Court has left Treveris and is probably in Arelate in the south by now. They had to leave hastily and they would've taken all the ready-to-arms cavalry and infantry units from Germania and northern Galliae with them as escort. Constans's only hope will be to mobilize the standing guards in the smaller towns and to lure as many of the comfortable retirees off their estates as he can. I imagine he'll have some success. He should be able to please his father with a reasonable show of force when they converge on Treveris in about ten day's time."

"What about Colonia and Mogontiacum?" Pinnosa asked. "They're both huge garrisons. Why haven't they managed to shore up the frontiers and contain these invaders?"

"Well, the big problem—as you know—is that they've both been severely depleted to help Stilicho with the Goths in Italia and the neighboring Provinces. We had reports, just after the big winter invasions, that Mogontiacum, for example, was down to less than a half a Legion with only ten Centurions. Now in my day—and the last time I was in that area was twelve seasons ago—Mogontiacum alone had well over three Legions and as many as a hundred Centurions on station at a time. We're not sure how many men there are in Colonia, but we do know they're sending a sizeable force to meet up with Constantine at Treveris. That includes the all-important cavalry units he'll desperately need if he is to rein in the tribes. They have already broken through and are wandering all over Germania and Galliae, wreaking havoc."

"How long will my daddy be away?" asked Trifosa, who had continued listening to the grown-ups.

"We hope they'll be back before the winter," The King said gently. He leaned forward again and re-assumed his earlier gentle air. "But it may take them longer to accomplish their mission than they—or we—would like. So, your father may not be back until next harvest."

"Next harvest?" Trifosa exclaimed and burst into tears.

"Why so long?" Cordula asked as she comforted the little girl.

"Well, he and the other men might have to go to the south of Galliae after they've secured the border against the Germans. Firstly, they may have to escort some of the German tribes across the mountains to Hispania, where there is more land for them to settle on. And secondly . . . ." He looked very deliberately at Ursula, who was listening intently. "They may have to go into Italia to help Emperor Honorius against the Goths."

"To *Italia!*" Pinnosa groaned. "Hasn't Stilicho got enough men?"

Ursula remained silent.

"I met Stilicho many years ago, in Rome," the King replied thoughtfully. "Without any doubt he is Honorius's best hope against the Goths. But, there was also something in his eye which I couldn't trust. He's ambitious . . . ." He paused and looked around the gathering. "Bah!" He shook his head and signaled to the attendants to bring more food. "This is neither the time nor the place to discuss such a subject. Let's just say there are many possible reasons why Constantine and his men may be drawn across the Alps."

"But, Your Majesty—" Cordula began.

The King raised his hand. "That's enough talk about 'maybes,' 'mights' and 'perhaps.' We'll have to be patient until we get the next reports. Now, I want to hear from you young heroines about something that has *actually* happened. We are all eager to hear about your recent adventures, aren't we?" The children nodded eagerly. "And, what is this 'woman's field army' that you seem to be so set upon? When do you intend to execute these plans?"

"We start tomorrow," Pinnosa said enthusiastically. "We will send out a call to all able-bodied women in the West Country—"

"All able-bodied *Christian* women." Brittola insisted.

Pinnosa smiled at the correction and continued: "All able-bodied, Christian women will be invited to join us. We'll form a field army—including cavalry units—to patrol the coasts and country around Hadrian's Wall throughout the vulnerable summer months. We'll train in the frontier lands beyond Magnis. Then, around harvest time, we'll embark on a full campaign up to the Wall and around to Eboracum. Then we'll make a return tour, and we'll be back home before the Hunter's Moon."

"As she says, Father," Ursula added tentatively, "we'd like to dispatch the first messengers tomorrow." She looked uneasy.

The others looked surprised by the humble tone of her voice.

Ursula continued hesitantly. "I know we haven't consulted you, Father. But could we . . . possibly . . . use your Seal?"

"Tomorrow, you say?" He held his daughter's questioning gaze.

She nodded.

"I wish Rabacie was here to see such enthusiasm." He smiled at Ursula. "You get it from her, you know." He looked away across the room at his hunting tapestry and scratched his chin. "Actually, I was thinking of going hunting tomorrow with all my guards."

Brittola started to look disappointed, but then she saw that Ursula was already smiling.

"That means my Seal will be out on my writing table from dawn till dusk with no one to keep an eye on it."

"Oh, Father!" Ursula clambered around the table and gave him a hug. "Thank you."

"Thank you, Your Majesty." Pinnosa took his hand and kissed it.

The others echoed their thanks and bowed.

The King broke free from his daughter's embrace and reached for his wine goblet. An attendant hastily filled it. "It would seem a fitting measure of these sad and desperate times that our women are having to do the work of the men. But I know you are fine women. Each one of you is worth more than ten of the old men, like myself, who are currently trying to protect this troubled Province. I can sense that the winds of change are blowing strong. We must bend if we are to survive." He stood up and held out his drink toward them. "I drink to you, my daughter, and to you, her trusted friends, as well as to all the other good women of Britannia, who will help guard our tomorrows while the men are away."

He clinked his goblet with Ursula's and proposed his toast.

"To tomorrow. To all our tomorrows. And, to whatever our tomorrows will bring."

They all raised their drinks high and cried, "To tomorrow!"

IV

"Wake up, Mistress!" Oleander shook Ursula from her sleep. The old attendant was clearly agitated. "I'm sorry to wake you when you must be very tired after the feast last night. I know it's barely dawn, but you are needed urgently downstairs. Mistress Pinnosa sent me for you. She is already there with Mistresses Cordula and Brittola. Mistresses Martha and Saula have also been sent for. They need you as soon as possible. The street is full to bursting!"

Ursula could hear the sounds of a crowd outside. She hurriedly dressed and rushed over to the window—and was astounded at the scene below. Oleander was right. The street was crammed full—as far as she could see in either direction—with women.

Ursula arrived in the Palace Courtyard at the same time as Martha and Saula. Pinnosa already had things organized. The women were entering the Palace one at a time led by attendants to a long table where they were interviewed. Pinnosa, Cordula and Brittola, each with a scribe by their side, were in position at one end of the table. There were three more empty places with stools for scribes at the other.

"Ah, there you are!" Pinnosa called over her shoulder. "Don't stand there gawking. Come and get started. We've been doing this since before dawn and they're still coming. Isn't it incredible? Word must have spread like the wind."

"What do we have to do?" Martha asked.

"Make a note of their names and where they're from," Pinnosa replied.

"Whether they're married and have children or not," Cordula added.

"And don't forget to ask them whether they're practicing Christians." Brittola chipped in, barely turning around. "That's important."

"Then ask them why they want to join us," Pinnosa continued. "Then make up your mind whether they're in or not, but don't tell them here and now. Make a discreet note after they're dismissed. We'll put up lists later. Now, come on."

V

"Good morning, Your Majesty." Martha had assumed a thick, country accent. She shuffled toward Ursula oafishly. "I'd like to join the army please."

The others laughed. It had been a long day. They had finally cleared the street by mid-afternoon and dispatched ten messengers with proclamations from the King before evening bells. Even though they had interviewed over three hundred women, only seventy were suitable. Of those, only a handful were strong candidates. Afterward, Ursula and the others retired to the Ladies' Chamber of the Palace. There they recounted the day's events while enjoying a hearty supper.

"What's that?" Martha continued. "Am I pregnant? Nah, o'course I'm not!" She acted puzzled. "Well actually, come to think of it—what time of the year is it?" She scratched her head and rubbed her imaginary fat stomach. "Oh—whoops—I might be!"

They all shrieked with laughter.

"What about the one with the pigs!" Saula squealed. The others roared at the memory. "I'm taking my pigs, Mistress. 'If *they* don't go, *I* don't go!'"

"I had one . . ." Cordula was chortling so much that she was having difficulty catching her breath, "who would only go if she could take her husband."

"I had one . . ." Saula blurted, "who would only go if we promised she could leave her husband behind!"

"There were several like that," Pinnosa said loudly over their laughter. "Good God in Heaven, we had all sorts, didn't we? Those who were too old! Those who were too young—remember that girl who said she was in her seventeenth summer? She had barely seen twelve!"

"Don't forget those who were too fat! Remember the Miller's daughters?" Saula giggled. The rest laughed.

Martha pulled Saula and Cordula to their feet. The three of them play-acted the Miller's plump girls as they had squeezed through the side door to the Palace Gate and waddled over to the interview table. The trio then portrayed how throughout their interviews one would slip off one end of the bench then nudge her way back on—pushing the third off the other end. It had been torture for them not to laugh at the time, but now they gave full vent to their mirth. Brittola fell to the floor, laughing hysterically.

It took a few minutes before Saula was able to continue. "Oh, I almost forgot. I had one strange woman who was obsessed with hunting down honey makers. She said she wanted to join our army so that she could rid Britannia of them." She pulled a funny face and said in a country twang, "It's the cause of all evil, y'know. And them's that makes it are the Devil's own."

"Oh, talking of the Devil," Martha said, suddenly becoming serious. "Did you see that strange woman who came in toward the end? The one with the evil eye?"

"Ooh, yes!" Brittola hissed in a fearful whisper. "She *was* evil, and a complete stranger, too. I've never seen her before. Who was she?"

"Well, she gave her name as Rune and this is what she told me." Martha's voice became thin and menacing, "I would very much like to join your army. I'm no stranger to the blade. I have the scars to prove it, see. There are people who would vouch for my skills in blade craft—if they could—but they can't because . . . because I've had to *deal* with them, see. And when I deal with people they—"

"It sounds like she's had a tough and sad life," Ursula cut Martha short because she could see Brittola was getting scared. "I had one woman who really touched me."

"Who was that?" Pinnosa asked, reading Ursula's signal to turn the conversation.

The laughter had stopped and Brittola was beginning to look very tired.

"She'd seen over forty summers I'd say," Ursula continued. "She said she'd like to join us because she wanted a chance to rejoin her husband. When I asked her what she meant, she said he was dead and was waiting for her in Heaven. He died in the army's last campaign on the Continent. Her two sons were on the same campaign, and they, too, went missing. Unlike her husband, she never received confirmation—official or otherwise—that they were killed. All she knew was that they never returned home. That was more than five seasons ago. She lost her father many years before and—being an only child—her mother was all she had left. Then her mother died in the same plague that took our mothers . . ." She looked at Brittola and Saula. "That was three winters ago. Since then she's been living alone. She said she was desperately lonely and tormented by the hope that her lost sons might yet return. She told me she'd reached her limit; that she had been about to kill herself rather than continue enduring the torture of her misery. Then, yesterday, she overheard her neighbors talking about our venture to raise a woman's army. She snapped out of the nightmare her life had become, and suddenly felt—for the first time in years—that something existed which she could be a part of; something that could give her a sense of purpose. It didn't matter, she said, if she died in the doing. All that mattered was that she was doing something . . . was part of something . . . something that mattered. 'All the better if I die on some far-away battlefield,' she said. 'It's how my husband died, and I could never do better than he.'"

"Will she join?" Brittola asked quietly.

"I think there might be a place for her in the ordnance crews—or perhaps as an attendant. But she was too old for active duty. She lacked strength and speed, and she wouldn't be able to move fast enough when she needed to. Her body was as tired and drained as her spirit . . . rather like you, my friends!" They chuckled tiredly. "You all look completely worn out."

"It's time we were in bed," Pinnosa said, yawning and stretching. "We need a good night's rest. I have a feeling tomorrow is going to be just as hectic as today." She ushered the others out, and they all said their goodnights. Just as she was leaving, she paused in the doorway and said to Ursula, "I'll be down in the courtyard before dawn. Will you be up in time to join me?"

"Join you?" Ursula replied teasingly. "I'll wake you!"

Pinnosa laughed and followed the others out through the ante-chamber.

As the footfalls of her friends receded into the night, Ursula's smile slowly faded. A grimness gripped her features making her look tired beyond her years. She stood up and wandered distractedly over to the writing desk at the back of the chamber. She picked up its lamp and—holding it close to her face—peered into a polished bronze mirror that hung on the wall nearby. She could feel the lamp's heat against her skin and hear its crackles and hisses.

"I'm here, Constans. I'm here for you my love, wherever you are." She looked into the yellow flame and imagined shapes taking form in its trans-lucent body. "Where are *you*—I wonder? What are you doing? What dangers are you facing or about to face?" She closed her eyes. "Are you thinking of me? I'm here. I'm here. Can you hear me?" She kept her eyes closed and strained with every sinew of her being to sense some message in reply, but, despite the heat of the lamp, all she could feel was a cold, empty nothingness. "Oh, God. Please don't let him die. Please don't let my life be like that woman's. Once so full and then so . . . so *empty*. Please find it in your Grace, God, to bring him back home to me safe and sound. I give you my life and my soul. Just have the mercy to keep him alive, and bring us back together. Please, God . . . bring him home."

A gentle cough from the doorway made her slowly open her eyes.

"Are you all right, Mistress?" Oleander gave her an anxious look.

"I'm fine," she said quietly.

"Nugget's here, Mistress. He's waiting outside."

"Then bring him in. Don't keep the poor man waiting."

Oleander led into the room a short, bald, stocky old man. He wore a leather working apron, which covered his body from his neck to his knees. His hands were permanently blackened and badly scarred, and two of his finger-tips were missing. He was Corinium's master metalworker and jewelry maker, and his family had been making the royal jewelry and household metalwork for five generations. He looked the same as he had for as long as Ursula could remember. He reeked of the fires and potions of his work. Like the rest of the city folk, she knew him simply as Nugget.

"Y'Highness," he growled in a deep, phlegmy voice. "How can I be of service?"

"Has Oleander explained what I'm looking for, Nugget?"

"Yes, y'Highness. An alloy, which looks like gold, but's as hard as iron. Here, y'Highness . . . ." He began fumbling in his apron pouch. She could hear the rattle of metallic clutter. "I brought you this." He produced a small trinket box and offered it to her.

She took it from him, and held it up to the lamp for scrutiny. In the soft light it gleamed with a yellowy glow.

"It's more or less the right color, and it's certainly heavy," she mused while turning it over. "But is it strong?"

"Oh yes, y'Highness. It's the strongest alloy I've got what'll pass for gold at a glance."

He took it back from her and placed it in the center of the writing table. Then he grabbed a hammer from the rear of his belt and brought it down hard upon the box with a loud clanging thud. Ursula picked it up and re-examined it. The surface was marked but its shape was intact.

"Perfect," she said. "Can it be fashioned into a thin blade? A razor sharp, thin blade?"

"It's poor man's gold, y'Highness," replied the old man with a toothless smile. "It can be made into anything you like."

"Very well. Here's what I want you to make." She produced a drawing on some parchment from a small drawer under the table and showed him what she had in mind.

VI

The messengers bearing the proclamation with the King's Seal had hardly been dispatched when women—mostly able-bodied, unmarried, women, professing to be Christians—started arriving from the nearby estates and townships. Some came alone with just their attendant, but most came in pairs or small groups. Many of them were on foot. A fair number, however, came on horseback, and most of the horses were of a working age and fit for duty. Within a few days Ursula and the others had recruited over a thousand.

On the morning of the sixth day, shrill trumpets could be heard coming from the road to the southeast. Ursula, Pinnosa and the others rushed to the parapet and a magnificent sight met their eyes. Heading toward them and filling the road, was a complete cohort of over four hundred women marching in full uniform. Cordula was the first to read the standards and declared that they were a combined force from the Calleva Atrebatum and Venta Belgarum areas.

No sooner had they entered the city, when more trumpets sounded, this time, from the southwest. When Ursula and the others rushed back to the parapet they saw a hundred and sixty fully armed and uniformed women on horseback approaching the city, following Lindinis colors.

The following day, Ursula had to issue a second proclamation announcing that no more volunteers were needed, since the response had been so good. They had recruited seven hundred and thirty foot soldiers and had assembled a cavalry unit over three hundred strong. In addition, they had gathered two hundred attendants and a further seventy women to work as ordnance crews. The combined total of almost fourteen hundred women filled a complete wing of Corinium's West Barracks.

Ursula, Pinnosa and the others were up with the slaves before dawn and spent the entire day at the barracks. In the mornings, they worked together, organizing the women into cohesive units and appointing Commanders and junior officers for each one. In the afternoons, they separated to attend to the various types of training in the drill yards.

Pinnosa oversaw all fighting drills, including battle formations and maneuvers. She devoted a lot of her time to training the cavalry units, though she left their field trials to Martha; and to Baetica from Lindinis—who was, indeed, an exceptionally good horsewoman. Saula concentrated on self-defense—shield, sword and spear-thrust practice. She also supervised the women's training in signal codes and semaphore skills. Brittola saw to basic marching drill and kit maintenance. Cordula spent her time working with the messenger corps and ordnance crews.

Ursula worked mostly with groups of officers to develop systems for the effective relayance of orders and messages; disciplinary procedures; and appropriate codes of practice and behavior—both on and off duty.

Just before dusk, each day ended with a full turn out on the Parade Ground for an inspection. Pinnosa checked the women's uniforms, weapons and equipment, and Ursula their bearing and morale. In the evenings the senior Commanders, comprising of Ursula and her friends, plus some others, worked with the King to plan the campaign's strategy and operational requirements—often well into the night.

As high summer approached, the army of women was ready to commence its campaign. They had completed their basic training and—thanks to Corinium's hard-working crafts folk—they were fully uniformed and equipped. On Alban Heruin, the summer solstice, the only men involved in the operation—the messengers—were dispatched to Viroconium, Luguvallium and Eboracum to announce the women's mission and initiate preparations. Soon afterwards, advance parties of ordnance crews set off with accompanying guards.

VII

A tremendous tantarara of trumpets blasted from the parapets of Corinium's city walls, shattering the quiet summer morning. The North Gate slowly opened. Standing rigidly to attention in ten divisions, each one hundred strong, the field army, dressed in cobalt blue cloaks with matching helmet plumage, was already assembled on an open area to the side of the Glevum Road. On the opposite side of the road were the cavalry wearing the same blue but trimmed in white. The disciplined ranks made such a magnificent display, the townsfolk who came running through the gate ahead of the Vanguard all stopped and stared in amazement.

From out of the gate came the procession. The trumpet and drum players were first, playing loud fanfares and drum rolls. The standard bearers followed, displaying a new insignia—three white lilies on a field of cobalt blue and capped by a small golden bear—which had been specially created for the new Legion. Only moments earlier in the Forum, the King, in another of his eloquent speeches, had formally presented the Legion's Commanders with their standards. He had also bequeathed upon the Legion its official name—the First Athena.

Behind the First Athena standard were the local standard bearers from Corinium, Glevum, Calleva Atrebatum, Venta Belgarum and Lindinis. Then came the special infantry forming the Guard of Honor for the Commanders looking splendid in their helmet plumage of high white feathers. Their freshly burnished, specially made, light leather body armor, reinforced with rib-like metal strapping shone like silver in the early morning sun. Next came the elite cavalry Vanguard itself. Their armor, too, gleamed resplendent beneath their blue and white cloaks.

True to Britannic tradition, the last to appear were the Commanders. Martha, Saula, Brittola and Cordula came through the gate in single file, dressed in identical uniforms to the rest of the Vanguard, though their horses' dress livery was completely white. Then came Pinnosa and Ursula—side by side. Their cloaks were the same as the others' except that the trim, like their helmet plumage, was a mixture of gold and white. In addition, Ursula had a streak of royal purple in hers.

Behind the Legion's Commanders, and acknowledging the crowd's loud cheers with waves of his hand, came King Deonotus and his guards on horseback. As they emerged from the shadow of the city gate, they formed a line across the roadway. The King drew his sword and raised it for silence.

Three short trumpet blasts not only quietened the excited on-lookers, they also acted as a signal for the Vanguard to come to a halt. Maintaining full, formal, straight-backed decorum, Ursula and Pinnosa turned Swift and Artemis around to face him.

"Go forth women of the First Athena!" the King ordered. "Go forth and add a heroic new chapter to the annals of Rome! Commanders! Lead the First and Second Cohorts of the Legion First Athena in the Army of Britannia on a patrol of the frontiers!"

Ursula and Pinnosa saluted. The King solemnly nodded in acknowledgement. They both turned back to face the ranks and Pinnosa gave the first operational command of the campaign.

"Women of the First Athena! *Forward!*"

VIII

The First Athena spent a full cycle of the moon in the mountains near the coast, training and patrolling. Their presence freed the few remaining men to take some of the galleys from Maridunum across the Hibernian Sea to make a show of force. Even though there were only enough men to crew five vessels, the exercise was effective. Not one single raiding party was seen.

Ursula and the others came to love the mountains and their wild, rolling beauty. Catching the wind fresh off the Great Ocean to the southwest, the area was prone to sudden, rain-filled squalls followed by bright sunshine. The ensuing array of colors wove a magical spell in their hearts. Ever after, they referred to their guard duty as 'Rainbow Mountain patrols.'

During their tours of duty, the women of the First Athena repaired several of the outpost forts and re-activated many of the encampments. Whenever Brittola was supervising the work, she also ordered small Christian chapels to be built. Each one was painted with a coat of lime wash and glistened white, inside and out. It was equipped with a rudimentary altar and simple stools for prayer.

The guardsmen returned from their patrol along the Hibernian coast just before Lughnasadh, the start of the harvest. When the women handed the rebuilt installations back to the men, they were utterly amazed at the transformation.

Lughnasadh signaled that it was time for the First Athena to commence their long march north to the Wall—and Pict—country. The legion mustered and marched well, reaching the first of the Wall's fortifications in less than a full cycle of the moon.

Ursula and the others were completely unprepared for the area's stunning beauty. The landscape wasn't as wild and rugged as that in the Rainbow Mountains; but what it lacked in stature, it made up for in majesty.

There was, however, another important difference. From the top of the high stone wall, which lay across the land like a giant sleeping snake, they looked out over enemy territory. They could see his wooded hills and valleys, his streams and meadows. He was *there*—facing you—and not safely tucked away below the horizon across a broad sea.

Ursula and the other Commanders could feel the effect of this presence on the women. They weren't singing as much as usual—especially during daylight hours. They were constantly on the alert for the sound of approaching invaders. Some of them resisted being sent out on patrol in details smaller than thirty. "It's as if the trees themselves are watching you," they muttered. Before long, even the Commanders were referring to the land beyond the Wall as 'Eye Country.'

The situation along the Wall was worse than they had expected. Only the main fortress towns had contingents of guards. Most of the men were old, retired auxiliaries. There were just one hundred able-bodied legionaries at the main garrison in Luguvallium. The cavalry unit there was down to less than fifty. If most of the fighting men hadn't been called to the Continent, those numbers would have been more than ten-fold. On the Wall itself, only one sentry tower in three was occupied. Great stretches were left unguarded and exposed to attack. Even when a tower was manned, it never had more than three men, all auxiliaries. Ursula found only one cavalry unit—five strong—at one of the mile forts. Horses were in such short supply, messengers were using donkeys or going on foot. The First Athena marched half the length of the Wall to the main fortress at Cilurnum. They were astonished to find it virtually deserted with only a caretaker guard unit consisting of thirty auxiliaries commanded by an aged Centurion who had taken his retirement purse twenty years earlier.

Ursula held an emergency meeting with the other Commanders. They decided to deploy the Legion immediately and commence frontier patrols, working in three separate divisions. Pinnosa and Cordula took the largest group of three hundred and fifty infantry and one hundred and fifty cavalry. Without a rest, they set off back in the direction they had come from to make a show of force in the vulnerable border country beyond the Wall to the west. The remainder was split into two groups of equal size. Ursula and Saula's division headed for Segedunum and took responsibility for the eastern section of the Wall. Martha and Brittola's women were to cover the western section and base themselves at Vercovicium.

Around mid-afternoon the following day, the Vercovicium contingent was the first to make contact with the Picts. Martha and Brittola were organizing the barracking arrangements, when a cavalry patrol came galloping back from checking a section of the Wall just three miles to the west. They reported a broken gate and clear signs of a raiding party.

All their weeks of strategic planning and exhaustive training finally came into play. Martha summoned a squadron of thirty cavalry. Brittola called out a fifty-strong infantry unit.

From the way Brittola was fumbling with her own uniform, Martha could see that her friend was troubled by nerves. While the force was assembling outside the fort gate, she rode up to Brittola, took her aside and whispered, "This . . . ."

Brittola leaned forward and finished the phrase with her, "May not be easy!" They shared a hushed chuckle and Brittola's fears dissipated. Then they both returned to their units, shouting orders.

The force quickly departed on its mission: the infantry taking the broad military road which ran a short distance behind the Wall, the cavalry taking a more direct route across the high ground between the road and the Wall.

The cavalry soon reached the broken gate and picked up the trail, which led across the military zone into the rich farmland beyond. From the freshness of the tracks they knew the raiders couldn't be far away. Sure enough, they caught up with them less than a mile from the road. There were about twenty men, all on foot, roving in loose groups of threes and fours and clearly on the lookout for easy pickings. They had already managed to grab three head of cattle, which they had roped together and drove along in front of them. The Picts were heading in the direction of some smoke coming from a settlement in the valley below.

Importantly for Martha's cavalry, the Picts were out in the open with nowhere nearby for them to take refuge. At her signal, Martha's unit splintered into three groups and gave chase. Sounding their horns, they bore down upon the raiders at a full gallop. The women quickly surrounded their prey and cut off any possible routes of escape. Once the Picts were trapped, the cavalry kept their distance and waited for the infantry to arrive.

The fierce-looking tribesmen formed a defensive cluster using the livestock as a shield. They readied their bows and shouted war cries. The warriors had long hunting spears, but Martha was sure they had other blades of some sort hidden beneath their long, gray wollen cloaks.

It only took Brittola's contingent a short time to appear. After a quick assessment of the situation, the two Commanders decided on their plan of action. The cavalry kept their distance and spread out in order to corral the Picts in on three sides. The infantry formed ranks on the fourth side, divided into defensive groups of ten.

Then, without hesitation, Brittola's unit began their advance. As soon as they were within range, the Picts let fly a volley of arrows. The women had made such tight 'tortoise shells' with their shields, however, that they were all deflected. The infantry pressed on. The Picts fired a second round of arrows, but again the shields did their job.

Once in hailing distance, Brittola shouted, "You are completely outnumbered! Throw down your weapons and we will escort you back to the Wall. You won't be harmed since you have not yet committed any serious crimes!"

The Picts' reply was a stream of foul abuse followed by a third wave of arrows. This time one of the women in Brittola's group was hit in the ankle. She had to be taken from the field by one of the cavalry. The Picts roared in triumph and waved their spears.

Brittola tried again. "I repeat! If you surrender now and throw down your weapons, you won't be harmed! We will escort you to the Wall and let you go! Now *please* throw down your weapons!"

A woman near her in the 'tortoise shell' lowered her shield in stared at her Commander in surprise. "Please?"

"Hush!" Brittola reprimanded. She gave the order to advance ten more paces, this time with swords drawn.

Drawn swords was the signal that Martha had been waiting for. Brittola's women had barely taken their first step when the cavalry charged. An attack on four sides at once threw the Picts into utter confusion. Martha's unit rode past the cluster of men, firing their arrows and aiming low. None of the Picts' spears hit their targets. The rain of missiles thudded into the ground, forcing the tribesmen to dance about to avoid them. Only three of them sustained injuries—one was pierced in the knee, another in the calf, and a third through his foot—but it was enough to reduce the Picts to submission. They released the livestock and threw down their spears and bows.

"*All* your weapons!" Martha shouted, indicating her sword. Twenty blades were pulled out from beneath their cloaks. "Take off your cloaks, too, so that we can see what else you've got under there!" They did not understand her command at first, but after she signaled what she wanted, they complied.

The women were astonished at what they saw. Without exception, the tribesmen were completely covered with tattoos. From their necks to their ankles, their skin was smothered with swirling blue and brown lines, which sometimes surrounded a childlike picture of a bird or an animal. Now that the women were close enough to see them clearly, they realized that the men's faces were also tattooed with yet more of the swirls curling around every facial feature.

IX

"I was so astounded," Brittola said. "I didn't notice they weren't wearing any clothes until we were about to set them free at the Wall. Then we had to give them back their cloaks!"

The whole company laughed.

Twenty days later, the entire Legion mustered at Cilurnum for the first time since the divisions had set out on their patrols. The evening inspections were complete and the Commanders were having a modest feast with some of the junior officers in the luxurious halls of the Imperial Chambers, a right to which they were entitled, since they were commissioned officers in the service of King Deonotus—who was *ipso facto* the Imperial Roman Governor.

Ursula and her friends were pleased to see each other again. Like Martha and Brittola's women, each of the other two divisions had been in action against Pict raiding parties. Some of the clashes had been with groups of tribesmen as few as ten. But one fracas, which Saula's women had contended with, involved over fifty Picts. All three divisions had sent cavalry detachments into enemy territory in order to search for weapons in Pict settlements and deter the tribesmen from attempting further raids.

The laughter at Brittola's admission died down and it was time for another tale.

"The trickiest moments we had were when we were doing house to house searches in their villages," Pinnosa said.

"House to house?" Martha interjected. "Sewage pit to sewage pit more like! Phew!" She quaffed a goblet of wine.

"We learned early on that it's best to do the searches in groups no smaller than ten," Pinnosa continued. "Our very first detail worked only in fives. One group inadvertently entered the Chief's hut. He was ready for them with two of his men. They were armed with those huge blades—"

"What happened?" one of the junior officers from Ursula's contingent interrupted. She was on the edge of her seat with anticipation.

"Fortunately, they all got out alive. But three of them were seriously wounded and had to be taken to Luguvallium for treatment. One of them lost an eye I believe." She paused, obviously still blaming herself for the incident. She leaned forward intent on making sure they all learned the same lesson she had. "The thing to do is operate in larger groups. Then, when you enter, go in fours—two facing each side. That was our mistake, sending the detail in, paired up—back to back. It wasn't enough. They were exposed on both sides. If you go in fours, your sides are covered."

"Here's another important tip which we had to learn the hard way," Saula said. "Don't trust the children. No matter how innocent they might look. On our first search, we had a serious injury caused by children with knives. One of our women decided to ignore the three 'little angels' she saw cowering in the corner and concentrated on the adults. Before she knew it, she had three huge gashes on her legs and two of her comrades were carrying her out. She couldn't walk or ride. We had to commandeer an extra cart to get her back to Cilurnum."

"I think the main lesson I learned on my first house-to-house," Martha said jokingly, "was to cover my nose!" They all laughed. "I use a wet cloth. What do you use?"

"I put a smear of fish oil on my upper lip," Saula replied, which elicited a chorus of 'eek's' and 'ooh's.' "It works!" she cried indignantly. "It smells foul and it makes your eyes water; but it acts as a barrier to that awful stench from the bottommost pits of hell . . . ."

"Ladies! Ladies!" Ursula rushed excitedly into the room. A short while earlier she and Cordula had been called out to receive a messenger. "I have some important news for you." The laughter stopped. "As you know, in addition to sending full reports to my father in Corinium, I have also been sending them to King Aurelius at Eboracum." She smiled at the sight of their expectant faces.

"A message has just arrived from King Aurelius. He congratulates us warmly on the success of our campaign, and informs us that he has managed to muster a force of five hundred cavalry and seven hundred infantry, which he is sending at once to relieve us." The women let out a loud cheer. Ursula waited for them to settle down again before she continued. "They should arrive the day after tomorrow. That means we can look forward to having a well-earned rest and enjoying the warm hospitalities of Eboracum—a fortnight ahead of schedule!" They all cheered again. "It also means we won't have to complete a return tour. We'll be returning home on the Fosse Way!" Their third cheer was the loudest yet. "By the time we return to the West Country, the summer will almost be over. Our only remaining duty will be to stand on station at Glevum and Viroconium for a few weeks, sending out a few routine patrols. Then we should be able to complete our tour of duty and disband as planned with no losses and only a few injuries." She reached for a glass of wine and raised it. "Ladies . . . Congratulations! It's beginning to look as if our campaign has been a complete success. I give you . . . the First Athena!"

They all raised their glasses and cried, "The First Athena!"

"Oh, just one more thing . . . ." Ursula had a gleam in her eye, which not even Pinnosa could quite interpret. "The special relief unit coming from Eboracum . . . ." she paused again to heighten their anticipation, ". . . is comprised solely of women—including the Commanders!"

X

The women from Eboracum—whose official title was the "Third and Fourth Cohorts of the Legion First Athena"—wore a livery as red as the Corinium women's was blue. Their standard was three white lilies on a red field. To represent their allegiance to the same Commander-in-Chief, it was also capped by a small golden bear.

Their leader was Princess Julia, a second cousin of Ursula's, whom she had once met when they were both young children. She was the daughter of King Aurelius.

Ursula received Julia out in the open with her officers in full dress uniform. The cohorts of both regiments were drawn up in formation on the opposite sides of a long, sloping field. While the officers exchanged greetings in the center of the field, the regiments looked upon each other with a mixture of awe, admiration, and—it must be said—not a little rivalry.

Being involved in ordnance matters, Cordula met her counterpart from Eboracum apart from the others. Once her business was concluded, she nudged her horse, Epona, a few steps away from the group so she could enjoy the spectacle. She took heart at seeing such numbers—such strength. As she watched, formal salutes were exchanged, and Ursula and the other officers returned to the ranks of the First and Second Athena before starting their march to Eboracum. The Vanguard of the Third and Fourth Cohorts lined the approach to the bridge to give the women from Corinium a special salute as they passed. It was such a touching gesture, Cordula thought she would burst with joy and pride.

She raced over the field to join her fellow officers at the rear of the column as they set off to cross the bridge. Drawing up alongside Ursula and Brittola, she could see that they, too, were feeling emotional. "Quite a sight, isn't it?" she said.

"Indeed," Brittola replied. "A sight to warm the weary. A sight to erase exhaustion and make you feel exhilarated. A sight to put the spring back in—"

"That's certainly true." Ursula interrupted. "But, I think the women will enjoy a good rest. I know I need one. And I intend to enjoy every minute of our stay in Eboracum. Have either of you ever been there?" Brittola and Cordula shook their heads. "There is no better place in Britannia for an army in need of replenishment, of body—or of spirit. Eboracum has it all!"

XI

In Eboracum, King Aurelius celebrated their arrival in grand style. He insisted that the entire First and Second Cohorts—not just their Vanguard—parade triumphantly through the great city. The streets were crammed with waving and cheering townsfolk, and the air was thick with fluttering flower petals and incense smoke.

One of the many huge barracks just outside the City Walls had been made ready to receive them. It was stocked with generous amounts of food and clean clothes. Ursula and the other Commanders were guests of honor and given quarters in the Royal Palace. On the first night, a huge feast was held in their honor in the Great Hall, which was big enough for twenty tables. King Aurelius—a gray-bearded, heavy-set, elderly man who had clearly been tall and handsome when he was young—presided over the merry making. Being late summer, the food was both plentiful and varied. The wine and oils were wonderfully fresh.

The entertainment surpassed anything they had seen at Corinium. There were oriental dancers, magicians with their strange costumes and un-usual music, acrobats and performing animals. Cordula and Brittola were particularly enthralled by the exotic beasts.

"Look!" Brittola exclaimed as a huge, long-necked creature was brought into the hall and paraded around for all to touch and stroke. "They say the reason for the long neck is because in the wild they eat big snakes like pythons whole; and its name means 'snake-eater'. Can you remember its name?"

"Zaraf, or some such," Cordula replied. "I liked the one with the humps on its back—"

"Oh, yes. What was it now? The gammel or camelus, or something—"

"Wasn't it ugly! And those hideous noises it kept making. You know who it reminded me of, don't you?"

Cordula puffed up her cheeks and crossed her eyes. "Gerontius," she croaked. They burst into uncontrollable giggles.

The following day, the King set off with Ursula and the other Commanders on a three-day hunting trip into the beautiful surrounding countryside. They stopped for a meal on the first day in a sunny glade. While the others were tending to their horses, he took Ursula aside.

"When you get home, Ursula, please give this to your father," he said. From inside his hunting bag he pulled out a sealed parchment. "Amongst other things, it tells him how proud we all are of you. Along with your remarkable friends, you have achieved great things for a woman—and one so young at that. You have already garnered considerable respect—even from a tired old campaigner like myself, who thought he'd seen everything and had little left to learn."

Ursula bowed as she took the scroll.

"It also tells him about Julia, and how I hope she proves herself worthy of being called Commander-in-Chief of the Third and Fourth Cohorts of the Legion First Athena."

"I'm sure she will, Your Majesty," Ursula ventured politely. "She seems a very capable leader. Did she organize the Eboracum contingent herself, or were you the main instigator?"

"Ha! Straight to the point, eh? I like that in a woman!" The King laughed before becoming serious again. "I must be honest. When I first heard of what you were planning in the West Country, I hung my head in despair. 'Is this what we have come to?' I thought, 'Are we so short of good men that our good women are having to do the men's work?' Ah, but then . . . ." He tapped his temple and smiled. "I saw the look in Julia's eyes whenever your adventures were mentioned. She's been hunting with me since she was ten. Like you and your friends, she's no stranger to horsemanship, map-reading, using a weapon—killing and blood. Like you and Pinnosa, she's happier in the wild outdoors than in the stifling containment of the city. There's nothing she hates more than petty court gossip."

"I know how she feels, Your Majesty," Ursula said with a smile.

"So when she heard you were out in the mountains, on patrol, chasing raiders, on the march . . . . You should've seen her! She was like a caged lion, pacing up and down, looking for a way to join the hunt. The day I received your message telling me that the country along the coast was safe and that you were heading for Wall Country, I said to her, 'That's not right! Our southwestern cousins are coming up here doing our work for us, just because we're short of men. What do you think we should do about it?'" He paused and smiled. "Do you know what? I hadn't had a kiss that big since I asked her mother to marry me!" They both laughed. "She had it all organized in under a fortnight. The Palace was a-buzz, I tell you. Messengers were sent out, and within hours the first volunteers started knocking on the Palace Gate. I've never seen anything like it! Orders for the livery, and weaponry, armor fittings, horses selected, training regimes. Then there were maps, maps and more maps! Briefing after briefing with her officers—"

"I know, Your Majesty," Ursula interrupted politely. "I know exactly what Julia had to do."

XII

After they returned from the hunt, Ursula, Pinnosa, Brittola, Cordula, Martha and Saula decided they would enjoy the delights of Eboracum. They left the Palace soon after morning bells and set off to explore the magnificent city. Between its public buildings of great splendor, they found bustling streets full of interesting shops and stalls. The merchants sold things—pottery, jewelry, food and clothes—they'd never seen in Corinium or Glevum.

At midday, as the noon bell sounded, they sat at the South Gate Fountain eating a new delicacy: a blood sausage cooked in a wine and mushroom sauce, then wrapped in a crust of butter-rich pastry. Pinnosa and Martha loved it, but Brittola loathed it. Ursula, Cordula and Saula didn't much care for it either, and got into a lengthy discussion of how it could be made more palatable for West Country taste. Suddenly they heard the shrill note of a messenger's horn coming from the Londinium Road beyond the city wall.

Cordula recognized the timbre of the instrument immediately. She dropped her pie and ran to the gate. As soon as it opened, Morgan came thundering in on Hermes.

"Morgan! It's me!" Cordula cried as he dismounted.

"Cordula! What are you doing here?" Morgan exclaimed with surprise, brushing a heavy coating of road dust from his hair and arms. "And what is that uniform you're wearing?"

"It's a very long story. It'll take at least a whole walk in the moonlight to tell." She laughed and gave him a huge hug. "What are *you* doing here?"

"I bring the first report of Constantine's expedition. I crossed the Channel and arrived in Rutupiae five evenings ago."

"Goodness! You've made good time," she exclaimed. "Any other messenger would have taken at least seven."

"It's thanks to Hermes's stamina—not mine." He patted the great horse's flank. "First I went to the Governor in Londinium before heading up the Great North Road to Lindum and then on to here. I still have to go to Ratae Corieltauvorum, Corinium and Calleva Atrebatum before my round is complete."

"Must you be constantly on the move? Can't you have some time for yourself?" she asked coyly, snuggling closer.

"I . . . I can't, my dear," he said, cupping her face in his hand. "I'll have to return across the Channel with important messages to Constantine that will wait for no man . . . or his woman."

"Then we shouldn't waste a moment," she sighed. Looking deeply into each other's eyes, they drew close for a kiss.

Looking on from the fountain, Ursula imagined it was Constans who had ridden in through the gate. Constans who had returned safe and sound. Constans, who had leapt from his horse and embraced his love. His voice filled her mind, *Only in your eyes—I see home.*

"Ahem!" The King's attendant, a lanky, sour-looking old man with a long, hooked nose, entered the Messengers' Yard and gave a loud cough of disapproval as he approached the couple.

Morgan opened his eyes and glared at the haughty courtier. He was about to berate him for his rudeness when he noticed Princess Ursula standing nearby. He hastily extricated himself from Cordula's embrace. "Y—Your Highness," he spluttered, straightening his cloak and bowing awkwardly.

"Ahem!" The long-necked courtier turned languidly to face Ursula and her companions and also gave a cursory bow. "His Majesty awaits the messenger's dispatch in his private chambers. He also graciously invites the Princess and her—ahem—senior officers to join him."

XIII

"Refreshments are on their way, Morgan. We're in no rush. Take us through things slowly. Tell us everything—each little detail, no matter how trivial. And . . ." King Aurelius raised his bushy eyebrows for emphasis, "whatever you do, do *not*—on any account—leave out anything you told the Governor in Londinium. Understood?" He arranged his cushions and sat back in the large stone chair that was the centerpiece of the Royal Reception Room.

"Yes, Your Majesty," Morgan replied, with a hint of a smile. He was seated directly across the table from the King. Ursula, Cordula and the others sat on a bench to the King's right. Their expectant faces were no less eager than the old monarch's.

"What luck," Ursula exclaimed. "Morgan can tell us about events that happened as recently as ten or twelve days ago. If we were in Corinium, his news would be fifteen days old at least!' Their bench was well positioned to enjoy the view through the window. *Cordula's lucky,* she thought. *Morgan really is quite handsome.*

"Are you ready ladies?" the King asked. They all looked at Ursula and she nodded. The King, in turn, nodded to Morgan. "Then please begin."

"His Lordship, the Supreme Commander of the armed forces of Britannia, Constantine, sends you all his loyal and heartfelt greetings and humbly craves . . . ."

Oh please get on with it! Ursula felt exasperated with the formalities. There had been a time—not long before—when she enjoyed such things. They were to be savored as some of the pleasures and pleasantries of civilized life. But, now they were just tiresome and irrelevant. *Where is Constans? Is he all right? When is he coming home?*

Fortunately for Ursula, Morgan was very adept at speeding up the formalities without appearing brusque, and he soon started recounting his news. Indeed, he was an excellent messenger in many respects. He could describe scenes and events with such precision and clarity his listeners felt they had actually been with him to witness and experience them. He also had an uncanny skill whereby he allowed just a touch of the sender's characteristics to enter into his voice and manner, enabling him—without degenerating into a vulgar impersonation—to create the feeling that the sender was addressing the audience in person.

"The crossings went well. Both Constans and Constantine successfully landed in Galliae without any difficulties. As King Deonotus feared, Constans experienced considerable difficulty in rallying local forces. The Seine valley was much more severely depleted of legionaries than they'd anticipated. The few remaining able-bodied men refused to leave their towns and estates because of the threat of imminent attack from the wandering German tribes. As a result, Constans had to ride further south than originally planned—to the Loire valley. The level of depletion wasn't so great there, and the fear of the Germans was less. He managed to raise a force of over three thousand, mostly infantry. Despite this success, Constans's diversion seriously delayed his reunion with his father.

"However, things did not go according to plan for Constantine either. Instead of heading straight for Treveris as intended, they were greeted at Gesoriacum with news from Colonia that the remaining men from that garrison had gone directly to Mogontiacum. They had to deal with a large group of Germans who were spotted coming down the River Main. That left the frontier between Colonia and Confluentes virtually unmanned, with damage from the winter breaches left un-repaired. Constantine went directly to the area to shore up the defenses before making his way to Treveris.

"The result was that Constantine and Constans did not succeed in combining their forces until after Alban Heruin, well into the summer and almost two cycles of the moon later than they planned. It took a fortnight before they finally met up with the remnants of the Colonia regiments at Mogontiacum. I am pleased to report, however, that the eventual combined numbers of the Britannic, Colonia and Loire veterans amounted to almost thirty-three thousand . . . ."

The women gasped. From hearing all the difficulties, Ursula thought Constantine couldn't have mustered more than twenty thousand, but now it appeared he had more than enough men to accomplish whatever was needed.

King Aurelius breathed a huge sigh of relief as Morgan continued, ". . . including a cavalry contingent surpassing *ten* thousand."

Ursula and her friends applauded and cheered with astonishment.

"Those Batavians," the King muttered to himself. "Thank God for them and their love of horses."

"Now they can really get down to work," Pinnosa exclaimed. "With numbers like that, Constantine should have no difficulty rebuilding the frontier defenses and getting Mogontiacum back into shape."

"As well as rounding up most of the German tribes that are now wandering all over Germania and Galliae," Ursula added enthusiastically. "Morgan? What news do you have of that situation?"

Morgan couldn't prevent a tiny flicker of doubt from crossing his face.

"It appears that the situation there is far more serious than we thought. The Seine valley people were justified in withdrawing to the walled cities. Constans came across one tribe while he was there . . . ." Morgan paused.

Ursula failed to suppress a shiver and the others looked at her. "Please go on," she urged and managed a weak smile of encouragement.

The others returned their gaze to the messenger, except Pinnosa who studied her old friend carefully.

"Constans said he was amazed at the sheer number of people. He estimated there to be many tens—possibly hundreds—of thousands. They were spread out in family groups, all with their livestock. Even though he had two hundred men with him, he was powerless to stop them. They rode through some of the outer groups but quickly withdrew to the safety of an overlooking ridge. Constans was worried about encountering one of the large bands of warriors who are known to roam the tribes. They can be quite fast moving—and quite formidable. He estimated he needed a force of at least two thousand cavalry just to escort the tribe to whatever lands they are allocated. In addition, he would need two thousand infantry in order to tackle the fighting men and subdue them, before an orderly deportation is possible. The last time he and Constantine spoke to me about the matter, they were seriously thinking of creating two special units of five thousand men—each half cavalry and half infantry—to dispatch on these missions."

"Only two units," Pinnosa interrupted. "But there are at least five of these tribes on the rampage!"

Morgan could only look at her and shrug. For a moment the gathering was silent as the immensity of the task facing the men became clear in their minds. The King simply shook his head. Ursula turned around to look out of the window.

Morgan continued, "I think it all depends on how successfully they can secure the frontier. East of Mogontiacum, there are complete sections, sometimes more than a day's march long, with no guard units whatsoever. What they face isn't simply the rebuilding of those defenses. They have to redesign them so they can be manned very sparsely by highly mobile cavalry patrols. I think that task alone is going to take the rest of this year and much of next. Every time a new tribe approaches them intent on invasion, our forces lose precious weeks—a whole season, even."

"Do you know what I had been naïvely thinking?" Martha said quietly, breaking the long silence that ensued. "For a while I actually thought our women were doing work similar to Constantine's army. I was feeling proud of the First Athena for succeeding in doing the men's work for them. It was somehow rewarding to think that what our legionnaires were accomplishing in far-off lands—we were achieving here at home. I was even going to tease them about it when they returned." She sighed and shook her head in despair. "But what is chasing small raiding parties of Picts or Hibernians compared to rounding up tens of thousands of Germans and escorting them to new lands? How can repairing a gate in a wall—or building a chapel—compare to re-crafting a stretch of the frontier a day's march in length?"

Cordula looked around at the others. Saula and Brittola were nodding in grim agreement with Martha. Pinnosa had a look of fierce determination on her face. Ursula, though, simply stared out of the window; her thoughts clearly far, far away. *She's probably thinking of Constans, and wondering when—and where—they will see each other again.* Ursula's eye was suddenly caught by something high up above. Cordula looked up, too. There, against the cloud-speckled blue sky, was the unmistakable silhouette of a hawk, circling high above the city. As the two cousins watched, it disappeared into the blazing disc of the sun. *Poor Ursula. I know you're hoping and praying to be together with Constans. You're aching to be with him—to have him home.*

XIV

Two winters passed. The long days of high summer found the Commanders of the First Athena back in the halls of King Deonotus's Palace at Corinium. They were there to hold a Great Feast in anticipation of Constantine's success—and the imminent return of the men. Just as they started celebrating, Morgan's unmistakable horn could be heard in the distance outside and, within a few moments, he arrived breathless in the Royal Dining Chamber.

"Welcome, Morgan!" King Deonotus exclaimed. "This is, indeed, an unexpected pleasure."

It had been almost a year since Morgan's last visit. Ursula and the others had become used to receiving news of events on the Continent from other—less reliable—messengers, not in their employ.

"I wish it was pleasure that brought me here, Your Majesty." Morgan bowed to kiss the King's hand before turning to address the gathering—fleetingly catching the eye of Cordula. "Unfortunately, I bring grave news regarding Contantine . . ." His gaze settled upon Ursula. ". . . and Constans."

Morgan began by reminding the gathering of the difficulties the men were facing the previous year. How the previous spring, the wandering tribes of Burgundians and Suevi had wreaked so much havoc in central and western Galliae that Constantine was forced to divert his attention, leaving the work they were doing rebuilding the frontier defenses unfinished.

To contain the threat of the tribes, Constantine had split his force into five divisions. There were two large mobile units, each five thousand strong. One was placed under the command of Gerontius. The other under Constans. It was their task to round up the two large wandering Suevi tribes and escort them across the mountains to Hispania. A third unit of cavalrymen was stationed along the newly rebuilt defenses. The fourth contingent was assigned the extremely difficult task of settling the Burgundians—a collection of small tribes constantly at war with each other—along the more southerly reaches of the Rhenus. As for Constantine, he accompanied the fifth contingent to the south of Galliae, to Arelate, in response to an urgent request from the Imperial Court for reinforcements against the threat of further menaces which might come across the Alps from Italia at any moment.

"The overall strategy worked well at first. Constans and Gerontius succeeded in subduing the Suevi warriors, and were able to commence escorting the two tribes—both numbering more than fifty thousand—south toward Hispania. The Burgundians were tamed so well, their internecine warfare almost ceased, and the new defense arrangements on the Rhenus-Danuvius frontier—though incomplete—appeared to be keeping other invading German tribes at bay. But then things started to go wrong . . . ."

As Morgan spoke, Ursula could feel a familiar coldness creeping up her back. *Is he ever coming home? Oh dear, sweet God, when will all this end?*

"I'm sure you'll recall that while we were all busy celebrating Lughnasadh, Stilicho, the Supreme Commander-in-Chief of the Emperor's armies, died unexpectedly in suspicious circumstances. Well, his death created a dangerous lack of leadership in Italia, which was especially perilous for Constantine, just over the Alps in Arelate.

"Prior to his death, Stilicho made no secret of the fact that he perceived Constantine's success in Germania and Galliae as a threat. He managed to convince Emperor Honorius of the need to take measures to stem Constantine's rise in influence in the region. Almost immediately after he died, more tribes of Burgundians, Suevi and Franks began pouring across the undefended frontier, laying waste to areas that had barely started to recover from the previous devastation.

"Constantine was forced to re-deploy the main contingent of his men from Arelate to try and cope with the new invaders. This left him dangerously vulnerable to attack from any would-be successors to Stilicho's crown, who wished to attempt an opportunistic foray into Galliae to prove their worthiness.

"Meanwhile, the relocation of the two large Suevi tribes to Hispania also ran into problems. Constans had driven his tribe along a coastal route, which led across the mountains far to the west. Then they came down from the mountains into a sparsely populated area of Hispania. Gerontius, however, followed the main trade route directly south to the powerful metropolis of Cesarauguta, where the Imperial Court had been none too pleased at having Galliae's invaders foisted upon them.

"Gerontius's diplomatic and leadership skills were far from up to the challenge. A local Hispanian cavalry unit joined forces with some of the men who were under his command. In a night of brute terror, they massacred over five thousand Suevi women and children. Having thus compromised Gerontius, the Court found themselves with a useful puppet. They used him in their power plays with their neighboring province, as well as with the Emperor himself—who always had to 'earn' Hispanian co-operation in whatever schemes he was pursuing." Morgan paused before concluding. "I'm sorry not to have better news to report."

"These are unfortunate developments, indeed." King Deonotus sighed.

All eyes turned to Ursula, who looked away. Pinnosa had been scrutinizing Ursula while Morgan was speaking, and saw her desperately trying to hide her horror at how bad things had gotten for the men.

"It would appear our feast to celebrate Constantine's success is perhaps a little . . . premature." Ursula's voice could not mask her disappointment—her inner turmoil.

For a long while, there was an awkward silence.

Morgan interrupted their brooding, attempting a lighter note, "What of tidings from here? How has the First Athena's campaign season been?"

Cordula looked to Ursula, who nodded for her to tell their tale. "Fortunately, we have some better news to impart," she said enthusiastically, also attempting to lift their spirits.

"The First and Second Cohorts have beaten off more than thirty Hibernian raiding parties so far this year. The Third and Fourth have kept the Wall Country so tame we were able to send a four-hundred-strong expeditionary force north to the Antonine Wall to make basic repairs to some of the forts and sentry towers.

"Then, in high summer, Ursula and Pinnosa's women went on an extended exercise in the high mountains far to the north of the frontier lands—to places and islands that are off our maps. They returned—safely—to Viroconium Cornoviorum on Lughnasadh itself. Just as they were settling into their quarters for a much-needed rest, they heard trumpets to the east. A force of over fifteen hundred women in dark green livery marched into the barrack complex to—"

"Dark green livery?" Morgan interjected.

Cordula could not help smiling at her beloved's quizzical expression, before continuing. "Yes. It was the Fifth and Sixth Cohorts of the First Athena—led by Princess Faustina, step-daughter of King Regulus, ruler of Lindum. Their addition to the Legion meant that the First Athena's numbers had almost doubled and are now well over four thousand!"

Faustina stepped forward and Morgan greeted her with the decorum due a royal Princess.

After the introduction, Cordula continued, her tone somber, "We need the extra numbers, Morgan, because since you were here last a new menace has arisen in the east—the Saxons!"

"The Saxons have invaded?" Morgan's voice was full of alarm. He clearly had not heard of this development.

"Yes, the Saxons have been upon us for almost a year now. They roam the countryside of Lindum in bands of up to three hundred—all hungry for plunder and eager for sport of the most vile and despicable kind. They are much more formidable foes than the Hibernians or the Picts. They are large men and good fighters. They're led by chiefs who have served in Roman armies. They know how to fight in formation and use tactics. We have been hard-pressed to defeat them.

"Yes . . . you would be." Morgan's slow, deliberate tone matched the apprehension in his grim expression. "Constantine will be most concerned by this development."

"Then, please tell him he needn't be!" Ursula snapped, her voice strong and assured—her haunting, dark fears brushed brusquely aside like a demon in a prayer. "We are more than a match for them." She nodded to her cousin. "Please continue."

"Luckily, Morgan . . ." Cordula glanced at Pinnosa and they exchanged smiles, which lifted everyone's spirits. "Pinnosa has devised a new tactic for attacking them. She and Baetica come at the enemy from two different directions, thereby forcing the Saxons to fight on separate flanks. The squadrons gallop hard with their long shields held out at arm's length to protect themselves against Saxon missiles. Just as they draw level with their targets, they drop their shields, swap their reins into the other hand, grab specially shortened spears that are strapped to their backs, take aim and let fly—all at a full gallop—"

Ursula broke in, "Once captured, we deport them in leg irons."

"I still think they should be put to the axe," Pinnosa said curtly.

"It was decided that the humiliation of being beaten by an army of women will deter them or their kinsfolk from trying again," Deonotus said, staring pointedly at Ursula.

Morgan could sense that the Saxons and how to deal with them was still a topic of much debate amongst the commanders of the First Athena.

"Be that as it may," Ursula retorted, deliberately changing the subject, "with the Lindum, Eboracum and Corinium regiments working together, the Province will most assuredly remain safe until the men return!"

Morgan raised his cup in salute, "Constantine will be most pleased to hear of your success!"

They all toasted one another.

"Don't you find it a little curious," Pinnosa mused, "that we have yet to receive a contingent from Londinium? I wonder why? Perhaps it's because they can't find a cloth yellow enough for their uniforms!"

XV

"Enter!" King Deonotus called.

Ursula pushed back the door and returned his warm smile of greeting. Her father was alone in his private chamber, which was full of maps and parchments. It was the first moon cycle of winter. He had just returned from a meeting of the three provincial kings with the Governor in Londinium, and he was still reading a parchment that Morgan had handed to him. As soon as he'd changed out of his kingly robes, he sent for her. For once, Ursula was out of uniform. They both wore thick, heavy, woolen togas, as they had in happier winters.

"Sit down, my dear," he said, after they had kissed and hugged. "I'm afraid I have a very serious matter to discuss with you." It was evident from the way he started pacing the room that something was troubling him greatly.

"What is it, Father?" She said, sitting gingerly on the edge of the couch beside the fire.

"It seems the Governor and you share an important sentiment in common. You both wish the men would return home soon."

She said nothing and simply raised her eyebrows in response, knowing full well that anything involving the Governor was never as simple and straightforward as it sounded. What started as good news, inevitably ended as bad.

"But that's about as far as you and he agree. Your reasons for wanting them home couldn't be more different." He stopped pacing, sat down beside her and took her hands in his. "What I'm about to tell you, Regulus will also be telling Faustina, and Aurelius will be telling Julia."

His manner reminded her of when he had broken the news to her that mother had died. She shivered, but not with the cold.

"The problem is, my dear, that Britannia simply can't afford to finance two armies any longer. You know—don't you—about the recent tax riots in Londinium and the southern towns?"

She nodded. Only a week before she had received an order from the Governor to dispatch a unit of cavalry to contain a revolt by some small holders near Durotrigum.

The King sighed and resumed pacing the room. "The whole Province is thankful for what you and the First Athena are doing. The citizenry know they need you and your women out on patrol, protecting them from invasion, but . . ." he paused and looked her in the eye, "they don't want to pay too high a price for it."

"Does the Governor want the Legion to disband and the frontiers to be left in the hands of the standing guard?" she asked tentatively, barely managing to disguise a sudden surge of the old fears she thought she'd conquered.

"Aurelius and I knew this would happen," he continued, speaking more to himself than to her. "We knew that crafty old rogue, Regulus, wouldn't be content to sit back and let his daughter be outshone by you and Julia. We knew he would encourage her to match your efforts. But at the same time we knew there was a limit to how much the people of Britannia were willing to pay." He spun around and kicked the embers of the fire in exasperation, raising a cascade of sparks. "Bah! We warned Regulus not to try and match the Corinium and Eboracum numbers. 'Send Faustina to join Julia,' we said. 'Let her wear the Red or the Blue,' we said. 'Oh no!' says he. 'If my Faustina is to fight for Britannia, she fights in the Green.' The next thing we knew, the First Athena had doubled in numbers. And it doesn't stop there, does it? With the number of volunteers you're getting, the First Athena could well reach eight thousand in strength next year—and we will still be paying for the twenty thousand men on the Continent!"

"What have you and the Governor decided to do?" Ursula asked quietly, forcing herself to remain calm.

"Well, there were only three possible courses of action open to us. To disband the First Athena was the first . . . ."

Ursula took a deep breath. She was finding it difficult to take in what he was saying. Her mind was caught up in a tangle of racing thoughts. *Please don't disband us—not now! Not when there's so much to do. If only the men were here. Oh, why did they have to leave? Where is my Constans? Why isn't he here? What will Pinnosa say?*

". . . but, the way things are going in Galliae and Hispania at the moment, the men won't be able to disengage in the foreseeable future. That means the First Athena will be needed for at least one more year. One more trip to the Rainbow Mountains for you, my dear."

He looked at her anxiously. In that moment, she knew he'd had to fight hard for her cause. She wondered who his antagonist had been. *Surely not Aurelius. And, it can't have been Regulus, no matter how "crafty" he is. It must have been the Governor. But, why? He of all people should be more concerned with protecting Britannia than with helping other provinces to defend themselves.*

"The second option was for Galliae to pay for the men, but the Court in Arelate is still financing their units in Italia. We received the Governor of Galliae's reply last week. A very emphatic 'no!' That was why I had to go to Londinium. And that left only one further possibility . . . ." His expression became grave. "Constantine is going to mint his own coins and pay his men with his own money."

Ursula gasped. "You mean—"

"Yes, my dear. He and Constans are going to take the laurels and put on the purple." He handed the parchment that Morgan had just delivered to her. "Here," he said wearily, forcing himself to manage a faint smile. "Read your first-ever personal letter from an Emperor. And, prepare yourself to become a future Empress."

XVI

I salute you and your fellow officers. Well done on your magnificent work protecting the good people of Britannia. Your deeds give the men and me great cheer and make us pine for the genteel rigors of the 'Rainbow Mountains'! Are you aware that your fame has spread? Tales of your exploits are being told and recounted throughout all of Rome!

Why, even Honorius on his high throne in Ravenna has heard of you: of the terrifying Pinnosa, the bane of the Hibernians; and the fearless Brittola, the scourge of the Picts. He'll be sending you to Africa next!

They all laughed. Even though each one of Ursula's friends had read it a dozen times, Constantine's letter never failed to raise their spirits, especially when Martha read it out loud.

"Now go ahead to the part about finances," Ursula urged, settling herself on a sun-warmed stone. She looked around the ruins, the very same old Christian temple complex by the sea where she and Pinnosa had first conceived the idea of the First Athena. Ursula had ordered the Commanders of the First Athena to muster there to plan the forthcoming campaign season. They were seated around the pool by the altar, drinking wine and catching up on each other's intelligence. They were reading Constantine's letter again for the benefit of Julia who had just arrived.

Martha found the relevant passage and continued:

I assure you the First Athena will not be curtailed or disbanded because of petty squabbles between Governors over finances. I hereby give you my pledge that the Legion will only disband when you have handed over your standards to Constans and me upon our return to Britannia—a day we all hope to see soon. Until that day, the Province needs you to carry on with your good work. Do not give money matters a moment's thought! Leave such thorny issues to us old men as we rummage through our vaults, rattling boxes and arguing over how much blood we can squeeze from stones.

"He must have suspected that he would have problems with Hispania when he wrote that letter," Julia said. Ursula listened carefully to her cousin's counsel, because Julia had a good understanding of Continental politics, having been to school in Treveris. She had also visited the western provinces in recent years with her father. "By all accounts, the Governor of Hispania is the only ruler in the Western Empire with substantial reserves. Father received a report from Hispania a few days ago. It said the Governor has refused to make any payments to Constantine for what he called a 'Gallo-Britannic' army. He says Constantine holds no claim to represent their interests. In fact, he has gone much further than simply refusing to recognize Constantine and Constans's imperial status. He has raised a little known nobleman from Cesarauguta—Maximus—to the purple and created a rival, Hispanian Emperor."

"Pah" Pinnosa exclaimed. "This is precisely why I have no fear the First Athena will be disbanded—at least not until its work is done. It's because he anticipated such financial problems that Constantine took the purple. I'm sure he can raise enough money for his men on the Continent—even without Hispanian contributions. That means Britannia could afford a First Athena *double* its current size." She looked pointedly at Ursula, who slowly nodded in agreement.

"What of our men in Hispania?" Martha asked. "Aren't they in a precarious position if the Province has raised its own Emperor?"

"I was coming to that," Julia said tentatively. She looked uncomfortable. "According to the report, Gerontius has declared his allegiance to the new imperial house in Cesarauguta. In return for his 'loyalty' he has been made Commander-in-Chief of all Hispanian armed forces."

"Hell's teeth!" Pinnosa snapped. "I should have cut that traitor's throat while I had the chance."

"Wait. There's more . . . concerning Constans," Julia said, looking pointedly at Ursula. "The same report said that at the time of these events, Constans was still far to the west of Hispania—in Merida. We know he's refused to acknowledge the new regime. But we have no idea what he might be doing in response. No further reports have been received from him. His communication lines have been severed. It would appear he's completely cut off from his father and surrounded by hostile forces. As far as we know, he's still burdened with the Suevi. We think he's having to protect them against the Meridans, who have risen against having the Germans foisted on them. Poor Constans has a fight on his hands whichever way he turns."

"I'm sure he'll find some way to extricate himself and his men from the situation. He'll get a message out soon," Ursula said calmly, almost managing to convince her friends she wasn't upset by the news. She quickly changed the subject. "Constantine was hoping to consolidate his position by embarking on a campaign into Italia to help Honorius against the Goths, but I imagine he will deem that to be unwise in the light of these developments. What do you think, Julia?"

Before Julia could answer, Pinnosa stood up. "It's a lovely evening. Why don't we enjoy the sunset while we continue our discussions?" She could see that Ursula desperately needed to have attention diverted away from her. Pinnosa led them out onto the terrace where she beckoned them to sit on its stone rim. There, seated in a line, they were forced to look out to sea rather than at each other.

"The Continent is in utter turmoil," Julia began. "It's all the fault of that schemer, Stilicho. He had long plotted to unite the Roman and Constantinopolitan thrones. He distrusted any rival powers in either half of the Empire, and the only other significant Commander of distinction in the West was Constantine. Unfortunately for all of us, when Stilicho died, his schemes didn't die with him. The result is that the Empire—especially the West—is in great danger of being torn apart."

She smiled ironically at Ursula. "He deliberately exposed the borders to invasion purely in order to weaken Constantine's influence. The result is, the Germans are ravaging Galliae at the same time the Goths rampage all over Italia. Our forces are over-stretched and barely able to cope. The only thing the citizenry can do is seek shelter inside their city walls in the same way that Honorius has taken refuge in Ravenna. Stilicho has turned us all into squirrels. We're all holed up in our nests with our winter stores until the weather improves."

"But what of Constantine and his campaign into Italia?" Pinnosa asked.

"Well, now that Stilicho is gone, Constantine—being the most able Commander in the West—is virtually the only hope Honorius has left to defeat the Goths. That's why he should take the core units of his army into Italia. With these recent developments in Hispania, though, I can imagine that Constantine's first priority will be to consolidate his position before attempting a campaign into unfamiliar territory. He'll have to wait for Constans to return. Until that happens, I very much doubt whether he will leave southern Galliae. He can't go into Italia and leave Arelate vulnerable to attack, and—I hate to say it, but—he can't depart for Britannia either. In short, until Constans and his father manage to reunite their forces, in a way they are both trapped."

For a long moment, they were all silent as they pondered the intricate complexities of Continental politics.

"Dear God in Heaven!" Saula cried, leaping to her feet. "Why couldn't the men simply repair the frontier defenses, escort the Germans out of Galliae—and return home? When will their expedition be over? Won't they *ever* come home?" She started pacing up and down behind the others. "I will see my twenty-second summer this year, as will many of you! Are we going to be doing the men's work for the rest of our lives? When are we going to have real lives? When are we going to marry and have children? When we're in our fortieth summer? And who are we going to marry and have children with, for goodness' sake?" She looked pleadingly at the others one by one.

"Lady Saula has a point, Mistress," Baetica said to Pinnosa. "I'm a little older than most of the other women, including yourselves, and I'm the only one here who's married. A lot of the women have been speaking like Lady Saula. They say the men will never come home because they're mostly unmarried, and unmarried men only make their home where they are well paid. The way things are going, that could be anywhere in the Western Empire apart from Britannia."

"'An army of spinsters,'" Martha added. "That's how one of my women put it. She said we'll still be doing this work when we're too old to have children."

"And if the best of the Province's fighting men and women fail to have children," Saula moaned, "who will take over our work in future years? We should be meeting and marrying our men soon, otherwise Britannia will—"

"There's something very special about this ancient place of peace . . . and healing . . . and learning," Ursula interrupted, as she stared out to sea. "I seem to be able to see matters much more clearly here." She pointed to the nearby rocks. "It was over there that the idea of creating a frontier army of women came to Pinnosa and I." She stood up next to Saula; the others turned to face her. "And now, I think I know what we should do next."

She had a strange, far away look to her eyes. "Ladies, we will soon be embarking on our third campaign season, and the way the men's situation is developing on the Continent, we will probably have to embark on a fourth. And then—possibly—a fifth." She paced silently up and down for a while before continuing. "There's something about this life we're leading which gets into your blood. The drill and the march become your daily routine. You cultivate a taste for simple camp food to the point where you yearn for it whenever you are over-indulged at a feast. You find you get a far better night's sleep in a camp roll or on a barrack board than on a stuffy old bed. Frontier work has become our way of life. I'm sure you agree." They all nodded. "When you're out on patrol, you are no longer away from your home, you are *at* home." She stopped pacing. "And that is where the men are, too. At their homes . . . far away."

"No!" Cordula exclaimed. "There's a big difference between us on patrol and them. We're patrolling our homeland. We are at home when we're on patrol. The men are far from their true homes . . . and I'm sure they miss them."

"I'm sure they miss their homes, too," Ursula said patiently. "My point is, though, that the longer the men spend on the Continent, becoming embroiled in the day to day events there, and getting more and more familiar with the terrain, the more difficult it will become for them to extricate themselves. I think there is a real danger they'll never come home. If that is the case, the women who fear having to guard the Province for the rest of their lives will have their nightmares come true."

"But what can we do to prevent that happening?" Saula sounded utterly exasperated.

"I think I may have an idea," Ursula said calmly. "But, before I tell it to you all, I'd like to ask Baetica a simple question. Baetica?"

"Mistress?" Baetica replied.

"I imagine your husband is the kind of loyal guardsman who yearns for the next campaign season. Is that so?"

"Yes, most certainly, Mistress. I'm more of a mistress than a wife, if you know what I mean."

"I'm sure he misses you when he's away, but when he is safely back home I imagine he misses life in the ranks even more."

"That's correct, Mistress. As a matter of fact, within a fortnight of arriving home he's usually so restless we have to go on a three-day hunt—even in mid winter! 'Bear hunting bear' I call it."

Ursula waited for the ripple of laughter to finish before continuing. "Under normal circumstances, when a legionary goes off on campaign, what is the most effective way of ensuring that he returns home as soon as the campaign's over and doesn't volunteer for extra duties?"

"Send word that he's a father," Baetica answered without hesitation. "Let him know there's an addition to the family at home . . . preferably a boy."

"But most of the men with Constantine and Constans are single." Cordula objected.

"And these aren't 'normal circumstances'" Saula cried.

"You are both absolutely right," Ursula replied, with a fierce gleam in her eye. She glanced at Pinnosa, who was smiling as if she knew what was coming. "What I'd like to propose is that we do the following: We expand the First Athena to equal the number of Britannic men under Constantine and Constans's command, and then—"

"But that's over twenty thousand!" Martha blurted.

"Please allow me to continue." Ursula placed a reassuring hand on Martha's shoulder. "We create a First Athena which not only matches Constantine's contingent in size, but also in composition, being comprised mostly of unmarried personnel. At the same time, we create a reserve Legion—the Second Athena—with approximately five thousand, the same as we had this season. That will all take the better part of a year to accomplish. The next stage of the plan couldn't be put into operation until next Alban Elued. It will be toward the end of the campaign season, but then . . . ."

She stopped pacing and looked around the group. Most of the women looked dumbfounded, except Pinnosa and Julia who were both grinning. "Then—with the Second Athena remaining behind to maintain Britannia's defenses—we'll take the First Athena to the Continent. We'll catch up with Constantine and hold a Grand Wedding, marrying all of the unmarried men and women together."

"A wedding!" Cordula jumped up and clapped her hands with delight.

"Two entire armies?" Brittola cried incredulously, as she rose.

All the woman stood and started talking.

"Equal numbers . . . ." Martha began mulling the idea aloud.

"A woman for each man . . . ." Saula said with a smile.

"Equally matched . . . ." Martha mused. "One to one."

Ursula could see from their expressions that her idea was taking root. A new hope was beginning to dispel their despair. After a long, deliberate pause, she continued, "There's a further stage to the plan. The women will stay with the men for however long it takes for them to become pregnant. Then, as soon as they are with child, they will return to Britannia, carrying the babies that will ensure their husbands' return . . . carrying the seeds of Britannia's future."

The Commanders were stunned into silence.

"I think it's an extremely ambitious plan." Pinnosa stepped forward and stood next to Ursula. "And I can see many problems and difficulties that we will need to overcome." She put her hand on Ursula's shoulder and was surprised to find that Ursula was shaking. "But it's a logical—if a mite extreme—extension of the First Athena's mission to defend Britannia . . ." she paused, before adding with a smile, "and I support it wholeheartedly—though I have no idea how to organize the training for the final stages!"

"I think you're absolutely right, cousin," Julia said after the laughter at Pinnosa's quip had died down. "Our situation warrants drastic action. As far as I can see, there is no other way. Not only does this plan ensure that Britannia will have a new army of strong young men in future years, it will also lure many—if not most—of our best men back to their homes. They'll know they have a real family waiting for them."

"More than that," Ursula added. "If, for whatever reason, the men fail to return, the mothers, being women of the First Athena, will ensure that the new army receives excellent training."

While the others began to talk excitedly about the prospect of training young sons in the arts of soldiery and the crafts of war, Pinnosa stood apart from the group and stared thoughtfully out to sea. After a while, she turned to Ursula and said, "I'd like to make one small amendment to the plan."

"What's that?" Ursula asked with a smile.

"You have your Constans, Cordula has her Morgan, and almost everyone here has her mind on some handsome officer who is currently serving far from home. But I really can't think of any fine young man—in Galliae or Hispania—I would like to marry and bear the child of." She took her eyes from Ursula's and turned to address the group as a whole. "I volunteer to be spared the marriage part of the plan, so that I can maintain the readiness of the First and Second Athena's while you're all busy rearing your young legionaries."

"I'll join you, Pinnosa!" Brittola stood by the old altar. She held her cross out in front of her as if to ward off something evil. "You're all talking about marriage as if you were breeding horses! 'Making a new generation of high quality leaders and fighters.' 'All getting pregnant at the same time.' 'Restocking our army.' May I remind you that marriage is a holy estate, the union of a man and a woman in their service to God. True marriages are built upon love, not . . . not breeding potential!"

She shook her head and lowered the cross, her anger spent. She looked sadly at her old friends and continued in a quieter voice, "I will go with you on this desperate mission because I am one of you and I love you as if you were my sisters. But I cannot—will not—take part in this . . . this cattle market marriage."

A strong evening breeze lifted their hair and ruffled their cloaks, as the women stood motionless, watching her in silence.

Brittola looked intently at Ursula. "You said you don't know why this place of peace and learning makes you have these ideas. Well I know why." She knelt down in front of the altar to pray, and as she began to intone her prayer the others dropped to their knees.

"Dear Lord and merciful God. You have chosen this holy place to seal our Fate. You have shown to us how, through Ursula, You reveal to us our True Mission in life. We will follow whatever Fate You have allotted us, Lord. We will succumb to Your Will. We will obey Your wishes with love and devotion, though we know not yet where our mission—Your mission—is leading us." Then, after a long pause, very quietly, she began to sing *Praise the Lord.*

The others joined in. By the end of the first verse they were all singing at the top of their voices.

Chapter 4

The Storm

Despite Ursula, Julia and Faustina's impassioned pleas, their fathers were slow to warm to the idea of the Great Expedition and the Wedding of the Legions. Of the three Kings, Deonotus was the most reluctant. He'd personally served in three previous overseas expeditions and experienced first-hand how easy it was for missions to become far more complicated than originally planned. Nevertheless, he agreed to attend a special assembly of the provincial Kings, convened by Aurelius in Lindum prior to their regular gathering with the Governor in Londinium to mark Alban Eiler, the Spring Equinox.

Barely had the Kings and Commanders arrived in Lindum, when Morgan rode unexpectedly into the city and rushed to the Audience Chamber. He dispensed with formalities—such was his urgency—and commenced his report while still breathless. "Emperor Constantine has been forced to turn back from Rome. There are too many Goths and too few legionnaires willing to help. The moment he crossed the Alps, all were suspicious of him. Stilicho managed to make sure no one would trust Constantine, and when—"

"Wait!" King Aurelius—his face full of alarm—raised his hand, forcing Morgan to stop and catch his breath. "What have you told the Governor about this in Londinium?"

"I have not been to Londinium, Your Majesty. Constantine told me to find you first as a matter of import!" Morgan's expression was dark with foreboding. "Before Constantine withdrew from Rome, he uncovered a plot between the rulers of Hispania and Londinium. They were both in the pay of Stilicho!"

The following day, the Kings' retinue set forth to Londinium. The riders included the Corinium, Eboracum, and Lindum Royal Guards, and the First, Fifth and Sixth cohorts of the First Athena.

Horns blaring, the riders made their way into the Provincial Capital, only to be met with the stares of the citizenry. Not one Centurion was to be found. At the Palace, they discovered that the Governor and his Court had been forewarned. They had fled, taking with them the contents of the Treasury as well as the Imperial Guard. By the time the Kings arrived at the Imperial Palace, their quarry was well on his way to Hispania.

Later, after the Kings had settled into the Governor's Palace, Deonotus told Ursula, "It's no use going after him, my dear. He really didn't get away with that much. For the last three winters, we've suspected something like this might happen. As a precaution, all of us kept payments to the Roman coffers at a minimum. As a result, well over three-quarters of Britannia's wealth remains in the Province, safe in the keeps of Corinium, Eboracum and Lindum. The citizens of Britannia are now free to spend their money and deploy their resources as they wish."

Deonotus paused, smiled and took a draught of the Governor's wine. "And, we all know what the greatest wish of the people is . . . ."

"You mean—"

"Yes, we have enough money to expand the Athenas."

"Father!" Ursula exclaimed as she rushed to hug him.

He returned her embrace and then pulled away, "Come now, there is work to be done. Aurelius, Regulus and I will need to stay in Londinium for a while to get things in order, and to ease communication with Constantine. And, we need to give some thought to where you and your legion ought best be based . . . ."

II

A full cycle of the moon later, Ursula, Pinnosa and Julia were once again in the Imperial Palace in Londinium, when one of the First Athena's messengers, Eithne, arrived from Lindum.

"The Saxons have invaded, Mistress! Faustina's units are badly outnumbered. She asks that you send reinforcements."

"How many raiders does she estimate?" Julia asked.

"Two thousand are already ashore, and still more were landing when I left, Mistress," Eithne replied. "The Saxons were crying out a challenge in Latin. They want the 'feeble men dressed as women' to come and fight."

"Two thousand!" Pinnosa stood up in alarm. "Last year, there were less than a thousand throughout the entire campaign season!"

"It's worse, Mistress," Eithne's grim expression presaged her serious news, "These Saxons have horses."

"Cavalry units!" Julia exclaimed.

"We told the Kings!" Pinnosa said angrily, glaring out the window, "We told them to maim the Saxons before putting them in their boats. Maybe this time they'll listen."

"I'd better go and inform them." Ursula said, placing a hand on Pinnosa's shoulder, "You are right. It does look as if the humiliating defeat at the hands of an army of women has acted more as a provocation than a deterrent."

III

Loud shouts and rhythmic, echoing rumbles caused Ursula, Pinnosa and Julia to rein in their mounts on a bank above the Tamesis. A training galley splashed erratically past—the officer bellowing frantic orders. Because it was below deck, the resonating beats of the pace drum became distorted into a strange bittern-like boom.

The galley rowed past a large island, which was the First and Second Athena's new home. The Holy Isle—so named for an ancient Druid temple for the Lady of the Lake that stood there, of which Brittola disapproved—was a day's journey upstream from Londinium, near a river crossing called the Bray. Here, the Tamesis ran slowly through flat land, spreading out into mud flats and shallows. In this shallow expanse of water sat an island big enough for an encampment housing over ten thousand. It had a narrow, slow moving channel to one side and a broader, fast moving channel on the other, which gave it protection from the kind of unwanted attention large numbers of healthy young women attracted. It was the perfect place to use as a training camp. In addition to being an ideal location for recruiting and training purposes, the Holy Isle was also perfect for the rapid deployment of active units to any area where they were needed.

Ursula and her fellow Commanders had ridden hard to the Holy Isle to make arrangements for the emergency expedition to Lindum—so hard they had left their escort far behind. They knew they had to do something urgently to relieve Faustina in Lindum, but precisely what had yet to be decided.

They were just downstream from the isle, at a point where the river currents picked up, making excellent water for swimming and galley practice. As far as they could see in either direction, the riverbanks were crowded with training detachments. Most of them were in the shallows practicing their swimming. Both training galleys were in use with several crews of sixty lining up to take their turns by two jetties that were near to where the Commanders had come to a halt. There were also several groups nearby practicing river crossings on horseback.

It had not been women from far afield who had so dramaticly increased the Athenian ranks. The regular comings and goings in and out of Londinium of units of the women accompanying their Commanders had finally roused the interest of the people of the Capital. At the break of dawn, just before Beltane, the lookouts on the Holy Isle had rushed to fetch the officers to see an extraordinary sight. Both banks of the Tamesis, as far as they could see in either direction, were flanked with women, all standing silent and still in their new Londinium livery. It had not been—as Pinnosa had mockingly suggested—yellow, but bright orange. There had been five and a half thousand of them, including one thousand five hundred cavalry.

"I think I know what we need to do," Ursula said, after they'd caught their breath. "We need to transfer as many of our best and most experienced women to Lindum as we can spare—and do it as quickly as possible."

"I was thinking that," Pinnosa said. "It has to be the First and Third Cohorts."

"But, they're needed in the Rainbow Mountains, and along the Wall," Julia objected.

Ursula smiled. "Not if we activate the Second, and send them to relieve the First."

"But the Second aren't ready," Julia exclaimed.

"They're as ready as we were when we went on our first campaign," Pinnosa retorted.

Julia paused to think, then nodded reluctantly in agreement.

"As soon as we get into camp, Julia, I want you to organize the messengers." Ursula turned to Pinnosa. "Round up all the experienced cavalry women that are here—including the trainers—and set off immediately. Even a small force of a hundred or so will be of help to Faustina."

"Take care, Pinnosa," Julia added. "Even with the Lindum cavalry you still won't have enough women to match two thousand Saxons hell-bent on a fight."

"The numbers don't bother me," Pinnosa said with bravado. "We'll whittle away at them whenever they break up into smaller groups."

"No!" Ursula snapped. "I don't want you to fight them until reinforcements arrive. That's an order." She looked fiercely at her old friend. "Limit yourself to monitoring the enemy's whereabouts. Concentrate your efforts on evacuating any settlements that lie in their path. We don't need any futile small-scale engagements up there, which result in nothing but heavy losses. I want you—and the entire First—intact for our Great Expedition. You are to wait until Julia and I arrive with reinforcements. Is that fully understood?"

"Yes, Your Highness," Pinnosa said, saluting with an exaggerated flourish.

"I mean it, Pinnosa. No adventures."

Pinnosa's expression became serious. "Don't worry. We'll play it safe."

Ursula continued, "I'll accompany half of the Second to the Rainbow Mountains and oversee their deployment. Julia will take the other half to the Wall and supervise the hand-over. Then we'll both lead the First to you as fast as we can."

The Commanders exchanged nods of agreement.

Pinnosa smiled. "Which one of you will get to Lindum first, do you think?"

Neither Ursula nor Julia rose to her bait, but they did allow themselves wry smiles. Just at that moment, their cavalry escort came into view, and all three Commanders hauled their mounts around to resume their ride into camp.

IV

"I did as you asked," Pinnosa said to Ursula almost a cycle of the moon later, a short ride from the ruined town of Causennae where Ursula, Pinnosa and Faustina's units had converged. "I avoided any direct confrontations with the Saxons—despite an eagerness on their part to do battle. Whenever the Saxons spot one of the First Athena units monitoring their movements, their cavalrymen leap on their mounts and give chase." She shrugged. "Of course, we get away easily. Our horses are much faster."

Brittola chuckled, "Tell her what they were yelling at you."

Pinnosa smiled wryly. "They were shouting, 'We want Pinnosa blood!'"

"They know who you are?" Ursula failed to mask her unease.

"The Saxons somehow found out the names of all the Athenian Commanders. They call out our names whenever we get close," Pinnosa replied.

Ursula tried to hide a shiver.

Pinnosa pretended not to notice and rolled out a parchment map on the board she'd set up next to the supply tent. "The Saxons are in three main groups—one large and two small—systematically working their way through the area between the Great North Road and the Fosse Way. There are hundreds of tiny hamlets—filled mostly with pottery and metal workers—which makes evacuating them extremely difficult. We're doing our best, but dozens of these people are being slaughtered each day. The devastation these invaders wreak is . . . is horrific."

Ursula was silent for a moment. "I think we need to attack the Saxons right away."

"Shouldn't we wait for Julia's contingent?" Cordula asked.

"Her unit is still a few days' march away," Pinnosa said. "The longer we wait, the more villagers die."

"Brittola," Ursula put her arm around her old friend, "this is your first encounter with the Saxons. They are far more dangerous than Hibernian or Pict raiding parties. We have no choice other than to put the women's safety first. You know what that means, don't you?"

"Of course," Brittola said without hesitation, "we aim to kill."

"You understand, don't you?" Pinnosa added, also putting her arm around the youngest Commander in the Athenas. "We have to keep the First Athena intact for the Great Expedition."

"What do you take me for—an idiot?" Brittola snapped indignantly. "These Saxons are the most dangerous beasts on God's earth. An arrow through the foot wouldn't stop one of them from breaking a woman's neck!"

"I wish Saula was here," Martha said.

Brittola said consolingly, "She'll be here with Julia's regiment in a couple of days."

"Ladies!" Pinnosa stood forward and raised her voice to address the entire gathering of officers. "I'm afraid we have an extremely serious problem on our hands. The tactic we used last year won't work. The enemy has far greater numbers this time, including cavalry units. We're going to have to devise a new strategy. Hand-to-hand fighting is out of the question. Much as I hate to admit it, we wouldn't stand a chance. They'd tear us to pieces."

"The only way is a rain of arrows," Cordula said emphatically. "But how? How can we get them to line up for us . . . in the open . . . down field?"

"I know just the place. I grew up around here," Faustina exclaimed. "The Witham Valley is near Causennae. If we could lure them down it, there is a point below the ridge where the woods open out into a huge meadow. It's a perfect place for a trap! We could hide whole cohorts of archers in the trees. They would be completely invisible."

"Perfect!" Pinnosa said, thumping a wagon's wheel. "And I know exactly how we could lay the bait . . . ."

While they were busy formulating their plans the skies darkened and big raindrops started to fall, plopping in the earth about their feet. By the time they remounted and were ready to set off, the rain was coming down hard. As they neared Causennae, it was a torrential downpour.

Despite the weather, the first stages of the operation went well. Pinnosa led a 'dummy' patrol of fifty cavalry—which included Ursula, Brittola, Martha and Cordula—and engaged the Saxons in a clearing to the west of the town. As soon as the invaders saw the women, they sent up a loud cry of, "We want Pinnosa blood!" Their cavalrymen rushed for their horses and the chase was on.

After a wild ride through dense forest, with the women sometimes having to deliberately slow down in order not to lose their pursuers, they crossed a ridge to find themselves heading west along the Witham valley. Sure enough, as Faustina had said, the woodland soon receded to expose a long, broad area of open meadow. Even through the driving rain, Ursula and the others quickly spotted two broken boughs arranged in a cross, which indicated where the archers were in place.

At that same moment, a scouting party of a dozen Saxons on horseback emerged from the trees at the other end of the clearing. They saw the women of the First Athena galloping directly for them. With a jubilant war cry, they drew their weapons and charged.

Ursula immediately saw the dilemma facing Faustina. If she let fly a volley of arrows to fend off the small scouting party, the main force of Saxons would be alerted to the trap. There was nothing she—or anyone—could do.

Upon recognizing Pinnosa, the scouts let out a loud, guttural cry of, "Kill Pinnosa!"

Pinnosa and two of Faustina's officers were about thirty lengths ahead of the rest, apart from Brittola, who was on her own in the middle between them and the main group. Ursula was back in the pack with Martha and Cordula immediately behind her. They were already galloping at full speed. She couldn't close the gap. As she watched, the Saxons converged on the three front women, yelling at the tops of their voices as they went in for the kill.

Both of Faustina's officers were felled as soon as the Saxons made contact. Their horses shied and ran off, leaving Pinnosa completely exposed to attack. She discarded her shield and drew both her swords. She was matching the yells of the men with her own great war cry, when one of the Saxons managed to duck beneath her wide side-swipes to hack at her thigh with his sword. His blade opened a terrifyingly long and gaping wound. Pinnosa arched in pain and dropped her long sword. As she did so, a second scout wielding a broad axe scored a deadly blow in the middle of her back. It knocked her to the ground where she lay on her side, motionless.

Brittola—screaming in wild fury and leaping from her horse—rushed to Pinnosa's side. She staved off the enemy's blows with her shield, and did what she could to prevent her fallen friend from being cut to pieces by the Saxon blades. Artemis' kicked her hind hooves ferociously, as did Brittola's horse, Feather. If it had not been for the two beasts' combined frenzy, those few fateful seconds would have seen both women killed.

"Martha! Cordula!" Ursula shouted over her shoulder. "Grab Artemis and Feather!" Most of the Saxon scouts had veered to one side and were readying themselves for their attack on the rest of the women. Their leader was still harassing Brittola and the two riderless horses. "The rest of you . . . . Keep going! Don't fight—and don't stop!"

Ursula went straight for the leading Saxon and set upon him. He spun around, slashing at her with his long sword. She brought her blade up in defense, barely managing to deflect the blow away from her head. As the weapons clashed, her arm was badly jarred. She could feel her grip weaken. Ursula knew she couldn't deflect another heavy strike. She could see he was about to hack at her again, aiming for her thigh as he had done with Pinnosa.

Just at that moment, Swift, sensing her mistress' danger, neighed loudly and sank her teeth deep into the Saxon horse's neck. The mount reared and, with blood streaming from its wound, shied away, out of control.

Ursula leaped down to Pinnosa's side. The rest of the women were obeying her order and riding past, but she could already hear the war cries of the main group of Saxons as they bore down upon them. Pinnosa was bleeding badly and barely conscious.

"Go," Pinnosa said feebly. "Go. I can't move. You, too," she said to Artemis, who was refusing to budge, despite Martha's best efforts. "Go." She waved her hand and the great horse finally responded. "All of you. Go now."

"Brittola!" Ursula cried, realizing the only course of action that was possible with the Saxons less than fifty lengths away. "Get onto Swift!"

"But what about Pinnosa?"

"Do as I say—now!" Ursula grabbed Pinnosa's shield, which was lying nearby, and laid it over the lower half of her friend's body. Brittola's shield was too torn to be of any use, so she laid her own over her upper half. "The arrows will start any moment now. Lie still!"

She jumped up onto Swift behind Brittola, grabbed the reins and urged the strong horse to fly.

The Saxons were only five lengths from trampling Pinnosa to death, when the first, massive volley of a thousand arrows rained down. Ursula needn't have bothered with the shields. The First Athena had trained well and all the arrows landed in the thick of the enemy pack.

V

"It's getting late," Ursula said, dabbing a wet cloth gently on Pinnosa's brow. The Physic had said it was too soon to tell whether the gash in her leg would cripple her. Fortunately, the cut was clean and there was no danger of losing the limb. Her rain-sodden woolen cloak had prevented the axe from doing too much damage. The wound was only skin-deep. But, there was a problem more serious than her wounds. A terrible fever had gripped her while she was being transported to Lindum. The Physic worried that it would consume her if it did not abate soon and allow her to drink.

Ursula turned to face the others who were sitting on the opposite bunk. "Please go. All of you. I'll stay with her for now."

"But Ursula—" Brittola began, then shivered. They were all still in their soaked uniforms, having stayed by Pinnosa's side in the hope that she would come around. Only Ursula was warm and dry, having been tended to by Oleander, who had wrapped her in a clean toga as soon as she entered the Palace.

"That's an *order*, Brittola," Ursula snapped. "Get out of those wet clothes, have a hot bath and sleep." They were about to rise when she added as an afterthought, "Cordula. Could you relieve me at midnight?"

"Of course," Cordula replied, standing up to lead the others out. "Come on everyone. What good will we be to Pinnosa if we fall too ill to take care of her?"

They rose and reluctantly exited the room. Brittola was the last to depart. As she reached the door she whispered to Ursula, "Don't let her die! You won't let her die, will you?" She was close to tears.

Ursula gave her a reassuring look. "Don't worry. I'll make sure she gets well." She indicated the door. "Now go."

Brittola left, closing the door behind her. Her voice came back from the corridor loud and clear, "Get well, Pinnosa! God is with you! He won't let you die! You have work to do!"

Ursula managed a faint smile as she heard the others 'shush' Brittola and lead her away down the echoing passage. Within a few moments the small chamber on the third floor of the Palace was absolutely silent. Only the occasional murmur of the wounded Commander punctuated the gentle hiss of the oil lamps.

Ursula reached for the cup of medicinal wine and lifted Pinnosa's head to try once more to make her drink. The fluid went in between her lips, but she was still too delirious to swallow. It trickled out the side of her mouth and down her neck. Ursula tried again and again. On the fifth try she muttered, "Drink. Drink. In God's Will, *drink!*" But still the wine wouldn't go down.

She put the cup aside, grabbed Pinnosa's hands and started rubbing them hard, desperately trying to break the fever and bring her friend back from the brink.

"Come on, Pinnosa. I know you can hear me. Wake up." No response. She slapped her gently across her face. "In God's name—*wake up!*" She slapped her again, a little harder, and then pulled her forward so that she could speak into her ear. "Pinnosa, I know you can hear me. You have got to wake up and take some drink, otherwise . . . ." She gripped her shoulders tight and shook her. "Otherwise . . . . Oh!" She flung Pinnosa back onto the bunk, stood up and stared at her in utter exasperation.

Pinnosa's head had rolled to one side. She was breathing hard.

Crazed with desperation, Ursula paced up and down, pleading with God to release Pinnosa from her torment. After a while, she calmed down, returned to her stool by the bedside and bent forward to retrieve the discarded wine. Tearing off a small piece of bedding, she soaked it in the wine and poked the dripping cloth into Pinnosa's mouth.

"Come on, old friend," she said gently. "It's Ursula, here. The others have gone. It's just you and me. I know you can hear me. You've got to fight this fever just as if it were a Saxon raider. You have to fight it! Please." She felt herself starting to cry, "Please . . . ."

There was still no response. She stood up again and resumed her pacing. "Oh, dear God! What *is* this life we're leading? Oh yes, it's taking us on some big adventures—that's certain . . . yet . . . every step we take toward glory seems to be a step further away from the very thing we're fighting for . . . further away from home."

She looked at her friend. "Where is your home, Pinnosa? You don't have a home any more." She looked away. "And what of my home? Where is that I wonder?" She went over to the room's only window, which was small and overlooked the dark street below. It was a cloudy, moonless night. There was nothing to see apart from shadows.

"All I know is that my home is in Contans' eyes," she said quietly. "In his eyes . . ." she paused, "wherever they are."

She rushed back to the bed and grabbed her friend's hands again. "Only in your eyes, I see hope, Pinnosa. Oh, Pinnosa! Don't die! Please don't die!" Ursula couldn't prevent herself from weeping any longer. She collapsed onto Pinnosa's lap as wave after wave of sobs engulfed her. "I can't do it without you, Pinnosa. I can't do it. You are my strength. You are my hope."

"Ugh. What a terrible taste," Pinnosa said hoarsely. She hacked a dry cough.

"Pinnosa?" Ursula sat up in amazement.

"The Saxons. What's happened to the Saxons?"

"Forget the Saxons." Ursula pulled herself together. "We'll take care of them. You concentrate on getting yourself back on your feet and re-building your strength. Here, sit up and take some of this wine. It's good for you."

"Ugh! It's foul stuff. I'd rather grapple with a Saxon than drink that witch's brew."

VI

The heavy *clack, clack* of the approaching Commanders' sandals' hobnails, the rattle of their weapons, and the clatter of their armor reverberated throughout the Great Hall in the Imperial Palace long before they came into view. Not all the Commanders had been summoned—only those of royal blood: Ursula, Julia and Faustina, as well as Cordula, whose mother, Sorcha, had been Ursula's mother, Rabacie's younger sister.

As the four royal Commanders entered, they saw the three Kings were seated at a long, broad table. Deonotus beckoned them to take a seat opposite. It was Lughnasadh, the start of the harvest season, and, in true Britannic tradition, they were all wearing 'corn crowns' made from ears of unripe corn and barley—even Julia, who was the most Roman of those present.

"What news of Pinnosa?" Deonotus asked as the women took off their swords and made themselves comfortable.

"She's doing well, Father," Ursula replied. "She's already walking unaided, and keen to get back in the saddle."

"The attendants daren't leave her for a moment," Cordula added. "Not because she's weak—because she's too strong for her own good."

The women smiled at Cordula's quip, as did Deonotus. Regulus and Aurelius, however, remained serious. There was something in their demeanor that put the Commanders on their guard.

"Too strong for her own good, eh?" Deonotus' smile froze. "I fear the same might be said about the Athenas."

"What do you mean, Father?" Ursula asked quietly.

Deonotus looked at Regulus and Aurelius. They nodded, indicating he should continue.

"We have come to a decision about the Athenas—an important decision—and that is why you are here." Deonotus's tone was grim.

Julia and Faustina shared looks of alarm with Cordula.

Outwardly, Ursula showed no emotion, but inside her fears raced to the fore, plunging her emotions into turmoil. *Please don't disband the Legion. It is the only hope I have—the only hope of ever—*

"If the numbers are getting too big, we can—" Julia began.

Deonotus raised his hand for silence. He took his eyes from his daughter to look at Julia and give her a reassuring smile.

"The numbers are *not* too big." He returned his gaze very deliberately to Ursula and looked at her intently. "And it is not our intention to disband it, either."

Ursula sighed with relief.

"Your successful campaigns against the Saxons have more than proven your ability to organize—and execute—complex military maneuvers against a well-organized enemy. The Athenas can never be too strong in that regard. But . . . ." Deonotus paused. He was clearly finding it difficult to continue.

Regulus cleared his throat and made ready to speak.

Deonotus rallied his thoughts and pressed on. "What I'm trying to say is that we think the situation both here—and in Galliae—is deteriorating . . . I mean the plight of the Province is getting such that . . . . Not that the Athenas aren't helping. Far from it! They're making all the difference. But then that's one of the reasons. It's just that—"

"Let's keep this simple, shall we old friend?" Aurelius gently placed his hand on Deonotus's shoulder. "For a whole host of reasons, we think the time has come for Constantine and Constans to return to Britannia."

Deonotus nodded in agreement.

Aurelius continued, "But, persuading them to abandon their mission won't be easy."

Deonotus nodded again.

"There is only one way it can be done. That is for the First Athena to embark upon its Great Expedition."

"You mean . . . we're to . . . ." Now it was Ursula who struggled to find the right words. She looked around at the others and instinctively clasped Cordula's hand.

"Yes, my dear," Deonotus said with a smile. "It's time to prepare for the Wedding of the Legions!"

VII

Despite Ursula's eagerness to embark on their mission, it proved impossible until the following spring. This was for several reasons. A fresh wave of Saxon invasions prolonged the campaign in the east and it was several weeks before the last of the raiders could be rounded up. By the time they returned to the Holy Isle, there wasn't enough of the campaign season left for them to plan and carry out such a large scale and elaborate expedition. The extended campaign in the east also meant that the recruitment and training of the Athenas fell far behind schedule. By the end of the summer the Second was two thousand under its required strength. The First only numbered fifteen thousand—of which three thousand had barely started their basic training. Another very important reason for delaying the mission was that Pinnosa remained in Lindum, recuperating. Embarking on the Great Expedition without her was unthinkable.

In addition to all these setbacks, they discovered that there weren't enough galleys left on the Britannia side of the Channel to transport the women across. Even after recommissioning several old craft that had not been used for many years—including an immense one-hundred-oar vessel that had been moored at Eboracum for as long as Aurelius could remember—the expedition was still five galleys short. This was a major problem that would take the entire winter to resolve. They had no choice other than to row three of the Maridunum galleys around the coast to the crossing point at Dubris, and then wait for two new galleys to be completed at Durobrivae on the River Medway.

"I don't know what the bloody world's bleedin' coming to." They all laughed at Martha's imitation of an old man at the boat yards.

It was the evening before Samhain, the festival to mark the end of the summer, and the Commanders of the First and Second Athenas were assembled on the Holy Isle to hold their final meeting before the Legions disbanded for the winter.

Martha had just returned from the shipyard at Durobrivae. She was recounting an entertaining conversation she'd had with an old shipwright. He had been entrusted with the task of adding a third position to each of the oar benches and she had met him while inspecting the hulls on their slipways. Martha mimicked his rustic, southern accent perfectly.

"I thought 'womanizing' was what the bloody apprentices did on their bleedin' trips to Londinium! I never thought it'd mean changing bloody war galley benches so that three wenches—er, 'scuse the expression, Mistress—'ladies' could work the bleedin' oars! I don't know what the world's bleedin' coming to, honestly I don't!"

She acted out the shipwright hitting himself on the thumb with his mallet. "Ow! Bloody shi—'scuse me, Mistress—Bloody! bleedin'—I hit me Bloody! Bleedin'—" She hopped about, feigning pain and repeating, 'Bloody, bleedin'' as she did so. The officers laughed so much, Martha repeated it several times.

"I mean to say, Mistress," she finally continued. "An army of women with women bleedin' Commanders! With all due respect, Mistress—what bleedin' next? Women bloody shipwrights? Do you know something Mistress? My Rachel! She wanted to join your bleedin' lot! What's it called? The First Athletic or some bloody thing. Well, I said 'No!' didn't I? You ain't joining no bleedin' army of women! Your place is here, looking after your poor father and your three bleedin' brothers. There's no bloody way you're leaving us to join that bleedin' escapade. *No bloody way!*"

"I asked him what his Rachel did in the end, and do you know what he said?" Martha said, drawing the story to a close. The others—their laughter abating—looked at her questioningly. "He told me she had joined."

Three shrill horn blasts from outside the Officers' Tent interrupted their laughter. They rushed to the entrance. There, on the opposite river bank, silhouetted against the sunset, was the familiar form of Pinnosa on Artemis. She blew her horn again, this time allowing the note to linger. As she did so, the huge mare reared in greeting.

Cordula said with a chuckle, "A rider with a disabled leg could never have stayed on for such a move. She has to be fully recovered!"

"It looks like the new cavalry units will have a full winter training schedule after all," Ursula said with a broad smile.

VIII

The winter was an extraordinarily mild one. When Morgan arrived in Londinium shortly after Imbolg, the coming of the spring, he was amazed to find his native island ablaze with crocuses and primroses. There was fresh fish on the street stalls instead of salted. He even spotted one trader with several brace of lambs for sale—for a premium price.

As he entered the Great Hall in the Imperial Palace, he heard his beloved's voice.

"Morgan!" Cordula cried. The last time she had seen him was a year and a half earlier, and she had convinced herself she wouldn't see him again until well after the winter thaw and the mountain passes far to the south had opened.

Quickly he ran to her embrace, then stopped, aware that many eyes were upon him.

The three Kings and all the Commanders of the Athenas tried not to smile.

"The preparations for the Wedding of the Legions are complete." Morgan had to pause while they all applauded his announcement. "Constantine has asked me to relay his heartfelt and profound support for the Great Expedition, and to make a point of telling the leaders of not 'the First Athena' but of 'the Women' that 'the Men' eagerly await them. Furthermore, he has sent messages throughout all Rome, both East and West, that Constans Caesar is about to gain a beautiful, royal bride and that the House of Constantine the Third will soon be blessed with heirs!" The accompanying round of applause was meant for Ursula, who smiled in reply. She hid the tingle of fear she felt at the thought of the effect such announcements might be having in certain dark quarters of the Continent.

"I, personally, relayed the plans to Constans," Morgan continued. "And, I bear a letter to the Empress-to-be." He produced a parchment from his bag, handed it to Ursula and bowed. Her courteous return bow barely concealed her excitement. "He says that he and his men are now doubly eager to complete their mission in Hispania so that they can be ready and waiting for their spring brides in Arelate. 'What mountains wouldn't we traverse?' he proclaims, 'What seas wouldn't we cross? What battles wouldn't we fight, to be at one with our heroic, Britannic women. To know the warm embrace of Home?'"

While he was relaying Constans's message, Morgan had been unable to prevent himself from addressing it to Cordula. Her eyes filled with tears and her lips quivered as she fought to contain her emotions and retain her composure. During the warm round of applause that followed his recital, Ursula gave her a gentle hug. It helped Cordula immensely to sense that her cousin was also having difficulties holding her sobs in check.

IX

My Dearest Love,

I am writing this in haste as Morgan needs to leave soon if he is to take full advantage of the night in avoiding our pursuers. I can't give you details of our mission in case this finds itself in the wrong hands. Similarly, I won't discuss the arrangements for our wedding except to say, Have no fear. I'll be there!

I'm so proud of you and the inspired work you are doing with the valiant women of the First and Second Athenas to safeguard the Province while we are detained with this messy business. How I envy the Saxons who have the honor of seeing you all in action! Take care, my love, as you embark on these campaigns. Promise me you won't put your personal safety at risk. Let Pinnosa lead the assaults. She is far more formidable in the fray than you. What enemy would not quiver at the knees upon witnessing her terrifying onslaught?

I assure you that it is the firm resolve of all the men under my command to relieve the Athenas as soon as possible—not only because we all wish to be home with our families and friends—but also because of the shame we feel at not being able to protect Britannia ourselves. Finally, my love, the thought of being with you again, of looking into your eyes, of listening to your voice, is all I live for. Every day that we are apart is a day away from home, and a day wasted.

All the love in my heart,
Your Constans.

Ursula held the letter to her chest—overwhelmed with her need for Constans. Suddenly, she recalled her shock at seeing Morgan's dark, lined, weather-worn complexion the moment he walked into view. Had he been roasted by the hot southern climes, or perhaps hardened by the grueling ordeals he's been through? *Goodness, there's no boy left in him!*

She glanced at her reflection in a nearby plate of polished silver and was shocked to see how she, too, had changed. *But then I imagine we've all grown—matured—a great deal as a result of these . . . these ceaseless campaign seasons. I wonder whether Constans has changed, too? Will I even recognize him? Will he recognize me?*

X

On Alban Eiler, the streets of Londinium were overflowing with people. Tens of thousands from all over Britannia had come to witness the departure parade of the First Athena and their splendor in full dress uniform. The entire Legion was due to pass through the heart of the city and over the huge bridge, which crossed the Tamesis in front of the Imperial Palace. Then they would be heading out of the city eastward, along Watling Street—the road to the Channel ports—where over eighty galleys were waiting for them. The river, too, was crowded with craft from far afield, all crammed with onlookers eager to enjoy the glorious spectacle and hoping for a glimpse of the Commanders.

The main body of the Legion was led on its march by Julia, Faustina and Baetica. Ursula, Pinnosa and the other Corinium officers weren't leaving until the following day with the women of the Vanguard in two new galleys that had just arrived from Durobrivae. Those ships were moored immediately in front of the Imperial Palace by the bridge. They each looked magnificent, draped prow to stern in streamers of the Legion's colors.

As cohort after cohort paraded past, the noise from the crowd in the Forum and adjacent streets was deafening. The air was full of drum rolls and the blasts and toots of countless horns, pipes and whistles. Ursula and the other Vanguard Commanders, who were with the royal assemblage on the steps to the Basilica, had never imagined that such a cacophony of sound was possible.

The march past took almost the entire morning. By the time Julia and Faustina's standards finally came into view, Ursula and the others' arms ached from so much from saluting.

Ursula was just about to cheer her fellow princesses when suddenly the air was filled with flocks of homing pigeons and doves released from the buildings surrounding the Forum. The flap of their beating wings added to the noise of the crowd.

Aurelius and Regulus exchanged congratulatory smiles.

"That was a nice touch," Ursula shouted to Cordula, waving to the Kings in acknowledgement of their surprise 'farewell' gesture to their daughters.

Julia and Faustina looked splendid in their dress uniforms. They completed their formal salute to the royal party and rode past, waving their helmets to the crowd as they went. As they exited the Forum down the short street, which led to the great bridge, the Vanguard Commanders and the royal ensemble mounted their horses and followed them.

The Royal Escort stopped on the bridge and, at a signal from De-onotus, a hundred horns on the roof of the Imperial Palace sounded a fanfare to announce the Commanders' departure. Julia and Faustina gave their final salute and left the bridge. As they did so, Aurelius gave another signal. Three thousand hunting hounds on the southern bank of the Tamesis were un-muzzled and allowed to howl. The noise reverberated the entire length of the city's waterfront and echoed deep into the metropolis' streets.

Julia and Faustina, however, had also arranged their own farewell. Just as the Commanders reached the point in Watling Street where they knew they would be disappearing from view, from special pens constructed amongst the trees sprang four successive waves of geese and swans. Hundreds of birds, each dyed a color of the First Athena, took to the skies. The first wave was blue, the second red, the third green and the fourth orange.

XI

"Ursula, my dear?" King Deonotus called to the figure on the balcony.

Ursula heard him, but didn't turn immediately. She didn't want to hurry in to the Farewell Feast. She looked down at the two large galleys moored below. Early the following morning, they would be taking her and the others to meet up with the rest of the fleet—and away from her home.

Her father paused a moment, watching her. The intense colors of the setting sun made her white toga look almost purple. Her long, blond hair, which was unbraided for once, flew out behind her in the fresh spring evening breeze like a pennant.

She turned to face him. He could see that she was crying. "What's the matter my dear? Are you nervous?" he said gently, putting his arm around her.

"Not nervous, Father . . ." She made an effort to stop crying and pulled herself up straight. "Terrified!" She grabbed his arm. "I'm terrified of what we're attempting. I'm terrified of not succeeding in our mission. I'm terrified of all that the Continent has in store for us. But most of all, Father, I'm terrified of not seeing you again and of never returning home. What if we suffer the same curse as all the other Britannic armies that have left the safety of this beloved Province, never to return?"

The old King did not say anything. He clasped his arms around her shoulders as tightly as he could, doing his best to keep his own tears in check. Then, slowly, he stepped back so that he could look at her.

"We haven't been completely honest with each other, have we? We've never discussed the real reason why you're doing all this. You're not Pinnosa. You are not the scourge of all barbarians. And deep in your heart you are not undertaking the Great Expedition for the benefit of Britannia." He paused and lifted up her chin so that he could look into her eyes. "You simply want to be with Constans."

She clenched her quivering lips and nodded.

"All that you've suffered these past campaign seasons—and all the magnificent things you've achieved—it's all been because you want to be back in his arms."

"Oh, Father, why couldn't I be happy to remain here and be patient, like Mother was while you were away. Why couldn't I be content to stay home and wait—and hope."

"But you *are* like your mother, my dear. Exactly like her. Like you, she had to be active. Like you, she had to be working her destiny and not having it worked for her by circumstance. Oh, she waited for me, all right. But at the same time, she worked with Constantine and others to shore up the Kingdom and make sure I had a secure home to come back to. And you? You're just the same. It's only the circumstances that are different. Her fight was to keep her family and her home. Your fight is to have them."

"But my home is here with you."

"No, my dear. Your home is somewhere far to the south—somewhere deep in Galliae or Hispania. When you depart tomorrow, you won't be leaving home . . . you'll be heading home."

"Oh, Father!" she cried and hugged him once more.

"Come now, my dear. The others are waiting." He gently led her inside. "By the way, how is your Latin? Did you have those extra lessons with Bishop Patroclus?"

She laughed. "Yes, I did, but I'm not sure how much use '*Voluntatem Dei iudicare Diaboli est*'—God's Will is for the Devil to judge—is going to be in getting us safely to Arelate."

As they left the balcony arm in arm, a strong gust of wind blew through the moorings below. The furled sails of the galleys rattled against their masts, and the streamers of the First Athena flapped frantically, like fish caught is a shallow stream trying to avoid the gaze of a heron.

XII

The preparations for the departure began soon after dawn. The horses were led down to the vessels from their stables at the rear of the Imperial Palace. In the stern of each galley, below the main deck, were special stalls, where up to thirty beasts could be strapped tight in harness frames. Artemis was the first to be led across the ramp onto the deck. She had never been on a vessel before. The unfamiliar noises and smells, plus the gentle rocking of the galley, made her nervous. As she was being positioned onto the loading platform, she flattened her ears and flared her nostrils. She struggled and kicked. Then, Swift, who was directly behind her, stepped forward and nuzzled her on the back, which calmed Artemis down enough for the platform to be lowered.

The junior officers and first rowing crews came next, the former to make a final check of all the provisions and equipment and the latter to settle into position and prepare the oars. Each galley had fifty oars, twenty-five on each side. The new fittings allowed three women per oar, which meant that a rowing crew numbered one hundred and fifty. Each galley had two rowing crews, which would rotate at hourly intervals.

The Tamesis bristled with onlookers eager to see the Vanguard depart on their highly decorated and splendid new galleys. Along both banks and across the great bridge, the pressure of the crowd was so great that some people fell into the water. The river itself was full of craft of every description, from the lavish barges of the nobility to the simple skiffs of the local fishermen.

As soon as the rowers were in position, the rest of the Vanguard boarded. Their appearance from the Guardhouse in full dress uniform roused a great cheer from the crowd. As they took up their ceremonial positions on deck, their armor and weapons reflecting the dawn's clear light, the cheers were even louder, joined by the now familiar accompaniment of drum rolls and whistles.

A great fanfare of trumpets and horns sounded from the roof of the Imperial Palace, heralding the departure of the Commanders. The first to appear was Ursula, with Deonotus by her side. She was in full dress uniform, and he was wearing his formal Royal Robes of Court. The multitude roared with excitement as she walked slowly to the leading galley, waving as she went.

Behind them came Pinnosa. She was by herself, striding toward the second galley, which was under her command. She acknowledged the crowd's cheers by unsheathing her long sword and brandishing it above her head, waving it slowly to and fro in great arcs.

Then, escorted by Regulus and Aurelius, came Cordula and Brittola, both of whom were joining Ursula on the first galley. Even though she joined Cordula in waving to the crowd, Brittola was clearly embarrassed by the enthusiastic welcome. The people knew the Commanders by name and the frenzied cries of 'Ursula,' 'Pinnosa,' 'Cordula' and 'Brittola' built up into a chant which crescendoed as Martha and Saula appeared.

Just as they were about to board Pinnosa's galley, the two friends paused at the end of the ramp. Saula pulled out some small pipes from under her cloak and accompanied Martha, who danced a little jig performed by West Country sailors for good luck before a voyage. When they finished, they bowed to acknowledge the crowd's warm round of applause before turning to march up the ramp, side by side.

Like the departure of the main body of the Legion the day before, there were no formal speeches. This time there were no surprise farewell gestures either. The officers on Ursula's galley simply said their final good-byes to the Kings, who then returned to the shore.

As Deonotus was about to leave, he took his daughter by the hand one last time, kissed her on both cheeks and said, "God goes with you my dear. Remember that I shall be praying to Him every day for your safe and speedy return."

She squeezed his hand tightly and kissed him on both cheeks. "Whatever my personal reasons are for doing this . . . remember, Father, we—the First Athena—are doing it for you, and for all Britannia. So, when you pray, pray for us all . . . including yourself."

He smiled, released her hand, and walked slowly down the boarding ramp.

As he did so, she felt an overpowering surge of her old fear. It made her tremble and she had to grab the galley rail, close her eyes and take two or three deep breaths before she could turn round to face her officers and crew. The instant she saw Cordula and Brittola looking expectantly at her, she felt better.

Ursula and Pinnosa gave the orders for the ramps to be removed from their respective vessels. The broad green sails unfurled in the breeze. Once the mooring ropes were untied, the tempo drums started beating. The oars creaked. Bystanders could hear the rowers grunting as they began the arduous task of getting the giant craft underway. The two huge galleys, in their colorful splendor, pulled away from the waterfront and slowly headed out into the main stream of the river.

Up on deck, the officers, including the Commanders, and the Ceremonial Guard all stood to attention. They maintained their formal salutes until they were well downstream and the great city of Londinium receded into the distance.

XIII

With a full wind in their sails they made good speed. By mid-afternoon they were already well into the broader waters of the estuary. They had just completed the seventh crew change when, suddenly, the lookout aboard Ursula's galley raised the alarm. As soon as Ursula and Cordula reached the prow they could see several large skiffs coming at them from the marshlands off the north shore.

"Pirates!" Cordula exclaimed.

Ursula shook her head. "Ever since Constantine's departure and the loss of navy patrols, the pirates have had free reign."

"So I've heard," Cordula said grimly. "Those shallow inlets on the north shore are perfect havens for them." She pointed to the fast-moving, flat-bottomed boats. "Look at all those oars! There are twenty to each skiff—that means at least forty fighting men."

"They don't usually prey on water traffic until harvest season. Perhaps this is an instance of the First Athena's fame acting as a bait for trouble," Ursula said as the alarm horn started to sound. She counted ten of the skiffs emerging from behind a long sand bar. Then, she noticed something curious on the leading skiffs. "Can you see those faint spirals of smoke on the bows of the three in front?"

"Yes. I wonder what that is . . . ." Cordula replied, shading her eyes and squinting.

"It'll be hot bitumen for fire arrows." Ursula's voice was full of alarm. "They use them to cause panic and bring the vessel to a halt." She spun around, and shouted orders, "Bring down the sails! Remove all flammables from the deck!" Then she rushed to the stern, where Brittola was on watch, to see whether Pinnosa was doing the same.

About five hundred cubits behind them, Pinnosa's crew were also lowering the sails and clearing the decks.

"They're signaling with their semaphore flags," Brittola reported. "Pinnosa wants us to stay on course. We're to slow down a little and keep our standards flying so that we draw the attack. She's going to veer around on our starboard. Then she'll come across our bow and meet them head on."

"Tell her we'll comply."

"Wait. Saula hasn't finished. She also says 'This - may - not - be - easy,'" Brittola said, smiling.

Ursula frowned. "Tell Saula to limit her messages to those given to her."

"But she was only—"

"No 'buts,' Brittola," Ursula snapped. "We're about to go into battle. The only messages to be transmitted are those essential to ensure survival and victory."

Brittola looked shocked at the sharpness of the rebuke. She had never seen Ursula like this.

"Now, do as I say. That's an order!"

XIV

Pinnosa had barely gotten her galley into position when the leading pirate skiff was upon the lead Athenian ship. Just as Ursula had predicted, the attack began with flaming arrows. Most of the first volley fell short, plummeting into the water and sending up huge plumes of steam. Three stuck into the galley's side, and one landed on the deck. The crew formed a bucket line, first filling the leather buckets with seawater, hauling them up the sides and passing them along until they could reach the flames.

A couple of the crackling missiles hissed their way in through the oar holes. Flames erupted in the close quarters of the rowing compartment. The women screamed and tried to get away from the fire, upending the benches and crowding the passageway to get out.

Ursula took charge of the situation, helping evacuate the rowers, then organizing the bucket lines to put out the fire. As soon as things were in hand she raced back to the prow to watch Pinnosa's counter-attack.

Her eyes widened as she saw Pinnosa's ship cut so closely across their bow, that three oars on her left side were snapped off. Almost immediately, Pinnosa met the clutch of pirate skiffs at full speed. Her prow rammed neatly into the center of a leading one with a steaming vat, lifting it completely out of the water. Men tumbled and boiling bitumen poured everywhere before the craft snapped in two and fragmented in Pinnosa's wake.

A handful of men managed to gain a purchase on the galley's oars and started scrambling up them. A unit of Martha's archers saw to it that none of them succeeded in reaching the sides.

While all eyes were looking forward, a heavy volley of burning arrows sizzled onto the deck. Two grappling hooks landed and bit into the planking. A second skiff had come around behind the starboard oars and managed to approach the galley.

Pinnosa rushed to the stern. Using her long shield to protect herself against the relentless hail of arrows, she hacked at the grappling lines with her sword. She was still trying to cut the second line, when yet another skiff maneuvered itself close to the galley's stern, joining the attack. The barrage of missiles intensified greatly. A third grappling hook took hold on the deck. The threat of boarding seemed imminent.

"*Archers!*" Pinnosa shouted over her shoulder as she ducked to avoid another salvo, losing her helmet as she did so. "Archers! For God's sake keep me covered!"

Martha's unit raced into position and let fly. Pinnosa climbed over the rail. With her sword and shield held high, she leaped from the galley's side. For a moment, she seemed to fill the air like some fearsome specter of a warrior of old; her cloak billowing wildly, her bright, red hair flowing free in the wind. Then she plummeted down on to the prow of the skiff below, landing behind the vat of steaming bitumen. Before the pirates could respond, she kicked the cauldron from its mountings, sending a crackling tongue of flames hissing along the entire length of the skiff. The only way the men could avoid being burned alive was to dive into the water. Within moments the skiff was abandoned and ablaze.

Then she leaped across onto another skiff, which had drawn alongside. This one had no vat of bitumen. Her only advantage was the narrowness of the prow, limiting her attackers to attacking one at a time. Martha's archers kept the pirates pinned down. In between each volley, one of the louts leaped up, yelping a war cry and charged Pinnosa. One brandished a huge, double-bladed axe, another a long sword. Pinnosa matched their brute strength with disciplined and measured force and dispatched four of them before they were beaten.

As soon as she sensed their submission, she reached for the last of the grappling lines, grabbed hold of it and cut it. The galley was still moving at speed. As soon as the rope was severed, she was yanked into the water. To everyone watching, Pinnosa seemed to stay under the water for what seemed an eternity. Martha and three of her archers, heaving with all their might, eventually managed to pull her clear of the deep and back to the safety of the galley.

XV

"You had absolutely no right to put your life in danger like that!" Ursula paced the end of a long wooden jetty where they'd moored for the night. They were on the southern shore of the Tamesis estuary, a place that usually only saw salt barges.

The two Commanders were alone. Martha and Brittola were supervising the camp arrangements inland. Cordula and Saula had taken the early watch on board their respective vessels. The sun had not long set and the sky was a great panoply of the last of the grand summer sunsets with its vivid reds, purples, blues, oranges, yellows and silvers. A strong southerly breeze made their cloaks flap. "Under normal circumstances an officer of your rank would be decommissioned and thrown out of the Legion for such irresponsible behavior," she shouted angrily. "What in God's name did you think you were doing?"

"'Under normal circumstances?'" Pinnosa snapped, "Under normal circumstances you and I would be sitting around a warm fire somewhere in the West Country eating pheasant and drinking wine—*not* leading twenty thousand young women to the far reaches of another Province so that they can get married and become pregnant."

Ursula took a deep breath and said more quietly, "You're right. These are not normal circumstances. But, they are *our* circumstances. We are the commanding officers of a large army. Above all else, we are responsible for our women. What you did out there put the entire expedition at risk just for the sake of your . . . your idiotic, suicidal pursuit of glory."

Pinnosa stepped closer and said, "Even though we were moving at full speed, they somehow managed to come around behind us and attach grappling hooks. We were in grave peril. If just one boatload of those pirates had boarded, we would have suffered severe casualties before we could have subdued them. What is more, one boatload would have only been the first. If hand-to-hand fighting had started, we would have slowed down, and then they would have all been upon us, like carrion for the kill. The moment those first grappling hooks took hold, I saw the very real danger of my entire crew being lost." She paused and shivered again at the memory. "I saw a chance to save the situation. Things were happening fast. I had to take the risk . . . ." She shrugged. "It worked."

"You're obsessed with following your father!" Ursula exclaimed, her face becoming red with anger.

"And *you* are obsessed with following your Constans!" Pinnosa snapped. "What's more, you're terrified of where you might be leading the women as you do so!"

Ursula spun around in exasperation. She looked out over the estuary. For a long moment there was silence as they both suffered the torment of the other's cruel words.

Pinnosa remained motionless, staring at Ursula's back. After a while, she moved to stand by her side. They stared out at the cold, gray expanse of water.

Although Ursula did not turn, she heaved a sigh. They both knew the anger had passed. "I want you to promise me that you won't put yourself in such danger again," Ursula said quietly. "The entire expedition would have to be called off if you weren't with us to lead the cavalry."

"I promise," Pinnosa replied in a voice that was equally as subdued. "In return, I want you to promise not to use my father against me again. It hurts all the more coming from you."

"I . . . I'm sorry. The cavalry aren't the only ones who need you, you know."

"I know."

They finally turned and hugged each other. Even though it was a clumsy hug—their cloaks got in the way and their helmet plumage became entangled—they held each other tightly for what seemed an eternity before they pulled apart. Then, they walked back to the galleys, side by side.

"Whatever made you think of leaping down off the galley like that?" Ursula said teasingly. "I was sure you were going to end up in the water."

"I *did* end up in the water. Now I know why Neptune never wears body armor. It's ten times as heavy in water—especially *cold* water!"

As they headed back to their galleys, linked arm in arm, they turned their backs on the distant glow. Had they been looking, they would have seen a huge bank of billowing dark clouds scud along the horizon and smother the final shimmers of sunset.

XVI

Three days later the main fleet of galleys were to assemble beneath and between the two great lighthouses built high upon the great white cliffs—the Pharos of Dubris—where they were to be joined by Ursula and Pinnosa's vessels, coming from Rutupiae to the north.

Ursula and Pinnosa arrived in Rutupiae the day before, giving Pinnosa enough time to find replacement oars for the ones she had lost in the pirate skirmish. She also had hasty repairs made to an oar mounting, which had been damaged in the entanglement. Soon after dawn they set off to cross the Channel.

The sky was clear and conditions were perfect for the galleys with calm seas and a mild breeze from the southwest. They were still well to the north of the South Foreland, where the coastline turned westward into Dubris waters, when the lookouts spotted a host of green sails out to sea. It was the main fleet, but they were further north than planned. That meant the crossing to Gesoriacum would take longer than anticipated. This alarmed Ursula and the other Commanders of the Vanguard at first, but then, as they cleared the Foreland and entered the open seas of the Channel, they realized what had happened. The wind had changed direction, and the same strong gusts from the southeast that had filled the sails of the main fleet and pushed them northward, began to buffet against their own vessels.

The Grand Fleet was an awe-inspiring sight with fifty full-sized war galleys and over thirty lesser supply craft. Even Ursula was astonished at the sheer size of the force assembled on the water. As their galleys drew closer to the main fleet, it looked as if the Channel was filled with vessels. Each one bore pennants in the bright colors of their First Athena unit. Ursula and Pinnosa took their crafts through the heart of the fleet in order to take up their position in the van with Julia and Faustina. As they passed each galley, the crews, with their freshly burnished armor and weapons glistening in the spring sunshine, let out a great cheer and raised their helmets in salute. Standing alone on the prow, returning the salutes, Ursula was so moved by their enthusiastic display of loyalty, she was nearly brought to tears. She had her own crew cheer in reply. Behind her, Pinnosa's women did the same.

The most inspiring and impressive sight, however, was Julia's gigantic, one hundred-oar galley. As it came into full view, towering above those around it, it dominated the rest of the fleet like a mother hen with her brood. When Ursula's galley approached, the three hundred women on deck in their Eboracum red cloaks let out such a resounding cheer of greeting it could be heard throughout the entire fleet.

During the long winter months in Londinium, the Commanders had spent many hours with two retired admirals meticulously studying every aspect of naval work, including fleet formations. It only took a brief exchange of semaphored messages for Ursula to establish which one she had decided to adopt. She directed the fleet to break into four flotillas. She commanded the Corinium galleys, taking the southernmost flank. Pinnosa led the Londinium flotilla, which had the largest number of war galleys, in the center. Faustina directed the smaller Lindum flotilla and took the northern flank. Julia managed the Eboracum regiment plus most of the supply galleys. Her group were to follow the other flotillas in a cluster, as opposed to their long, straight lines.

In order to get into formation, Faustina's galleys had to maneuver first and peel off to the north. Ursula's galleys then steered to the south. Separating the Londinium galleys from the supply vessels wasn't so straightforward, as it involved several of the large war galleys having to make huge circuits in order to allow the slower vessels the space to arrange themselves. The maneuvers took a long time to execute. It was while the Eboracum flotilla were in the process of heading back toward the Britannic coast in order to clear the Londinium galleys that the weather started to change.

The wind picked up and switched direction so that it was coming directly from the south. Ursula realized that in such conditions the sails were more of a hindrance than a help, so she had her flotilla strike them and switch to oars. She signaled for the rest of the fleet to do the same. Her command was relayed down the line to the rear, which was still within semaphore range. Within a few minutes she saw the Londinium vessels lowering their sails. She thought she could see the Eboracum vessels doing the same, but she wasn't certain, her galley was already too far away. She couldn't see the Lindum galleys at all.

By the time the Londinium and Eboracum flotillas had assembled in formation and the Grand Fleet was finally ready to embark upon its crossing, the sky was gray. Some dark and menacing clouds appeared on the southern horizon. More worryingly, the southerly wind was blowing in stronger and stronger gusts.

"Might it not be an idea to turn about and head for shelter in Rutupiae Bay?" Cordula asked tentatively. She and Brittola were standing behind Ursula, sharing anxious glances.

Ursula didn't reply at first. She stared at the distant clouds as if she was daring them to come any closer.

"Rutupiae Bay is only—" began Brittola.

"We've taken the entire morning to arrange ourselves in a formation set for Gesoriacum," Ursula interrupted without turning around. She looked up at a bright patch of sky overhead and squinted as she spoke. "It's a little after midday now. We'll be there before sunset, as long as this wind doesn't become fresher. It'd take us a long while to turn about. Rutupiae Bay is half the afternoon away." She looked out at the sea. "The swell doesn't seem to be getting any heavier. That could indicate that these gusts are just isolated ones, and those are harmless rain clouds . . . not storm clouds."

"I don't think it's worth the risk," Cordula said with more than a touch of anxiety in her voice. "Look at those clouds. They're moving fast. By my reckoning, we'll be under them shortly. That means we're going to be out in the middle of the Channel when we find out whether they're storm clouds or not. That's the worst possible place to get caught in a squall. I say we turn back."

"I agree," Brittola said. "There's not just a storm coming, I see a message in those clouds, too. It's a warning from God. He's saying 'don't come this way—not today.'"

"Messages from God are never so simple," Ursula said thoughtfully.

"We could head due east for the northern beaches of Galliae," Cordula suggested. "They're not too far away."

A junior officer approached them and saluted. "Message just received from Lady Pinnosa, Mistress."

"What is it?" Ursula asked, keeping her gaze fixed out to sea.

"It was difficult to read because of the swell. We missed some of it, but we managed to catch, 'Why wait for the wind?'"

"Thank you. That'll be all." She finally turned to face Cordula and Brittola. They could see her expression was grim with a determination fiercer than any they had seen before. "You both know full well what it means for us to have reached this point." She indicated the shore with a nod of her head. "The people of Britannia are all praying for the First Athena to succeed in its mission. We are the last hope the Province has left. I'll not disappoint them now by turning the Great Expedition around—just because of the weather." She paused and looked at each of them. Then she turned back to face the distant clouds. "The next stage of our mission is to cross to Gesoriacum, not to the northern beaches of Galliae. Gesoriacum is waiting for us with barracks and stables all prepared. After two days' rest there, the whole Legion will be refreshed and ready to commence their long march south. On the other hand, if we were to cross an area that was unprepared for our arrival, we would be risking a hostile reception. We would also be denying the women a much needed rest." She turned back to face them. "I know what Pinnosa is saying—'We know which way we want to go. Why wait for the wind to make up its mind?' My mind is made up. We shall pray those are simply rain clouds and not a storm. Proceed as planned.

"Yes, Mistress," Brittola couldn't hide the doubt and worry in her voice.

"And, Brittola," Ursula said with a sudden smile, "add at the end, 'This may not be easy.'"

XVII

They made good progress for quite a while, holding formation and putting a great deal of distance between themselves and the rapidly receding white cliffs of their homeland. In the middle of the afternoon the wind intensified, the sky darkened and the first squalls of rain started to beat down. Heavy sea swells made Ursula's galley judder fiercely, swaying from side to side. Ursula ordered all loose objects tied down securely and had the order relayed throughout the fleet. The signal captain reported that she was unsure it reached Faustina's flotilla as they had drifted north to the limit of signaling distance.

Soon, the full fury of the storm was upon them. Fearsome gusts of wind beat at them that could lift a woman off her feet and throw her across the deck if she wasn't holding tight. The driving rain became a wall of water. With the poor light, it became impossible to see further than the next galley in line. The sea became a tumultuous, heaving mass of waves that reared up to monstrous heights on all sides of the galley. They crashed down onto the deck like a god in rage, intent on destruction.

The fifth such mountain of water had just smothered the entire craft, when Brittola came struggling back to the prow from attempting to dispatch the order, 'Hold course,' to the galley behind. She was completely drenched—as were they all. Her long hair hung in wet flaps across her face like seaweed. "It's no good! We couldn't send the message!" she shouted "But we received one from Pinnosa just before the waves got too big!"

"What did she say?"

"'Hold course'!"

They were about to laugh when the prow plummeted into a huge trough. The sudden downward lurch threw Cordula hard against the rail. Ursula, who had been the only one holding on, fell to her knees. Brittola fell flat on her stomach, her arms and legs splayed; she was winded and unable to move. Ursula reached forward to help when the next wave hit.

XVIII

Ursula coughed out seawater and shouted, "Help! Someone come and help!" She struggled to maintain her grip as she dangled off the side of the galley. Her right arm and leg were hooked around two rail posts—and more importantly—her left hand gripped Brittola's calf, which was the only thing that kept the young Commander from plunging into the raging waters below. The pitch and roll of the vessel caused Brittola to alternately dangle in mid-air or smash, face first, into the craft's side.

"Keep still!" Ursula yelled to Brittola. "Don't struggle!"

Cordula clambered under the rail and reached as far over the side as far as she could, but to no avail. Brittola's other leg was well beyond her reach.

"Get a grappling hook! I can't hold her much longer!" Ursula cried.

Cordula disappeared.

Even though Ursula was straining as hard as she could to keep hold of Brittola, the violent movements of the vessel were too strong for her. Horribly, she felt her hand slipping down Brittola's leg.

Just as Ursula's grip slid to Brittola's ankle, Cordula reappeared. She dived beneath the rail, throwing her whole body over the side. She managed to grab Brittola's other ankle with both hands. As soon as Cordula had her in her grasp, the two junior officers who were holding onto Cordula's legs hauled both Cordula and Brittola up the galley sides.

Two more women grabbed hold of Ursula and within moments all three Commanders were back on deck. As soon as the helpers withdrew, Ursula and Cordula, grimacing with pain and gasping for breath, managed to pick themselves up and lean against the rail. Brittola, however, remained crumpled in a heap, unconscious. Ursula was about to tend to Brittola when the officer in charge of the rowing crew, fighting against yet another crashing wave, came struggling along the deck towards them. Her face was filled with wild terror.

"Emergency!" she yelled. "Come quickly!"

"What is it?" Ursula cried hoarsely.

"The waves are snapping the oars and mountings like firewood!" she shouted, beckoning frantically for them to follow her below. "We've already lost half of them—and the oar port seals are torn. The sea is pouring in!"

Part Two

The Continent

Britannia

The Long
Coast

Londinium
(London)

Delta

Rhenus
(Rhine)

**the
CONTINENT**

Noviomagus
(Nijmegen)

Aquae Matticae
(Wiesbaden)

Gesoriacum
(Boulogne)

Colonia
(Cologne)

Mogontiacum
(Mainz)

Confluentes (Koblenz)

Lutetia
(Paris)

Treveris
(Trier)

The Limes
(Empire Frontier)

Germania

Danuvius
(Danube)

Galliae

Castra Regina
(Regensburg)

Vindobona
(Vienna)

The Alps

The Pyrenees

Arelate (Arles)

Cesarauguta
(Zaragoza)

Hispania

Italia

Rome

Chapter 5

Colonia

Report to Augustus Constantine III, Emperor of the West and Grand Commander of all its armies, from Princess Ursula, daughter of King Deonotus of Corinium and Commander-in-Chief of the Legions First and Second Athena. Noviomagus on the Rhenus. Hail Constantine! Spero fore, ut magni mensis Martis venti spirent tibi omina fausta bonamque fortunam in vitae viam, et ut dulcedo Aprilis animos leonis commoveat ad relinquendum denique cubile hibernum—I hope the strong winds of March blew good omens and fortune in your path, and that the warm caress of April entices the spirit of the lion to finally abandon its winter lair. I regret to inform you that the First Athena will be delayed in its Great Expedition by a minimum of a full cycle of the moon.

A powerful storm of savage ferocity caught us in the middle of the Channel and scattered our fleet to the four winds. Our galleys were driven eastwards and strewn along the coastline of northern Galliae—mostly, we believe, into Batavian waters. By the grace of God, my galley was spared the depths and is still seaworthy . . . .

II

Slowly, Ursula opened her sore, bloodshot eyes. She found herself looking at a patch of yellow light. Not one yellow but many different shades flecked with golds, silvers, purples and reds. They were moving—ever shifting—ever changing. It felt as if the swirl of colors was going to engulf her.

A wave of dizziness overwhelmed her. She was forced to close her eyes and roll her head forward. Feeling nauseous, she looked back up, determined to focus on the cause of her torment. Slowly, her vision cleared and she recognized the glow of a distant dawn.

She became aware of strange sounds. It took effort to concentrate, but soon she realized they were being made by birds on water. There was the *kleep* of an oyster catcher. The babble and quack of a multitude of ducks in chorus—first here, then there—like choirs in competition. The ducks' song was punctuated intermittently by the stentorian honks of great crested grebes barking their feeding cries. Over all this, there was a lugubrious flapping of a host of tired wings followed by a long, sibilant splash as an early flock of geese arrived from the south. Not far from the galley, on the nearest wading ground, a Sentinel of the Marsh—a red shank—started its piercing yelps.

Her eyes slowly scanned the deck about her. Apart from the occasional creak as it rocked gently in the shallows near a long sandbank, the galley itself was utterly silent. The only other women visible on deck were the two lookouts, one to the fore and one astern. They were both fast asleep at their posts and wrapped in heavy woolen blankets.

A light breeze caressed Ursula's face and blew away the final vestiges of sleep. She shivered—and realized she was cold.

The storm! Her eyes widened at the thought. *There was a great storm!*

She was amazed to discover she had managed to sleep while sitting cross-legged on the deck near the stern with her back against the rail. Brittola's head was on her lap, her body stretched out to one side. Someone had arranged Brittola's arms across her chest as if in death. Ursula looked down and saw Brittola's cut and bloodstained face. It was badly swollen on the right side and framed by spikes of sticky, matted hair. *Oh, dear God. Look at you!* She freed her hand from the covers and touched her friend's forehead. It was warm. *Don't worry, Brittola. The storm's over. We're going home soon. Don't worry.*

Like the rest of the crew, Ursula had fallen asleep only a few hours earlier. The storm raged well into the night, though the skies had been so dark she couldn't tell when daylight had ended. It felt as if they had entered Hell and been doomed to spend the whole of Eternity fighting the Devil's forces, which attacked them with relentless savagery from the surrounding waters.

Most of Ursula's crew formed lines and struggled with the bailing buckets to keep the ship afloat. The few remaining rowers with oars and mountings intact did their best to do battle with the terrible waves. Several of the women had to deal with the panic-stricken horses, which were frantically trying to free themselves from their stalls. Just as most of the women had been on the verge of collapse, the winds weakened and the seas slowly abated, taking the storm's horrors with them back into the depths.

Ursula feared being smashed on rocks in the darkness. As soon as the galley stopped pitching and rolling, she and Cordula rallied the few women still capable of work and set about dragging the anchors, hoping to bring the crippled craft to rest. The fore anchor almost immediately bit into something solid. Within moments the aft line also became taut.

Ursula became aware of a great thirst and tried to cry for Oleander. But her voice had been shattered by the seawater and the shouting of the night before. The only noise she could manage was a faint hiss, which was instantly lost in the breeze. Gently, she lifted Brittola's head and lowered it onto a piece of blanket, which she bunched into a pillow. Groaning and wincing with the sudden pain of her cramps, cuts and bruises, she grabbed hold of the rail above her head and hauled herself up. As soon as she let go of the rail, a great surge of dizziness and nausea overcame her. She fell back against it, gagging for breath.

A fragmented image of the night before suddenly came to her. Oleander had been on deck, bringing blankets and—Ursula looked down to her left—a leather flagon of water. There it was, tied to the rail. She fumbled clumsily with the stopper, fell to her knees and drank, taking slow, deliberate draughts and doing her best not to gulp. The cool water soothed her cracked lips and washed the dryness from her parched throat, bringing the sinews of her drained body back to life. Her thirst quenched, she leaned over Brittola and held the flagon to the younger woman's cut and swollen mouth. Brittola flinched in pain, but did not wake. A vague recollection of some dim memory prompted Ursula to pour some of the water onto a corner of the blanket and gently squeeze the drips onto Brittola's partially opened mouth. She smiled when Brittola responded by licking her lips.

"You'll be fine, Brittola," she said hoarsely. "A few days' rest and a good bath, then you'll be back in the saddle . . . ." Her smile froze, then disappeared. She looked up. The dawn was now bathing the galley in its cold, yellow light. "You'll soon be home, Brittola. Constans and I will take you."

Ursula laid the flagon by Brittola's side and carefully stood up. Though she was still shaky and nauseous, she knew she could walk as long as she held on tightly to the rail. Slowly, she began making her way toward the stairs that led below. At the head of the steps, huddled in the alcove for the duty officer on watch, she found Cordula wrapped in a blanket and fast asleep.

"First, Brittola, and now, Cordula," she muttered to herself. "Oleander must be here somewhere." She looked out to sea again, this time peering into the black wall of night that shrouded the western horizon, away from the glow of the dawn. "The others can't be far. We'll probably see them once the sun is fully up." Then, with very careful and deliberate movements, she started to descend the steps.

Ursula could hear the gentle lap of waves against the hull. Somewhere toward the prow a piece of floating debris was tapping intermittently against the vessel's sides. It echoed throughout the craft like the taunts of an intruder. As she reached the last step, her foot dropped into water—the cold, harsh brine of the Channel in spring. Its chill shot through her body, making her shudder and catch her breath.

It was almost completely dark on the rowing deck. There were no lamps lit. The only illumination came from the jagged swathes of dim yellow-gray light coming in through the torn leather seals around the oar ports. It took a few moments for her eyes to adjust. What she saw made her reel back against the steps in shock. On every bench were huddled, motionless forms, shrouded in blankets. It looked like a sea of the Dead. Their gray faces stared at her with hollow, sightless eyes. Two of the nearest ones looked up at her with mouths agape, as if they had died begging for nourishment. As she stared at them, Ursula's own eyes grew wide with horror. But then she saw movement. They were breathing—not dead—just sleeping.

Why are you here—in this hell? This is no place for young girls like you! How old are you? Sixteen? Eighteen, perhaps? Why aren't you at home with your families? Another wave of dizziness and nausea forced her to close her eyes and steady herself. *Who are you, and why are you here, anyway?*

Just then a faint whinny came from the storage area to her rear. As if in a trance, Ursula drifted toward the sound. Slowly, she walked up the ramp to the raised platform in the stern. She heard the rustle of straw, and felt it sticking to her feet. The horse in the first stall was Brittola's Feather. The lively mare was fully alert and pleased to sense a familiar person nearby.

Where's Swift? she thought, coming to a halt. Then she remembered. *Oh, that's right. Swift's with the others.* She took another step toward Feather and began to reach out to hold her, but then she hesitated again. *What others? Where?* She shook her head dismissively. *Well, wherever she is I hope she's well. I hope . . . they're all well.*

She put her arms around Feather's neck and gave her a hug. The horse nuzzled her in reply. The light was just strong enough for Ursula to see long grazes across Feather's flanks, which she had gotten from being thrown against the stall posts. "You had a bit of a rough ride, didn't you?" she whispered quietly. "Poor Feather."

"Poor *Feather!*"

Ursula jumped. She hadn't heard Oleander come up behind her.

"Beggin' your pardon, Mistress, but what about the poor First Athena!"

III

As more of the early morning light filled the lower deck, the women began to stir. Slowly, they eased their stiff and aching bodies into action. *They are like phantoms rising from their tombs,* thought Ursula, *It's a miracle that not one of them was lost in the storm.* Brittola's injuries were the most serious. Many of the crew, however, were also suffering from cuts and head wounds caused by falls or being hit by wild oars as the sea wrestled them from their grasp. *Thankfully, no bones are broken and no amputations will be necessary.*

Still in shock, Ursula withdrew to the prow, where she stood silently for most of the day, wrapped in a blanket. Her hair hung over her shoulders and down her back in lifeless, flat streaks, making her look like one of the mad women who begged in the Forum at home. She scoured the horizon to the south and west, only pausing to take a swig from her water flagon. If anyone tried to approach her—even Oleander or Cordula—she waved them away.

Ursula did turn to watch with interest whenever Oleander tended to Brittola, who remained unconscious until just before midday. She even managed a weak smile when her young friend eventually came 'round while Oleander was gently washing her hair. As Ursula watched, Brittola managed a few sips of water, then fell back to sleep.

Through her daze, Ursula sometimes overheard Cordula organizing the crew, but throughout the morning she did not interest herself in their recovery, preferring instead to maintain her scrutiny of the far horizon.

Only a handful of women were fit for duty, and even they were weak. After Oleander had attended to some with minor injuries, there were enough to form two work gangs, each twenty or so strong. Cordula had been badly cut and bruised herself and needed Oleander's attention before she was capable of moving without too much pain. Once Cordula was in action, however, things started to happen. The more seriously injured women, including several attendants, were brought up on deck and made comfortable on the stern. Those who weren't actually injured, but were otherwise unfit for duty due to exhaustion or shock, were detailed into bailing crews. They formed long lines leading from the depths of the rowing deck to the sides of the galley, and spent most of the morning passing the large leather buckets to and fro.

Some of the remaining able-bodied attendants were assigned to getting the vessel's contents back into order. Others saw to the horses, tending their wounds and fixing their stalls. One of the work gangs, under Cordula's supervision, set about clearing away the debris in the rowing deck. They did what they could to reposition the oars. By mid-morning it was clear that only nineteen were in full working order, ten port and nine starboard. Many oars were missing and others were damaged beyond repair. The main problem, however, was the number of broken mountings.

The crew's tasks were made easier by Oleander's foresight the previous day. As the storm loomed, she had remembered something her husband taught her many years before. Leading the other attendants in gathering all the perishable and dry goods they could find, they wrapped them in bundles and secured them fast against the beams, which formed the ceiling of the lower deck. Thus it was that the miserably cold and wet women had dry clothes to change into and food that had not been ruined.

By early afternoon, most of the chores were done. Everyone was exhausted and sat on the deck, wrapped in their cloaks or blankets, trying to sleep. Cordula then roused the work gangs once more for the final task; hoisting the sail to allow it to dry out. The dead weight of the wet cloth was incredibly heavy. Chanting and sweating, it took all of the able-bodied women to heave it to the top of the mast. After much difficulty, they managed to tie it into place. The moment came for them to discover whether it had been damaged by the storm. The damp stays required several hefty tugs to be released, but, finally, it slowly unfurled. The entire crew cheered as the great green sail bellied in the wind, without so much as a small rent.

While they were celebrating, Ursula, remained on the prow, watching the distant horizon—seemingly oblivious to events on board.

Some members of the crew muttered resentment at her apparent disdain, and a couple of them, believing she was completely distracted, eventually commented out loud.

"She's only a Commander when she wants to be," one young woman said openly to her friend. "When there's glory in the offing."

"That's right," her companion sneered. "As soon as there's dirty work to be done, she's just a poor little Princess after all." They started to snigger.

"That's enough you two!" Ursula heard Cordula snap. "For that insolence you can go and relieve the attendants who are cleaning out the horses. And, if I hear any more talk like that, I'll flog you myself. Now go!"

As the two women skulked off in shame, Oleander went up to Cordula. She whispered in her ear, "Excuse me, Mistress. I think I know how we can bring Princess Ursula back from her nightmares."

IV

"The women are ready for inspection, Commander." Cordula stood to attention and saluted. Three nearby horns blew a short fanfare.

Ursula slowly released her grip on the rail and turned around. There in front of her were Cordula and two junior officers in full-dress uniform, giving her a formal salute. Behind them, lining both sides of the deck, was the rest of the crew—even the wounded. They were standing to attention in their Corinium blue cloaks, with their helmets tucked neatly beneath their right arms and their left hands on their sword hilts. All were, indeed, ready for inspection.

"Your cloak, helmet and sword, Commander." Cordula held them out for her. The helmet and sword were neatly arranged on the cloak, which had been correctly folded.

For a few moments, Ursula just stared at her cousin with a bemused look on her face, as if she wasn't sure what was happening, or what was expected of her.

Unseen by the company, Cordula smiled and gave an imperceptible nod of encouragement.

Ursula looked once more around the deck. "Why is the sail unfurled?" she asked with childlike innocence. "Are we preparing to go somewhere?"

"It's merely drying, Commander," Cordula replied, quietly but firmly—thrusting the cloak forward. "Now please put on your uniform. The crew is waiting."

Ursula bent down to place the flagon of water on the deck. While she was stooping, she loosened the blanket and let it fall away, exposing her leather tunic and arm bands. Then she closed her eyes, took a deep breath and stood up straight. Slowly, she took hold of her sword and carefully fastened it around her waist, taking the time to adjust the hilt until it rested firmly and correctly against her hip. A little faster, and with a modest flourish, she opened her cloak, swung it over her shoulders and fixed the clasp neatly in place. As she took her helmet, she looked Cordula in the eye and whispered, "Thank you."

Ursula made a point of checking the women's wounds and their dressings rather than their uniforms during her inspection. Before finishing and moving on down the line, she held each woman's gaze, nodded and smiled. Without exception, each woman smiled back.

Mid-way through the circuit, as she was crossing the deck, Ursula stopped and bent down to check on Brittola, who was tucked inside the alcove formed by the bulwark at the top of the steps. "How are you doing, old friend?" She took Brittola by the hand and smiled.

"I hope to God I don't look as bad as you do," Brittola whispered feebly. She tried to return Ursula's smile, but her swollen face was too sore.

Ursula could see that the old fire was beginning to burn in Brittola's eyes. She left her, feeling confident that the youngest Commander in the Legion was well on her way to recovery.

With the inspection complete, Ursula joined Cordula, who was standing by the galley's mast. Cordula handed her a cord and gave the signal for the horns to blow another fanfare.

Realizing Cordula's intent, Ursula gave the cord a sharp pull, looked up and smiled. From the top of the mast unfurled two long and brightly colored pennants—the blue of the Corinium cohorts and the white, gold and purple of their royal Commander-in-Chief.

V

The overcast sky of the late afternoon seemed to mirror their spirits as Cordula briefed Ursula on the state of the galley, the crew and the horses. They discussed where they might possibly be on the coast of Galliae, and decided that without a scouting party, they could form no clear idea.

"You look tired," Ursula said once their decision on how to proceed was made. They were by themselves on the prow with Oleander seated nearby. "Go and rest with the others. I'll take over from here."

"Yes," Cordula replied wearily. "I think I will."

"One more thing before you go." Ursula placed her hand on Cordula's arm. "I want to say thank you. Brittola and I both owe you our lives. And I . . . owe you much more." She gave Cordula a long, affectionate hug. "Thank you for everything."

As they separated, Ursula had a broad smile on her face. "Oleander, make yourself useful," she said jovially. "Can't you see I'm famished? What's more—I'm sure the crew is as eager for some fresh, hot food as I am. Now, I'm going to lower the boat and take a hunting party over to those wading grounds. While I'm doing that . . . rig up the deck grate, light a fire and, prepare the cooking utensils!"

The crew reveled in their feast, eating their fill and breaking into song as soon as they had sated their hunger. As the sun began to set, they started singing sadder songs about lost loves and homes far away.

Suddenly, the lookout on the stern shouted, *"Boat ahoy!"*

Ursula and the other officers rushed to the rear. Brittola, who was able to walk with Oleander's help, followed. There, coming toward them from the north, was a small rowboat. As it drew nearer, Ursula's crew let out a great cheer. The occupants were wearing Corinium blue.

VI

"I can't come aboard, Commander. We have to return before it gets dark," the officer in the rowboat shouted. Ursula recognized her at once as Viventia from Calleva Atrebatum, one of the Second Cohort's more capable leaders. "We need your help. We've lost our commanding officer, Lollia Similina. We've run aground on a steep sand bank about two or three leagues that way." She pointed northeast.

"That is grave news indeed about beloved Lollia," Ursula called down to the boat in reply. "How about the rest of your crew? And your galley—is it seriously damaged?"

"Our mast is down—it was the mast falling that killed the Commander. Many were injured. We lost some oars and many more have broken mountings, but we are still seaworthy—if only we could get ourselves off the sandbank. I think it should be possible at high tide."

"We'll be there first thing in the morning."

"Thank you, Commander. The others will be pleased to hear that—especially when they know it's you," Viventia said enthusiastically. "Thank goodness you lit your fire. If you hadn't, we would never have known you were here."

Cordula quickly scoured the northern horizon before turning back to Viventia. "Why can't we see smoke from your fires?"

"Everything's too wet. The crew made camp on the sandbank. We're trying to get everything dry, but without any fire it's very difficult."

"You said many were injured. Do you have any who are seriously wounded?" Ursula asked.

"Not really, Commander. No amputations—thank goodness. Only three women who can't walk. Our biggest problem is the cold."

"Stay where you are for a moment." Ursula turned to Cordula. "Do you feel up to it?"

Cordula looked down at the shivering women on the boat below them, then back at her cousin. "Yes, I do." she replied resolutely.

"Good. Take the five best women we have and follow them back to their galley. Be sure to return here at first light, though. We'll need the boat to pilot us through these sandbanks and shallows. Understood?"

Cordula nodded, saluted and set off to round up her crew.

Ursula turned to Oleander. "I want you to load these two boats up with all the dry clothes and blankets, and as much cooked food as we can spare."

As Oleander bustled off, she smiled and muttered under her breath, "She's back to her old self."

Ursula overhead her remark, and smiled, too. Then she returned her attention to the women below. "We're going to send our boat with you," she shouted. "We have some spare provisions you can take."

"Thank you, Commander. But we must make haste. It will soon be dark."

"Have no fear. They'll be with you in just a moment. Tell me—can you see any sign of any other galleys from where you've gone aground?"

"Just as we were preparing to come here, one of our lookouts thought she saw another wisp of smoke further to the north. But we couldn't confirm it. The light was too dim."

"How about inland? Can you see any signs of civilization?"

"Nothing, Commander. Not even a sheep."

Cordula reappeared with her crew and they climbed down into the rowboat. Oleander and the other attendants lowered several brace of cooked birds plus some bundles of clothes and blankets down to the two boats. Both craft pushed away, the crews rowing as hard as they could in order to beat the night.

As they disappeared into the gathering dusk, Brittola tapped Ursula on the shoulder. "Do you realize," she whispered, her voice still weak, "that if all the galleys are spread out a few leagues apart, that means the First Athena could be scattered along hundreds of miles of coastline?"

"Ah, but you're forgetting that we were the southernmost flotilla. We took the brunt of the storm. I'm sure Pinnosa has managed to rally the others and they're probably moored in a cluster just up the coast. I wouldn't be surprised if we made contact with them sometime tomorrow," Ursula said, trying, but not succeeding, to sound reassuring.

VII

The following day, most of the crew was fit for duty. Apart from Brittola, only a handful of women were still too weak to work.

When Cordula returned soon after dawn, the galley was bustling with activity and a chorus of *Praise the Lord* could be heard coming from below. It took them most of the morning to row to the beached galley. They had to proceed slowly in order to avoid running aground themselves. Three times the pilot boat's sounding line warned them of a hidden sand bar, which they had to circumnavigate. The third such diversion was the most frustrating. They were less than a third of a league from the other women—whom they could already hear cheering—when the sounding line struck bottom. This final sand bar, however, was the continuation of the same one the other galley was aground on, and it seemed to be endless. It took Cordula almost an hour to find a channel deep enough for them to use. Ursula's galley had to execute several tight turns in order to follow her.

When they eventually managed to break through into the right channel, they rowed as fast as they could to their compatriots. The stranded crew greeted them with wild cries of joy.

The bow of other galley was grounded squarely on a high spit of sand, shingle and mud that sloped dramatically downward, leaving the stern in clear water.

The tide was already at its zenith, so they lost no time in making preparations for the rescue. Ursula began by maneuvering her galley into position so that the two vessels were stern to stern. Cordula and Viventia in the small boats quickly set about connecting the craft with two long ropes, one on each side. When Cordula gave the 'all clear' signal, Ursula knew they were ready.

At the sound of a horn from Ursula's galley, the women on the spit waded as far as they could into the freezing water, carrying their oars to use as levers and push-poles. As soon as they were in position, Ursula ordered the signal—three rapid horn blasts—to be given. The moment it sounded, all the women—rowers and pushers alike—began to heave as hard as they could.

Ursula's first rowing crew did their best to build up as much speed as possible before the slack in the ropes was taken up. At the same time, the women in the water pushed or levered with all their might. There was a tremendous jolt as the two ropes went tight, bringing Ursula's galley to an abrupt halt. The horses in both vessels whinnied frantically. Almost immediately, a loud cheer went up from the women in the water. From Cordula's signals, Ursula learned the other galley had slid a complete cubit.

Ursula's second rowing crew took the oars and slowly rowed back to position the galley for another pull. To maximize the rowing distance, Ursula maneuvered so close to the other one she could hear the women in the water shivering. This time she two craft came into contact and wood started to splinter, before raising her hand for the horn to give three more blasts.

Ursula heard the lead rower shout, "Come on! We can do better than the others!" With the help of the extra slack Ursula had given them, they succeeded in building up more speed than the first rowing crew. Ecstatic cries from the other galley meant their craft had been pulled farther out. The jolt, however, was too strong for one of the ropes. It snapped with a loud *crack*. The severed ends whipped through the air, almost hitting one group of women, forcing them to bob like ducks into the bitter cold water.

The remaining rope pulled Ursula's galley around to the right. The Commander and her women ran to the side rail to see the results of their efforts. The stricken galley seemed to take on a life of its own. Slowly at first, but then building up speed, it began to pivot on its port side. The women in the water started to scream as they felt the silt shifting beneath their feet. The strong suction of the currents created by the sliding hulk started pulling them under. Ursula and her crew could only look on helplessly as several of their comrades struggled frantically to avoid being sucked under. Miraculously, one by one, they each managed to escape the depths and scramble—exhausted— back to safety.

Finally, the huge craft—moving as if under the spell of some powerful unholy spirit and with a chorus of grotesque creaks and groans—completed a tight turn and slithered sideways into the deep channel. Once afloat, it rocked to a standstill. The echoing cries of the horses in its stern resounded across the sudden stillness like the forlorn wails of a Siren in torment.

VIII

"It's no use!" Cordula shouted from the pilot boat. "We have to go about! Make a tight turn to port!"

Ursula thumped the rail in exasperation and turned to Brittola, who was standing beside her on the prow. "I'm certain we've explored this channel before. I recognize that sandbank."

"How can you be so sure? They all look alike to me," Brittola replied. Her voice was back to full strength. The swelling on her face had diminished considerably.

It was mid-afternoon of their second day with the other galley and progress was slow. The pilot boats were doing their best. Indeed, Cordula and Viventia were becoming very adept at their task. But the endless maze of channels, sandbanks and spits was proving to be a nightmare of treacherous currents and shallows. The complete lack of proper landmarks was making navigation impossible.

Early on, they learned to use the waterfowl as indicators of the presence of hidden shallows. However, they were now surrounded on every side by swirling masses of birds as far as the eye could see. There was no obvious route out. The incessant noise of the birds was also driving many of the women—including Ursula—to the point of distraction.

Apart from the diversion of hunting and fishing, the only thing to revive their spirits had been the improvement in the weather. The clouds had dispersed and the skies were a vibrant, spring blue.

"If only we could see some sign of land," Ursula muttered angrily to herself, as she paced to and fro. "Just one sheep or a goat would—"

"*Boat ahoy!*" cried the lookout.

Ursula and Brittola rushed to the stern and joined the rest of the crew in shouting with delight at the unmistakable sight of a small white sail. It was about three leagues distant and moving rapidly towards them.

"Full dress uniforms!" Ursula ordered. "Tell the other galley to do the same. And get Cordula and Viventia back on to the galleys as a precaution."

As soon as Cordula was on deck, she rushed excitedly to the stern to join Ursula and Brittola in scrutinizing the approaching vessel and speculating on who the occupants might be. It was a strange-looking craft with two sails—one main and one to the fore. It moved rapidly for a vessel which was barely big enough for a crew of five or six, but it zigzaged far more than necessary, even in these treacherous waters. From this evidence, Ursula and the others concluded they were most probably Batavians, who were known to inhabit such waters and had built special vessels for use in them. They studied it while it approached them.

"Such a craft might be put to good use in the vast wet lands beyond Lindum." Ursula commented to Cordula and Brittola.

As the craft neared them, they could see it contained a crew of only three, which made the speed they were achieving even more impressive. The crew consisted of a man and two teenagers who looked to be his sons. They were wearing attire Ursula and the others had never seen before. Their white cloaks were shorter and their clasps more elongated than Britannic ones. On their heads, they wore curious leather skullcaps with a fur trim and flaps for their ears. Their garb confirmed Ursula's suspicions that the visitors were indeed Batavians and not from Galliae.

"*Salavete, amici*—Greetings friends," Ursula cried, as they came alongside. "*Pacis amantes sumus.*—We come in peace."

The man shouted his reply in a rich, booming voice, which was plain to hear, but the words were completely unintelligible.

"*Salvete, amici,*" Ursula repeated, and then continued slowly in Latin. "We come in peace. We are from Britannia."

He repeated his reply equally as deliberately, adding at the end a sentence that seemed to include the word 'Britannia.' But his speech was heavily accented and his message still eluded them. He made to grab the rope boarding ladder.

"Guards!" Ursula commanded.

A fierce display of arms by three women at the top of the ladder deterred him. He pushed his boat away from the galley side with an oar. Then he shouted a new message, this time with an obvious note of annoyance in his voice.

"We come in peace," Ursula called out once more in Latin. "But we won't allow unidentified or unauthorized personnel on board. This is a military vessel on a mission."

She turned to Cordula in frustration. "It's no use. He doesn't speak Latin. Are there any women on board who speak Batavian?"

"No. I'm sure there aren't."

"Send a message to Viventia and ask her," she ordered. "I'll do my best to keep him talking."

While Cordula rushed to the stern, Ursula tried once more, stressing each individual syllable just in case it was her accent that was causing the problem. "We come in peace. Are you Batavians?"

He didn't reply. It was clear from his manner not only that he failed to realize she had asked him a question, but also that he was tiring of the situation.

"We need to get to Gesoriacum. I repeat, Gesoriacum. Can you help us navigate out of these . . . Oh 'shallows,'" Ursula muttered to Brittola, glaring at the deck in frustration. "What's Latin for 'shallows?'"

"I don't think it matters," Brittola replied. "He's leaving."

Ursula looked up and saw that the two teenagers were using small paddles to turn the craft around. At the same time, the man was positioning his main sail to catch the slight breeze that was coming steadily from the southwest.

"Wait! Please don't go! We're checking to see whether there's someone on board who can speak Batavian," Ursula cried, but it was too late.

The craft completed its turn and moved way. As it picked up speed, the man turned to face them, and—using hand signals—indicated in no uncertain terms that they should stay where they were, and that he would return.

Ursula hugged Brittola, laughing as she did so. "He'll be back. I know it. He's going to fetch someone who can speak Latin."

IX

"We can't wait here any longer," Cordula exclaimed. It was mid-morning the following day. "Our drinking water is getting dangerously low. We must resume our search for land immediately, otherwise we'll die of thirst."

Ursula had been holding the galleys at anchor while they waited for 'the Batavian' to return. The sky was still clear, but a strong wind had begun to blow from the southwest, making the both the horses and the women restless. Ursula had been standing on the stern since dawn, her gaze fixed on the point where he had disappeared the day before, hoping and praying for his return. "How many more times must I tell you, Cordula?" Ursula's voice, like Cordula's, was strained and tense. Tempers were beginning to fray. "You didn't see his gestures. He was emphatic that we should stay here."

"Would you mind showing me the 'stay here' gesture again?" Cordula asked impatiently.

With a heavy sigh, Ursula complied.

"I'm sure that was just his exasperation," Cordula insisted. "He was probably saying, 'stay here and rot for all I care!'"

"But then he did this," Brittola interjected, copying the Batavian's unambiguous 'I'll be back' gesture. She looked pleadingly at both Ursula and Cordula. "Can I suggest we wait until midday?"

"Very well," Ursula said with a sigh of reluctant resignation. "If there is no sign of him by midday, we will up anchors and head in that direction." She pointed over her shoulder toward where the Batavian had disappeared. "And if we—"

She stopped as Cordula's expression suddenly changed from anxiety to amazement. Ursula spun around.

There, on the distant horizon, was a small white sail.

X

. . . We were rescued from the treacherous sandbanks of the Batavian coast by the good people of a small fishing village called Veere. Their mayor, Udo, found us and, with the assistance of the village priest, Maxian, he guided us through the endless maze of shallows to their harbor. Udo and Maxian informed us that their people and other Batavians encountered more of our galleys out in the shallows and that some of them were seaworthy. Since then, we have been making good use of the Batavian light craft to relay messages to the other crews. They are to muster here in Noviomagus, which has adequate facilities to repair our damaged fleet, barrack the women and tend to our wounded.

Since Noviomagus is the first major military base up the Rhenus after the river converges, it is also a convenient rallying point, which should prove easy for the other galley crews to find. Indeed, when we arrived here yesterday afternoon, there were six of our vessels in the harbor waiting for us. From their reports, we have now accounted for twenty-seven galleys, over eight thousand women and approximately eight hundred horses.

The death toll from the storm so far is thirty-seven women and almost two hundred horses. Among those lost are Lollia Similina, daughter of Titinius Similina of Deva, and Magunna of Luguvallium. We have three hundred serious casualties receiving treatment here in Noviomagus. Only seven amputations have been necessary so far and the rest of the wounded should be fit for duty within a fortnight.

Cordula and Brittola are with me, and are well, plus a very compe-

tent officer, Viventia Martius from Calleva Atrebatum. There is no news yet of Julia, Faustina, Pinnosa, Martha or Saula, but we do know that Baetica is safe. Her galley is aground on a sand bar, which is connected to land about half a day's march from here. Because she has valuable supplies, she won't abandon it until another vessel comes to relieve her. I shall be sending Cordula and Viventia to accomplish this shortly.

Along with this message, I am also sending a light vessel to Britannia in case any of our fleet was forced back by the storm. I dispatched riders to Gesoriacum to inform them of our situation. It would seem that no further messages are necessary since the Batavians have remarkably efficient communications! Not only was Noviomagus expecting us, Colonia, Mogontiacum and Treveris have all been informed of the arrival—and plight—of the First Athena, and Colonia has even replied. I have a brief—and rather curt—message before me from a certain Rusticus, who claims to be your good friend. It says that if the 'highly esteemed' women of Britannia are unable to endure the prospect of the long and arduous journey to Arelate, they can be assured of an even warmer embrace in Colonia! He sounds like a crude sort and I can't say I shall be sorry not to accept his offer.

I estimate we shall need a further three weeks for the First Athena to complete its muster and be in a position to recommence the Great Expedition. The Batavians have already promised to replace our lost horses. They have huge stables here and plenty of stock (and yet they tell me the Noviomagus facilities are small compared to those in Colonia!).

Finally, when you relay our news to Constans, please be sure to add that the storm has strengthened our resolve. Once the Great Expedition is resumed, nothing more will prevent the First Athena from fulfilling its duty.

You are both constantly in my prayers,
Ursula

✳ ✳ ✳

My dearest daughter.

It was with great relief that I received your report. For the sake of Aurelius and Regulus, please send another dispatch as soon as either Julia or Faustina are sighted or accounted for.

Philip Griffin

We first knew of the storm when a messenger arrived from Gesoriacum telling us that no vessels from the Great Expedition had arrived
or been sighted. The moment we received the report, Aurelius, Regulus
and I rode in haste to Rutupiae in order to organize the search for galleys, but to no avail. Not one vessel from your fleet has been sighted
on this side of the Channel. Regulus, who spent many years on naval
patrols in Batavian waters and who knows the conditions well, says the
galleys could be scattered as far as the Long Coast, which stretches for
many miles to the north of the Rhenus.

You did not mention in your report the exact nature or extent of
the damage to your vessels, but we presume the main problems you
have are broken or lost oars and perhaps fallen masts. If this is the
case, limit the repairs to the oars only. Do not ask the shipwrights at
Noviomagus to replace masts or repair damaged hulls. That would be
too costly and time consuming. There are plenty of vessels on your side
of the Channel, which you can commission to bring the First Athena
safely back.

I have one piece of good news, which should bring you some cheer.
We received a report two days ago that the Third and Fourth Cohorts
of the Second Athena, under the capable leadership of Claudia Mar-
cia, successfully routed a fifty boat Hibernian invasion along the West
Coast, putting over a hundred of the murderous swine to the sword and
sending the rest back in leg irons, minus their thumbs as you instructed.
Only twelve of the infantry and three of the cavalry were killed and
less than thirty women were wounded. It would seem that the rigorous
training you and the others put them through was highly effective.

That's all for now, my dear. I hope all goes well with the muster,
especially your search for the missing Commanders. You are constantly
in our thoughts and the whole of Britannia is praying for the successful
re-commencement of the Great Expedition.

Your loving father,
Deonotus

* * *

From Augustus Constantine III, Emperor of the West and Grand
Commander of all its armies, to Princess Ursula, Commander-in-Chief
of the Legions First and Second Athena. Arelate.

Hail great Princess and Commander! Aestatis tepores augeant tibi animum repleantque libertate!—*May the early warm breezes of summer be lifting your spirits and filling you with freedom! I hope this finds you fully reunited with the brave women of the First Athena and that you have recovered from your great adventure on the high seas. The Channel can be surprisingly vicious for such a narrow stretch of water.*

More importantly, I hope this reaches you before you embark on your long march south, for I fear I must order you to postpone the Great Expedition. You have not been the only ones suffering setbacks in recent weeks. While the hidden forces of the depths were seeking you out for battle, an unholy alliance consisting of armies from Hispania, plus a large band of Suevi tribesmen, sneaked through the mountains and laid siege to Arelate. They are ostensibly under the leadership of our old 'friend' Gerontius and a certain Maximus who claims the title "Emperor." But these are mere puppets. Pulling the strings are busy hands—hands gubernatorial and ex- gubernatorial—hands imperial as well, I suspect.

Normally, I could crush such a rabble in one swift and decisive attack. But recently I had to send twelve thousand of my best men to the Rhenus in order to deal with yet more Burgundians, who seem to be intent upon ravaging eastern Galliae. I sent urgent messages ordering their recall, and am awaiting their return as I write. It is also possible that Constans might come to my aid. He was on his way here for the 'Wedding of the Legions.' He should have received my message, which I sent by trusty Morgan, a few days ago. I'm optimistic he will arrive very soon.

Reluctantly, I have to order you and the entire First Athena to stay where you are. I know Noviomagus well. It is a safe place. The people are warm-spirited and kind. It is a good, safe distance from the troubled areas of Germania, northern Galliae and the frontier. I am sending a dispatch to the mayor, Dagvalda, whom I have known for many years, instructing him to make the necessary arrangements for yourself, your fellow officers and the rest of your women. He is a trusted friend, and I have every confidence he will ensure you are well-treated.

So, you have heard from that rascal Rusticus? Have no fear of him, unless you fear hospitality itself! I won't attempt to describe him. He defies description. Suffice to say that he is one of those all too rare people who are a welcome counterbalance to the world and its troubles.

His letter does raise one very serious and important point, however. There are forces on the other side of the Alps that count me as their enemy. This means they most assuredly see you and the First Athena as a threat, too. For this very reason, for your own personal safety and for the safety of the First Athena, I therefore order you not to go to Colonia under any circumstances. From Noviomagus, Colonia is the first step to Rome, and the nearer you get to Rome the greater the physical and political dangers become.

From where you are now stationed, there are only two possible routes for you to follow. The first—head directly south across central Galliae to Arelate as planned. The second—go back to Britannia. Any other route—especially the route to Rome—is most certainly a path to ruin and disaster.

Do not go yourself to Colonia. Do not send a patrol there. Do not even send a dispatch via the city. The risks are far too high in each case. Instead, you—all your officers and the entire First Athena—must stay in the relative safety of Noviomagus. Complete your muster, let your wounded women heal, keep up your training and enjoy Batavian hospitality.

I'll send for you when the time is right, which should be soon. I know how disappointed you will be to receive these orders, but you have persevered well these past three years. I know you have the discipline to be patient for just a few weeks more, while Constans and I finally put a stop to Gerontius and his antics.

In the meantime, I'll leave you with this happy thought: Arelate is at its best in high summer, perfect for weddings and young couples!

Until then, may God be with you,

Constantine.

XI

The galley was back to its full splendor. All of the Commanders from the entire fleet of galleys were assembled on deck enjoying a cloudless, bright blue sky and a warm summer's breeze. It filled the sail and pushed the craft along the crystal clear waters of the river that led them back home. They all smiled as they ate their pheasant.

Oleander was busy readying the grate for the next delicious course.

She sang a lively summer song as she bustled with her work. Martha and Saula accompanied her, playing on their sailor's pipes and joining in the chorus.

Off we go!
A-sailing, a-sailing
Off we go!
A-sailing along

Take damsons and raisins—
and all things nice
Take bully beef and salt it—
salt it thrice
Take the best wine and cork it—
adding some spice
And off we go sailing
A-sailing along

Suddenly, Pinnosa spotted a lone stag on a nearby hilltop, looking like the master of all it surveyed. "Come on everybody," she cried. "Let's go hunting!"

Oleander kept up her song and all the women joined in chorus as they rode their horses across the water and hard up the hill, giving the stag the chase of its life.

That's strange, Ursula thought. *Why is Oleander leading the hunt?*

Off we go!
A-hunting, a-hunting
Off we go!
A-hunting along

Take arrows and daggers—
and all things keen
Take the high ground and low ground—
but don't be seen
Take your meat as you find it—
but keep it clean
And off we go hunting
A-hunting along

When she reached the point where the stag had been standing, Ursula stopped and let the others ride on without her. The sounds of their singing mingled with the pounding of their horses' hooves and faded into the distance. She took in the magnificent view. It was a vivid panorama of hills and valleys richly coated with the deep, vibrant green of luscious woodland. Here and there she could see a waterfall beneath a full crescent rainbow. A nearby valley poured forth a trickling stream, which ran over moss-covered boulders into the river where the galley was moored.

She could hear the sound of birds in the trees as they chirped and chirruped their way through the long, summer's day. As she listened, from way on high—somewhere in the heart of the sun—came the piercing cry of a hawk.

What is it about this place? she thought. *I've never been here before, and yet it has the unmistakable feeling of 'home' about it.*

"You *are* home."

Pinnosa's voice made her jump. She turned to face her and they were standing so close she could feel the heat of her friend's breath.

"Remember? Only in your eyes—I see home," said a voice behind her. "And only in your voice—I hear family."

She turned back, and now she was looking into Constans's deep brown eyes. She could see his pink tongue flickering behind his perfect white teeth as he spoke.

"Oh, Constans." She leaned forward to kiss him, yearning with all her being to feel the warm touch of his soft, sweet lips.

"There's no time for that," Contantine bellowed. "Come! We have to save the townsfolk from the great, black bear."

Ursula started to run as fast as she could because she knew the great black bear was the most dangerous beast on God's earth. People had to be saved from its terror. She and Constans ran together, and while they were running she could feel his hand holding hers tightly. Even though they were running as hard as they could, Pinnosa and Constantine were always somehow in front—just beyond reach—and running harder than anyone else.

Looking back, she saw Martha, Saula, Julia, Faustina, and Brittola—but, curiously, not Cordula—all running, faster and faster, leaping over rocks and fallen branches. Some were crossed—perhaps to make a signal. Behind them, she could see her father and the other Kings in their full regalia, all running like the wind, and she even caught a glimpse of her mother bringing up the rear with a lumbering Bishop Patroclus.

Ursula stopped running and found herself in a huge, cavernous, dark space—the black bear's lair. Her footfalls reverberated and echoed far into its hidden depths. It took a moment for her eyes to adjust. Suddenly, she lost hold of Constans's hand. The shock of losing him filled her with the starkest, most horrifying fear she had ever felt. She started to scream.

A faint noise penetrated her screams and she stopped. It was the clamorous murmur of a multitude of voices in the dark. Slowly, she turned around to face the sound. There in front of her was the First Athena. Twenty thousand women, all of them wet and cold, all wrapped in gray blankets. They were pointing their fingers at her in accusation.

Brittola was their leader. "There it is," she cried. "There's the black bear! There's the monster that's killing us all!"

They started to approach her, obviously intent on revenge. As they drew nearer, Ursula realized that the only way she could survive was by becoming one of them. The only way she could become one of them was to turn around, and point her own finger. But, she knew that the only direction she could point it in was toward Constans and Constantine who were behind her.

"I will not," she cried. "I can not!"

A voice from somewhere deep within whispered, *You must! You have no choice! They have betrayed you just as you betrayed the First Athena!* The voice was her own, but it was also Pinnosa's.

"*No!*"

Ursula spun around so violently, she felt nauseous. And then—she pointed.

She became one of the multitude of women clamoring for retribution. The act of pointing her finger gave her a joyous feeling of relief.

As Ursula and the rest of the women closed in on the two men, Constans started to cower in fear—much to Ursula's shame and disgust. "No! Not me! It wasn't me," he whined like a small boy, as he fell in a pathetic heap at his father's feet.

Constantine stood firm and defiant, with his cloak thrown back over his shoulder and his hand upon his hilt. He drew his sword with a mighty flourish, and shouted, "*Stop!*"

The women paused, but only with great difficulty. They were filled with a momentum that had an awesome power of its own. Ursula, like the other women, knew they had to move forward.

"I am not the great black bear that you seek," Constantine cried, now beginning to show concern. "But I am sworn to protect you from it. Stand back!"

The mass of women edged forward, barely able to contain the ranks upon ranks of women behind them. A tremendous force was being unleashed. A force that could not—would not—be denied. To Ursula it felt like a constant pressure that was both pushing from without and pulling from within.

"Stand back I say! Seek not the great black bear! For if you seek it, in turn, it will seek you. It will seek to kill you! Mark my words . . . *It will kill you all!*"

The sea of women moved closer still. Their hands reached for his arms, his body—his face.

He cowered and reeled as he tried to fend them away and fought against being engulfed. "Come no further in this direction," he cried in desperation. "Beyond me lies the great black bear!"

Then, just as he was about to be smothered by the indomitable force of women, Constantine, too, finally turned and pointed—with his sword—into the darkest depths of the cavern.

With the final obstacle overcome, the awesome pressure was released. Wave after wave of the women plunged into the darkness. Not one of them knew what lay ahead.

As she fell, Ursula wasn't frightened. She knew that the women's force was an all-conquering power, which could never be contained. It was an invisible and inevitable force—like the spring. Now that she was part of the body, the darkness held no fear for her—only freedom.

Just as she was beginning to enjoy the sensation of flying through the darkness, there seemed to come from everywhere at once, a hideously loud roar. The awful sound filled her ears with physical pain. The roar became a deep, reverberant voice, hacking the air with its venomous laughter, torturing her mind with its chilling, evil menace.

"Is that the great black bear?" Brittola shouted by her side.

"Yes. And I think the great black bear is really the Emperor."

"I don't," Pinnosa cried from Ursula's other side. "I think it's God!"

At that moment, a dim, silver light appeared in the center of the darkness and began to grow. Ursula's heart filled with anticipation and excitement. She knew they were about to find the answer. The laughter began to fade and the ever-brightening light was about to engulf the entire great cavern, leaving her free to fly wherever she wished . . . .

Someone pulled at her cloak, impeding her flight.

"Let me go," she cried. "Can't you see we're about to find the truth? We're about to find out the cause of all our suffering!"

Ursula looked behind her. The sky was full of the women of the First Athena—thousands of them—all wearing long white cloaks, all riding beautiful white horses, and all galloping forward at full speed into the wonderful, welcoming, silver light.

"The white riders!" Ursula cried, leaping up from the chair.

Oleander was knocked to the floor, the corner of Ursula's cloak slipped from her hand.

They were alone in her private chamber to the side of the Officers' Hall. Cordula was away with Viventia searching for the missing vessels. Brittola was down at the waterfront checking the galleys.

Oleander looked concerned as she picked herself up. "Were you having a dream again, Mistress?"

Wiping sweat from her brow, Ursula saw her anxious glance. She could imagine Oleander's thoughts. *Perhaps my mistress can no longer perform her duties. Perhaps her judgement is clouded.* Ursula had recently been waking up from her sleep feeling more tired than when she went to bed. As a result, she had been drifting into the restless world of her tortured mind whenever she was left alone and allowed to rest.

"If you don't mind me saying so, Mistress, you shouldn't let yourself fall asleep like that. It's not healthy for a young person like you to doze during the day. You should save your tiredness for the night." Oleander bent down and picked up the parchment that had fallen from Ursula's lap—the order from Constantine to wait in Noviomagus indefinitely. "Anyway, Mistress, it's almost evening bells. You should get yourself down to the galleys for your inspection. Mistress Brittola will be waiting for you."

Ursula gave a distracted nod, then, with some effort, deliberately bustled herself into action. She rearranged her cloak and straightened her clasp. Oleander tidied her mistress's braids. Then Ursula buckled her sword 'round her waist, grabbed her helmet and started to leave. As she opened the door, she came to a halt, staring vacantly into space.

Oleander walked slowly over and took her by the hand, just as she had for many years. "I'm sure all the other mistresses are safe and well: Mistress Martha, Mistress Saula, and, especially, Mistress Pinnosa. And, I'm sure you'll get the order for the Great Expedition to resume soon."

Ursula snapped out of her trance. She returned Oleander's reassuring smile, squeezed her hand, then turned away and left the room.

XI

"Ten craft are still unaccounted for, of which six are supply vessels and four galleys, including Pinnosa's and Faustina's." Brittola announced, reading somberly from the scroll that had just been given to her. It was Viventia's latest report. Then Brittola smiled. "Good news! Julia's galley has been found, or . . ." Her smile faded, "what's left of it . . . ."

"Julia's huge galley was splendid, but very old," Ursula interjected with concern, while Brittola read ahead.

"Apparently, it broke to pieces as soon as it grounded on a sand bar to the far west of the Rhenus delta. Miraculously, only three women died. But they lost all of their horses as the cold water of the Channel claimed the stern. The crew survived for a full three days in the wreckage until one of the Batavian skiffs spotted them. The Batavians led two smaller galleys—both from the Lindum flotilla—to their rescue."

"How is Julia?"

"Still badly shaken, and refusing to speak about the crew's ordeal." She looked up at her Ursula. "Do you think you'll be able to persuade her to talk about it?"

"Perhaps," Ursula said softly.

Brittola turned back to her parchment. "The overall death toll from the storm now stands at almost four hundred. A hundred and sixty were from two of the old supply craft, which were seen to sink, each taking with them their complete crews."

"That doesn't bode well for the missing supply vessels that were of a similar type," Ursula mused.

"Nearly one thousand seven hundred of the First Athena are still unaccounted for, plus over four hundred horses. Forty-three vessels were wrecked, most of them beached, and a few completely broken like Julia's. Several of the older craft sprang leaks and sank in the shallows. The crews were forced to swim ashore, abandoning their horses to the water. Only twenty-six vessels—seventeen of which are war galleys—survived the storm intact and are seaworthy. These are safely moored in Noviomagus' naval harbor, well guarded by sentry towers and floating port booms to keep unwanted craft away.

"As King Deonotus suggested, the shipwrights were commissioned to rectify the damage to the oars and their mountings only. The work is now complete and the craft are ready for inspection as of . . . today!" Brittola smiled as she finished reading through the report and rolled up the parchment.

"That *is* good news. We'll do it immediately." Ursula said decisively, leaping to her feet.

Ursula and Brittola had just completed their inspection of the seventeenth galley, when they heard a familiar voice boom out from the quayside.

"Ahoy there! Are any of these galleys heading for Gesoriacum? I have an urgent appointment to keep!"

"It's Pinnosa!" Brittola cried excitedly. "Pinnosa! You're safe!"

"Why, oh why, does my Christian conscience always have to state the obvious?" Pinnosa teased.

Brittola and Ursula ran down the ramp and gave her a huge hug. The three women held each other tightly until they heard awkward shuffling noises behind them and remembered the guards.

"Where are Martha and Saula?" Ursula asked as they pulled apart. "Are they all right? Are they here?"

"They're fine, but they won't arrive until late tomorrow. They're with Faustina, leading three galley crews here from the north. I thought you might be a little worried, so I came on ahead to let you know we're safe."

"Faustina's all right too?" Brittola reached up to touch Pinnosa's face.

"You really must stop restating what we already know, Brittola." Pinnosa playfully tousled her hair. She turned to Ursula. "Oh, I almost forgot. I did bring two others with me, whom I thought you might be pleased to see." She let out a shrill whistle. From behind a nearby workman's hut two loud neighs could be heard in reply. Two mares—one black, one gray—walked into view.

"Artemis and Swift!" Brittola cried.

"You've done it again!" This time Pinnosa gave Brittola a playful nudge in the ribs.

As the other two started to mock-wrestle, Ursula stepped off the wooden jetty onto the dockside. She stared at the two great horses, both of which looked to be in good condition after their ordeals. For a long moment, they stood still and simply returned her gaze, as if they too were finding it hard to believe they were being reunited. Then, Swift neighed loudly a second time, gave a little prance and a kick, and cantered eagerly over to Ursula, obviously pleased to be back with her mistress. Ursula gave her almost as big a hug as she had given Pinnosa. Swift snorted and nuzzled her in reply.

Artemis walked quietly up behind Ursula. She took Ursula's cloak in her teeth and gave it a sharp pull. Brittola and Pinnosa joined in Ursula's easy laughter, and all three women made a fuss over the frolicsome black mare.

"Come on, you two," Ursula said, after the embraces were over. "Let's return to the Officers Hall and have a simple meal. We'll enjoy a big feast when the others get here tomorrow."

"Simple, yes. . ." Pinnosa said as she mounted Artemis. "But, can we please have some red meat? I've had enough waterfowl to last me till the moon turns blue!"

XII

While they ate that evening, Pinnosa told them of her adventures in the storm.

"Stripped of our mast, and virtually without oars, our galley drifted for three days before sighting land. When we finally made it ashore, we set up camp. I sent out scouting parties to make contact with crews from other vessels. Just two days later, Martha's scouts heard horns blowing, and around a headland came a group of Faustina's women on horseback.

"Many had been injured—some badly—in both crews. Lacking their masts and hauling gear, the hulls of both our vessels had to be partially dismantled in order to free the horses. All of which meant it was over a week before we were able to assemble into one contingent, six-hundred-strong, and ready to march to find the rest of the Legion."

Pinnosa leaned back against the pillows and cushions, picked meat from her teeth, and held out her goblet for more wine. "We assumed we were on the coast of northern Galliae, so we headed north, thinking we were heading toward the Rhenus. It was another week before we met some Friesian seal fur merchants who told us—in the most appalling Latin!—we were heading the wrong way. The storm had actually blown us much further north than I'd estimated—clear to the Long Coast north of the Rhenus. We were marching *away* from the river, and civilization, rather than toward it, heading deeper and deeper into Friesian territory."

"Friesian territory!" Brittola exclaimed excitedly. "Aren't they very dangerous and unpredictable?"

"The ones we met were very hospitable and friendly—almost civilized." Pinnosa smiled and continued her report, "Even though we turned around immediately, it took us a full seven days to get back to our wrecked vessels. A few days later, we came across a scouting party from the other Lindum galley, although we didn't reach it until the next day.

"Their galley also lost most of its oars, but it had kept its mast and hoist, which enabled them to unload their horses easily. The craft had been beached, but, unlike ours, it was re-floatable and could still be used. Saula offered to lead a special detachment to stand guard until it could be rescued, but Faustina reckoned we were in enemy territory and safety had to come first. After much discussion, I reluctantly gave the order for it to be scuttled."

She took a long draught from her wine. "It was an emotional moment for the Lindum cohort when their galley was towed out into deep water and had its hull stoppers removed. I led a prayer, pleading with God to have spared the First Athena's Grand Fleet such a fate, as the proud vessel disappeared beneath the waves."

"You . . . prayed?" Brittola asked incredulously.

"Yes, I did," Pinnosa pretended to look hurt. "Possibly to the same god as you."

Ursula laughed, "And I pray, too, that you please . . . continue."

"Three days later Martha's scouting patrol met a band of Batavian merchants heading north. The men told them that the First Athena was mustering around 'the most beautiful Commander-in-Chief in the entire Roman army' at Noviomagus, and gave us directions how to get here.

"Soon after that, we found the road that led inland from the Long Coast and headed straight for Noviomagus. I rode ahead, not only to let you and the others know we were safe, but also to make arrangements for nine hundred exhausted women, their horses and their attendants.

"Once they're collected from the far bank of the river and ferried the final leg of their journey . . ." Pinnosa paused as she reached for another haunch of venison, "they will all need a long, hot bath, a good meal and—at long last—a well-earned rest."

XIII

"Good evening, ladies! Your Highnesses! Allow me to introduce myself. My name is Decimius Rusticus Amorius Pantheus Maximus, though my friends—and I know we will soon be very good friends—usually call me Rusticus. I come from the greatest city north of the Alps—glorious Colonia—where I am not only the Praetorian Prefect, appointed by a very dear mutual friend of ours, the Emperor Constantine the Third, but I am also one of the most well-known, respected and—dare I say—'loved' of its denizens."

He laughed a rich, baritone laugh, then adjusted the sleeve of his bright red toga and struck a serious pose. "As you can hear, I speak perfect Britannic like a native. This is because I come from a huge family and one of my many aunts—my beloved Aunt Phoebe—was Britannic. I loved her dearly and she taught me well."

Rusticus took several steps further into the Commanders' Room in the Officers' Hall. His ample frame seemed to fill the room. He took in the officers with a flicker of his mischievous eyes. His white-toothed grin broadened beneath his dark, curly beard. He made a gracious bow, which made him look like an oak resisting the wind, then looked around the gathering before continuing. His eyes settled upon Brittola, who was standing in front of him, apparently transfixed. She blushed.

"So you are the mighty Britannic women who formed a great army. You beat off the murderous Hibernians and kept those hideous wild Picts at bay. You even defeated powerful Saxon armies! Now, you have survived a great storm, only to land here in Noviomagus. This is a little off route perhaps, but basically on course for your rendezvous with Constantine's men in Arelate—hopefully before Lughnasadh—but not until after he has joined forces with his son, Constans, and driven the evil Gerontius into the ground where he belongs. Am I right?"

"Uh . . . y-yes," Brittola stammered.

"You are remarkably well informed, Rusticus," Ursula said.

He turned, slowly and deliberately, in her direction. "And you, Your Highness . . . for I take it I am addressing Princess Ursula, daughter of King Deonotus of Corinium?" She nodded. "I once campaigned with your father many years ago. He is a man for whom I have the utmost respect. And if I may say so, Your Highness, you are every bit as beautiful as your much-lamented mother, Queen Rabacie."

Pinnosa laughed. "He caught you there, Ursula! A compliment for a compliment, eh, Rusticus? Then who am I, if you're so well-informed?"

He turned his large round face toward her. His grin grew even broader. "You—fearsome lady with the bright red hair—you must be the legendary Pinnosa, horsewoman supreme and the scourge of the enemies of Britannia. Am I right?" She smiled and nodded. "Ha! I knew it! They say the man who can tame you can only be found on Mount Olympus!"

"And you . . ." He returned his gaze to the young woman before him and lowered his voice. "You are the youngest and sweetest of the bunch. You must be Brittola."

As if they had a life of their own, the fingers of both Brittola's hands grasped her cross. Without saying a word, she bowed with great decorum.

He returned her formal bow, then turned to address the entire gathering. "As for the rest of you lovely ladies . . . I'm afraid you'll have to introduce yourselves."

"Introductions can wait until later, Rusticus," Ursula said politely but firmly. "First, I think we would all like to know what brings you here."

He reeled as if from shock at her words and raised the back of his great hand to his receding hairline. "Ah, but Your Highness, it has been a tiring journey for me to come and see you today. Would you deny a humble guest some refreshment before taxing his tired mind with difficult questions? I have brought some amphorae of excellent wine with me from the cellars of the Imperial Palace at Colonia. May I suggest we dine and get to know each other a little better before we discuss . . . shall we say. . . matters?" His smile broadened once more as he cast his eye around the group.

Ursula looked at Pinnosa, Julia and Faustina. They each gave surreptitious nods in reply.

"Very well. Please forgive us, Rusticus, for forfeiting our duty to an honored guest in favor of caution." She finally returned his smile and added jokingly, "Even if he does arrive uninvited, unheralded and unannounced."

He smiled back and bowed again, but this time she thought she detected some genuine humility in his manner.

"We wouldn't wish you to think the officers of the First Athena lacking in basic civilities." He made to comment, but she cut him short. "Now please excuse me while I attend to some pressing matters." She turned to address the others. "Ladies! Please introduce yourselves to our new friend, the honorable Rusticus of Colonia. Indulge him for a short time until the feast is ready. Remember our Emperor praises him greatly as a host, so do your very best to entertain him with true Britannic hospitality."

"Your Highness," Rusticus called after Ursula. "To dine with the officers of the First Athena will not be a matter of receiving simple hospitality. It will be like dining in Heaven!"

XIV

The kitchen had spent all day preparing a celebratory feast, and the spread of food was magnificent. On the tables was hot and cold food of every description: great steaming mounds of cooked vegetables, fruits, fish and eels were offered up on huge silver and bronze salvers. There were large bowls of freshly steamed shellfish and dozens of smaller dishes full of sauces and dainties.

The day before, Baetica had rescued the crew of the final missing galley from the Londinium flotilla. The muster of the First Athena was complete and there was finally something to celebrate. As the women and Rusticus took their positions, an endless stream of attendants issued forth from the kitchen with the meat to place before them. Platters of mutton, pork and venison were followed by calf, bear and stag, which had cooked slowly all day on spits. The whole beasts were carried around the tables for diners to cut off what they wanted. There was a great variety of waterfowl, cooked properly with sweet sauces and stuffing.

Pinnosa took a bite and declared, "I had forgotten there was any other ways to prepare wild bird besides burning them over a campfire! Delicious!"

As if the plethora of rich smells wasn't enough to excite their taste buds, the full-bodied, aromatic red wine from Colonia warmed the palate perfectly and created an anticipation in the mouth that turned the fullest appetite into a ravenous hunger.

Along with the other Commanders sharing his table, Ursula watched Rusticus with a mixture of revulsion and amazement. He did not eat so much as graze. Bishop Patroclus, the only other 'ample-bodied' man Ursula had ever dined with, like most Britannic men, either ate, talked or sang—but only one at a time and to the exclusion of the others. Rusticus, on the other hand, gnawed distractedly on a bone while talking or singing. Sometimes he interrupted himself in mid-sentence to pop a dainty into his mouth. Pausing only to strip the meat from a wing, he would continue chewing throughout a conversation, stabbing the air with the bones to emphasize his point. At one point, he held a half-eaten flank of venison in one hand for the duration of three separate conversations—and a song—before eventually returning to it and finishing it off. All this was punctuated with so much wine, she began to think he was Bacchus incarnate.

He was clearly in his element at a feast. His repartee had the whole company laughing raucously, especially after he discovered they were all chaste. Then he began making quips about women and marriage. At one point he leaned forward to Ursula, who was reclining on the couch next to his, and pinched her on the arm.

"Ow!" she cried, more surprised than hurt. "What was that for?"

"That's what the first bite of marriage feels like. Simple wasn't it? Just a delicate little pinch. But suddenly you're no longer a virgin—you're a woman." He looked her cheekily in the eye. "Hopefully a married one! Ha!"

Long after the women had finished eating, his appetite eventually waned. As he adjusted his position on the couch to one where he could continue quaffing his beloved Colonia wine, Ursula felt the moment was right for questions. "Rusticus," she said, as she too adopted a more comfortable drinking position, "I think it's time you told us the real reason why you are here."

"Very well, Your Highness." He frowned. "Unfortunately, there is more to life than pleasures such as this." He raised his voice to address the entire gathering. "Ladies! I'm afraid it falls upon me to be the reluctant bearer of unfortunate news." He paused to down another goblet of wine. Then, with all the women looking at him in anticipation, he held the vessel out for more and waited for it to be filled before continuing.

"Three weeks ago, another large tribe of Burgundians came down the River Main and broke through the frontier below Mogontiacum, intent on heading south to join their cousins who are causing Constantine such serious problems. Eight thousand men from the Colonia Garrison, including three thousand cavalry, went to join forces with the few legionaries left at Mogontiacum in order to attend to the matter. Unfortunately, since their departure, we have received reports that yet another tribe—Franks, we believe—have gathered along the frontier defenses just beyond the Taunus hills. They seem to be intent on heading toward Colonia itself. They could be upon the city and its surrounding area any day now. Yet, we only have what is left of the Garrison—less than a thousand men, with only a few hundred cavalry—to protect us."

Rusticus looked around the head table, as he paused to take another swig of wine. "I have come here today, Your Highness, to ask the First Athena—as the only sizeable field army in the area—to come to Colonia's aid in this, one of the great city's most miserable and darkest hours."

Ursula kept her eyes fixed firmly on Rusticus and watched him as he looked nervously around the group of Commanders. She knew he could see them exchanging glances of concern and shaking their heads. "I'm afraid we can't comply with this request," Ursula finally replied, firmly. "Our orders are to remain here in Noviomagus until it is safe for us to proceed south."

"With all due respect, Your Highness, your orders are over a month old. Events have overtaken circumstances. I'm sure if Constantine were here and could see for himself the desperate situation Colonia is facing, he would authorize the deployment immediately."

Pinnosa turned her goblet thoughtfully in her hand. "It is only by luck that we're here, Rusticus. What would Colonia do if there was no First Athena?"

He held her gaze before replying quietly, "Close its gates and pray."

"I can't believe the great city of Colonia is so defenseless," she contended. "Surely you can round up enough men—retired legionaries and so forth—to mount a credible deterrent? Can't you even put together two thousand cavalry to rein these Franks in and turn them around?"

"Please do not forget, Commander, that the people of Colonia, like those of Mogontiacum and Treveris, are well experienced in handling Germanic tribes. Why, most of us are of German origin ourselves. We understand their thinking, and we know what it would take to stop them. To 'rein these Franks in and turn them around,' as you say, would take a force of at least eight thousand men, including a minimum of thirty-five hundred cavalry. Even with your recent unfortunate losses, I'm sure the First Athena can more than match that number." He returned his attention to Ursula. "The expedition would only take a month," he pleaded. "You could still be in Arelate well before Lughnasadh."

There was a long silence. All eyes were on Ursula, who looked grave as she pondered his request. Finally she said, "There is sense in what you say, Rusticus. The First Athena is ready for action, and I'm sure we have the numbers to achieve what you ask. However, Pinnosa is right, too. We are here only by coincidence—by ill fortune, to be precise. Our mission is not to reinforce the Rhenus frontier. We are to go to Arelate and then return to Britannia, which is also in desperate need of reinforcement against invading tribes." She looked down the table to some of the junior officers before continuing. "And, anyway, I will not disobey the orders of our Emperor, no matter what the circumstances."

"Emperor? Pah! He's only wearing the purple because he needs to control the mints!" He took an angry swig of wine, obviously embarrassed at his loss of discretion. "Bah!"

Ursula and Pinnosa exchanged a look.

"I'm sorry, Your Highness. I didn't mean to offend you." He leaned forward. "You must realize that Britannia doesn't stand a chance on its own if the frontier is allowed to crumble. Constantine knows that better than anyone. If the frontier falls, Germania and Galliae will fall. If they collapse, Hispania will fall. If Hispania falls, Britannia will be surrounded by hostile tribes on all sides. And if the Germans combine forces with the Hibernians and the Picts, how long do you think your Island Province could resist the onslaught? A year, maybe two?"

Like the rest of the women, Ursula remained silent. She looked at their drunken guest with pity as he held out his goblet for yet more wine. She could see that in better times he would shun such serious talk in favor of fun and merriment.

While all eyes were still looking at him, a new idea came to Rusticus.

A smile returned to his face and his eyes regained some of their old mischievous sparkle. He looked up from his goblet and sat up straight. "My humble apologies, Your Highness. I have just realized that I have sadly been remiss. I've been concentrating so much on my mission I have completely forgotten another—entirely separate—matter. Prince Jovinus of Colonia asked me to convey his greetings to our royal visitors: the Princesses Ursula, Julia and Faustina. He asked me to extend his personal invitation for you to come and visit him while you are camped on the Rhenus. The hunting is excellent at this time of the year and the Prince is most eager to return some of the generous hospitality shown to him when he and his father toured Britannia several years ago."

Ursula looked at Julia and Faustina. They shared an expression of pleasant surprise. Rusticus's manner had been so convincing, for the briefest of moments their Commanders' roles were completely forgotten and the three Princesses found themselves warming to the royal invitation.

Then Ursula snapped them back to reality. "Kindly thank Prince Jovinus for his most generous invitation, and tell him that under normal circumstances we would be more than happy to accept. Unfortunately, however—"

"Just a moment," Pinnosa interrupted. "May I have a quiet word with you, Princess?" She turned to address Julia and Faustina. "And with Your Highnesses?"

The four women withdrew to an antechamber, where Pinnosa drew then into a corner and spoke in a hushed whisper, "I think it would be a very good idea if you accepted this invitation."

"What?" Ursula and Julia cried loudly together in disbelief.

Pinnosa shushed them, as they were still within earshot of the head table.

"You know what Constantine said about Colonia in his orders," Faustina hissed.

"Yes, but think for a moment." Pinnosa leaned closer to make doubly sure they weren't overheard. "We didn't study maps of the defenses along the Rhenus before we left, and we didn't bring any with us. It's an ideal opportunity for you to explore the area and become familiar with the terrain. You'll also be able to make your own assessment of possible manpower strengths and deployments."

Ursula and Julia nodded slowly.

"But, we can rely on the Batavians and others for such information," Faustina objected.

"I disagree," Pinnosa replied. "I don't think we can rely on anyone. Our 'friend' in there has proven that to me beyond doubt this evening—with his display of 'loyalty' to Constantine. I wouldn't trust him any more than I would trust a Pict with a baby. The only information we would ever get from Rusticus would be that which he deemed important—and that which he thought would bend *our* means to *his* ends."

She paused and looked at them one by one. "We've all discovered recently what it's like to be completely lost with no first-hand knowledge of the area." Julia shuddered. "I, for one, would feel much more at ease with our current situation if we had our own reliable information on things like the fortifications along the Rhenus further upstream and possible crossing points. Or, about Colonia itself—its defenses and the surrounding lay of the land. You could even take up this offer of a hunting trip and see for yourselves what the frontier lands look like on the other side of the river. We could make our own assessment of how quickly a German tribe could travel through them." She paused to let her suggestion take root. "The more I think about it, the more value I see in you going. I only wish I could go with you, but one of us needs to stay here. Anyway, I think you ought to go as the invitation intended—as Princesses without a military escort. Leave your uniforms and weapons here. Just take your hunting kits."

"What if orders come through from Constantine while we're away?" It was clear from Ursula's voice that she was already convinced and was now only thinking through the details.

"You know as well as I do we won't hear from Constantine until some-time in the next cycle of the moon. But even if orders did come through, by all accounts, Colonia is just a short ride away. I'm sure you could be back here before the preparations for the long march were complete."

A few moments later, the four women returned to the Commanders' Room. Ursula didn't even wait for them to be seated before making her an-nouncement. "Rusticus: Julia, Faustina and I have decided to accept Prince Jovinus' kind invitation. We will leave with you first thing tomorrow morning and head straight for Colonia."

XV

"*Pro iucundissima omnium in orbe urbium!*—Here's to the most exhilarating city in the world. Long may she be the greatest jewel in Rome's crown north of the Alps." Ursula raised her glass in yet another toast. "We have enjoyed our three days here tremendously."

As she sat back down, she reflected that this trip had temporarily removed all the cares of recent years. She was once more a royal Princess, instead of the Commander of an army.

A few days earlier, Ursula's initial impression of the great city of Colonia had been one of wonder. Its sheer size was almost overwhelming, especially for she and Faustina, who had never been outside Britannia before. The city was about the same size as Londinium, but, because of its strategic position on the frontier of Rome, it also had a huge military complex—one that rivaled that of Eboracum. Indeed, "Londinium and Eboracum combined," was Faustina's apt description of it.

Ursula was particularly struck by the stark contrast between the military and civilian areas. As the royal party—consisting of the royal Princesses, Rusticus and Bishop Clematius—rode through the outer districts, Rusticus made a point of taking them through the huge barrack complexes on both sides of the river. Row after row of empty and deserted buildings, both personnel quarters and stables, made her realize how weak and defenseless the city was.

The haunting stillness of the military complex was replaced by a hectic, bustling, cosmopolitan city as they entered one of the city's main gates. Colonia was crammed with people, goods, and beasts from every corner of the Empire—the innocent, provincial eye would be forgiven for confusing it with Rome itself. Ursula heard so many languages being spoken she wasn't sure which was the local German dialect.

As they rode slowly through the crowded streets, Ursula was astonished at what she saw. The most remarkable sight was a troupe of performing creatures she had heard of, but never encountered, called apes. They were dressed in mock uniforms and performed comical tricks. The apes' owners were dark-skinned men from a province called Africa who wore exotic clothes in hues she'd never imagined existed. The men sang tunes full of strange sounds while the apes performed their acrobatics.

The royal party stopped before a great machine, which played music, powered by a donkey on a treadmill. A man—who spoke a most peculiar form of Latin—approached them and enthusiastically explained how it all worked. A complex series of bellows forced air through pipes that were mounted in rows along the top. They made a shrill noise that was almost deafening. There was an equally complicated system of gears, levers and pulleys that worked the sticks to beat the drums and bells, which formed the main body of the contraption.

As they rode away, and its inharmonious sound receded into the distance, Julia said, "It's the machine itself—rather than the hideous music it produces—that is the actual attraction."

Everywhere they went, they discovered goods for sale that were new to them. Of special interest was the exquisite glassware for which Colonia was justly renowned. Being surrounded by so much exotica, the three Princesses dismounted and, accompanied by their escort, made their way on foot, wandering slowly from street stall to shop in a leisurely manner.

Eventually, they arrived at the great Imperial Palace at the heart of the city, where Prince Jovinus received them in an elaborate reception. Ursula had met him once before, when he was a mere boy of twelve. She barely remembered him, having only been eight at the time. When he appeared from behind a column, walking with Bishop Clematius, she was pleasantly surprised to find herself exchanging greetings with a rather handsome, tall, red-haired young man. Moreover, it was clear from the outset that he took great pleasure in the company of the three Princesses—especially her. They had no difficulty in persuading him to make immediate arrangements for a hunting party to go out deep into the nearby Taunus hills.

She came out of her reverie of the last three idyllic days to hear Jovinus reply to her toast in elegant Latin, "And here's to Britannia. Long may she continue to produce such remarkable women."

Her smile faded as her mind filled with thoughts of the First Athena and home. She downed her wine and stood up. "I'm just going to check on Swift," she said quietly. She headed for the nearby woodland stream where the horses were grazing.

"I'll come with you," Jovinus said, leaping eagerly to his feet. "We're in bear country and you shouldn't go off alone."

Before she could stop him, he had taken her by the arm and was leading her toward the trees. She looked back at Julia and Faustina and noticed their exchange of smirks. She poked her tongue out at them over her shoulder, which made them giggle.

"When do you think the First Athena will commence its long march south?" he asked.

"Hmm?" she replied distractedly. She had been enjoying walking arm in arm with him through the dappled pools of sunlight that filtered through the canopy of leaves overhead, and had drifted into a daze.

"All right, I'll be more direct . . . ." He stopped walking and pulled her round to face him. "When will you be leaving?"

"I . . . I'm not sure. We really ought to get back to Noviomagus as soon as possible."

"Why don't you let Julia and Faustina return to Noviomagus, and you stay here for a while longer?" He grabbed her by the shoulders and moved closer to her. She tried to step back but there was a tree behind her and all she succeeded in doing was allow him to pin her against it.

"But . . . but I couldn't," she said clumsily, her mind beginning to race as she realized his intentions.

"Why not?" He put his hand under her chin and lifted her mouth toward his. "You know you want to, just as I want you to."

She tried to wrestle her head away from his looming face, but his grip on her chin tightened, and the only measure she could take was to pull herself back tight against the tree trunk.

"I want you to stay in Colonia, and—"

His lips were almost upon hers. She could feel the heat of his breath.

"Stop! Say no more and do no more!" she shouted.

He looked nervously over his shoulder in the direction of the camp.

"Now, please, let me go," she said through gritted teeth.

He took one look at her fierce expression and stepped away.

"Thank you," she said quietly but firmly. "I'm going to check on the horses. I strongly suggest that you go back to the others and tell them to get ready to leave. Tell them also that we're going to ride to that high point you've been telling us about, which is just a few miles from here. All right?"

He made to say something.

"All right?" she snapped.

He nodded, turned and walked sheepishly away.

Ursula closed her eyes and began to tremble.

XVI

"What a magnificent view!" Faustina shouted over the roar of the wind.

The tallest hill in the Eastern Taunus hills was more like a small mountain. The top had been cleared and a lookout tower built on the highest point to take maximum advantage of the elevated position. All six of the hunting party were standing on its upper platform. A strong, northerly wind was blowing their hair and cloaks out behind them as they turned to look north, deep into the German wild lands.

Rusticus pointed out the valley of the River Main in the distance. They could also make out the *Limes*—the extended line of palisades and fortifications, which formed the frontier. It stretched from Confluentes on the Rhenus, over two hundred and fifty miles southeastward to Castra Regina on the Danuvius.

Rusticus was telling them a long humorous tale about his last journey into the wilderness, when Ursula interrupted him. "Look!" She pointed down to an area immediately below them. "What do you think is causing that?"

As they watched, it seemed as if the entire forest between themselves and the Limes five miles to the north was alive with movement. Birds were shooting out of the trees, and the clearings seemed to be full of creatures of the forest—all running scared. Then they spotted them.

The Germanic tribes.

Faustina pointed to a clearing about a mile from the base of the hill. It was full of people in and around carts. Behind the crowd in wagons came a small herd of cattle driven by three figures on horseback. The whole group was moving slowly in the same direction—toward the royal hunting party.

Ursula noticed another clearing further away with a small river running through it, also full of people on the move. She could even see groups of children playing in the water as they went.

Great God, Ursula thought as she surveyed the disturbed landscape. *If all that movement is Germans, they must number in the tens of thousands—if not more.* She scoured the distant horizon. *They are already well inside the frontier, with nothing between them and Colonia. The city hasn't got a chance!*

Her mind leapt to a wild ride to Magnis and a people under threat. She recalled the wide, staring eyes of a frail old man, scared beyond his wits by the sounds and horrors of death, and the look on Pinnosa's face as she realized her family might have been killed. *It only took the actions of a mere handful of young women to restore the peace, and give defenseless people the security they craved . . . security and hope . . . .*

"Its the Franks!" Jovinus shouted. "We must leave at once! We're in grave peril here! Their advance scouts travel in bands of up to a hundred and they always head for high land."

Ursula barred the top of the steps and the way back to the horses. "As soon as we get back, I shall order the First Athena's deployment to Colonia—so that we can contain these Franks."

Even Rusticus gasped at her sudden decision.

"One more thing. . ." She looked pointedly at Jovinus before continuing. "Having experienced the delights and distractions of 'the greatest city north of the Alps,' the women shall be confined to barracks . . ." Ursula shifted her gaze to Julia and Faustina, and added in Britannic, "including the officers."

Chapter 6

Mundzuk

Scouts from both the Mogontiacum and Colonia Garrisons, disguised as woodland folk, monitored the progress of the Franks as they made their way through the Taunus hills toward Colonia.

From their reports, Ursula determined that the tribe was guarded by five main groups of fighting men. Four of the bands appeared to be mobs of untrained and undisciplined youngsters, each about a thousand in strength and led by a small group of elders on horseback. At the heart of the tribal horde, attached to the royal party, was a fifth—and much better organized—military unit. This was a sizeable corps of well-trained, well-armed infantry plus an elite cavalry unit of Royal Guards about three hundred strong.

The First Athena laid their trap in an area of gentle hills and valleys that were part of the elevated plateau to the east of where the Rhenus ran through a long, twisting gorge on its way from Mogontiacum to Confluentes. Rusticus advised that the operation should take place early in the morning when most of the tribesmen, especially the younger ones, would still be sober. They would be easier to deal with than when they were filled with "liquid courage."

Soon after dawn on the legion's third day in the area, Ursula gave the orders for the operation to commence. It began with decoy cavalry units, led by Saula, Brittola, Faustina and Viventia entering the fringes of the tribe's sprawling camp area at four separate points in order to draw away the large bands of untrained men.

In each case, the Frankish leaders fell for the bait. They gave chase on horseback, only to find themselves led into clearings where they were surrounded by archers and a large force of cavalry. By the time their men arrived on foot, the leaders were disarmed and made captives. Thus leaderless, the

Frank mobs submitted to defeat and surrendered their weapons, including their fearsome throwing axes.

All readily accepted defeat except for a group of fifty or so teenagers, still full of "ale bravado" from the previous night's carousing, who chased after Viventia's squad. When they realized they were encountering the famous First Athena, they rushed at the Roman archers. They managed to hurl their large and vicious spiked axes before being felled by a well-aimed volley of arrows. Several of the First Athena were hit. Four were killed.

Elsewhere, Martha and Baetica emerged with their units of decoy cavalry from a small gully into the very valley—a narrow and twisting gorge— where the Frankish King had made camp. The royal party, including children and elders, were bathing in the stream that ran through the clearing when Martha's women sounded their horns.

Before the Frankish guards could make for their weapons or their horses, Martha and Baetica's cavalry thundered out of the forest. They attacked using Pinnosa's short spear maneuver, before racing off down the valley toward the Rhenus, leaving behind several wounded. Looking back over her shoulder as they galloped for cover, Martha was pleased to see the plan working. The entire Royal Guard, led by the King himself, was giving chase.

As the summer's sun appeared over the eastern ridges, Ursula, Pinnosa, Julia and Rusticus set forth with the core division from where they had spent the night hidden amongst the crags overlooking the gorge. They had with them a cohort of men from the Colonia Garrison as they set off along the hunter's track that took them directly to the Frankish royal party's camp. Following Ursula and Pinnosa's lead, they rode at full gallop through the dense forest and down into the valley. Their aim was to press home the attack as swiftly as possible and take best advantage of the opportunity Martha's and Baetica's units had afforded them.

Ursula's cohort burst from the trees and emerged into the clearing to find the nobles and their guard of infantrymen still in disarray after Martha and Baetica's onslaught. With Ursula and Pinnosa to the fore, they raced across the clearing and made a single, decisive pass that felled several more of the Frankish men, before regrouping and taking up position by the First Athena standard on the high ground along the tree line.

With no cavalry in support, the Frankish infantry immediately surrendered and allowed themselves to be disarmed by the men from the Colonia Garrison without any real resistance. The Colonia men barely finished tying up their captives, when they heard the sound of thundering hooves. It was the King and his Royal Guards returning from their futile chase of Martha and

Baetica's legionaries. As soon as the King's cavalry entered the clearing and saw Ursula's force, they become wild with fury. The King managed to rally most of his men into a group at the opposite end of the clearing, but several of the more frenzied ones galloped over to the disciplined Roman ranks, brandishing their axes and letting fly their arrows.

Seeing the possibility of unnecessary casualties on both sides, Pinnosa, leapt from Artemis and grabbed an old woman from among the royal party, who bore a strong resemblance to the Frankish King. The old crone squawked with pain as Pinnosa dragged her to the back of an abandoned cart that was lying in the open ground between the two armies. Forcing the woman's right hand open on the cart's backboard, Pinnosa brandished her sword on high before bringing it down to slice off the old woman's little finger.

"*Aiyee!*" the old woman shrieked.

"Tell him that his infantry have been disarmed, and that his family are being held by the First Cohort of the Legion First Athena," Ursula called to Rusticus. "Then tell him that I'm going to count to three. If he and his men haven't put down their weapons by then, I'll order my Commander to slit her throat."

Early on, Rusticus had determined that the only way to deal effectively with the Franks without too much bloodshed would be to capture the women-folk of the leaders and use them as bargaining tools. Indeed, Rusticus had proved invaluable to the mission, especially with his ability to speak fluent Frankish. "One of my many aunts, Aunt Aiga, was a Frank," he told Ursula back in the Commanders Room in Colonia. Obviously forcing his melancholy, he stared deep into his goblet of wine. "I loved her dearly, and she taught me well."

Now he gave Ursula a formal salute and rode from the Roman ranks to shout her message across the clearing. The Frankish cavalry were struggling to reel their horses into formation. Many were still shouting their war cries.

The Frankish King, a big man wearing leather and chain body armor, with a brace of throwing axes tied to his waist, raised his hand for his men to be silent. He rode slowly toward Pinnosa. When he was about twenty cubits away, he stopped. For what seemed an eternity, he scrutinized her.

Pinnosa glared defiantly back, her sword still drawn and poised. Finally, he glanced down at the poor old woman, who had collapsed to her knees in agony. Then he shouted his reply. Rusticus also shouted his translation, "He'd heard that the Roman women from Britannia were brave and fought like men. Now he can see for himself that they are just gutless and devious wenches who deserve only to be trodden into the ground like the vile vermin they are!"

"*Start counting!*" Pinnosa demanded without taking her eyes from her adversary.

"*Ünus!*" Ursula shouted before Rusticus could translate.

The King went for one of his axes.

Pinnosa grabbed the old woman by the hair, and pulled back her head, exposing her throat.

His hand stayed on the axe, but he didn't pull it out of his belt.

"*Keep counting!*" Pinnosa cried, again without looking around.

"*Duo!*" Ursula called out.

Pinnosa raised her sword. "Tell him to order his men to drop their weapons again, Rusticus," she commanded.

Rusticus repeated the ultimatum.

The Frankish King appeared unmoved.

"Tell him it'll be the children next," Pinnosa snapped.

Rusticus hesitated.

"*Tell him!* Tell him he'll lose both his past *and* his future."

Rusticus hastily shouted the translation, his voice becoming almost shrill with urgency.

The King's cold eyes took in the ranks of the First Athena. He saw his family bound tight in their grasp. He turned to survey his captured infantry, kneeling on the ground beside their wounded. They all had their hands on their heads and were closely guarded by the Roman horsemen. Then he looked back at his own cavalry, axes drawn and ready to charge.

"*Count!*" Pinnosa shouted.

"*Trës!*" Ursula cried at the top of her voice.

Pinnosa placed the edge of her blade against the old woman's neck and made to cut.

The King shouted an order. After staring at each other, his men dropped their axes.

"*And* their swords . . . as well as his own weapons!" Ursula shouted.

Rusticus frantically bellowed the translation.

Reluctantly, one by one, they complied.

II

"The reason my tribe is heading west is because we are seeking refuge in Roman territory," Sunno, the Frankish king, told Ursula and the other Commanders through Rusticus later as they sat in a campaign tent together. "We were forced to leave our homelands by invasions of people who were being driven out of their homes from even further east. They were fleeing from an even greater terror—the Huns.

"The eastern tribes were once rivals, but not so long ago they joined together—they call themselves the Alemanni—in order to resist the murderous Huns and their relentless pursuit of plunder.

"The Huns!" he snarled, "The Huns are the cause of all the ill fortune that has befallen us!"

"Who are they? What do they look like?" Pinnosa asked.

Sunno hunched closer and said in a quieter voice, "I have heard from some of the Frankish merchants the Huns aren't human. They are hideous creatures that have escaped from the underworld. They have big, square heads and long, pointed faces. My soothsayers tell me, the Evil Ones who crave suffering in our land—the ones who thrive on hatred and war—it is *they* who set the Huns loose upon the world."

Sunno paused; a look of loathing clouded his face. "I have even learned of their leader's name," he said through Rusticus's translation.

Ursula felt the hairs on her arms start to rise. Even before he spoke, she felt she knew what he was going to say.

"Mundzuk."

The sound of that name coming from Sunno's brown-toothed mouth made Ursula break out in a cold sweat. She reached for Rusticus's ever-present flagon of wine and took a sizeable swig to prevent herself from fainting.

While she fought to retain her composure, Sunno continued. "Many, if not all, of the Alemanni tribes follow behind us. They also seek refuge in Roman lands. Only Rome is powerful enough to protect them—and us—from the Hun menace.

"When do you think the Alemanni will reach here?" Ursula asked through Rusticus.

"They will cross the River Main and break through those puny defenses you call the Limes sometime before two more cycles of the moon are complete."

Ursula politely thanked Sunno for his information. Then, solemnly, she announced she was about to inform the King Sunno of his status in the eyes of the Roman authorities.

Rusticus produced an Imperial Decree and handed it to Ursula. She read it out loud, in Latin, pausing after each article to allow Rusticus to translate it into Frankish.

"This comes directly from Augustus Constantine the Third and Prince Jovinus of Cologne. I, Princess Ursula, Commander-in-Chief of the First Athena and Decimius Rusticus Amorius Pantheus Maximus, Praetorian Prefect of Cologne, are authorized to act as the Emperor's agents in any dealings with you. That includes whether to resort to force if you, or any other tribal leaders, fail to comply.

"By order of Augustus Constantine the Third, the Franks are denied permission to cross the Rhenus. However, you are invited to take on Roman Federate status as long as you and your people agree to settle in the triangle of frontier lands formed by the Rivers Rhenus and Main and the Limes. Most importantly, you must swear an oath of allegiance to Rome.

"You will then assume, as your primary duty to Rome, the defence of the Limes between Confluentes and the River Main. In the exercise of this duty, you will agree to be subject to the authority of the senior Commanders of both the Mogontiacum and Colonia Garrisons.

"Finally, assuming you agree to these terms, as federate citizens of Rome, your army will be allowed to carry weapons—including your axes. You will also be given training and material support from the Garrisons at Mogontiacum and Colonia."

After Rusticus completed translating the final sentence, they all looked to Sunno for his response.

At first, the Frankish King simply returned their gaze without any expression. Then, slowly, he lowered his eyes to the ground and began to nod and smile. Suddenly, he stood up.

Ursula, Pinnosa and Julia leapt to their feet and drew their swords.

Sunno burst into bellicose laughter. "Do you take me for a *fool?*" he cried, as Rusticus rapidly translated. "Look at you! A 'Roman army' of women! An 'Imperial agent' with more wine in his veins than blood!" He leered into their faces. "Is this the 'majesty and might' of Rome that we are now 'entitled' to become a part of?" They looked at him in silence. "Your 'Emperor' Constantine, your 'Prince' Jovinus and whoever *really* wrote that 'Decree' can continue writing as many pretty pieces of paper as he—or she—wants."

He hawked his throat loudly and spat a huge globule of phlegm onto the matting before Ursula's feet. "It's all Roman *spit!* That's all it is! And like you and your precious First Athena . . ." he waved his hand dismissively at the nearby ranks outside the tent, "it will mean nothing to the likes of the Alemanni when they come here. Or to the Huns when they follow! The Burgundians have proven how feeble you Romans have become. The Suevi, too—and, yes, the Goths—who are now knocking on Rome's door . . . just as the Saxons are knocking on Londinium's."

"I take it then, that you reject the Emperor's offer." Ursula's voice sounded resolute, but while her words were being translated she could feel the strain of her facade as she struggled to disguise her fears. Deep down inside, she knew what Sunno had said was true.

Rusticus, obviously feeling uncomfortable, translated the Frankish King's churlish reply in hushed tones. "You may take it—pretty girl—that the Franks, like their other German cousins, will do exactly as they please. There is nothing the likes of you can do to stand in our way. We won't be caught off guard again and allow you to nibble away at a few fingers!"

Both Ursula and Pinnosa made to reply, but Sunno held his hand up for silence. Deliberately ignoring them, he turned pointedly to address his son. "As I see it, Clothar, we have a simple choice. Either we join the Alemanni and pick the bones clean of the fine feast that once was Rome." He turned back to face Ursula. "Or we work with this Roman . . . 'army' to defend what is left of the crumbling Empire *against* the Alemanni. Who would you rather fight, my son—the fierce tribesmen of the Alemanni or these women pretending to be—AHH!"

Sunno was so intent upon bullying Ursula and Pinnosa that he hadn't noticed Julia sidling round behind him. As he leaned forward to emphasize his taunt, Julia lunged between his legs and grabbed hold of his testicles. His eyes watered as he cried out with unbearable pain. He tried to twist around to grab his attacker, but she squeezed tighter. He squealed, understanding that to move at all meant excruciating agony.

His son tried to leap to his aid. Pinnosa was upon him in a second. She knocked him to the ground and pinned him there with her sword. Its tip pricked his neck and said in no uncertain terms, 'Don't move a muscle!'

"Please tell our esteemed visitor," Ursula said calmly to Rusticus, "that he seems to have forgotten something. No—better still—ask him *whether* he has forgotten something."

Rusticus mopped the sweat from his brow and translated.

Sunno hastily nodded in reply.

"Good. Now ask him if he knows what it is that he has forgotten."

After the translation, Sunno grunted, but didn't reply.

Ursula nodded. Julia squeezed even tighter. He gagged. "Ask him if he would like us to remind him."

Sunno began to nod frantically well before Rusticus finished his translation.

"Please point out that this humble army of Roman women has got his tribe—and its leader—by the balls. He was right about one thing; they do have two choices. They can remain barbarians. In which case, they won't be protected by Rome's laws. There will be nothing to stop us killing them all right here and now. Or they can become federate citizens of Rome, protected by Roman law and granted a measure of citizen rights as long as they uphold their duties as outlined in the Emperor's offer—oh, and Rusticus . . . ."

"Yes, Commander?"

"After you've translated that, please finish with just one simple question."

"And that is?"

"Will he accept the Emperor's terms? Yes or no?"

III

From Augustus Constantine III, Emperor of the West and Grand Commander of all its armies, to Princess Ursula, Commander-in-Chief of the Legions First and Second Athena. Hail great Princess and Commander! Utinam fortis aestatis sol illuminet te et calefaciat omnia quae vis.—*May the high summer sun be shedding illumination and warmth on all you survey.*

Your report on the situation along the Limes saddened me greatly and added much to my burdens. It would seem that all our hard work has proven futile and fruitless. The Limes seems to be acting more as a lure than a deterrent to these German tribes and would appear to be more porous than resistant!

First of all, I exonerate you and the First Athena from disobeying my orders. I have also received reports from Rusticus and Jovinus and it is now clear that the Franks posed a great threat to Colonia, which the city couldn't have resisted without your help. I was clearly wrong to think we could afford to keep nineteen thousand seasoned veterans, including some of the best cavalry units in the Roman army, out of the thick of things. Indeed, you and your women deserve full credit for the way you handled the campaign. I don't think we men could have achieved what you did with so few casualties. As Rusticus says, "These incredible women remind us all that there is much more to fighting than missiles and blades!"

Secondly, I now order you to deploy the First Athena to Mogontiacum. This is for two reasons. First, you need to supervise your new 'friend,' Sunno, very closely. Not only because he is himself untrustworthy, but also because his loyalty—if he knows such a concept— may be elsewhere. The other reason is that this approaching body of Alemanni is a very serious threat indeed. If they break through into Germania and Galliae, it will be no exaggeration to say that the West is lost!

I therefore want you in Mogontiacum where you will be in a much better position to deal with the problem as it develops. You and the others and Rusticus (I'm encouraged to hear you work well together) need to think very carefully about your tactics with the Alemanni when they appear. You can be sure that the techniques you used so effectively with the Franks will now be known to them. They will be taking measures, such as disguising their noble women as peasant folk and replacing them with substitutes.

Your biggest problem will be the sheer number of armed men—especially the large cavalry units from some of their more eastern tribes. I suggest you look for an opportunity to make a massive show of force. In my experience it is the only way to halt their advance. If you had four times your actual number of cavalry this would pose no problem!

Finally, a warning. Now that you are caught up in Continental events, you must exercise even greater caution and be less trusting than ever before. The Franks and Sunno are a case in point. They may very well be in the pay of one of the Emperors from the House of Theodosius. Honorius is still holed up in Ravenna. His half-nephew, Theodosius the Second, is now back in Constantinopolis after a short campaign into Persia. Either of them could be planning with Sunno for the Franks to turn on you—as so many 'federate' tribes have done recently.

We now know, for example, that many of the Burgundians, who are the bane of eastern Galliae and have been tying up most of my men, have been 'encouraged' by one or the other of our Theodosian friends—and quite possibly both! More than that, I now have conclusive proof that the House of Theodosius is behind this Hispanian insurrection, which still has us penned in like a yearling, by Gerontius and Maximus's interminable siege.

Most seriously, Constans has had problems with treachery from most, if not all, of his auxiliary Suevi units. Their true loyalty would seem to stretch back over the Alps. In fact, he has been so caught up with overcoming the rebellious units, he has yet to emerge from the mountains to come to my aid—though I am expecting him to do so any day now.

Even these Huns wreaking so much havoc beyond Rome's borders, are probably working for Theodosius the Second. He has a strong interest in keeping the West weak and pre-occupied. We now know with certainty, for example, that this monster, Mundzuk, assembled the core of his force more than two winters ago along the northern shore of the Black Sea, within easy reach of Constantinopolis.

Incidentally, do not succumb to this wild panic that precedes these Huns. It is their most potent weapon. Apart from their gruesome appearance—they apparently place their babies' heads in block clamps during their formative years which gives them their horrifying looks—they are no more fearsome than any other Barbarian tribe, and just as vulnerable to attack from a disciplined Roman army.

Hopefully, we'll soon crush all these pests that are currently bothering us so that your Great Expedition can be resumed. Arelate is just as beautiful in the autumn as it is in the summer. As the campaign season will be almost over, it should be possible for the 'army of newlyweds' to winter together and keep each other warm!

Until then, may God be with you,
Constantine

IV

I suggest you look for an opportunity to make a massive show of force. In my experience it is the only way to halt their advance. If you had four times your actual number of cavalry this would pose no problem!

The words from Constantine's letter kept repeating in her mind as Ursula sat alone in the Commanders' Room in Colonia poring over maps and reports, trying to think of a strategy for dealing with the Alemanni. The first tribes were reported to be less than five days' ride from the Limes. They were moving very slowly, which meant the First Athena still had some time to formulate a plan and implement it.

She was interrupted from her thoughts by the sound of familiar steps approaching. She looked up and smiled.

"Good day to you, Your Highness," Rusticus exclaimed as he strode in through the door a little early for their daily exchange of news. "The weather's perfect for hunting. You should be outside with Swift gathering game, not imprisoned with your charts gathering far too much information for such a beautiful, young head!" He handed his bright red cloak and even brighter blue riding hat with its extended plume to Oleander.

"Good day to you." Ursula found it difficult not to laugh at the sight of him adjusting the wide riding belt round his ample girth and trying to get comfortable. "Rusticus, I'd like to ask you something."

He breathed a sigh of relief as his bodily bulges assumed their natural positions. "Hmm?"

"How many women are there in the First Athena?"

Rusticus grabbed a handful of bread and cheese from a nearby bowl and reached for the wine. "What a question coming from you." He looked at her askance as he poured his draught. "You might as well ask me how many angels there are in Heaven."

"I am curious to hear your answer. To your knowledge, what are the exact numbers of the First Athena . . . infantry and cavalry?"

He walked over to the planning table and held her gaze for a moment. Then he sat down and placed his food before him. "You *are* serious, aren't you?"

She nodded. "Have you ever known me not to be?"

"Let me see . . . ." He took a swig from his goblet and looked up at the ceiling. The fingers of his free hand ran through his whiskers while he gave the matter some thought. "I would estimate you have around . . . fifteen thousand infantry . . ." He looked out of the corner of his eye at her to see whether she reacted.

She stared at him inscrutably.

"And about . . . three thousand cavalry?"

"How many people in Colonia would share those estimates, besides you?"

"Apart from myself? There's Jovinus, of course, the Commander of the Garrison, the ordnance official of the barracks maybe—although you do your own purveyance . . . ." He seemed to run out of possibilities. "Bishop Clematius, perhaps . . . that is assuming all you good Christian women go to confession!" In his vexation, he quaffed more of his beloved wine. "Oh, I don't know. It's difficult to say. You've kept the security around the barracks and stables so tight."

She thumped the table. "*Exactly!*"

Rusticus was so startled he spilled wine down his front.

"What about Mogontiacum? How many of the First Athena are they expecting?" She placed both hands on the table and leaned forward in earnest.

"I . . . I don't know." He shrugged. "Mogontiacum's barracks and stables are even bigger than ours . . . and emptier. The fact that we've accommodated you without any problem would be sufficient information for their preparations. To answer your question, they're probably expecting no less than ten thousand—and no more than thirty."

"Ha! Perfect!" She pummelled the table with her fists in excitement. "Last question, Rusticus, and the most important one: How about the Alemanni?"

"How big do they think the First Athena is?"

"Yes."

"Well, they probably think of you as 'big enough to crush the Franks and the Saxons.' If they have a number in mind at all, it will be even vaguer than the one the people of Mogontiacum have."

"That's *it*, Rusticus!" She rushed round the table and threw her arms around his shoulders, making him spill even more of his wine. "I know how we can contain the Alemanni!"

"That's *what*?" His bemusement turned to exasperation as he wiped his chest. "*What's* it? *How*?"

"By making the Alemanni believe the First Athena is much bigger than it really is."

Rusticus laughed and took another swig of wine in celebration. "By the way," he asked with feigned casualness. "How big is the First Athena, exactly?"

Playfully, she tweaked his bulbous nose. "How many angels are there in Heaven?"

V

The First Athena was ready to embark on its re-deployment to Mogontiacum within a week. Their most important requirement—if their plan was to succeed—was horses. They needed as many horses as they could find. With Rusticus's help, within four days they commandeered the entire remaining stock of horses in both the Noviomagus and Colonia stables, amounting to just over three thousand head.

Meanwhile, under Pinnosa's supervision, the cavalry Commanders set about training three thousand of the infantry in enough basic horse handling skills so they could parade convincingly on horseback and act as an escort for a marching army. By the time the horses were ready—so were they.

Instead of having a Grand Parade through the city as they had done in Londinium, Ursula had all three thousand cavalry—along with the three thousand decoy cavalry—leave Colonia in six smaller detachments, each a thousand strong, throughout the course of the day. Under cover of darkness, they returned to the city's barracks along the opposite bank of the river. Then they departed again the following day, creating the impression that the First Athena's cavalry numbered twelve thousand. Once the Legion had finally assembled—twenty miles south of Colonia—they set off along the broad military road south to Mogontiacum.

Three days later, the blue silhouette of the Taunus hills started to loom large before them. The rise marked the end of Roman territory, the limit of Roman rule and—just beyond—the beginning of the never-ending sea of barbarianism.

Evening bells were just sounding as they crested the last hill on their route. There, immediately before them, was Mogontiacum—the largest, most powerful fortress north of the Alps—its massive yellow and red stone ramparts set aglow by the setting sun.

Ursula and the Commanders paused on a promontory and looked in awe at the immense garrison fortifications. The whole military complex straddled both shores of the Rhenus, adjacent to its confluence with the River Main, where the great river completed a sweeping bend to head west toward Colonia. The city at the heart of the complex nestled against the water's edge on the southern bank of the Rhenus beneath a long, natural ridge that followed the river's southern shore. The ridge's jutting bedrock formed the foundation of the fortress's huge battlements and towers. They completely dwarfed the city, enveloping it on all sides like some gigantic, ever vigilant guardian.

The fortifications were orientated northward, against the threat of German invasions. It was an intimidating presence on the landscape, like an indomitable sentry on eternal duty.

"You can almost hear that place warning would-be invaders," Ursula said to Faustina, "'Halt! You are now approaching Roman territory. You may not enter without due permission from the Roman authorities. You may not proceed unless you abide by Roman laws and obey Roman orders.'"

The First Athena didn't actually enter the city itself. Instead, the Legion circuited the city walls along the waterfront and crossed the great bridge over the Rhenus to the military buildings on the northern shore. The First Athena could choose from the row upon row of empty barracks and stables, which had the capacity to house as many as a hundred thousand legionaries. Ursula repeated the deceptive ploy they used in Colonia and had both the real and the dummy cavalries arrive a second time the following morning. Somehow, though, the maneuver seemed a flimsy gesture beneath the imposing structures of the huge fortifications.

A number of reports were waiting for Ursula when she arrived. One informed her that the first of the Alemanni tribes would be reaching the Limes within days. Another more recent one alerted them that Roman patrols had already encountered several Alemanni scouting parties less than one day's ride from the frontier.

Working closely with the Praetorian Prefect of Mogontiacum, Julian Florentius, Ursula, Pinnosa and Martha immediately set about organizing the local woods people into "spy networks" to gather as much first-hand knowledge of the approaching menace as possible. At the same time, the elite Vanguard of the First Athena was divided into six reconnaissance units, each led by one of the senior Commanders. They headed off across the Taunus hills into the wild lands beyond the Limes with local guides to gain an understanding of the terrain they were about to operate in.

The reconnaissance patrols had barely reported back, when Rusticus arrived by boat from Colonia, joining them once again to act as translator. Even though the Alemanni peoples spoke a wide variety of languages, only two tongues were used when their leaders held meetings. It just so happened that Rusticus could speak both of them fluently. "My aunts Uta and Gorda were from Alemanni tribes," he had said forlornly over a glass of red wine. It had been late in the evening in Colonia, after they formulated their plan. "I loved them dearly, and they taught me well." After which he wiped away a tear and blew his nose into his toga.

The following day, the plan—which they had taken to calling the Grand Deception—was put into action. The First Athena set forth on its task to convince the Alemanni that the Legion was double its actual size with, crucially, an accompanying cavalry unit of four times its real number. It took two days for the women to get into position, during which time the foremost tribes of the Alemanni began to make their camps in the military zone adjacent to the Limes.

Ursula sent official delegations into each of the tribal groups to greet their leaders and inform them that the Commander-in-Chief of the First Athena, Princess Ursula of Britannia, the official representative of the Emperor, Augustus Constantine the Third, would like to convene a meeting to discuss their approach of Roman territory. The meeting was to be held two days later at a special point where three rivers met just north of the Limes. The Chieftains all readily agreed and the delegations returned safely without incident.

Then the Grand Deception truly began.

As the tribal ambassadors and their accompanying escorts of armed guards made their way along the three valleys that converged upon the designated meeting point, each one caught sight of a number of contingents of the First Athena cavalry monitoring their movements from high vantage points. As Ursula intended, once the Alemanni reached the clearing where the assembly was to take place—and while they were waiting for the Imperial Delegation to arrive—the Chieftains quickly exchanged reports. They determined that each valley was patrolled by four cavalry units: blue, red, green and orange. Each unit appeared to be approximately one thousand strong. Their conclusion was that the First Athena had a total of at least ten—and possibly as many as twelve—thousand cavalry. By the time Ursula and the Imperial Delegation arrived, the Alemanni concluded the information they had received from the Franks suggesting that Mogontiacum and Colonia were defenseless and ripe for plucking, apart from a few over-ambitious women, had been completely false.

After due ceremony and an exchange of gifts, Ursula, through Rusticus, began the negotiations. She laid out the terms of the Imperial Decree which offered federal status, special rights and incentives as long as the Alemanni agreed to settle in the Taunus hills beyond the Limes and act in concert with the Roman Garrisons of Colonia and Mogontiacum to keep further invading tribes at bay. The Chieftains made a show of resistance, which Ursula could see was only token. After some minor wrangles, they unanimously and unconditionally accepted the Emperor's offer.

Up until the conclusion of the talks, the Grand Deception seemed poised to be a great success. The trouble came just as Ursula and the Imperial Delegation were preparing to leave. One of the tribal leaders—a very tall man called Luethari—expressed a strong desire to see some of the renowned prowess of the women of the First Athena in "the arts of war".

"What better way to demonstrate and strengthen our new allegiance to Rome," he declared enthusiastically, "than by challenging the best of the young Amazons to a friendly contest—champions against champions!"

Ursula, smiling politely, whispered urgently in Britannic to Rusticus, "We can't agree to this. What, in God's name, are we going to do?"

"Keep smiling and pretend to laugh with enthusiasm at the prospect."

Rusticus hastily demonstrated and forced a hearty chuckle as if relishing the prospect of what was being suggested.

"The longer we stay here," Julia said, forcing a broad smile and adopting a false light-hearted tone, "the greater the risk of the truth being exposed." She feigned a lighthearted laugh. "I say we leave right now."

"Ha, ha, ha . . ." Rusticus guffawed to keep up the charade. "We can't decline. To do so would be a grave insult. It would put our alliance with them in utter peril—not to mention our lives . . . . Ha, ha, ha."

Ursula joined in the pretend joke and added her own mock chuckles to the round of false laughter that ensued. "Very well, Rusticus," she said, realizing she could hesitate no longer. "We'll agree to a contest, but do your best to keep it short. Keep the First Athena well away from their men."

After Ursula smiled and nodded her agreement, preparations were completed swiftly. The ceremonial guards withdrew from the center of the huge clearing, creating an open arena for the contest, across which the two rival banks of onlookers faced each other. One side was eager with anticipation—the other full of trepidation. Ursula led the tribal and imperial delegations to one end, leaving the other as the stage entrance for the participants.

Viventia, Baetica and Pinnosa commenced the games by representing the First Athena in a display of horse riding skills. Viventia went first, entertaining the Alemanni by standing on her horse's back at full gallop, then by sitting sideways on her horse and firing arrows into stationary targets. Baetica made a similar show of expertise in horse-womanship except that she rode backwards instead of sideways. Like Viventia, she drew an enormous roar of cheers from the Alemanni ranks as well as warm applause from her comrades.

Pinnosa decided to demonstrate the superiority of Roman horses. She entered the arena on foot, alone, carrying in her hand some birds' eggs that she'd found nearby. She whistled a sharp, high note and Artemis appeared, without any trappings, at the end of the clearing. At a second whistle the great horse reared. Another started Artemis trotting around the clearing, and at the next she broke into a gallop. A final shrill note brought the handsome and well-groomed mare to her mistress.

The Alemanni shouted, banged their shields with their swords, and cracked their whips in the air in appreciation.

While they were still applauding, Pinnosa took the eggs she had been carrying and carefully placed them in Artemis' mouth. Then she leapt upon the great horse's bare back and rode over to the tribal leaders who were sitting with Ursula. By guiding Artemis with pressure from her knees and by leaning forward so that she could whisper simple commands, Pinnosa directed the powerful mare to delicately place an intact egg—one by one—into each chieftain's outstretched hand. Pinnosa then had Artemis back-step the entire length of the arena to the edge of the clearing, where the great horse reared several times with dramatic, air-punches of her hooves—each rear accompanied by a great roar from the men—before finally departing. Her spectacular exit ceremonially marked the end of the First Athena's display of horse riding expertise.

Next, it was the turn of the Alemanni. They fielded a group of riders to demonstrate their skills in battle. Men leapt from their horse's backs to dismount foes. Then they rode leaning off their horses from one side or another to avoid missiles that were fired at them.

With the riding demonstrations complete, it was time for the true contest to begin. The first round of games was to be a test of marksmanship.

While the preparations were underway for the arrow and spear competitions, Rusticus, resuming his fake, jovial facade, leaned over to speak with Ursula, and Julia, and Pinnosa who had just rejoined the dignitaries. Pretending to laugh merrily, he said, "I hope you realize we're in grave peril!" He pointed surreptitiously at a ferocious looking chieftain who was leering salaciously at an extremely nervous-looking Brittola.

Pinnosa chortled at the pretend joke. "Yes, I know. Any moment now, one of their guards is going to get near enough to our patrols to notice what they're wearing," she said, referring to the women's reversible, two-colored cloaks. "They may have fooled the Alemanni from a distance—but they won't close up."

"Not only that," Rusticus continued, his chuckle beginning to sound tired and forced, "the next round of the contest will be man-to-woman combat."

"We'll simply *refuse* to participate!" Julia blurted angrily, momentarily breaking the delicate facade.

Rusticus laughed loudly to counteract the tense silence of suspicion that Julia's outburst had elicited. "It's not as simple as that. It would be a great insult to them, which would place the whole alliance in jeopardy."

"But if we go ahead and participate, the alliance will also be undermined," Ursula mused quietly, limiting herself to an indulgent smile. "Look at the size of some of those men. They'd be more than a match for even the biggest and best of our women. That would make the First Athena beatable in their minds."

"It depends what kind of hand-to-hand they have in mind," Pinnosa suggested.

"Don't even think about it," Ursula hissed through a stiff grin. "We must find a way to disengage from the rest of the contest without insulting them. It's the only answer."

"But, ha—ha—how?" Rusticus tittered nervously. The way he tugged on the neck of his toga betrayed how uncomfortable he was feeling.

Throughout the marksmanship competition, Ursula and the others racked their brains for a way to end the contest without either side losing honor. Both teams performed well and appeared to be equally matched. The crowd roared as the scores kept pace with each other. By the time the games were drawing to a close, Ursula was becoming almost frantic to find a plan.

Then, during the final round of archery, a strong wind blew up from the west. The sky filled with ominous black clouds and large raindrops began to fall. Undeterred, some of the Alemanni took the field to display their skills with whips. One of the tribesmen had just started knocking stones off short poles in the ground, when the heavens opened.

The downpour made it impossible for the contest to continue. Ursula and the others were—at last—able to depart, their dignity, their deception—and their newly-formed alliance with the Alemanni—intact.

VI

Upon their return to Mogontiacum, Ursula declared a day of rest for the entire First Athena. At Rusticus's suggestion, the Legion went to a large open-air baths not far from the garrison complex in the foothills of the Taunus Mountains called Aquae Matticae. There was a special grotto reserved for senior officers and high-ranking officials, the centerpiece of which was a huge, open-air bath—a *natatio*—decorated with dark blue, red and gold mosaics. Behind the natatio and raised slightly above it were the *laconica* and *caldaria*—the hot and tepid baths. The baths lay beneath a dense, dark canopy of leaves from the overhanging trees that trapped the steam, causing it to linger in great voluptuous clouds. The source of the hot spa water was a natural spring that oozed from a large crevice in the rocks between the roots of two huge towering oaks, and was a rusty red in color. Wisps of the steam drifted out from the trees across the natatio to the more exposed cold water pools, or *frigidaria*, which were fed by crystal clear mountain water.

The area to the side of the natatio was the massage area as well as the way out to the stables and the narrow track that led to the Mogontiacum

Road. It was here that Ursula and Brittola retired, leaving the others in the pool playing with Rusticus. He was in his element, languishing naked in the bathing water, drinking his beloved wine and enjoying the antics of his fellow bathers—twenty nubile young women.

Brittola and Ursula lay stomach-down on adjacent wooden trestle tables for their massages. Their attendants kneaded warm, aromatic, herbal oils into their necks, backs and shoulders. They could hear Martha, Saula and Cordula giggling as they played some game in the pool. Pinnosa's hearty laugh would erupt periodically accompanied by the sound of thunderous splashes.

"This place would be perfect," Brittola said, "if only it had a chapel."

"It would be perfect . . . if it was back in the West Country," Ursula replied drowsily.

"Mistress?" Oleander's voice had a strange edge to it.

"What is it?"

"I think you should sit up, Mistress. There's someone here to see you." The attendant's unease communicated itself to Ursula and Brittola. Without speaking, they both sat up, fully alert, and followed Oleander's gaze.

As soon as Ursula saw the familiar silhouette, she froze. Standing in the entrance and casting a long shadow, was Morgan. He had paused to let his eyes adjust to the darkness after coming in from the strong, late summer sunshine. There was a tension about his presence, which was immediately apparent. It spoke of unwelcome news.

Fear took hold of her with a viciously cold chill, and Ursula started to shiver uncontrollably. In a daze, she donned her bathrobe and went to receive him. Focusing solely on Morgan, she didn't hear Brittola order the attendants to fetch the others and call for Cordula.

Morgan took a step toward her. In that moment, Ursula knew, deep inside, what he had come to tell her. It was as if Morgan's presence and the message he bore was an event that repeated itself endlessly throughout the whole of eternity. This, the enactment, was merely a ritual.

Morgan said nothing at first. He bowed low and straightened, looking somberly into her eyes. His sad gaze conveyed far more than the words that were to follow. It was to be his sorrowful expression, more than anything else that she would relive again and again in her dreams. He reached out, took hold of her right hand and delicately placed within it a small wooden object.

She didn't need to look down to know what it was.

While the crowd were still laughing and enjoying Constantine's joke, Ursula strode boldly down the steps to Constans, clasped his face in her hands and kissed him full on the lips. The hoots and shouts for "More!" were almost deafening. She needed no further bidding and did as they demanded. This time he wrapped his arms around her and held her tightly in his embrace. Unmindful of the crowd's roar, she pulled back slightly and handed him the small trinket she had been working on.

"What is it?" he had to shout.

"It's a tiny portrait of me, which Brittola painted. I had it set in a silver frame and encased in wood. I decorated it myself. It's something for you to remember me by." While she was speaking, she placed it around his neck. For a moment it dangled awkwardly on its black cord against his breastplate, looking a little silly. She smiled and tucked it inside against his chest. Then she looked up at his face.

"I shall never take it off. Even when I'm bathing." He took her firmly by the shoulders and looked deeply into her eyes. "Always remember this. Only in your voice—I hear family. Only in your eyes—I see home."

"There was a great battle, Your Highness." Morgan's voice finally pierced the icy silence, which had become all the more intense as the others drew near. "Constans was down to only two thousand men—his Vanguard and a loyal detachment of Batavian cavalry. The others had deserted him, believing the rumors that Constantine was about to be ousted. It was said that a huge force from Italia was coming—possibly led by Honorius himself, but certainly sent in his name. Only those loyal to the House of Theodosius would be rewarded—or even spared.

"Constans was determined to come to his father's aid and join forces with him in order to crush Gerontius's army. But the defectors knew too many of his secrets—mountain paths, caves and camps. Gerontius was able to set a trap. As they tried to use a narrow mountain pass to slip past the enemy, Constans and his men rounded a bend and found themselves facing a force of six thousand with another four thousand rapidly emerging from hiding places to the rear. Even though—"

"No! It can't *be!*" one of the younger women shrieked. Several of the guardswomen began to cry.

Morgan continued. "Even though they were outnumbered five-to-one and at a complete disadvantage, the enemy lost over half their number before the fighting was over.

"Constans himself was one of the last to succumb. They found his body still kneeling in the midst of many slain Suevi warriors—all of whom perished by his sword. The standard of the First Horse was tucked under his right arm—for he'd used it as a crutch after he received his first wounds. His left hand was so tightly clasped around that . . ." he nodded to the object in Ursula's grasp, "those who found him had to cut it free."

"Was there . . ." Ursula paused, took a deep breath, and began again. "I mean, did he send a final message?"

Morgan shook his head and pointed to her hand as if to say, 'you have it there.'

He turned to face the others and addressed them in a louder voice. "As if this tragedy wasn't enough of a burden to convey, I'm afraid I bring even graver news that affects not only us—but the entire world."

"Go on." Pinnosa said resolutely as she walked over to Ursula and put an arm around her.

"When I arrived in Mogontiacum, seeking the Commanders of the First Athena, an urgent—and most terrible—report reached the city from beyond the Alps." He looked down for a moment, obviously gathering strength for what he needed to say next. Slowly, he brought his head back up and proclaimed, "The Eternal City has been assailed, ransacked and pillaged by that curse of the West—Alaric and his Visigoths!"

Several of the women wailed in anguish.

"You mean. . . ?" Rusticus gasped.

"Yes. Rome herself has been razed to the ground. It still smolders— like a great sacrificial pyre—as we speak."

VII

Ursula paced up and down in the little white chapel Brittola had built behind the Officers' Hall at their barracks in Colonia. In the months since Morgan delivered the news of Constans's death, she had shut herself away, leaving strict orders not to be disturbed. Tiring, she sat cross-legged on the floor, staring at the altar, her eyes empty of expression. After a while, she leapt to her feet to begin pacing again. Unconsciously, her hands tugged at her hair and plucked at her dress. Loudly, she called out to the Heavens, "Dear, merciful God. Where *are* You? Where is Your Light? Please give me Your Light that I might see You, for I am withering in the darkness. I am drowning in the shadows!" She stopped pacing and fell to her knees. "I know now that my great sin is selfishness, Lord. All that I did, I did for my own ends. I formed the First Athena—taking twenty thousand of Britannia's best from their homes and families and denying them natural lives. I brought them on this . . . this cursed mission—all because I wanted to secure a home and a family for myself. You've seen fit to punish me for my sins and deny me that which I sought. All I ask, Dear Lord, is that you punish *only* me. Punish me, and spare the others."

"Amen," Brittola said, startling Ursula. She lingered in the doorway, unsure whether to enter.

Ursula remained kneeling. "Why are you bothering me? What do you want?"

Brittola forced a smile as she walked hesitantly over to the small altar and knelt down beside her. "May I join you in prayer?"

Ursula simply nodded and returned to her own, now silent, communion.

Brittola produced her cross from under her cloak. She closed her eyes tightly and began to pray aloud. "Dear Lord, Princess Ursula of Corinium, dutiful daughter of King Deonotus and Commander-in-Chief of the First and Second Athenas, thinks she was the instrument that created the Legions of women and set them on their mission. Please find it in Your Mercy to make her see that in all that she has done she has been *Your* instrument, working in *Your* service. Please enable her to understand, Lord, that it was Your Will that plucked us from our homes and families. It was Your Will that sent us on this mission. But most importantly, Lord, make her realize that without her at its head—without her as Your instrument—the First Athena can't continue on its Great Expedition, which the people of Britannia—and of all Rome—now need to succeed . . . more than ever." Brittola opened her eyes and looked at Ursula, who remained motionless, staring ahead sightlessly. "Amen."

Ursula half-turned to glance at Brittola, with a look of irritation on her face.

Brittola smiled. "You're giving me one of those looks."

"What look?" Ursula murmured.

"Like you used to give me when we were children, when you wanted me to keep quiet. Remember?"

Ursula smiled faintly and dismissively.

Brittola pressed on. "I could be noisy in those days, couldn't I? If I didn't get what I wanted, I used to whine and complain—"

"Whine? *Squeal* more likely." Ursula stood and wandered over to the little window behind the altar. Almost as soon as the words were out of her mouth, she looked as if she had lost interest in the conversation.

"I suppose you're right," Brittola continued carefully. "What I meant to say was that whenever you were busy with something, no matter how trivial, the important thing was that you weren't to be interrupted. You *hated* being distracted. Do you remember that time when you were arguing with Bishop Patroclus about a letter he received from that wily old fox, Pelagius, about the duties of Man and the duties of God? Remember? You were intent on going through it, point by point, and pulling apart the reasoning. I was keen for you to prepare for my father's feast at the time, but you—"

"I wasn't to be distracted?" Ursula said as if speaking in a dream.

"Heavens, no! Indeed, if anyone dared to divert you, it was as if they had committed the gravest of sins, and you would—"

Ursula spun around. "Brittola. You've been a great help. You're right, I *am* nothing but God's instrument. And, it is *I* who have committed the greatest sin of all . . . *distraction!*"

Her look of fierce determination told Brittola she was returning to her old self.

"Now I know not only what God wants me to do, but also how He wants me to do it . . . I'll *not* be distracted again!"

Ursula looked back out of the window and scanned the early evening sky in search of the North Star that would direct her to the little constellation of Ursa Minor—her namesake. "Constans was—and still is—my only true love. I would have devoted my life to him, and to our life together. But now God, in His Divine Wisdom, has seen fit to deny me the life of my dreams."

She smiled as she found her star. "My true mission—God's mission for me—is to lead the First Athena and ensure it succeeds in whatever task God puts before us." She lowered her voice and spoke in a quiet murmur as if speaking to another in secret—to someone no longer there. "I thought it was the storm and our diversion into Germania that was the distraction from our task—and that our task was the Great Expedition. But I was wrong. Our *real* task—God's task—was to come to these ravaged lands and do what the First Athena was originally created to do . . . frontier patrols. Indeed, it may even be the Great Expedition itself that is the true diversion now."

Ursula turned back to face Brittola, who smiled, pleased to see the old flames burning bright in Ursula's eyes. She knelt in front of Brittola and took her hands. "As you have always said, old friend, our true mission is to do the work that God sets before us—nothing more, nothing less. Now I know that my personal mission is to serve Him by leading the First Athena in whatever tasks that befall it. To serve Him to the best of my ability. And, to serve Him . . . *exclusively.*"

Ursula looked Heavenward. "I will never again be distracted from my service—to God or to the First Athena. The only man worthy of justifying such distraction is dead. There's only one way I can avoid being ensnared in the clammy grasp of another man's ambitions. There's only one way I can escape the clutches of . . . of princes and other would-be emperors . . ." she turned and gripped Brittola tightly by the shoulders, "and that is to wear the White."

Brittola gasped.

"I'll never be distracted from my mission again! I'm going to Bishop Clematius tomorrow and ask him to administer my Vow of Chastity."

"I'd like to take the Vow with you," Brittola said quietly, without hesitation. "That is, if you don't mind."

Ursula scrutinized her old friend as if she was only truly seeing her for the first time. Then she smiled and nodded.

"Moreover, I think some of the others may want to follow too, but . . ." Brittola looked uncomfortable, "there is one who can't follow us."

Ursula stared at her quizzically.

Brittola stood up and moved over to the altar before delivering her news. "There's something you should know, which I only just discovered. It's why I came here to see you . . . to tell you . . . ."

"What is it?" Ursula said, rising.

"Cordula will also be with Bishop Clematius tomorrow. But she'll be seeking forgiveness and mercy."

"Why?"

"She is with child."

VIII

From Augustus Constantine III, Emperor of the West and Grand Commander of all its armies, to Princess Ursula, Commander-in-Chief of the Legions First and Second Athena. Hail great Princess and Commander! Utinam magni Martis venti spirent tibi omina fausta bonamque fortunam in vitae viam.—*May the strong winds of March blow good omens and fortune in your path.*

Please accept my full apologies for not writing sooner. I will refrain from expressing my grief, for in Constans's death I know we both share a loss of the same magnitude. Suffice to say I hope the time will come soon when we can comfort and console each other in person, and alleviate some of the pain together.

Unfortunately, we must not only mourn his death, we must also grieve his defeat, which was a major setback in terms of our fight against Gerontius and his Rabble (his undisciplined mob does not merit the title "army"). As Morgan's reports have informed you, I took advantage of the winter months to slip out of Arelate undetected and personally survey the situation with our nemesis, the Burgundians. No less than fifteen separate tribes are now wandering throughout the upper Rhenus and Rhone valleys, keeping the main force of my army fully preoccupied! I have just returned to make preparations for the forthcoming campaign season, which I don't mind admitting I dread.

Our situation here in southern Galliae is becoming more and more perilous. When I returned from my reconnoiter of the Burgundians, I discovered that a further five hundred of my Imperial Guard had deserted to Gerontius's ranks, apparently believing they will be better rewarded there. With the complete loss of Constans's division and the depletion of my main force due to the near constant run-ins with Burgundians, I can now only count twelve thousand men loyal to me—of which less than five thousand are cavalry.

My greatest fear is what might come at us from over the Alps. After their victory at Rome, the Goths are now acting like true conquerors and might attempt an expansion into Galliae. More worryingly, Honorius, instead of joining forces with me to rid Italia of its pestilence, as he should, is about to receive some reinforcements from Constantinopolis—which he may then use against me.

Oh, the tragedy of Rome and the absurdities wrought by our thirst for power! When will we realize that ultimately our fellow Romans are more than our greatest rivals; they are also our greatest allies?

On to matters concerning you and the First Athena: Firstly, I discovered on my surveillance mission, that the Grand Deception you used so effectively with the Alemanni may now be working against you. Several of our informers told me that the Burgundians are convinced a great army of over thirty thousand women is patrolling the Limes. I have also received reports from Italia that suggest the same beliefs are held there. Beware! You can be certain that Honorius and Theodosius the Second are following your feats up there in frontier country very closely. If they perceive you to be a formidable force loyal to me, you can expect them to be scheming your downfall.

I think the greatest potential threat you should keep on the alert against is Mundzuk and his ever-growing Horde. They are wintering on the banks of the Danuvius just west of Vindobona. Theodosius positioned them there to keep Honorius's forces divided. Now that the

Goths have the run of Italia and are keeping Honorius fully preoccupied, the Huns are no longer part of Theodosius's design. Mundzuk and his warlords may be feeling restless and spoiling for a fight. In which case, the prospect of taking on a large, mobile force of Roman women may be too tempting to resist!

This brings me to a sensitive topic: whether or not the First Athena should disengage from the Continent. I am no longer optimistic that the Great Expedition can be recommenced. I do not think, at this stage, that the First Athena should continue to be deployed along the Rhenus, or, for that matter, anywhere on the Continent where you are at great risk from hostile forces such as Mundzuk's Horde. I shall refrain from ordering your return to Britannia in this dispatch, but I would like your comments on the matter in your next report so that I can make a final decision before the campaign season gets properly under way.

Finally, a personal comment on your decision to take the Vow of Chastity: I have to confess that in my mind's eye you are still a young teenager full of joy, hope and happiness. You used to play such games with your friends and family when I saw you at feasts. I sometimes find it difficult to reconcile that image of you with the highly resourceful and respected Commander of Legions I now know. But then I remember a stalwart young nineteen-year-old woman who stood up to me behind the Officers' Hall in Corinium two nights before we departed. Then, two mornings later, you held yourself with such dignity and grace as your beloved and betrothed, Constans, made what was to be his final farewell. It was always clear to me that you have all the warmth and compassion of your father as well as the fierce determination of your late mother (indeed these were the qualities I welcomed in my son's choice for his bride). Now I realize there is something in you that was put there by God to equip you for the great challenges that you were to face. Whatever this quality is in you, I know that it is something I cannot fully fathom, having never encountered anything quite like it before in a woman. Perhaps it is this quality that has guided you to your momentous decision.

As your Commander, I fully respect your decision. In my eyes, your Vow of Chastity does not compromise your effectiveness as an officer in any way. Indeed, it may even enhance it! As the father of Constans, I would like to say to you that a love such as yours was made in Heaven, and I believe that he took your soul there with him when he died. Without your soul, no other relationship would ever hold meaning for you.

This explains to me why you have chosen to forego other men in what is left of this, your mortal life. Constans, I know, is with you in this, as he will always be with you. Moreover, he is the only one who can truly appreciate what it means to you.

May God be with you.

Augustus Constantine III.

P.S. I wasn't surprised to hear of Brittola's decision to join you, but I'm curious to know why Martha has taken the Vow, and even more curious to know why Saula didn't. Don't those two always do everything together?

✳ ✳ ✳

Report to the Emperor, Augustus Constantine III, Grand Commander of all the armies of the West, from Princess Ursula, daughter of King Deonotus of Corinium, Commander-in-Chief of the Legions First and Second Athena. Hail Constantine! Spero fore, ut magni mensis Martis venti spirent tibi omina fausta bonamque fortunam in vitae viam, et ut dulcedo Aprilis animos leonis commoveat ad relinquendum denique cubile hibernum.—*I hope the strong winds of March blew good omens and fortune in your path, and that the warm caress of April entices the spirit of the lion to finally abandon its winter lair.*

I thank you for your kind words about Constans. I, too, look forward to the day we can mourn him together. Which is why I was so saddened by your suggestion that the First Athena should disengage from the lands of the Rhenus and return to Britannia. I do not share your pessimism concerning either your position, or ours, or, indeed, of the prospect of our recommencing the Great Expedition. Your numbers might be down to twelve thousand, the Burgundians may be keeping you embroiled in the provincial matters of Galliae more than you anticipated and Gerontius may be proving more tenacious than anyone expected, but I am positive the tide will turn in our favor soon. Allow me to refresh your memory concerning the more positive aspects of our situation: Firstly, the frontier along the Rhenus is secure, with the Alemanni and the Franks now proving themselves to be credible allies in keeping other tribes at bay. Secondly, Jovinus, after much prompting by Bishop Clematius, Rusticus and myself, is finally making use of the new-found security of the frontier to entice several cities in northern Galliae to release their standing guards in order to march south to reinforce you. He is making the rounds personally and should have accumulated at least seven thousand men—including three thousand cavalry—by the time he sets forth in July. Thirdly, all the reports we receive here from Italia suggest that the Goths and Honorius are keeping each other so busy, there is little or no possibility of either of them being capable of crossing the Alps to strike at you, certainly not before Jovinus arrives with his reinforcements. Finally, now that the frontier is holding and no further tribes are breaking through, the Burgundians should settle down on the lands you have allocated them in the Rhenus and Rhone valleys. Your main force should be free to assist you in breaking Gerontius's siege, around the same time as Jovinus heads south.

My optimism is possible because the First Athena is making good use of the improved military roads you built four years ago. We are able to maintain cavalry and infantry patrols that represent a credible Roman presence. This, in turn, keeps the Franks and Alemanni in check.

I would now like to relay to you our recommendations concerning the Legion's deployment, which we have discussed at length here. Firstly, now that your numbers are down to under twelve thousand we don't see the need to maintain more women on the Continent than would be needed for a reduced Great Expedition, so we recommend that around six thousand infantry and five hundred cavalry return to Britannia to reinforce the Second Athena. The Legion may well become stretched this year if the rumors of a Grand Alliance between the Hibernians, Picts and Saxons are true. Julia has volunteered to lead the force, and I strongly recommend we appoint her to the task and make her acting Commander-in-Chief of both armies. The Second will benefit greatly from her experience and skill as a leader. I would also like to send Baetica back as head of the cavalry. Apart from Pinnosa, she and Viventia are the only Commanders who could extract the necessary respect from the Second Athena.

Another reason why we think it would be a good idea to send some of the women back is that it would give a much needed boost to the morale of those left behind. About a third of the women are finding their task here difficult and the conditions unpleasant. I can't help feeling that if we allowed them to return to Britannia, the morale of the remaining two thirds—who are still fully intent on the Great Expedition—would improve dramatically.

My second recommendation concerns the duties of the remaining eleven thousand of the First Athena. I propose to continue our patrols of the frontier, sending a deployment of two thousand cavalry per month down the full length of the Limes as a show of force. Additionally, I will send two smaller detachments of a thousand infantry plus five hundred cavalry per month into northern Galliae to reassure the cities and towns of our presence. We will implement these plans twenty days from this date unless we receive orders to the contrary.

Thank you for your kind words concerning my "new uniform." It fits beautifully and I feel much better because of it. It's a great shame that you can't make the same choice, otherwise I would heartily recommend it!

Incidentally, your messenger's wife is doing well. The baby is due in July. She has discharged herself from the Legion but refuses to be separated from her friends, despite Morgan's pleas for her to return to Britannia. We have made a special home for her in the Messengers' Courtyard from where she supervises the ordnance crews. Some of Rusticus's many aunts visit her there and fuss over her like an empress!

Finally, a note to explain something that we shouldn't expect a busy Emperor to be aware of: Martha's young man, Blussus of Glevum, was killed with Constans, whereas Saula's young man, Lucius Brigionis, is still with you in your Imperial Guard.

You are always in my prayers.

Your ever faithful

Ursula

IX

Ursula held regular meetings with the other Commanders and the Alemanni tribal leaders in Mogontiacum. Though there were many vacant Officers' Halls in the garrison complex, they always met in the Augustus Room, with its imposing colonnade and huge circular oak table. At every gathering the reports about Mundzuk and his approaching Hun Horde became more plentiful, detailed and gruesome. In early summer, things seemed to be coming to a head.

"It is said that the leaders take cruel pleasure in skinning and burning their victims alive," said Gunderic, chief of the Vandals, who was a visitor at the meeting. The Vandals were a particularly nomadic and war-like people whose allegiance to Rome was almost as strong as their propensity to attack it. However, like the Alemanni, they were currently looking to Rome to protect them from the even more ruthless Huns. He continued in his thick, dark voice. "Then, while the wretched souls still breathe, they tear their innards out with their bare hands and eat the offal raw—before the victim's very eyes."

Upon hearing this, one of the younger Alemanni princes had to withdraw from the chamber. He could be heard retching as soon as he disappeared from sight.

"What bothers me most," the tall chieftain, Luethari, said, "is that Mundzuk organizes his Horde so that it travels and fights in one massive unit of over thirty thousand men—not separate divisions like German tribes. When they approach you intent on attack, they are utterly and absolutely . . . unstoppable."

Neither Ursula nor Rusticus could think of anything to say to counteract the mood of doom and dismay that enveloped the gathering. For once, not even Pinnosa's indomitable spirit could find the words to prevail.

Gunderic interrupted the uncomfortable silence, "As you all know, we have scouts patrolling the Limes—"

Pinnosa let out a loud, mocking "Hah!" Everyone present knew what she meant by it: *Looking for opportunities to raid, you mean!* However, she refrained from saying anything, content to let her expression do the talking.

Gunderic looked quizzically around the gathering, then continued. "It is abundantly clear to us the Horde is using the abandoned Limes fortifications and their broad, treeless military zone as a road to lead them directly to the Rhenus." He leered menacingly at Ursula. "It is said that they are lured by the prospect of an encounter with the legendary fighting women."

Ursula felt distinctly uncomfortable. The Alemanni were plainly nervous—and hostile. It was now her turn to report, and all eyes turned to her. They all stared hard, with naked aggression. Gone were any vestiges of the deference they'd previously displayed.

She'd been intending to report that the ranks of the First Athena had recently been depleted and a number sent home to bolster the defenses of Britannia. She was also supposed to be informing them that the remaining detachments of men from the Colonia and Mogontiacum Garrisons were about to set off for Arelate and would probably not be back until the autumn.

"Friends, allies and esteemed guests . . ." *Now isn't the time*, she thought, looking at their faces. *I'd better keep this simple.* "I have come here today to inform you that we have—temporarily—had to curtail some of our routine patrols along the Limes and deploy units of the First Athena and the Colonia Garrison . . . elsewhere."

The Alemanni started to talk amongst themselves, some quite animatedly.

Pinnosa "shushed" them quiet and nodded for Ursula to continue.

"Throughout the summer months you, the Alemanni—along with the Franks—will have to take on a much larger share of the frontier responsibilities. This includes the maintenance of border patrols, which—"

A burly man with a thick beard and a face like gnarled wood, one of the senior chiefs, called Botilin barked, "Which are the ones most likely to be the first to run into Mundzuk!" He stood up and cracked his whip across the table at the Roman delegation. "We, the Alemanni, are the world's *greatest* fighters! But we fight best in small, mobile groups no larger than a thousand!" He paused to glower at the head of the table where Ursula, Pinnosa, Saula, Rusticus and Viventia were bunched together before continuing. "How do you—our honored and esteemed Roman fighting women—suggest we stop this murderous beast with thirty thousand heads that can flick even the fiercest fighters from its flanks as a bear does a troublesome gnat?"

Muttering something to Ursula about nipping a rebellion in the bud, Pinnosa suddenly leapt to her feet and drew her sword. "That's *enough!*" she cried, and, with a swift downward swipe, she severed the lash of Botilin's whip before he could snatch it back.

The Alemanni erupted into consternation.

"I will have *silence!*" she shouted in a voice that forced all others into submission.

The Alemanni resettled resentfully. Not one of them could withstand her ferocious glare.

"You don't attack a beast with thirty thousand heads," she said calmly once their silence was complete. "You watch it carefully . . . and you study its habits. That's how you discover its weak points. Only then are you in a position to know how to defeat it."

The tribal leaders looked at each other and began to sneer dismissively at her battle-less plan.

Pinnosa walked around to Botilin, flipped her sword over so that she was holding it by the point and knelt down before him to offer him the hilt. As she did so, she said in softer, almost deferential, tones, "We, the women of the First Athena, will help you to study Mundzuk's Horde. We will work with you to devise a plan by which we can defeat it and capture—or kill—Mundzuk himself." She thrust the hilt forward, proffering her peace, and smiled.

After looking nervously around the gathering, Botilin awkwardly accepted her gift, with a clumsy attempt at graciousness.

From then on, the rest of the meeting was relatively constructive.

Afterwards, as they made their way back to the garrison buildings housing the First Athena, Rusticus warned Ursula and Pinnosa against placing too much trust in the Alemanni and the Franks. "They can take up the life of wandering just as easily as they gave it up. When they agreed to fight for Rome, they thought it would only mean keeping out their own kind. When these Huns and their Horde arrive, don't count on the Federates to stand by your side. If the Huns are after Roman prey, as far as the Germans are concerned, that is a Roman problem. My advice to you, should events turn out that way, would be to move the First Athena inside the fortress if you're at Mogontiacum or inside the city walls if you're at Colonia. From there you can allow yourselves to hope that the monster with thirty thousand heads gets bored toying with the caged bird that it can't get its claws on and moves elsewhere, looking for easier pickings."

"Don't forget, Rusticus," said Ursula with a wry smile and a wink at Pinnosa, "even we birds have claws!"

X

The following morning, Rusticus rose early to depart for Treveris to rendezvous with Jovinus. He was to join the new army the Prince had raised for their long march south to relieve Constantine, whose need for a skilled interpreter was now greater than Ursula's. When he emerged from his chamber, he was dressed as if for a pheasant hunt, not a military campaign. He wore a red cloak and a bright green hunting hat with an even brighter long spume of orange plumage.

Ursula and the others watched sadly as he and his attendant commenced their usual struggle to heave his full frame onto his horse. They were all sorry to see him go. Ursula couldn't help feeling a sudden surge of panic, like a child understanding for the first time that her father was off to war and might not come back.

"Take care of yourself, Rusticus!" she called up to him as he took up the reins of his horse. He offered her his hand, but instead of shaking it, she kissed it. "Be sure to give our regards to Jovinus and tell him to have courage."

"And if by chance you meet up with Gerontius on your travels," Pinnosa added jokingly, as she, too kissed his heavily bejeweled hand, "kindly slash his throat for me! But before you do, please remember to say a few short words first."

"What are they?"

"'This is a thorn from a young Britannic rose.'"

"Will that mean something to him?"

"Oh, yes! It will mean something, all right. It'll remind him of something he'd rather leave forgotten—and hopefully will add to his torment in Hell!"

Saula pressed forward to kiss Rusticus's hand and said, "When you see Constantine, will you please be sure to impress upon him that the First Athena is ready to recommence it's Great Expedition at a moment's notice? All we need is his word."

"Don't worry, Saula. We'll get you young Brittanic people together for your mass wedding as soon as we can." Rusticus smiled and looked over toward the assembled ranks of the Vanguard that had been called on parade in order to send him off. The sight clearly moved him.

His gaze returned to the Commanders who were huddled around his horse like children. "It has been an honor and a privilege to work with you this past year and a half. You have not only shown me what women are truly capable of, but you have also made me realize it is wrong to despair even when it seems that all hope is lost." He looked at their faces, one by one, before continuing, "You have taught me well, and I love you all dearly."

The women were all close to tears—even Pinnosa.

"Anyway," he added with a mischievous grin, "I want you to promise me that one day—when all this turmoil is over—we'll get together and return to the hot springs at Aquae Matticae to resume our brief respite from Duty that was so rudely interrupted."

"We will, dear Rusticus. We surely will!" Ursula replied emphatically. "On behalf of the entire First Athena, I hereby promise! Now go! And fare well in Galliae!"

He nudged his horse and started to move off, but after a few steps he turned around and called over his shoulder, "Don't worry about me in southern Galliae. My Aunt Thebis is from there and she told me all about the area—"

"We know!" Ursula shouted, and the others joined in chorus, "You loved her dearly—and she *taught . . . you . . . well!*"

XI

"Oooh! Look at those tiny little fingers," Saula cooed at Cordula's baby boy, "and look at all that dark hair!"

"He's so cute," Martha chuckled. The old friends from Corinium along with Faustina and Viventia and a few junior officers were huddled around a wickerwork crib. Cordula had placed her son on the table by the window in the Commanders' Room at the barracks in Colonia so they could admire him.

Saula leaned over the baby. "We all know who *your* father is, don't we, you little fidget midget?" She tickled the baby's tummy and made him giggle.

They all chuckled at the sound.

While they were laughing, Ursula pulled Pinnosa away, leaving the others to carry on with their innocent fun. It was mid-August, yet the July patrols had barely been completed. Indeed, Pinnosa's frontier patrol had only just returned that morning and this was Ursula's first chance to speak to her alone.

"I am so pleased to see you," Ursula said in hushed tones as soon as they were apart from the group. "I was beginning to get worried."

"We had a bit of trouble with a rogue unit of Vandals, which took us a bit further east along the Limes than we usually go—"

"East? Along the Limes? Any sign of—"

"No, nothing. If there is a Horde, it's a Horde of rumors. Anyway, I understand we weren't the only ones who were waylaid. What's this I hear about you having to make a special trip to Mogontiacum?"

"Tongues wag fast around here, don't they?" The last vestiges of Ursula's smile dissipated, and her anxious frown returned. "It's the Alemanni. The closer You-know-Who gets, the more restless they become. Once again they threatened to march into Galliae. And they insisted on meeting with me personally. Reassurance after reassurance. They *crave* reassurance!"

"At least they acknowledge your authority."

"That is small comfort. It wasn't only our patrols that were delayed, you know. Martha and Faustina had to go to Treveris to bolster the standing guards, who were about to disband following the departure of Jovinus." She looked anxiously at Pinnosa. "Do you think we're in danger of being stretched too thin? We're being expected to cover ever more duties . . . ever more ground."

"I think our main problem is the Alemanni. Constantine was right in his misgivings. It's difficult to gauge who is the most uncomfortable—them as our 'guardians' or those whom they 'guard.' I sometimes think our job would be easier without them."

"And, what exactly is our job these days? I'm not sure I know anymore. I sometimes think—" Ursula paused, and both she and Pinnosa looked awkwardly around at the others. They had all gone quiet as they had overheard the exchange between the two senior Commanders.

"Well, I think our job is most definitely to protect this area and all its peoples—Christian or barbarian—from the scourge of the Huns!" It was Brittola who broke the uncomfortable silence. "Mundzuk and his minions are the biggest monsters on God's Earth! There is nothing they wouldn't do to satisfy their lust for plunder!"

"That's true. She's right," Faustina said, nodding. "The Limes is theirs to wander—and plunder—as they wish. I hear they spent the spring laying waste to many of the estates in Noricum, an area neither Honorius nor Constantine have the resources to police. There is no one to stand up to them there. But there is someone here . . . . Us!"

"You say 'laying waste' as if it was nothing more than a housewife's chore!" Brittola's voice was shrill with emotion. "Have you heard what they actually *do* to people? It is said they—"

"Come, come!" Ursula strode briskly over to Brittola and put her arm around her. "Not in front of the baby, please." She turned very deliberately to Cordula. They could see she was determined to change the subject. "What will you call him?" she asked, taking Cordula by the hand, "Will you give him Morgan's father's name?"

"No, we've already decided against that." Cordula looked magnificent in motherhood, like a rose in full bloom. She was dressed in a plain, brown *chiton* or maternity tunic, in stark contrast to Ursula's more elaborate and ornate, pure white robe. "We both feel we'd like a name which stands for a completely new start—the beginning of a new world." She picked the baby up. His eyes were open wide and he appeared to grin at the sight of the bright, white lady before him, which made them all laugh. "Anyway, his father hasn't seen him yet. How can he name a child he doesn't know? When he does—"

"Your Highness! Ladies! I bring you grave news!"

They all spun around to where the familiar male voice had come from, and were astonished to see Morgan, the father of the baby, standing at the entrance to the Commanders' Room. He was dressed in what looked to be a monk's garb. They could sense at once that something momentous must have happened.

Ursula stepped forward. "Morgan. We were just admiring your new-born son." She gestured for the cluster of officers to move aside, and said gently, "Cordula?"

Cordula emerged from between the others to stand facing him with the baby in her arms.

Morgan moved toward the pair, his face momentarily filled with wonder. He was just about to reach out for both mother and child when the burden of his duty returned to him. He paused in trepidation. The magical moment was shattered, leaving Cordula to stare wide-eyed at her husband in shock.

"Constantine is dead!" he blurted out, causing several of the women to gasp. "They're *all* dead—or worse than dead . . . . Many have turned traitor!"

XII

Morgan was obviously exhausted, having ridden Hermes hard—almost non-stop day upon day—to deliver his terrible news. He sat resting on a bench with Cordula and the baby by his side. The rest of the officers were seated on the floor about his feet. Ursula and Pinnosa both stood by the window, staring out at the parade ground, watching as a late-summer squall sprinkled the dry, gray earth, yet listening intently to his heart-wrenching words.

"As you all know, Honorius had a momentous stroke of good fortune in the untimely death of Alaric. He suddenly found himself back in complete control of northern Italia with a full force of ten thousand well-armed and fully trained Roman legionaries at his disposal. Half of them were on loan from Constantinopolis and under the leadership of Constantius, a ruthless and highly capable Commander known by friends and enemies alike as 'Iron Fist'—and he was ready to crush his master's nemeses.

"The Goths were still in torpor after their leader's death and were safely contained for the moment in the far south of Italia, where they posed no immediate threat. We, on the other hand—although considerably weakened by the attrition and inter-army fighting Honorius had engineered—looked dangerously poised to muster new forces. Honorius was especially concerned that we might be reinforced at any moment by the incredibly resourceful Legion of women on the Rhenus. Thus strengthened, he feared Constantine might make another foray into Italia in the pretence of going after the Goths.

"So, Honorius decided to send Iron Fist and the newly-formed Italian field army across the Alps to retake Galliae. We heard tell that he half-expected the arrival of an Italian army to persuade our men to renounce Constantine and join the campaign against the Goths. How badly he underestimated Britannic loyalty and resolve . . . or so we thought!

"Whatever their intentions, Iron Fist emerged from the Alps without any warning and marched straight for Arelate. We had just managed to assemble five thousand of our men and were in the process of attempting a rout of Gerontius's forces when the army from Italia arrived, catching us—and Gerontius—completely off guard. Gerontius, in his dim-witted confusion, presumed that Iron Fist was reinforcing us, and took flight. Thus, he left to the mercy of Fate his puppet emperor, Maximus, and the 'federate' German tribes, who were now completely confused as to where their allegiance should lie.

"In the midst of all the mayhem and confusion, Iron Fist caught up with Gerontius and pinned him down in a small fortress in the foothills of the Pyrenees. The sad, debauched, old dog committed suicide rather than face justice. The remaining Roman legionaries from Gerontius's force then accepted the clemency offered by the Italians and marched back with them to Arelate—to confront us.

"By this time, we were in extreme difficulty. While we had been out in the field, the Imperial Court in the city of Arelate had taken heart in the surprise presence of a considerable force finally coming from Italia. In a show of allegiance to Honorius, the 'true' emperor, they closed the city gates on the 'usurper' and his army, denying us a safe refuge. We were suddenly a brave but weary—and hungry—army just five thousand strong pitted against a force of ten thousand fresh legionaries from Italia, reinforced by three thousand traitors.

"The battle barely lasted an hour. Only a few of the Brittanic divisions actually fought. I was standing beside Constantine when at one point we saw a whole cohort throw down their standard and run to join the opposing ranks—so blatant was their treachery!" Morgan gasped a ragged sob that threatened to tear Ursula's heart in two. He forced himself to continue, "The spirit of the men had waned ever since the fateful decision to head south and support the Court at Arelate. . . . But it was the defeat of Constans last year that placed so much doubt in their hearts.

"As soon as Constantine saw which way the wind was blowing, he gave his last order. Again, I was standing right next to him, so I can repeat it verbatim. He said, 'Brave and loyal men of Britannia, we have to concede that the day is lost and that all we have tried to achieve these past few years is about to be destroyed. Our only chance now is to flee this field of shattered dreams and meet again in a long lost land that we once proudly called home! I have no other choice on this God-forsaken day but to issue the most cowardly of orders . . . . *Flee!* Make your escape as best you can! Your greatest danger now is in staying together in large groups that can be easily pursued and destroyed. Whatever you do, don't band together until a safe distance is between you and this miserable place. Then make your way to Britannia. With God on our side, hopefully some months from now, we can re-group on home soil, and begin to rebuild—perhaps with the help of our valiant women in the First and Second Athenas. Now, go! All of you—*go!*'"

Morgan started to sob with the pain of his memories. Cordula put her arm around him and coaxed him to continue. "We . . . we had left it too late. We were the victims of our own foolish pride. The decision to flee should have been made much earlier. The enemy was too near . . . and we were too weak. Most of the officers were caught before leaving the battlefield and beheaded. The few who did manage to escape didn't get far, and were soon dead, too.

"Constantine and I did manage to escape from the battlefield, to-gether—just the two of us. In fact, we had a small stroke of luck. With twenty Italian riders in hot pursuit, we ducked into a heavily wooded valley and stum-bled upon a tiny, out-of-the-way monastery where we were able to disguise ourselves as priests. In fact . . . Your Highness?"

"Yes?" Ursula turned to face him. Her face seemed to have aged ten years and her white uniform, silhouetted against the green light of the window, made her look more like a temple priestess than a Commander-in-Chief.

"Even though the enemy was so close at hand that we could hear their shouts and horns in the surrounding woods, Constantine—our Emper-or—made a point of kneeling before the altar in the tiny chapel and saying a short prayer out loud. He said, 'Oh, Holy Father, Some people will say it was my misplaced Faith that brought me to this . . . place. Others will say it was Fate. But you know as well as I, Father, that it was neither that led me here. It was one thing and one thing only—*Duty*. And apart from you, Father, and my dearest Constans, only Ursula will understand what that truly means . . . .'" He paused. "Does that mean anything to you, Your Highness?"

"Yes . . . yes, it does." They all looked at her expectantly, but she simply added quietly, "Thank you for conveying his words so faithfully. Please continue."

"There isn't much more to tell. The following morning, we were rid-ing next to each other along a narrow road, heading north, when suddenly we heard the horns of our pursuers approaching from behind. 'Go!' he shouted to me, 'Make sure Ursula and the others hear of our demise! Go, for Heaven's sake, *Go now!*'

"I obeyed him, but stopped on the first ridge to look back. The problem was, of course, our horses. Priests don't ride such steeds. The search party didn't even bother to check whether he was a real priest or not. They rode down hard upon him with their swords drawn. He let out a spirited yell and raised his great blade in reply."

Morgan paused again, to ensure he was fully composed for what he about to say.

"He died as he always lived—fighting with all his strength!"

XIII

"Ursula," Pinnosa called from the doorway. The Commanders' Room was almost empty. Ursula and Brittola were seated at the planning table and Oleander was on a stall by the window, sewing. It was the middle of the afternoon the day following the awful news. The other Commanders were in the baths, cleansing themselves as part of their respect for the Day of Mourning that Ursula had declared. "There's an Alemanni girl here whom I think you should see. She's one of the women from the gate, but she was making such a fuss when we wouldn't let her in that I was called over to hear her case. I decided you ought to hear it too."

Ever since they barracked at Colonia, the First Athena was plagued by two unwanted groups: "gawkers" as Ursula called them, and local volunteers. The gawker problem had started while they were still in Britannia on the Holy Island. The women of the Athenas were trained to ignore the large bands of onlookers, many of whom had traveled great distances to see the famous "fighting women."

In Colonia, however, the problem had risen to a far greater magnitude. Whenever they left their barracks, the First Athena women were mobbed by large groups of well-wishers trying to bless them, or souvenir hunters offering purses for their cloaks, swords or plumages whenever they went through a civilian area on patrol. Indeed, several dozen of the women sent back to Britannia with Julia had been those who succumbed to the temptation to profiteer from the fame of the First Athena. When Cordula took over the ordnance depot, she heard tales of organized rings—particularly amongst the Londinium women—that sold plumage feathers in sets of the four colors of the Legion for large amounts of silver.

The second problematic group was the endless stream of women camping by the barrack gates pleading to join the Legion's ranks. Some were very young girls, who often approached the gates in groups of up to thirty in number. Others were mature women, most of whom looked as if they had good reason for wanting to devote their lives to the world of weaponry and war.

Ursula adopted the policy with both groups of completely denying them access to the camp or barracks. She relied on the regular patrols of the Colonia Garrison to move them on. The gawkers were simply a nuisance. But the volunteers could be very problematic, even threatening suicide if they weren't allowed to enter and join. Because of this, Ursula made a point of handpicking the gate and perimeter sentries. She selected only those with the necessary strengths to be immune to the many ploys and often dramatic ruses they encountered in the course of their duties. As a result, their gate security record was excellent. There had not been one single incident of a breakthrough or of riotous disorder in the street outside.

This request from Pinnosa represented the very first time an exception had been made to the strict codes of practice. Ursula knew she wouldn't have authorized it without a very good reason. "Very well," she said resignedly, sharing a raised eyebrow with Brittola, "Show her in."

Into the room came a short young girl, barely seventeen years of age, with her hair bunched on top of her head in a fashion typical of the more eastern Alemanni tribes. She was accompanied by one of the women of the First Athena in Londinium orange, a talented linguist called Cunoarda, who was brought in to act as translator. The Alemanni girl was clearly nervous to the point of terror at being in the presence of Roman officers—but she was also in obvious physical pain. She tried to walk toward them with a normal healthy gait. But there was an eerie stiffness to her steps, and she failed to suppress a grimace as she bowed. Seeing her discomfort, Brittola dragged over a bench and indicated she should be seated.

It took quite a while for the girl to recount her misadventures and make her plea. By the time she finished, Ursula wasn't sure whether it was the girl's story or the impassioned way she told it that influenced her the most.

Her name was impossible to pronounce, but it translated into "amber," which was what they decided to call her. Amber had the misfortune of being camped with her family near the Limes, by a tributary of the Main, about three days' ride north-east of Mogontiacum, when they were ambushed by a scouting party from Mundzuk's Horde. All of her tribesmen were killed instantly. Amber, her mother and her two sisters were taken prisoner. They were herded back to the Hun's camp to be offered to the warlords as playthings.

Amber still found it difficult to talk about the horrors she experienced in their hands. Several times she started to sob uncontrollably as she recalled some particularly violent memory, at which point either Pinnosa or Brittola would console her and coax her to continue.

She and her sisters were forced to watch her mother being raped, not just once, but many times by the complete group of the "ugly head" warlords. Then it had been Amber and her sisters' turn. The loathsome, violent drunkards tortured them when they tried to resist.

At this point in the story, Amber drew up her tunic to show her back and legs. Ursula and the others saw her appalling wounds. There were gouges and sores, some of which would clearly never heal. The worst was a gaping trench across her upper right thigh where the flesh had been completely stripped off.

Amber went on to tell them how she and her younger sister, being especially "sweet and delicate," were thought good enough for the monster, Mundzuk, himself. He joined the orgy later and Amber could sense who he was by the fear he generated amongst the other ugly heads, even though they were drunk by the time he arrived. He exerted a power over them with an ominously evil aura that seemed to emanate from every portion of his being. Most evil of all—she recounted with a fearful flinch—were his strange, heavily-lidded, deep-set eyes.

Mundzuk only stayed with the rest of the ugly heads long enough to eat some of their foul, dried meat and drink some of the Alemanni ale they had plundered that day, before he grabbed Amber and her sister. He carried them, one under each arm, back to his tent, which she remembered was set apart from the others. Once there he threw Amber's sister to one side, obviously intending to save her for later, after "enjoying" Amber first. Then, showing great delight, he took up a container of boiling hot oil, stood over her and poured it on Amber's open wounds. She remembered screaming in sheer agony, but the pain was so intense she passed out.

When she woke up, she found herself lying in a pile entangled with the bodies of her dead mother and sisters. They were by the small river near the Hun camp. It seemed that once the ugly heads had their sport, they simply discarded the bodies like leftovers from a feast, before moving on. In great pain, Amber crawled to the river where she found an old, but usable, boat hidden in some reeds. Believing that the craft had been put there by one of the gods—the God of Revenge perhaps—Amber had just enough strength to push the boat out into the current before she collapsed.

The next thing she knew, she was awakened by a fisherman from

Mogontiacum and his two young sons. They took her into their home and saw to her wounds. A week later, as soon as she could walk, she had set out for Colonia to find the only people who could help her get revenge—the fighting women of the First Athena. Her hope was that by being in the one army that could stand up to Huns, the same god that gave her the small boat would also give her an opportunity to plunge a dagger deep into Mundzuk's innards.

She finished her story by swearing an oath to kill Mundzuk, knowing that only his death could cause the Horde to fall apart and the evil menace that was perpetrating such horrors daily in its relentless pursuit of plunder to dissipate.

When Amber had finished, Ursula called Oleander over and sent her out on an errand before addressing the young Alemanni girl. "Please tell her there is very little the First Athena can do to help her, because . . ." she glanced awkwardly at Pinnosa, "because we are about to depart for our homeland in the west."

"*What?*" Pinnosa exclaimed, glaring wide-eyed with astonishment at Ursula.

Ursula raised her hand for silence, forcing Pinnosa to curb her outburst while the message was being translated.

Pinnosa fumed, obviously angry at the announcement of a plan she'd had no part in.

Ursula continued, "And now please tell her we will treat her wounds in—"

Amber threw herself on the floor at Ursula's feet, screaming. "She says we can't go, Commander," Cunoarda hastily translated. Brittola pulled Amber away and helped her back on the bench. "She says we've got to stay and fight. Otherwise all the women along the Rhenus will go through what she and her sisters went through—and all the men will die!"

"I thought that was what she was saying." Ursula's voice sounded more than a little strained as she studiously avoided Pinnosa's fierce gaze. "Please inform her; firstly that she can't join the First Athena; secondly that her audience is over, and thirdly that she will receive treatment for her wounds."

Amber continued to plead though her sobs.

"But, Commander . . . ." Cunoarda protested, obviously feeling concern for the Alemanni girl.

"You have performed your duty well," Ursula interrupted curtly. "Now, you are dismissed."

Badly shaken, Cunoarda stood up and grabbed Amber by the arm to lead her away. They were halfway to the door when Oleander re-appeared carrying Ursula's old Corinium blue cloak to give to the Alemanni girl. Amber looked at it in wonder. As she held out her arms for Oleander to put it over her shoulders, Cunoarda spun on her heels and shouted at Ursula in frustration and anger:

"Just because the men are gone and the Great Expedition is off—doesn't mean there's nothing for us women to do! All the homesick cowards went home in May. Those of us that stayed behind want to *fight* this . . . this Evil" she pointed to Amber's wounds, "not run away from it!"

Pinnosa held out her hand for Cunoarda to stop. "All right, you've said your piece now—"

Before she could finish, Amber interrupted, speaking in hushed, gentle tones.

Cunoarda was still full of emotion from her outburst and had to fight hard to regain her composure, before she could translate. "She says thank you for the present. She says it'll give her something to remember us by and prove that we weren't a just a dream after all." Then the guardswoman saluted her officers, took Amber by the arm, and left.

Ursula, avoiding Pinnosa and Brittola's angry looks, stood up and went over to stand beside Oleander by the window in silence. It was one of the stern, imposing silences she often used to control difficult situations.

Oleander, who had seen her use it to great effect over the years—even as a child, smiled.

"Beggin' your pardon Mistress . . ." Ursula turned and glared at her, but Oleander wasn't going to be intimidated, "if we are going to be leaving before these Huns get here, shouldn't we begin making preparations soon?"

"Hold your *tongue!*" Ursula snapped.

"Yes, Oleander," Pinnosa said, "you're right, we should. And we should start by making the *decision* to leave!"

Ursula turned to face Pinnosa and for an awful long moment they glared fiercely at each other, their eyes boring deep into the other's soul.

Unable to bare such open hostility between her two old friends, Brittola asked quietly, "What made you say we were going back to Britannia?" She caught Ursula's eye. "Is *that* God's Will now?"

Ursula sighed, lowered her gaze to the fire, and, in slow, deliberate tones, began to explain. "It's not a question of God's Will. It's a question of reality. These Huns are not the enemy of Britannia nor of the First Athena. If we leave Galliae, so will they. I say we let our true enemy—the House of Theodosius, who brought the Huns out of the wilderness to be the bane of Rome's borderlands in the first place—deal with them."

"If we leave now," Pinnosa retorted sharply, "everyone will say that we ran away from the rabble like cowards. That we failed in our sworn duty to defend Rome against the barbarians. If we leave now, and we abandon the people of the Rhenus to this merciless Mundzuk and his murderous Horde, we will leave in shame and the House of Theodosius will have a complete victory over the armies of Britannia. If we leave now, and we shy away from our duty, all that we have achieved—all that we have worked hard for—will amount to *nothing!*" Pinnosa smashed her fist down hard on the table. The blow set a bowl of fruit in the center wobbling, and a cascade of freshly picked apples toppled onto the floor.

"'All that we have worked for.' 'All that we have achieved.'" Ursula said mockingly, "That for which we were working . . . is *gone!* And we have 'achieved' . . . *nothing!*" She, too, thumped the table hard with her fist. More apples tumbled to the floor.

The two enraged women both leaned forward across the table, barely an arm's reach apart, each burning their will into the other with their wild stares. The scattered fruit lay between them—the casualties of their verbal assault.

"But, that's not true, Ursula," Brittola's plaintive voice broke the tension.

Ursula and Pinnosa slowly turned to look at her. She was holding her cross as she always did when she was nervous and in need of comfort.

"That's simply not true. We've created a magnificent army of women who fight for order and who stand for peace." She looked them both pleadingly before continuing. "Now, as the Commanders of that army, may I suggest you think calmly and carefully about how it is best deployed? You have no higher authority to refer to now, apart from God. So, may I further suggest you pray very hard before you decide?"

Ursula and Pinnosa both sighed and started pacing the room—Ursula by the window, Pinnosa by the fire.

Ursula was the first to speak. Her voice was faint—fragile, even. "I . . . I admit that we could be seen to have a duty . . . to stay here. . . to protect these people . . . maybe even to fight—or resist—this Evil that is drawing closer by the day. But I also feel . . . that we have a greater duty . . . to the First Athena . . . to the women themselves . . . now that Cons—I mean, the men—are. . . ."

"*Forget the men!*" Pinnosa had been pacing away from Ursula, but now she spun around and took several purposeful strides toward her. "They are *dead!*"

Ursula visibly flinched as if the words were being stabbed into her heart. Seeing this, Pinnosa deliberately repeated them, "They . . . are . . . dead!" She strode round the table and grabbed Ursula by the shoulders. "Even before they died, you knew the Great Expedition would never take place, didn't you?"

"No, I—" Ursula pulled herself free from Pinnosa's grip and turned away.

"You knew the First Athena had found its true mission—to defend the frontier lands. Didn't you?"

Ursula looked frantically at Brittola, like a child trying to evade being caught as the culprit. "Well, I—"

"*Didn't you?*"

Ursula appealed with her eyes for Oleander to help her. But the old attendant could only stand by open-mouthed at the scene before her. Ursula looked again at Brittola. Then Pinnosa. Then back to Brittola. "Yes," she whispered finally.

"And, you know in your heart *that* is what the First Athena should do now." Ursula tried to wrest herself free from Pinnosa's grasp, but her old friend tightened her grip. "Am I right?"

Ursula nodded.

"Then, let's get the others in here and begin making some *real* plans." Pinnosa started walking toward the door.

"No, wait!"

Pinnosa halted and turned back to face her.

"It's not as simple as that." Ursula took a deep breath and steadied her voice. "You might think it's obvious what we should do, and I . . ." she took a tentative step toward Pinnosa, "I *might* agree with you." She took a second step. "And under normal circumstances, if you and I agree that something should be done—it *is* done. But not this time."

Pinnosa and Brittola both looked bemused. Ursula continued, "This isn't a decision that we alone can make. I'll not lead a single woman against the Huns who would rather return to Britannia—to her home. These Huns are a formidable foe, the likes of which no Roman army has ever encountered. I don't mind admitting that I'm frightened of them—terrified even. The First Athena can try to overcome them, but there's a very real chance . . . that we might not succeed."

She paused to allow the import of her words to settle in their minds, before adding gravely, "I only want to lead an army—even an army of peace— that is following me willingly and knows full well where I'm leading."

She returned her gaze to the empty parade ground outside. "I'm going to give the First Athena the choice on this issue. Each and every one of them—officer or legionary—will have the freedom to choose their fate. We'll see if that young Londinium lass was right about what they want to do. I'm going to ask for volunteers."

Pinnosa and Brittola looked at each other in astonishment. Then, slowly, Pinnosa began to nod.

Ursula, meanwhile, continued in a quiet voice as if she was speaking to herself, "And if they do volunteer to take on this . . . this Mundzuk and his Horde, I think I may have a plan that might . . . just . . . work. . ." She fell silent, but it was clear to the others that her mind was working again, and possibly on a new—and daring—line of thought.

Satisfied that nothing more needed to be said, and with a purposeful gleam in her eye, Pinnosa signaled to Brittola and quietly led her out.

XIV

Ursula called the officers together in the Commanders' Room soon after dawn the next day. She ordered an assembly of the First Athena in full dress uniform for an important announcement at morning bells. Martha returned soon after to inform her that several cavalry units had already departed on escort duty. A complete assembly wouldn't be possible until after evening bells.

Slightly disgruntled, Ursula resigned herself to the situation and allowed Brittola to engage her for the rest of the day. In the morning, they composed reports to Britannia and to Jovinus. His force was now in the precarious position of being the matter of utmost importance for Iron Fist and his army from Italia. In the afternoon, Ursula and Brittola were joined by Cordula. They went over various contingency plans for their ordnance requirements, depending on what the will of the Legion was to be. Then, just before evening bells were about to ring out, Martha came in to the Commanders' Room to report that the entire First Athena was assembled and ready for Ursula's address.

"At last!" Ursula muttered to herself as she headed down the long pillared corridor toward the Entrance Hall. She was still preoccupied with adjusting her helmet and plumage as the door slowly opened. When she finally looked up and stepped out over the threshold, the portico revealed a sight that made her gasp. Ursula was so astonished that Brittola had to gently nudge her to go out onto the steps overlooking the parade ground.

She slowly stepped outside and beheld the entire First Athena—infantry and cavalry—dressed in new white uniforms that mirrored her own, Brittola's and Martha's. The evening summer sun, illuminating the Legion from the side, made them appear to shine like freshly burnished silver.

Ursula stood still on the steps for a moment to enjoy the wondrous sight. As she did so, the trumpeters sounded a loud fanfare and the entire Legion stood to attention. All eleven of the infantry cohorts were lined up before her in their disciplined ranks. Behind them were the cavalry divisions standing in neat rows. To the fore of each cohort were its standard bearers and officers. To Ursula's left and facing the rest of the army was the Vanguard cavalry unit. They were arranged in two rows and mounted, and were all bearing their swords across their breastplates in ceremonial display. In front of the Vanguard were the senior officers in a line, which Brittola and Martha now left her to join.

The only member of the First Athena missing was the Commander of the Cavalry. Just as Ursula noticed her absence, a second fanfare sounded and Pinnosa appeared at the far end of the parade ground. She was astride Artemis and led Swift by the reins. Like the others, she was also dressed in a uniform of the purest white. Ursula stared at her in astonishment.

The parade ground fell absolutely silent. The attendants, who were gathered at the opposite end from the officers, made not a sound. Even the birds were hushed and still. It was as if Time itself had commanded "full attention" for a moment of such significance.

With the lightest of touches, Pinnosa urged Artemis forward. All that could be heard was the steady *clip, crunch, clip, crunch* of the horses' hooves on the loose stone surface. While she approached, Ursula descended the steps.

Pinnosa brought Swift up before Ursula, and as she prepared to mount the proud gray mare, Ursula looked up at Pinnosa and gave her a wry smile.

In reply, Pinnosa pretended to scrutinize her new uniform. She noticed an imaginary speck of dirt on her cloak, and made a great show of removing it daintily—with her little finger raised.

Ursula spluttered with a quiet laugh as she hoisted herself up.

Starting with the Vanguard and the senior officers, then moving around to the eleven cohorts, the two Commanders made their circuit of the parade ground. As they passed each unit, the standard bearers raised their insignia and the entire cohort saluted.

The sun was setting and shadows were beginning to lengthen by the time the inspection was finally over. Ursula and Pinnosa returned to the portico for the Commander-in-Chief to make her address. At a signal from Ursula, they rode Artemis and Swift up the steps. The entrance to the Officers' Hall faced west and as a result was usually steeped in shadow. But as Ursula and Pinnosa turned their steeds round to face the gathering, from between the two central pillars, they were caught by a ray from the evening sun. To every woman in the Legion, they appeared to shimmer with an awe-inspiring presence. Such was the spectacle that many of the attendants gasped and one of them audibly uttered, "They look like goddesses on a mountain top!"

"Women of the First Athena—*I salute you!*" Ursula cried. Her voice was amplified by the rock walls of the portico, and could be heard in every corner of the parade ground. She waved her arm in a wide sweep that encompassed the entire gathering before continuing. "The First Athena is surely the most magnificent Legion in all of Rome's armies! You are truly Britannia's best! Today—as I look at you in your splendor—I see you shining forth like a great beacon in these dark times. You are a light forcing all our nemeses to run for the shadows or risk being burnt to ashes by your radiant heat! You . . . ." Ursula hesitated, suddenly overcome by her emotions. She looked down and saw that Brittola, too, was clearly having difficulty holding back tears.

"May I address the Legion?" Pinnosa said quietly, leaning toward Ursula and smiling, "I believe I might be able to save us some time."

Ursula looked at her old friend in her new white uniform—and nodded.

"Women of the First Athena! You all know that you have been called here today because your Commander-in-Chief wishes to share with you a difficult dilemma. Now I call upon you to let her know your faith in her judgment." She looked back at Ursula and gave her a reassuring smile. "All those who wish to return to Britannia—with their honor intact—stand down and assemble to my left. All those who wish to risk their lives in the defense of the peoples of Germania and Galliae, and attempt to turn back this murderous Horde of Huns that is wreaking a path of devastation—raise your swords!"

Ursula was about to protest that Pinnosa had not given the women of the Legion a full picture of their predicament. It had been her intention to explain that facing the Huns meant risking the real prospect of death. She wanted to be certain they understood that choosing to return home was not cowardice—that they could do so without shame.

Before she could say anything, the entire Vanguard and the officers, whose weapons were already drawn in salute, raised their swords to the sky. At the same time, from all across the parade ground could be heard the clicks and rattles of blades being pulled. Then—as one—they filled the air with a sea of flashing metal that burnt bright like fire as it caught the last rays of the sun. Not one woman went to stand at Pinnosa's left. The "vote" was unanimous.

Ursula took a deep breath, as much to steady her voice as to make herself heard. "Women of the First Athena—I salute you yet again! You have shown your courageous strength, which comes from your discipline and honor. You have also demonstrated your willingness to stand up and fight for what is right—even though it is not you who are wronged!" She paused to drink in the magnificent scene one last time.

"I will go now and work with the other Commanders to formulate our plans. Rest assured we will do out utmost to ensure your lives are not placed in unnecessary jeopardy as we maneuver to wrestle these lands from the Huns' tyrannical grip!"

She glanced over at Pinnosa and they shared a broad smile. "Women of the First Athena, I am proud of you all! And I say to you now .. . . *Salute yourselves!*"

In one voice, they all cheered an almighty "*Huzzah!*" The cry of their eleven thousand voices filled the military complex and resounded beyond. It startled the people of Cologne, and could even be heard down river by those of the Franks and Alemanni camped along its banks.

XV

Shortly before Lughnasadh, Mundzuk and his Horde crossed the Main River and moved deep into the Taunus hills on their way to the Rhenus at Confluentes. This was well within the area under the auspices of the First Athena. As the Horde drew nearer, it came under close examination by Pinnosa and Martha's scouts. From their reports, Ursula saw a pattern emerge. The Hun leaders enjoyed their hunting and would leave the main body of their Horde in the valleys and take a smaller group of warriors up into the hills for their sport. Ursula realized that this was the chance they needed and ordered that her plan be put into action at once.

So it was that one bright autumn morning, Ursula and Pinnosa watched as Mundzuk, accompanied by several hundred of his men, came riding hard into a highland clearing. They were in pursuit of a clutch of deer led by a particularly nimble buck. As they reached the crest in the clearing, Mundzuk and the hunt leaders pulled up short. Ursula could clearly see him frantically signaling to the others behind to get quickly into formation.

Ursula smiled to herself. She knew what he had seen. She looked down the line to appreciate the awesomeness of what had stopped Mundzuk in his tracks. The entire First Athena cavalry—all three thousand of them—were stretched in a long line across the clearing. They were all dressed in their uniforms—and stood absolutely still with just the gentle flap of their cloaks in the light breeze. Ursula thought they looked like a bank of white clouds caught in dawn's rays.

Within moments, the Huns had formed their line. The two armies stood motionless, scrutinizing each other from a distance like two great bears—one brown, one white—preparing to wrestle.

Ursula nodded to Pinnosa to ride out. As planned, she was accompanied by Viventia and two Alemanni tribeswomen—one of whom was Amber—each carrying a white flag of truce. Slowly, they rode into the center of the clearing.

Ursula observed that Mundzuk chose a man with a horrendous diagonal scar across his face to meet with her delegation. She knew from reports that this was Mundzuk's half-brother, Rugila. He had apparently learned to speak basic Alemanni—no doubt from some poor victim. She watched as Rugila chose three men and then came forward to meet Pinnosa.

While the two groups of riders approached each other, Ursula narrowed her eyes and peered intently at the figure of Mundzuk. She knew as she did so that he, too, was staring back. She could see his deformed, elongated head—a feature he shared with several of those around him.

So this is the monster—here at last. And these are his men. He is, indeed, a beast of a man—but a man nevertheless . . . .

Suddenly, a young boy from the Hun ranks yelled and whipped his mount forward. He galloped across the clearing, past the two delegations, and over to where the ranks of the First Athena were assembled. The women looked on anxiously as he rode boldly along the length of the women's line, well within spear throwing distance. He came to a halt barely twenty cubits from Ursula and stared at her with obvious contempt.

He called out in fluent Latin, "*Esne Ursula, virgo regina, dux Primae Athenae?*—Are you Princess Ursula, the leader of the First Athena?"

His voice had not yet broken and Ursula found herself at once amused and admiring of his youthful audacity. But his alien appearance startled her. She studied his skull, which seemed cruelly deformed, and looked deep into his hideous, un-human eyes before replying in Latin, "It is customary for an uninvited visitor to introduce himself first. Whom do I have the honor of addressing?"

"I am Prince Attila, son of the great Mundzuk, ruler of all the lands beyond Rome! And soon he will cross the Alps, crush the puny Goths and add the Great Sow, Rome herself to the beasts under his control!"

He threw back his head with great pomposity as he spoke, and proclaimed, "One day I will be King of the Huns and I will rule over all my father's minions from The Black Sea to Hispania! After today, that will include you—assuming you do the sensible thing and surrender!" He pulled out a vicious-looking hunting knife and brandished it threateningly.

Martha and the others of Ursula's personal guard drew their bows in readiness to fire. Ursula held up her hand in restraint. She said to Attila, "Be not so hasty to make enemies, Prince! We Romans are of far greater value to you as your friends."

Slowly, he returned his knife to its sheath and looked at her with renewed curiosity.

Ursula smiled and continued in a more gentle tone. "Please tell me, Prince Attila; how did you come to speak such perfect Latin?"

"We have one of your Roman priests among us who teaches us many things about your strange ways, including your god, Christ, who preferred to suffer rather than fight!"

"So he did . . . but I think there is another way to view that." She looked at him thoughtfully before continuing, "You could say he preferred to win rather than fight."

"In the same way that you do?"

Ursula did not answer. Instead she gazed at him, offering no challenge. She saw a kind of understanding in his eyes.

"You don't intend to fight my father, do you? What do you intend to do?"

Ursula laughed out loud at his impudent quick wit.

His nostrils flared with a startling anger and he reached for his knife again. But then he must have remembered the guards and their bows, as his hand slid away from the sheath.

She stopped laughing and said curtly, "Such big questions from one so small. Now go back to your father quickly, before he thinks I've taken you prisoner! You'll find out soon enough the intentions of the First Athena."

Attila turned his horse around and made it give a defiant prance as he galloped off. As he rode back across the clearing, the pugnacious little prince decided to show off by doing a handstand on his mount's back.

The women of the first Athena chuckled thinly, disengaged their arrows and lowered their bows. The falseness of their merriment made Ursula realize how tense the boy's visit had made them all.

Attila returned to the Hun ranks at the same time as Rugila. The consternation caused by Rugila's news clearly saved the young prince from the thrashing his stormy-faced father had obviously intended to give him. As Rugila made his report, Ursula could plainly see Mundzuk's expression change from dark thunderous menace to sheer open-mouthed astonishment. She smiled. She knew what Rugila was reporting would be a complete surprise to Mundzuk—and she knew her plan was going to work. In her mind, she went over the message she and Pinnosa had carefully worded and practiced a hundred times.

"Princess Ursula of the Britons, Commander-in-Chief of the Legion, First Athena, comes here today not to fight, but to see for herself whether the Huns are worthy of her breaking her Vow of Chastity in order to marry their renowned leader—the Great Mundzuk—master of all the lands north of the Empire. She therefore challenges the Huns to put on a display of their prowess so that she can assess their worthiness as aspirants to having a Brittanic queen."

There was a long silence while Mundzuk studied her across the clearing. Although she couldn't see his eyes clearly, Ursula could feel their cold gaze—and her smile waned. Then, unexpectedly, he smiled. He turned to speak to Rugila, and, with a cursory wave of his hand, sent him back with his reply.

Riding to the center of the clearing, Rugila announced in a loud voice, "The Lord Mundzuk is more than willing to let the First Athena see some true Hun horse riding and fighting skills. He asks, however, whether the renowned Roman women would favor us with a similar display?"

Ursula's smile returned. She feigned a brief discussion, with Pinnosa and the other leaders, before sending Amber forth to proclaim in reply, "The women of the First Athena will be honored to show Lord Mundzuk what they are made of."

Within moments, the Huns commenced their display. To begin with, the horsemanship skills they demonstrated weren't dissimilar to those displayed by the Alemanni, and Ursula speculated with Pinnosa about who had learned what from whom. But then they produced the weapons Ursula had heard much about—their lariats and whips—which she knew they could use with deadly effect in battle. She looked on in amazement as, with seeming effortlessness, they showed how they could ensnare both horse and rider at full gallop and bring them to the ground.

The final display featured Rugila himself. He placed five attendants in a row about ten paces apart, then rode along the line at full gallop. As he approached each attendant, he threw an egg into the air. With a loud crack of his whip, Rugila broke each one, splattering everything in its proximity.

As soon as he had finished, Pinnosa rode out to the center of the clearing with Amber to interpret. Speaking to Rugila but raising their voices so the rest of the Huns could hear, they relayed the message, "Princess Ursula congratulates the Lord Mundzuk and his remarkable men on such an impressive—and worthy—display!" Pinnosa lowered her voice and said to Amber quietly, "Now please instruct our honored *friend* to return to his ranks and tell his master that the First Athena's demonstration is about to commence." While Amber translated, Pinnosa smiled sweetly at the short and stumpy 'ugly head'.

Rugila did as he was told and returned to his master's side. Mundzuk and the other Hun leaders leaned forward in their saddles, eager with anticipation. Many of those closest to the women's ranks even leered openly at them.

There was a long pause, during which the line of the First Athena remained completely motionless. Mundzuk and the other Huns were just starting to share glances of uncertainty and bemusement, when all of a sudden a wondrous thing happened. The entire First Athena cavalry turned into a swirling mass of white birds that filled the far side of the clearing like a shimmering, sparkling haze before flying up into the clear September sky and disappearing from view.

XVI

Almost a full cycle of the moon later, the Commanders of the First Athena were reclining around the feast table after their meal. It was now mid-October, and Ursula had a serious dilemma. After the First Athena 'disappeared' in front of Mundzuk and his warlords, the Huns had vanished, too. From the day after their trick with the doves, ducks, geese and swans no one had seen a single Hun. Consequently, no one knew whether they had swallowed the bait and were heading for Colonia.

Not knowing the Huns whereabouts had at first been a little like a game. The entire Legion had taken to speculating on where the first report would come from. Indeed, some of the Londinium women even started taking wagers on the likely first contact. But after three weeks, it was beginning to weigh heavily on their minds. Each night, conversation revolved around the same questions: "Where are the Huns?" "Has Mundzuk set the Horde's course for Colonia?" "Has the Horde split up and the menace dissipated?" "Can the First Athena at last leave Germania and depart for Britannia?"

Ursula, too, was vexed by the same nagging thoughts, but she dared not voice them to the others—not even Pinnosa—as she didn't want to undermine their determination to stick with their plans should Mundzuk appear. Instead, she confided in Cordula, who had taken to keeping her cousin company after the others had turned in. Often long into the night, in between reminiscences of home, the life that was and the life that could have been, they would ponder the same questions that were on everybody's mind: "What should we do now?" "How much longer should we wait for Mundzuk?" "Should we muster the First Athena and leave for home—possibly leaving Colonia undefended?"

Morgan's arrival one evening with news of events in the south came as a welcome diversion. He was in surprisingly good spirits, which raised the morale of the women, and to perpetuate the lighter mood, he took his infant son in his arms, and pretended to address his report to him. "Do not be fooled, my little friend," he said, adopting the lyrical rise and fall of Rusticus's distinctive voice, which everyone instantly recognized. "Those horrible Huns are in the German wilderness somewhere. They most certainly have not headed back down the Limes. The frontier may not be defended, but it is still closely watched. A Horde of thirty thousand Huns won't go unnoticed for long. In fact, our people keep us fully informed of what's happening along the frontier, while we deal with these Burgundians—some of whom are with us and others are with Iron Fist . . . ." Morgan pulled a funny face that looked just like one of Rusticus's favorite expressions. "But, I never had a Burgundian aunt, so I can't tell which is which!"

By the time he finished, not only was the baby in fits of giggles, but the officers present were laughing, too. Even Pinnosa joined in, who normally took military messages very seriously.

While everyone was laughing, Martha stood up and bowed theatrically. She had perfected a comic routine in which she impersonated a confused Mundzuk busily looking for the birds of the First Athena and falling into the empty pits they'd been hidden in. She performed it now for the benefit of the gathering.

As Ursula looked on, the laughter and merriment reminded her of happier times with her old friends back in Corinium. Back then, when Martha and Saula would put on little comic plays, she would laugh so much her sides would ache.

Play-acting over, Martha whispered something to Saula and the others knew they were in for more entertainment. Saula produced her lute and handed Martha a little drum. As soon as Saula plucked the opening refrain and Martha started tapping the rhythm, the rest of the women applauded, because they recognized the little ditty the two friends had created and taught the others.

Everyone joined in, including Ursula. They all banged the table with their fists while Martha sang the verses then burst into rousing singsong for the chorus.

Mundzuk come
Mundzuk Hun
Mundzuk play
But he no fun!

Mundzuk come from far away
He come to visit—can't stay
He see big mountain—can't climb
He walk around—save plenty time
He see big water—can't swim
He walk around—he not dim

Mundzuk come to visit Rome
We say "Not welcome! Go home!"
He take a bath—not clean
He chase a princess—not queen
He go to Heaven—not dead
God say "wrong place—ugly head!"

While Martha was singing the final verse, one of the night watchwomen entered the room. By the expression on her face, it was clear she had come to deliver an urgent message. As she made her way to Ursula—who was sitting slightly apart from the main group by the window—one by one, the entire gathering noticed the guard's presence. Martha ceased her performance, and everyone went quiet with anticipation.

When the watchwoman completed her report, she stood to attention. Slowly, with a somber expression, Ursula rose to address them. "Ladies! It appears that Mundzuk is more resourceful than we gave him credit for. We have just received a rather dubious report . . ." she looked at Pinnosa in a way that suggested they had some rather urgent work to attend to, "that apparently he didn't disappear into the wilderness." She paused for emphasis. "If this report is to be believed, he took his Horde and crossed over to the hills on the western side of the Rhenus—into Roman territory!"

Gasps of astonishment and disbelief pervaded the room.

"If all this is true, it would seem that he has since been deliberately toying with us by lying low in the one area of dense forest he knew we wouldn't send scouting parties to. One thing we know for sure . . ." she raised her voice and her junior officers caught a rare glimpse of their Commander-in-Chief's anger and frustration, "he *deliberately* disappeared in order to exact revenge for our 'little trick'!"

A deathly silence took hold of the gathering until Faustina asked, "How do we know all this?"

"Good question." Ursula looked back at the watchwoman. "From two sources it would seem?" The woman nodded. "Please tell the others how we came by this intelligence."

The guard was clearly nervous at the prospect of addressing the senior officers and she was unable to prevent her voice from wavering. "Well, first, Commander, we got sight of this rider coming at us fast across the bridge. Then we saw a second one close behind him. They was obviously one in pursuit of the other . . . ." She paused and looked uneasily at Ursula.

Ursula nodded encouragingly.

"The first one rode straight up to the gate and leapt from his horse, screaming, 'Let me in!' in Germanic. But of course we didn't." She looked around the room, swallowed hard and continued, "Anyway, seeing that the other was right behind him, he screamed at us: 'They're upon us! The Huns are upon us! They're coming at us from the *south!* I stumbled upon them on the military road. They'll be here in less than a week!' He didn't say any more, because at that point the other one caught up with him and speared him in the back."

This time it was Brittola who broke the stunned silence. "Who was he?"

"We don't know, Mistress. He was dressed in Roman garb, and he spoke the same German as those from Colonia. He had seen at least fifty winters I'd say. Maybe he was a member of the standing guard or just a citizen on his travels in places where he shouldn't've been. We've sent for the Colonia Guard. They'll probably be able to identify him."

"And then what did the second rider do?" Ursula prompted gently.

"He greeted us in Latin—bad Latin—and told us he was an emissary from the Great Mundzuk sent to relay the King's gracious greetings to his bride-to-be, Commander. We wouldn't let him in, so he told us what you've already told the other officers. Except he didn't say they was 'hiding' in the hills. He said they was 'hunting' in them, 'gathering game for the wedding feast' and such like."

She paused, swallowed hard again, then asked, "Beggin' your pardon, Commander, but we're still holding him in the Guard House. What do you want us to do with him?"

Ursula looked grimly at Pinnosa and nodded toward the door.

Pinnosa stood up and shouted for their cloaks.

Ursula replied to the watchwoman, signaling that she should return to her duties, "We'll be along shortly. But while he's waiting, give him some refreshment. If he really is an emissary from Mundzuk, and not just some drunken prankster, we don't want to treat him badly, do we?"

XVII

Ursula and Pinnosa met the strange emissary, who was dressed in a curious mixture of Hun and Frankish garb, and listened to his tale. He claimed he was a messenger who had been traveling with a companion. They'd befriended the Colonia man whom they met on the road. When it was time for them to go their separate ways, on the other side of the bridge, the Colonia man suddenly turned violent and tried to rob them. The Colonian killed the messenger's companion and threw his body into the river before trying to escape. The messenger had at first been too shocked to save his friend. Then, when he caught up with the villain outside the gates, too crazed with rage to show mercy.

Ursula and Pinnosa went to the far end of the corridor, away from the room where he was being held, to discuss what to do.

"He's definitely one of Mundzuk's men," Pinnosa declared, her voice thick with disgust. "That much I *do* believe!"

"What do you make of this business with the Colonian?" Ursula asked quietly.

"I'm not sure. Perhaps our friend in there isn't an emissary, but a spy. Maybe he wasn't on his way here with a message, but on his way back with one. Who knows?" Pinnosa's eyes narrowed. "We could try to get the truth out of him."

Ursula shook her head fiercely. "No. There'll be none of that. He may or may not have been an emissary before, but he's certainly going to be one now." She grabbed Pinnosa's arm. "I think we may have ourselves the bait we need to lure our monster with thirty thousand heads from its lair!"

XVIII

The next three days felt like the longest in everyone's lives. The preparations for the 'wedding' had been completed two weeks earlier. The only thing they could do now was hold station and wait for Mundzuk to arrive.

In order to divert the Legion's thoughts from their fear of the approaching menace and to alleviate the sheer frustration of having to bide their time, the officers of the First Athena busied themselves with plans for their return to Britannia. They soon realized that within two or three weeks the weather would deteriorate and conditions in the Channel would become too harsh to attempt a crossing. As soon as this became clear, Brittola led the senior officers in prayer for a speedy solution to the Hun problem so that they wouldn't have to delay their departure for home until the following spring.

Ursula endeavored to distract herself from darker thoughts by making several attempts to write a letter to her father. But each time she tried, she realized things with Mundzuk had to be resolved before she would have anything to report. So her quills remained dry and her styluses cold.

Then, in the middle of the afternoon on the fourth day after the emissary was released, they received a flurry of reports that the Hun Horde had been spotted. They emerged from the hills to the southeast of the city and were beginning to cross the broad flat plains, which led to Colonia. That evening, the southeastern horizon glowed blood red with their fires. Ursula knew with certainty that the day they had planned for was imminent.

Late that night, long after the officers' meal was over and the women had retired to their chambers, Ursula walked pensively out onto the south-facing portico of the Officers' Hall. She wanted to take one last look at the red streak in the dark, which seemed to cut through the night like an open wound. She was still in her white uniform, but, untypically, had her hair clipped back in a bunch, which exposed her slender neck and made her look much younger.

She was startled by the sound of footsteps coming toward her from the loose stones beyond the paving. From out of the shadows came Martha, Saula, Cordula, and Brittola. "You should all be in bed," she said quietly. "It's going to be a long, hard day tomorrow."

"*You're* the one who should be in bed." Pinnosa's voice came from behind a pillar on the opposite side of the portico. She moved into the light coming from the open door. "After all—you *are* the bride."

"Ursula, we were just wondering," Martha said quietly, as she stepped forward and affectionately held Ursula's arm, "There's one thing that still bothers us about tomorrow's plans." She looked deeply into Ursula's eyes. "How exactly are you going to kill him?"

Ursula smiled. "Do you know something, Pinnosa?" she said cheerfully without taking her eyes away from Martha's, "You're right. I should go to bed early before my wedding day. But I can't. My mind is full of excitement and . . . and I feel a little hungry."

She turned and called, "Oleander!" The old attendant appeared in the doorway. "Fetch me the most appropriate food for a bride-to-be . . . an apple!"

Oleander hurried off, and the old friends from Corinium sat down on the cool stone steps. For a long, still moment, they stared at the ominous distant red glow.

Without turning around, Brittola broke the silence. "Ursula?"

"Yes?"

"Please answer Martha's question. Apart from putting that wounded Hibernian out of his misery at Pinnosa's villa, you've never actually killed a person before, have you? At least not—"

"Why should that affect what she's about to do tomorrow?" Pinnosa interrupted. "This is a foul Hun we're talking about—not a human being!"

"No, Pinnosa," Ursula said firmly, "We should talk about it. Brittola's right. I've never killed an able-bodied foe before. But you have, Pinnosa? In fact, you're the only one of us who has. I'm curious. What is it like? How does it feel to cut open another's body?"

"Can't we *please* talk about something else?" Pinnosa pleaded, but they continued looking at her, waiting for her reply. She sighed. "It feels just like cutting meat except it's warm instead of hot or cold," she said dismissively, and turned back to face the horizon. Then, after a long silence she lowered her gaze to the steps in front of her and added in a quieter voice, "And it's wet—not oily."

The silence continued for a while. Then, almost imperceptibly at first, Brittola began to weep. "Oh, God! Why must we live in a world full of death and killing?" She looked up to the stars and burst into uncontrollable sobs. "When will all the killing stop? When will all the dying stop?"

Pinnosa moved over and put her arms around Brittola. She rocked her gently saying, "There, there." But as she did so, Ursula could see a tear roll down each of her cheeks.

Cordula, sounding tense and awkward, said, "Ursula. I won't be with you tomorrow, and I . . ." She paused.

"What is it?" Ursula said gently.

"I'm just not ready to say . . . goodnight yet." She, too, started to choke with tears. This time it was Saula who did the comforting.

Ursula looked at Martha and saw that she was also struggling not to cry. As she reached out to hold her, Oleander returned with the apple.

"Ah! Thank you, Oleander. Just what I needed." Ursula placed the apple in her lap, reached up to unclip her hair, then picked up the apple again. "Would anyone like to share this with me?" The others were all too upset to answer. "Come on, Brittola! You look like you could do with something to take your mind off things. Have a nice piece of apple," she said holding out the fruit.

Brittola shook her head.

"Cordula, how about you? A nice, juicy slice of apple?" Ursula offered the fruit to her, but she shook her head, too.

"Oh, Ursula!" Saula exclaimed with emotion. "Can't you see that no one—apart from you—is in the slightest bit interested in that blasted apple!"

"I'll have a piece." Pinnosa said, opening her eyes with a look of understanding.

"Good. That's settled then." Making sure everyone was watching, Ursula squeezed the fruit in her hand. It fell into her lap in two pieces—neatly sliced in half.

They all gasped.

Brittola broke away from Pinnosa in amazement, "How did you do that? Was it already cut for you by Oleander?"

Ursula didn't reply. Instead, she picked up one of the halves and closed her hand tightly around it. Again it separated into two cleanly cut pieces. "Perhaps we should all have a slice each?" she suggested and started to laugh. She flipped her hand over and exposed the fine, crescent-shaped blade that was cupped across her palm and held in place by what looked like half a ring around her two middle fingers. "And *that* by the way . . ." she looked pointedly at Martha, "is the answer to your question." She produced the rest of the elaborate hairpin that Nugget had made especially for her back in Corinium and allowed them to examine it.

"I'm very pleased to see that it works. Not one of you had any idea I had a sharp blade in my hand, did you?" They shook their heads. "If five senior Roman officers could be fooled, I think I have a very good chance with our 'King' Mundzuk." She looked back at Pinnosa. "The only thing I'm worried about is that the first cut has to be the killing cut. I'm not sure which is the most lethal." She motioned across her neck. "To cut here . . ." she nodded toward her crotch, "or there? What do you think?"

XIX

It was almost the end of October, 411. The weather was autumnal but clear. Soon after dawn, trumpets sounded from the four walls of Colonia, warning those outside that the gates would soon be closed and secured.

By morning bells, the outer city beyond the walls was completely deserted. Not a soul was to be found in the artisans' workshops or scholars' colleges. The apprentices and slaves who were usually bustling about on their masters' errands, had vanished. Travelers' hostels were empty. The myriad of brothels that catered to every taste were abandoned. Not even a stray dog wandered the streets.

By mid-morning all the preparations in both the city and the military complex across the river were complete, and the entire region settled into an uneasy silence. Ursula could see that the battlements were crowded with people—from the highest officials to the lowliest sewer slave—all scrambling for the best view, and waiting for something to happen.

On the opposite bank of the Rhenus, the officers of the First Athena were gathered on the roof of one of the halls. They were watching the flag-poles over the city's East Gate, as they waited for the series of pre-arranged signals that would inform them of the enemy's approach. The rest of the Legion waited in their barracks and the parade ground was deserted, apart from the occasional attendant going about her tasks.

Then, just before midday, the drums began.

At first, like the heavy rumble of an approaching eight-wheel cart fully laden with rock from a quarry, the sound was something they felt, rather than heard. The moment the pounding was clearly distinguishable, the first black flag went up over the city's East Gate. Shortly afterwards, the women of the First Athena could hear and feel it for themselves—an ever-growing and ever-nearing *baroom-boom-boom*. They knew the Huns were coming.

It seemed a long, long time before the Horde came into view. Many of the city folk were to recall later that, of all the horrors they experienced that day, it was the relentless pounding of those invisible drums, marking time for untold numbers of unseen feet, that filled them with the greatest fear.

Just after midday, Ursula saw the second black flag go up, signaling that the Horde was in full view. This was followed soon after by a single white flag, which meant they were—as the Alemanni had foretold—moving as one body, thirty thousand strong, and not divided into separate units of any kind. It was fortunate that the harvest was over, otherwise the huge mass of men would have trampled down the farmer's crops as they approached the city from the south.

"I can't see any sign of burning," Pinnosa observed after scouring the southern horizon, "I'm surprised! I thought they laid waste to everything in their path."

"They must be on their best behavior," Martha quipped. "A sign of respect, perhaps, for their master's bride!"

They all laughed nervously.

Some time later, the third black flag went up, signaling that the leaders of the Horde were entering the city's outer perimeters. Soon the Huns would be walking on the deserted streets and encountering the white bunting that would lead them to the site of the wedding. This was the signal the officers had been waiting for.

Ursula gave the order for the First Athena to assemble. Within moments the parade ground was full with the eleven thousand white-clad women, standing to attention. The Vanguard took their position at the end of the cohorts nearest the gate, ready to lead the women out.

Pinnosa brought Swift up to the base of the steps of the portico to the Officers' Hall for Ursula to mount, but this time there was no inspection. Instead, Pinnosa simply saluted and rode off to the head of the Vanguard.

Ursula urged Swift up to the top step where she turned to address the Legion alone. "Women of the First Athena, I salute you!" She drew her sword and raised it on high. "You are truly the most magnificent and splendid Legion in *all* of Rome's armies! I am proud of each and every one of you! You have served Rome better than it deserves. You have served the peoples of Germania and Galliae better than they could ever have hoped. You have served Britannia better than we ourselves dared believe at first. You have served yourselves with great valor—and great honor! You have proven to yourselves you are worthy of living the rest of your lives with pride in your hearts and dignity in your manner! For even when you are old and all that we have been through together is but a dim and distant memory, you will always be able to hold your head up high and say in triumph, '*I was in the First Athena!*'"

A rousing cry went up from the ranks, forcing her to pause. It was with difficulty that she managed to quell the cheers.

"But above *all* else, you have served our Lord God to the best of your abilities. And now, before we embark upon the most dangerous mission we have ever faced, I ask you to join me in prayer." She turned her sword over and held the silver and gold hilt before her like a cross.

As she did so, Pinnosa bellowed, "First Athena! Swords *out!* And, kneel!"

The infantry knelt on one knee before their iron hilt crosses. The cavalry held their embossed sword hilts before them, with their heads bowed reverentially forward. Brittola was the only exception. She drew her sword but held it to her side and reached under her cloak for her cross. She clasped it tightly under her chin in her free hand.

"Dear merciful, ever-lasting God. We, the humble women of the First Athena, are gathered here before you to prepare to meet a truly hideous evil! They have been sent to plague these lands by dark forces that would seek to be the undoing of Rome and all that she stands for. We pray with all our hearts that You give us not only the strength to face this monster, but also the power to defeat it. For we fight this day not for Rome, not for Britannia—not even for ourselves! We fight so that your Divine Rule can prevail, so that the horrors of these times—the horrors that this troubled world has witnessed—might cease. So that Peace in your name, Lord, can finally reign . . . . Amen."

The warm reverberation of the women's' "Amen" filled the parade ground. It seemed to last forever before fading into the very soil beneath their feet.

Then, after a long pause, Pinnosa shouted, "First Athena! *Attention!* Face right!"

Ursula joined the other Commanders in front of the Vanguard, and the gates opened.

Pinnosa cried, "*Forward!*"

A resounding cheer went up from the top of the city walls at the sight of the white-robed First Athena emerging from their barracks. The Legion marching over the bridge toward the city in parade formation was a wondrous spectacle, which filled the hearts of the city's folk with hope. As the officers reached the city shore beneath the battlements, they could hear the people calling to them in a mixture of Latin, German and even Brittanic:

"Kill the Ugly Heads!"

"Go with God, Ursula!"

"Pinnosa Bloodhair! Bathe in Hun blood tonight!"

Following Pinnosa's lead, all the Commanders took off their helmets and waved them in reply to the cheers.

"If only there were just cause for such celebrations!" Saula shouted to Martha over the din as she waved and waved again.

"Oh, we'll give them something to celebrate," Martha cried in reply, "Have no fear!"

XX

The North Gate of Colonia opened out into a shallow valley that sloped down to the river's shore to a place called Shepherd's Meadow. Farmers used it to graze their sheep and cattle when they brought their herds to market. The area immediately below the city walls was a graveyard, which had a small Christian chapel. Around it was a modest grove of fruit trees that created a peaceful place of rest.

As Ursula led the First Athena into the Shepherd's Meadow, she saw that the final preparations for the 'wedding' had been carried out as ordered. The entire valley floor was covered in dried white flowers, making the hollow gleam like freshly polished alabaster. In the center of the white "carpet" was a small, ornate white tent.

Ursula came to a halt beside the temple complex. The cohorts assembled in their ranks behind her, forming a long white line along the water's edge. The last of the legionaries were just falling into position when the first Hun appeared along the top of the ridge, at the opposite end of the hollow.

Within a very short time, the entire ridge was dotted with men on horseback, acting as markers around the periphery of the white carpet of flowers. Then, as the Legion watched, the foot soldiers came up behind and filled the spaces between them, thickening the line into a concentrated mass of menace, bristling with weapons of every description. A short while later, the gathering was complete. Some thirty thousand wild and ruthless warriors from far distant lands arrayed in an uneven line along the ridge, faced eleven thousand women in white, standing, weapons sheathed, in disciplined ranks with their backs to the broad waters of the Rhenus.

The drumming suddenly stopped. An eerie silence settled. All that could be heard were the rattling harnesses from restless horses and the piercing cry of a lone hawk high above.

With a shrill fanfare of trumpets, Ursula and the other senior officers rode forward to a point halfway between the ranks of the First Athena and the small tent. Almost immediately a cacophony of drum rolls, cymbal clashes and clamor from foreign percussion instruments the Romans had never heard before burst the air. An opening appeared in the Hun line and a big man, dressed completely in black fur and riding a huge black stallion emerged, accompanied by three others of his kind in identical dress. It was Mundzuk. Like Ursula, he rode to point between his ranks and the tent.

The drumming and clattering clashes ceased. Rugila rode forward and addressed the gathering in his newly learned, heavily accented and faltering Latin. "The Great Mundzuk, King of all lands north of Rome, bids his greeting to the . . . the . . . valiant women of Britannia. He especially bids his greeting to the beautiful Princess Ursula!"

Pinnosa urged Artemis clear of Ursula's group and gave the reply, "Hail Mundzuk and his worthy Hun lords! We are honored indeed by your presence here today! Princess Ursula is most humbled to meet the great King!" She bowed as much as her ceremonial armor would allow. "Let the Royal Marriage commence!"

Pinnosa turned Artemis around and returned to the others. As she was taking up position next to Ursula she said in a voice just loud enough for them to hear, "The time has come." She and Ursula exchanged a look. There was so much they wanted to say, so much they had to say. All Pinnosa added was, "Good luck."

One by one, the others said the same. Brittola was the last. As Ursula's eyes met hers, she was too upset to speak.

Ursula forced a reassuring smile and said, "Good luck, Brittola. Good luck, all of you." Then she turned Swift to face the Huns and urged her forward.

Swift had barely started to move when Brittola found her voice and cried, "This . . . ."

They all joined in, "May not be easy!"

Brittola added, "God goes with you!"

Ursula glanced back over her shoulder and nodded. Then she turned away and slowly rode—step by step—up to the tent. There she dismounted and discretely attached Swift's harness to a cord that was hidden under the carpet of dried flowers. While she was doing so, she happened to glance back toward her friends and the rest of the First Athena. They all looked so beautiful, calm and peaceful in the afternoon sun—like a picture painted on a wall.

Suddenly, Ursula was filled with a cold, paralyzing panic. She had an overwhelming urge to run back to them and lead them all far away. For a moment she imagined being with them in the sunshine—hunting, fishing, singing songs and drinking wine. Then her terror returned—a tightening knot in the pit of her stomach. She gagged for breath and struggled not to vomit.

"Mistress!" Oleander whispered urgently from the tent opening, "Come inside—*quickly!*"

Ursula started taking deep breaths as she struggled to quell her churning stomach. But still she couldn't move.

Oleander rushed out and grabbed her by the arm. Smiling nervously at Mundzuk's delegation who weren't very distant, she led Ursula inside, saying under her breath, "Come on. You have to be brave now, Mistress."

Once inside the tent, Ursula couldn't stop talking. "He's almost *here!* I am *not* ready! My hair! We have to prepare my hair, Oleander. Quick! Where's that hairpin? Oh, Oleander—where *is* it?"

"It's *here*, Mistress. Now stand still while I put it in for you."

The old attendant carefully removed Ursula's helmet, then began brushing out Ursula's hair and arranging it in the style best suited for the ornament.

"Make sure it's in the right way, will you? You know, just as we practiced."

"Yes, Mistress."

A large drum boomed loud, cymbals clashed and hunting horns sounded, indicating that Mundzuk had dismounted.

"Oh, God! He'll be here soon! Have the tent ropes been done properly?"

"Yes, Mistress. *Please* keep still!"

"I can't do this! I can't!"

"Yes, you *can!*" Oleander gave Ursula's hair a tug, just like she used to when the young princess was being a naughty child. "You *can* and you *will!* The others are depending on you."

Ursula took a deep breath, clenched her teeth and closed her eyes.

Oleander resumed her usual gentle tone, "That's better, Mistress." She continued her work and for a moment they were both silent. "There. That's got it."

Ursula reached back to check the weapon was firmly and correctly in place, and nodded.

"Then I'd best be going, Mistress. The sooner I leave, the sooner it'll all be over." Oleander started to walk stoically toward the tent opening, but just as she reached it, she looked back. Ursula was standing as motionless, utter horror in her eyes. Oleander began to cry. "Oh, what have we come to, Mistress? You are such a beautiful young woman with such soft, blond hair—and beautiful blue eyes that can fill a room. You are in the prime of your life, and absolutely ripe for a *real* marriage." She ran back and put her arms around Ursula's waist in a long, loving hug.

Ursula returned the embrace, then, slowly, stepped back a pace. She looked deeply into the short, old woman's tear-filled eyes.

"I love you, Mistress . . . ever so much." Oleander tried to bury her sobs in Ursula's white cloak.

Ursula gently but firmly held her away. "I love you, too," she replied quietly.

Ursula nodded toward the opening. Oleander wiped her tears and with a final squeeze of her mistress' hands, moved toward it. She opened the flap and looked back. They both smiled, and Oleander left.

Ursula was alone.

She looked around the tent and noticed that the bright, white panels of the sides and roof were catching a breeze, and moving rhythmically—in and out—like a person's chest breathing beneath a sheet. In the center was a platform that had been placed and arranged according to her explicit instructions. She knew she needed to check it, but she couldn't bring herself to look at it.

Suddenly, the sides of the tent billowed in toward her. They heaved in great bulges as if something—a monstrous storm perhaps—was trying to tear through the cloth and burst in upon her to rip her tortured soul from her body with its wild swirls of terrifying ferocity.

"Look at the bed," she urged herself. "Look at it!" she repeated through gritted teeth.

Slowly, the gust of wind abated. Ursula finally turned her eyes to the raised platform. It was covered with fine, lace-trimmed bedding and cushions—all in white and cream silks. It looked beautiful and perfect enough for a real wedding night.

A wave of calmness came over her, the tent sides were stilled, and everything faded into a gentle white haze. A figure coalesced and there before her, in the stillness and soft light, was Constans.

On a sunny October day, another lifetime ago, he was lying on his back with a blade of grass between his teeth, looking up at the sky. They were seventeen and had been left alone together during a hunt in the hills north of Corinium.

"Come here," he said sweetly, "Let me kiss you."

As they kissed, she could feel tiny tingling sensations when he ran his fingers through her hair and gently touched her neck and shoulders. She looked into his eyes—his deep, blue eyes that were so close, so big . . . so real.

Then they were saying good-bye in the Forum. She was kissing him again and the crowd roared. She saw again the little trinket she had fashioned for him. There was the tear on his cheek during the speeches. Once more she heard her father's parting words. She recalled how her heart ached as she watched Constans's plumage in the distance, disappearing down the road to Londinium.

She remembered how Cordula pleaded with Morgan as he rode out upon the same road earlier that day.

There, in the haze of the tent, was Pinnosa's face as they fought the Saxons. Even injured, she scraped her blade on the stones, sending up a great rain of sparks as she prepared to lunge forward. The rain fell down on the battlefield and Brittola shielded Pinnosa against the fierce Saxon blows.

She heard Oleander say again, "You have to be brave now, Mistress."

She recalled Cordula's face as she said on deck, "The women are ready for inspection, Commander," and then saluting in a way that made Ursula remember her duty. She smiled as she thought about Rusticus and all his dear aunts. Martha and Saula dancing a jig before marching up the gang plank . . . .

The sound of pipes filled her mind and forced it into such a whirl that she felt dizzy and nauseous. Images flashed before her: drunken Hibernians; a disemboweled boy on a rope; tattooed Picts; Saxon war cries; the Franks and their arrogant King; Alemanni and Huns doing tricks on their horses; the cavalry racing through the trees; six young women flying along the road to Glevum; the white riders . . . .

She heard a shrill neigh from outside the tent. "Swift!" Mundzuk must be approaching. "I can't do this!" She clasped her hands before her and doubled forward in anguish. "I can't," she sobbed.

Then, as if from the very air itself, softly came Brittola's voice singing, "Praise the Lord." The sound was warm and sweet like honey mixed with wine. It soothed away Ursula's fears like a balm with its salvation.

There was Pinnosa's voice, loud and clear. Martha and Saula joined in—so full of life. The air became vibrant with the hymn as the entire First Athena began to sing. It seemed as if the tent, the valley, and the whole world were filled with the rich power of their voices.

Ursula relaxed her hands by her side and stood up straight. She was ready.

Just then, the tent flap was thrown open and Mundzuk strode boldly in. He looked at her and grunted something in his native tongue—which to her sounded like a dog growling. As he walked toward her with a big grin stretched across his hideously deformed face, he reached out to grab her by the arm.

She backed away and said, "No!" very firmly. Then she indicated that he should go to the marriage bed.

He turned his horrifying, other-worldly eyes toward the platform and then snapped them back to face her.

For a terrifying moment, Ursula thought he was going to spurn her offer. He was looking at her with what seemed to be suspicious scrutiny. She returned his gaze, feeling as she did so that she was looking into the eyes of Hell.

Mundzuk said something else in his gruff tongue and burst into a surprisingly high-pitched laugh. Abruptly, he tore off his furs and stood before her—naked. His scarred torso was surprisingly hairless, apart from his groin, which—much to her relief—had a profusion of hair that still hid what she did not wish to see. What little she could see filled her with revulsion. With a lascivious grin, Mundzuk leapt onto the platform with so much force he almost broke it. Lying on his back with his arms outstretched, he beckoned for her to join him.

Ursula smiled at Mundzuk with what she hoped looked like a nervous bride's look and turned away. *He's completely unarmed.* She loosened her cloak and let it fall to the ground. *And he's in the perfect position.*

She turned to face her enemy, deliberately allowing the sight of her nakedness to distract him while she reached up to unclip her hair.

Suddenly, Constans filled her mind again. "I'm coming home, my love . . ." she said aloud as she circuited the platform, smiling reassuringly at her prey, "I'm coming home."

Chapter 7

The Petal Field

High up in the lookout tower adjacent to the North Gate, which was reserved for the city's nobility, Bishop Clematius pushed a couple of lesser nobles aside so that Cordula could stand at the front. There she had a clear view of the entire "petal field"—as the people of Colonia were calling it.

Cordula hugged her sleeping baby and smiled again at the blanket he was wrapped in. It was the very same freshly bleached white wool that the First Athena were dressed in. She looked down at them, arrayed in disciplined ranks along the waterfront below and to her right. Like most of the nobles and the crowds along the town's parapets, all eyes were upon the small tent in the middle of the flower-strewn field.

A shriek from the parapet below startled her and woke the baby.

"Look! A woman has fallen from the ramparts," a city official next to Cordula said. "It's terrible, the crush down there. The rabble is constantly shoving each other. No wonder some of them fall off."

"There are far too many of them on that parapet," his companion, another official, complained. "I fear many more will die before the day is done. Who allowed so many up there? Where are the guards? There aren't enough guards these days to—"

"*There!*" Cordula yelled in anguish, pointing at the ranks of the First Athena, "There are your guards! And it is they who might die if—"

"Hush, hush, my child!" Bishop Clematius moved to position himself between Cordula and the officials. "You're frightening the baby. I must say, he looks well-wrapped up in his fine white linen," the Bishop said, making a fuss of her child, "Do you remember when we had to make it all in time for the parade after the mass Vow of Chastity?"

Cordula nodded and smiled. "Yes, I remember. The bleaching yards worked throughout the night. It was a good thing Ursula didn't inspect Faustina's women too carefully. They hadn't had their final rinse and the smell was horrendous. She—"

A cry went up from the crowd. There was movement at the small tent in the middle of the petal-covered field.

Cordula shuddered. *Where is Morgan? He should've been here by now. He should have returned yesterday.*

Far below, Ursula emerged. The crowd fell silent. Her toga and cloak were smeared with red streaks. She moved clear from the tent, stood still for a moment and then held something aloft in her left hand.

The First Athena let out a great cheer.

"She's done it!" Cordula cried, "She's done it!"

"Done what?" Bishop Clematius asked.

"Wait! You'll see!" she replied. Then she cheered again, prompting the nobles around her to cheer, too, even though they didn't understand why. Soon, all of Colonia was cheering.

Down in the petal field, Ursula leapt upon Swift and urged her to move. The long-legged mare started tossing her head and tugging hard at the rope that tied the tent. When it yielded, Swift lifted her head and sidestepped, heaving the taut canvas from its pegs. The cloth stretched tight like a galley sail before coming loose and flopping to the ground. As the canvas fell, a sight was revealed which caused the citizenry of Colonia to gasp with amazement and the Huns to let out an ominous, guttural cry.

There for all to see was a naked, blood-covered Mundzuk, lying on his back on a raised platform. His head and right arm were dangling over the side. Large pools of blood flowed from his neck and groin. It was plain to everyone what it was that Ursula had been holding up. The Scourge of the Northern Provinces was clearly dead—and emasculated.

Ursula cut Swift free, then rode toward Pinnosa and her friends. For a moment Cordula wished she was down below with them so she could share in the jubilant embraces that would shortly ensue. But then, as everyone looked on, Ursula did something which wasn't only unexpected it was also . . . strange.

Ursula veered Swift round, urged her into a gallop and started heading for Rugila and the Hun delegation, still brandishing Mundzuk's genitalia.

At the sight of Ursula's fierce approach, Rugila and his retinue hastily withdrew to the safety of their ranks.

Ursula didn't stop. Instead she urged Swift to go faster and rode hard after them in pursuit.

"*No!*" Cordula cried.

This time the crowd knew why Cordula had cried, and they echoed her, "No! No!"

As Cordula watched, her worst fears became a reality. From out of the Hun ranks flew a single, well-aimed and powerfully thrown spear. It pierced Ursula's leg just below her knee and penetrated well into Swift's side. The great horse reared in agony. Ursula's face was a mask of pain as she tried desperately to pull the weapon out. As they each struggled with their pain, Ursula and Swift moved closer to the Huns. Suddenly, a volley of arrows rained down upon them. Two of the vicious missiles embedded themselves deep into Swift's flanks. Another tore open a great gash across Ursula's unprotected shoulder.

"*URSULA!*" Pinnosa's powerful cry could be heard throughout the valley. "*URSULA!*" She tightened the reins on Artemis and the great black mare leapt forward into a full gallop.

"*No! Pinnosa, don't!*" Cordula shouted almost as loudly.

Then, as Cordula watched, feeling utterly helpless from the battlements, Brittola, too, shouted, "*Ursula!*" and spurred Feather on to follow.

"*No! Brittola! No!*" Cordula's sobbed.

In her anguish, she had clutched her baby tightly, his head against her shoulder. His deep blue eyes were fastened on the happenings below. Noticing this, she held his head up next to hers so they could face the scene together, and said into his ear, "Look on, my son, and remember well, for you will never see the likes of these fine women in white again."

Martha raced off after Brittola with Saula close behind. All four of her old friends were galloping hard across the petal field toward Ursula. Unlike her, they were in full armor. As a hail of arrows assailed them, they used their arm shields to protect themselves. Their freshly burnished body armor gleamed beneath their flying white cloaks—making them almost too bright to look upon as they charged forward in their fury.

Ursula and Swift had stopped. The pain was clearly too much for both horse and rider. Ursula made no attempt to extract the spear. Instead, she leaned forward and spoke into Swift's ear as if coaxing her forward.

Just as the others were approaching her, another flurry of arrows rained down. One penetrated Ursula's upper arm, which she was using to shield her face. Another pierced Swift's neck, it's shaft firmly embedded just under her mane.

Pinnosa cried "*Ursula!*"

Ursula looked back.

Cordula thought she saw Ursula feebly wave the others away. Then, with her friends barely ten lengths distant, she turned back and urged Swift forward. Rider and mount mustered all of their remaining strength and the two went—heads held high—into the Hun ranks at the point where Rugila and the delegation had disappeared. Large pikes, spears and blades of every description poured in upon them and they disappeared—engulfed by the mass of men.

From the far end of the petal field, Faustina and Viventia led the charge of the Vanguard cavalry to save their four senior officers. Behind them the entire First Athena advanced.

The Huns with their first taste of blood broke into an undisciplined stampede, preceded by a huge volley of arrows and spears. Pinnosa, being the nearest to Ursula, was the first to become surrounded. Her terrifying war cry held the Horde at bay for a moment. She managed to spur Artemis several strides through them. Suddenly, a huge pike caught Artemis in the chest. The huge, black mare died instantly, falling to her knees. Pinnosa was forced to leap from Artemis's back to avoid being crushed.

Cordula could see Brittola urging Feather on, desperately trying to come to her friends' aid, despite having received an arrow in her leg. Close behind her, Saula started slashing away with her long sword at a group of tribesmen carrying long pikes. Martha struggled to avoid a second group of pikemen in order to break through to Pinnosa and rescue her.

Brittola was the first to succumb. She was so intent on going straight for Pinnosa that she forgot to watch her left, unshielded side. A pikeman found himself in the perfect position for a deadly thrust. The roar of war cries from the Horde was far too loud for any one death scream to be distinguished, but Cordula was sure she recognized Brittola's sweet voice cry "Dear God! Have mercy!" as she went down.

Then Cordula saw that Saula was surrounded by pikemen. Just as she tried to fend them off, something hit her exposed neck. Saula's hand flew to her blood-covered throat before she, too, toppled out of sight.

Faustina, Viventia and the Vanguard joined the fray. For a moment, as they charged into the Hun ranks with swords flashing left and right, Cordula's spirits soared in the hope that somehow the enemy could be forced back. But, when she allowed her eyes to scan the broader scene, she saw thousands upon thousands of battle-thirsty men swarming over the ridge and down the slopes toward the Athenian cavalry, her heart sank again. Then, immediately down below, she noticed a close-knit group bearing the Hun standard—indicating that Rugila, along with the other warlords, was withdrawing around the corner of the city wall, like a huntsman leaving the pack to its kill.

The sound of Martha shouting orders to Viventia turned Cordula's attention back to the bloodshed. Clearly Martha had a strategy in mind, but before she could carry it out, her horse was felled from beneath her. Still brandishing her sword, she was engulfed by a mass of spikes and blades.

Incredible as it seemed, Pinnosa was still standing. She'd lost her shield and so had to use Artemis' dead body to protect her back. She held her ground with both swords drawn, the bodies of five dead Huns lay at her feet. Screaming her defiance, she dared the hesitant tribesmen who formed in a loose semi-circle around her, to attack.

As the Vanguard entered the battle, she shouted orders to Faustina and Viventia. Before they could respond, a young Hun with a dagger leapt over Artemis's body and came at Pinnosa from behind. She spun around and made short shrift of him with her long sword, but while she was doing so, a massive pike was launched from the Horde. It hit home right between her shoulders and went in deep. She fell to the ground instantly. Cordula was sure Pinnosa was dead before the mob was upon her.

By the time the mid-afternoon bell sounded, it was all over. Faustina, Viventia and the Vanguard fought valiantly and took many men—both foot soldiers and cavalry—with them before they, too, were overrun. As Cordula watched, she almost became immune to seeing death after tragic death. But still she held her son in front of her, hoping that somehow the images would burn themselves into his mind, even though he was far too young to comprehend what was happening.

Behind her, she heard Bishop Clematius chanting prayers in Latin. Whenever she recognized one, she would join him as she stared in despair at the slaughter of her friends. To her distraught mind, a white, radiant light, that had burned bright for so long, like a beacon in the darkness, was being extinguished right before her very eyes by a smothering black cloud.

The white petals on the field turned red with blood, before being trampled into the earth. White cloaks, torn from their wearers' necks, became nothing but bloody shreds. Bodies were strewn across the field like discarded cuts of meat in a market. Cordula continued to watch as the Huns pored over the bodies of the dead horses and women, stealing anything of worth.

The once proud and powerful First Athena, which had meant so much in life, now seemingly meant very little in death, if anything at all.

Epilogue

"Trittola," Cordula said, gently rocking her young daughter to comfort her. The little girl had been sobbing intermittently ever since hearing the part about Constans's death, but as her mother brought the sad tale to a close, she burst into a full flood of tears. It wasn't just the story that made her cry, it was also the pain she could sense in her mother; the way the final words in particular seemed to be rent from her very soul.

"Do you remember that large hawk that swooped down from high in the sky and caught one of the doves in the kitchen garden?" she said tenderly, and her little daughter nodded. "Well, it was just like that in a way. A beautiful, delicate white thing was swallowed up by great big black thing. A bit like the way your brother described it to the Bishop." She looked at her son, who was sitting upright at the end of the bed, and asked, "Do you really recall something of what happened that day?"

She could see that her son, too, was upset. All he could manage was a firm nod. Cordula stretched her free hand toward him. He needed no further bidding. He flung himself at his mother, and, for a long while both children lay cradled—one under each arm—buried deep in her tunic, weeping.

All the while Cordula held them tightly, she stared at the entrance to the West Room, as if others were standing there, witnessing the scene.

Eventually, their sobs diminished.

"Mother?" her son asked quietly.

"Hmm?" she said distractedly, breaking her silent vigil with the invisible watchers.

"I know Father wasn't there, but sometimes he says things which make it sound like he was." He looked up at her pleadingly. "I don't understand."

"Your father arrived the very next day, long after the last of the Horde had gone—returning to the wasteland that is their home. He had been on his way back from Prince Jovinus and heard from a merchant he met on the road that the Huns were upon us. He pushed Hermes hard—right through the night—to reach us. Even though he missed the . . . the awful day itself, he still saw enough of the aftermath to comprehend all that had happened.

"I remember it well. Like many of the people of Colonia, I was wandering through the remains of the petal field looking—hoping—to find something . . . some tangible object that would help me to make sense of what had happened. Then all of a sudden, I heard his voice call my name, and there he was, dismounting from Hermes. It was like waking from a dream . . . a terrible, terrible dream. I—"

"I like your name, Mother," Brittola's little face peeped out from Cordula's tunic, where she had been nestled, making Cordula grin. "But, I've decided I'm going to call my first daughter, Ursula."

"That's nice. In memory of your illustrious Aunt?"

"Yes, in memory of her, but also I like 'Little Bear.' It sounds nice. Much better than 'Big Bear' here!" She gave her brother a playful punch.

"I like 'Arthur,'" he protested. "It's a strong name—a brave name!"

"And so it is, Arthur." Cordula tousled their hair, pleased that they were perking up. "Oleander suggested it, you know."

"Did she?" he asked incredulously. "I never knew that."

"Well, in a way she did . . ." Cordula smiled as a happier memory came back to her, like a wispy white cloud chasing a storm. "In fact, it was while we were still there on the petal field. Your father had already found her before he found me. After he and I embraced, I asked him what we were going to do and he said, 'We're going home.' He told me he'd arranged for a galley to take all the attendants home . . . 'including our new one.' I asked, 'Who might that be?' Your father beckoned, and out from behind Hermes came Oleander. She looked awkward at first, and she said she didn't want to appear ungrateful, but a master didn't have the final say when it came to looking after a child—it was a mothers' decision. Then she looked me in the eye and asked politely, 'Will you have me, Mistress?' I said, 'What a question Oleander! You may as well ask, 'Will the summer have the sun?'

"She gave me such a hug! Then she took you in her arms and said, 'Do you know, Mistress, I always wanted to care for a boy.' I shall always remember what happened next—she looked up at your father and I, and said, 'Don't you think it's about time this baby boy was given his name, Mistress? He needs a strong, brave name like Arthur or Victor or something.' I looked at your father, and I knew immediately that he was thinking the same as me . . ." She ruffled her son's hair and gave him a playful cuddle, "We both said it together . . . 'Arthur', and so you were named. I remember Oleander saying it over and over to you while she rocked you in her arms. 'Arthur, Arthur,

Arthur' she went—you know the way she does. Then she looked up and said, 'It's the perfect name for him, We need a great bear to follow the little bear.'"

"I miss Oleander," Brittola whined, her lip beginning to quiver again. "Why did she have to go like that?"

"Her years with us were good, happy ones, and she wanted it to end that way. She didn't want to be a burden when she became too old to work. She's very happy in the hospice in Corinium. It's near the Palace, where she has so many fond memories, and she—"

"We can go and see her tomorrow, if you like!" Morgan's voice made all three of them jump. He appeared in the doorway, smiling broadly, and holding the riding boots that he'd taken off in order to creep up on them and give them a surprise. The children yelped with excitement and rushed over to hug their father.

"Y'know, Arthur, I remember the day we named you as if it was only yesterday," he said, picking up his daughter and taking the children back to their mother. "You were christened that very evening by Bishop Clematius in the small chapel in what was left of the grove by Colonia's North Gate."

"It was a beautiful ceremony," Cordula said, reaching up to kiss her husband, "Many of the people from the city joined in, and they told me afterward that celebrating your naming was like celebrating a rebirth after . . . all that had happened."

"And at the end of the ceremony . . ." as Morgan continued, he gently eased the children back into bed with their mother and pulled the blanket over them. "the Bishop said, 'I expect there'll be a multitude of Arthur's and Ursula's in the coming years—and so there should be! We should fill the world with them, in memory of the glorious women—like your mother—who followed the greatest 'little bear' of all . . . the true and mighty Ursula.'"

Historical Note

In Cologne, Germany, at the back of the main station, just off Ursula Strasse and tucked away in an unassuming cobbled square called Ursula Platz, is the modern-day church of St. Ursula. It is a pleasantly re-constructed Sixteenth Century church well worth a visit in its own right should you ever be in the vicinity. What should interest you more, however—and what should cause you to linger in the Platz, close your eyes, and try to imagine—is what happened there around fifteen hundred years ago—a thousand years or more before the church was built. For on that ground, beneath the anonymous cobbles—which in ancient times lay immediately outside one of the main gates to Colonia, "the jewel of Rome north of the Alps,"—something truly terrible took place.

Whatever *did* happen there on that fearful ground, most probably transpired sometime around the Fourth or Fifth Centuries AD. This was the time of the collapse of Rome; the time of the Germanic invasions; the time of the Chaos that led the whole of Western Europe into the Dark Ages. Many awful things were happening at that time, in many places and all at once. Only some of them were properly recorded. History's front page was full and this story simply did not make it into the record.

Turn sharp right as you enter the modern-day church and enter the Golden Chamber. See the bones of the victims stacked high, literally from floor to ceiling. See the skulls—skulls of women brutally murdered—wrapped in Medieval packaging to be sold as relics. There were so many bodies in the mass grave that this House of God was built over, it was a veritable factory of reliquaries with more than enough raw material to sustain a thriving industry. For several hundred years, bits of Ursularine bone were what brought most visitors to Cologne. Indeed, as icons go, Ursula and her "virgins" were the Fourteenth Century equivalent of Elvis!

Back in the main chamber of the modern church, set in the wall and about the size of a large TV screen, is the enigmatic Clematius stone, it's difficult-to-decipher, ambiguous Latin inscription*, carved soon after the appalling event, provides us with the only historical evidence for the atrocity that occurred here. Apart from giving us the sole name we have that is linked with the real-life episode—Clematius—it alludes in vague terms to the martyrdom of many virgins, and fails to enlighten us with any useful information about who they were or why they were there. But that in itself is enough! It is testament that something *did* happen here—something involving the death of many women.

It may not have been written down and recorded, but such a powerful story about some undoubtedly incredible women simply *had* to be told. And so it was! The Romanized Germans of the Rhineland made it their own. As bear-worshipping folk, they probably changed the name of the women's leader to Ursula, "little bear." They passed it orally down through the generations—no doubt elaborating here, embroidering there—and the truth as well as the distortions became preserved in the ageless aspic of myth and legend.

Then, several hundred years later, Latin scholars—hagiographers from the Vatican—came to the Rhineland on an important task: they sought pagan heroes they could turn into saints, thereby satisfying the Church's ambition to expand and become truly catholic—truly all-embracing. The papal clerics made their own interpretation of the stories they heard from the Rhineland folk, and "Saint Ursula" was created—the forlorn, fateful woman who led eleven thousand "virgins" to their deaths on an unfortunate "pilgrimage." But the German scholars who accompanied the officials noted a different story and recorded references to the women being armor-clad, weapon-bearing, horse riders, who were "well-versed in the arts of war." And indeed, even the priests could not resist the iconized image of Ursula depicted clutching an arrow—or even a brace of them. Let there be no mistake, all agreed, Ursula and her "virgins" were no strangers to weaponry. What the Church preferred to ignore, however, was that the women were not on a "pilgrimage" of any kind. They had formed an army and were on a mission!

The truth is . . . the truth is lost. The actual story of whoever the real women were and whatever really happened to them is something we shall never know. I have, nevertheless, attempted to piece together the few fragments of the real story that have come down to us and incorporated these, plus the main elements of the Ursularine legend, into this purely fictional account. There almost certainly was a real Pinnosa, as well as a real Brittola, Martha, Saula and Cordula. These names survived in the oral tradition and were recorded by both the papal hagiographers and their accompanying German scholars. And who knows; maybe there really was amongst them a truly unique and remarkable princess from Britannia, who led an army of women on a campaign to the

Continent, where they met a horrific death outside a heavily-fortified city's gates at the merciless hands of the Huns.

One last note: History records that Mundzuk, father of Attila the Hun, was emasculated on his nuptial bed by an unnamed "western princess."

* The Latin inscription on the Clematius Stone reads as follows:

DIVINIS FLAMMEIS VISIONIB. FREQVENTER
ADMONIT. ET VIRTVTIS MAGNÆ MAI
IESTATIS MARTYRII CAELESTIVM VIRGIN
IMMINENTIVM EX PARTIB. ORIENTIS
EXSIBITVS PRO VOTO CLEMATIVS V. C. DE
PROPRIO IN LOCO SVO HANC BASILICA
VOTO QVOD DEBEBAT A FVNDAMENTIS
RESTITVIT SI QVIS AVTEM SVPER TANTAM
MAIIESTATEM HVIIVS BASILICÆ VBI SANC
TAE VIRGINES PRO NOMINE. XPI. SAN
GVINEM SVVM FVDERVNT CORPVS ALICVIIVS
DEPOSVERIT EXCEPTIS VIRCINIB. SCIAT SE
SEMPITERNIS TARTARI IGNIB. PVNIENDVM

(**A certain Clematius, a man of senatorial rank, who seems to have lived in the Orient before going to Cologne, was led by frequent visions to rebuild in this city, on land belonging to him, a basilica which had fallen into ruins, in honor of virgins who had suffered martyrdom on that spot.)

** English translation courtesy of: *The Catholic Encyclopedia, Volume XV* Copyright © 1912 by Robert Appleton Company